SAFETY LAST

Miss Caroline Lexham could have stayed in her country home and wed the honorable if uninspiring Squire Richard Marchand, instead of going off to the unknown world of London society.

Caroline could have turned and left for home when she heard the odious terms of her unpleasant late uncle's will, and realized that the legacy upon which her hopes rested could be snatched from her without a chance of saving it.

Caroline could have abandoned her love for Sir Henry Seymour when she saw that not only did he hold a social position high above hers and was hopelessly entangled with a titled beauty, but also gave every indication that he had no intention of stooping to be conquered by her.

Caroline could have done all these things so easily—but dismayingly, she did none of them. . . .

A COMMERCIAL ENTERPRISE

SANDRA HEATH
A COMMERCIAL ENTERPRISE

A SIGNET BOOK

NEW AMERICAN LIBRARY

NAL BOOKS ARE AVAILABLE AT QUANTITY DISCOUNTS WHEN USED
TO PROMOTE PRODUCTS OR SERVICES. FOR INFORMATION PLEASE
WRITE TO PREMIUM MARKETING DIVISION, NEW AMERICAN LIBRARY,
1633 BROADWAY, NEW YORK, NEW YORK 10019.

SIGNET TRADEMARK REG. U.S. PAT. OFF. AND FOREIGN COUNTRIES
REGISTERED TRADEMARK—MARCA REGISTRADA
HECHO EN CHICAGO, U.S.A.

SIGNET, SIGNET CLASSIC, MENTOR, ONYX, PLUME, MERIDIAN
and NAL BOOKS are published by NAL PENGUIN INC.,
1633 Broadway, New York, New York 10019

First Printing, September, 1984

2 3 4 5 6 7 8 9 10

PRINTED IN THE UNITED STATES OF AMERICA

Chapter 1

It was a lonely part of Dartmoor where the winding track from Selford Village passed over the stream by way of a narrow stone bridge. Floodwater from the melting snow on the high tors foamed in a torrent down through the rocky, tree-lined combe, the sound echoing around the naked branches. Cold, windswept, and desolate, it was a favorite place for highwaymen. All travelers, even the swiftest of horsemen, had to go slowly in order to negotiate the bridge, and highwaymen could wait with ease in the shelter of the concealing trees.

An old post chaise approached the bridge on its way down from Selford to join the main Exeter highway in the valley far below, but the roar of the swollen stream drowned the sound of the little hired carriage. It was a poor vehicle now, although once it had been the proud possession of a marquis. Its panels were a scratched and faded blue, and the heraldic emblems which once graced the doors had been completely obliterated. Perched on the more robust of the two horses, the yellow-jacketed postboy looked anything but cheerful as he glanced nervously around the combe for any stealthy movement which might give warning of someone lying in wait. Called a boy, Charlie Hargreaves was in fact forty-five years old, and he loathed having to turn out in such inclement weather simply to convey a young woman, whom he regarded as stubborn and willful, to the White Boar Inn on the first stage of an unnecessary journey to London. It was ten miles to the inn, miles which were hazardous and which offered too many hiding places for the so-called gentlemen of the road, and he could only view with apprehension the prospect of the next hour or so. On bitterly cold February days like this, only fools and the idle rich ventured forth into such risks; glancing nervously through the tangle of trees again, he urged the team across the bridge, pondering how his passenger, Miss Caroline Lexham of Selford Manor, apparently did not fall into either category.

A solitary horseman waited in the lee of a holly tree, his face hidden by the brim of his tall hat, his damp cloak billowing in the icy wind. He was not a man of fashion, his riding boots were well made rather than modish, and his leather gloves were substantial but hardly elegant. His attention was on the chaise, and in particular upon the mud-spattered window, where he could see the paleness of a woman's face. As the carriage reached the holly tree, he urged his horse directly into its path.

Charlie's face became instantly ashen as he brought the chaise to an abrupt halt. "Let us pass!" he cried fearfully. "We've nothing of value for you!"

The horseman dismounted, his face at last revealed as he looked up at the terrified postboy. "You've never had reason to fear me, Charlie Hargreaves, and you've no reason to do so now. I merely wish to speak with Miss Lexham." The wind almost snatched his voice away and his cloak flapped wildly as he made fast his horse's reins.

"Squire Marchand?" Charlie was taken aback, looking down in amazement at the young master of Selford Manor. "Will you be long, sir? Only Miss Lexham said I was to be as quick as possible as she had to meet the Exeter mail and—"

"I will take as long as is necessary to persuade her to abandon this foolish journey."

Charlie fell silent, watching as Richard Marchand turned toward the door of the chaise, hesitating a moment in obvious doubt. At twenty-eight, he was tall and well built, with tousled blond hair and clear blue eyes, and by any measure he was considered to be a catch in these parts. As master of Selford he could have had his pick of the daughters of nearby landowners, but everyone knew his heart was set upon his cousin Caroline, who at twenty was eight years his junior. Since the death of her mother she had lived alone in a house in the village, with a cook-housekeeper to look after her, and her handsome cousin had long been determined to put an end to that lonely existence. Everyone in Selford knew that he wanted to marry her, and an announcement had been expected for some time; the fact that there had so far been no such announcement was regarded by many as a blessing, for although Miss Lexham was very well liked and respected, she was nevertheless thought to be unattractively overeducated for a female. This fault in her upbringing had led to her being possessed of a singularly independent nature, and no sensible fellow would wish to endure such willful spirit in his wife. It was at the feet of Miss Caroline's late mother that most of the blame lay for this lamentable state of affairs, for she had sought to instill in her daughter all the qualities of a lady of rank, and being unable to afford a proper governess, she had engaged the services of Parson Young. The parson had by some dreadful coincidence also believed that a female should be as well educated as a male, and he had done his best to fill his pretty pupil's head with all manner of facts and figures, from a knowledge of astronomy to a thorough grounding in algebra and geometry. Of what possible use were such things to a woman destined to be mistress of a manor high on Dartmoor? It was not a female's place to be learned and knowledgeable, it was her function in life to find herself a husband, make him happy, and be a mother to his children. Of one thing Squire Marchand could be thankful, however, and that was that the good parson's command of the French language had been appalling and he had therefore not been in a position to instruct his charge in this fashionable tongue. Richard Marchand would therefore be spared constant lessons in history, geography, and arithmetic, which could then be repeated in in the language of England's hereditary enemy!

Charlie huddled himself against the elements, thinking to himself that never had Miss Caroline Lexham's mulish, overeducated, unfeminine traits been more in evidence than at present, for here she was, setting off on an unnecessary journey all the way to London on her own. And for what reason? She intended to be present at the reading of her uncle's will—an uncle she had never even met and who certainly had not entertained fond thoughts of his niece.

Richard still hesitated at the door of the chaise. He knew that what he was about to say would not be well received, for he and Caroline had had many heated arguments ever since her ridiculous and stubborn decision to go to London. Her insistence had angered him, and he took refuge in blaming her upbringing, but in his heart he knew that his anger was born mostly of the recent unease which had sprung up between them. She had begun more and more to want the freedom to conduct her life as she saw fit, not as someone else dictated, and he took this as an implied criticism, an unwarranted criticism of his manhood which he resented deeply. He had said hurtful things to her, he had tried to impose his will upon her, but she had stoutly held her ground. Now, at this eleventh hour, he had to try one last time to make her change her mind. Taking a deep breath, he flung open the door and looked inside.

The interior was gloomy. The drab upholstery was worn and there was straw upon the floor. Caroline sat in the corner, toying nervously with the strings of her velvet reticule. She was very beautiful, although she had never seemed conscious of the fact; perhaps that was part of her charm. Her eyes were large and gray, and the curls peeping from beneath her high-crowned brown bonnet were the color of warm honey. She looked almost lost in her voluminous traveling mantle, the ribbons of which were tied only loosely so that he could just make out the heavy chased silver of her grandmother's necklace, the only item of any value she possessed. Like Richard himself, she could not have been called fashionable, but where he was unmistakably a country squire, Caroline Lexham had the fragile, delicate features associated with ladies of quality. There was something very arresting about her, from the gracefulness of her slender figure and the tilt of her head to the candid expression of her wide eyes. Those eyes met his now, and they were a little reproachful. "Richard?"

"I think you know why I've stopped you, Caroline."

"It will serve no purpose; my mind is made up."

"I must persuade you to turn back to Selford, for apart

from anything else, journeying two hundred miles in these conditions is madness!''

"I am going to London, Richard," she said quietly. "And I do not see why you try so hard to prevent me. I'm only going for a short while."

"Are you?" The words slipped out before he could stop them. He searched her pale face. He was afraid to let her go, afraid that he would lose her forever once the sophisticated gentlemen of the *beau monde* saw her beauty. He was afraid too that after the excitement of the capital she had long yearned to see, the dullness of remote Selford would bore her. "Please stay, Caroline," he begged, his voice barely audible above the roar of the water thundering over the rocks nearby.

She found it hard to withstand this entreaty, but she knew that she must, for both their sakes. "I will not be gone for long," she repeated.

"Damn you!" he cried, his helplessness making him harsh again. "I demand that you stay here!"

Her eyes flashed in angry response. "You are my cousin, Richard, not my keeper!"

"I want to be more, I want to be your husband!"

She couldn't reply, and she lowered her eyes to the reticule lying on her lap.

He struggled to be gentle again, reaching over to put his gloved hand over hers. "Caroline, we grew up together, we've *always* been together, and since your mother died it's been assumed that in time we would—"

"Perhaps that's the trouble, Richard," she interposed quickly. "We've been together too much and now when I look at you I see my brother, not the man I wish to have as my husband."

"I don't believe you mean that, for I know that when I see you I see the woman with whom I wish to spend the rest of my life. My feelings for you are anything but brotherly, I promise you that."

She could only look at him. *Why* wouldn't he listen? Why did he refuse to hear when she tried to tell him the truth?

His fingers tightened a little over hers. "Please stay here, Caroline, forget this foolishness about London."

"I cannot." Her voice was quiet but firm. She loved him, but not in the right way, and in recent months the pressure to marry him had become almost unendurable. She had to escape from Selford for just a little while.

He snatched his hand away, his quick anger sweeping to the fore again. "You think that because you carry the exalted Lexham name that once you reach London your aristocratic relatives will welcome you with open arms! Well, you will be disappointed, for as far as they are concerned you are nothing but a lowly Marchand! They've ignored you all your life and they are not about to change now. Your father was the late earl's only brother, but he scandalized and infuriated them all when he took my aunt as his wife. Catherine Marchand may have been very sweet and beautiful, but by Lexham standards she was virtually a pauper!"

"It was a love match," she said defensively.

"For Philip Lexham it was a grave misalliance. Only if he had married a servant, a divorced woman, or a Cyprian could he have sinned more in their eyes. They never forgave him and he died disinherited, spurned by his own flesh and blood. They will never forgive you for being a living reminder of an episode they would prefer to sweep under the ancestral carpet. Don't go to the reading of that will, Caroline, for it will avail you of nothing and may even prove painful to you. Please listen to me."

She toyed once more with the strings of her reticule. He was right about her relatives, and she knew it, but how could she tell him that she was determined to go to London as much to be free of Selford and free of him for a while as to hear the last will and testament of a man she had never known? She needed time to herself, time to put things into perspective. More and more of late she had come to realize that she chafed at the close-knit rural existence which was all she had ever known. Now she yearned to see something more of the world. She was tired of conversation which turned solely on farming and prices, on cattle and sheep, on the vagaries of Dartmoor weather, on hunting and foxhounds and all the other interminable sporting activities followed with such obsession by country squires like Richard. It was a world for men and there was no place for women of Caroline's spirit. Such an existence forever more would stifle and frustrate her as the years passed and would make any marriage between her and Richard Marchand a very serious mistake. She didn't want to hurt him; she just wanted him to understand and accept the truth, but he didn't want to know what she felt or why she felt it. He was supremely confident that if she married him, then she would be content to forget her stubborn restlessness, which he regarded as mystifying female nonsense anyway. In his blind, unthinking way he was as arrogant as he accused the Lexhams of being, but he would have been appalled had he known she thought such things of him. He simply did not understand her, and she doubted very much if he ever would. She, on the other hand, understood him only too well, and knew that the barrier was insurmountable. As cousins they could be close and loving; as lovers they were as unlike as chalk and cheese, too opposite for there to be any hope of a successful and happy marriage.

Her long silence disturbed him. "Caroline?"

"I intend to go to London, Richard, and nothing you say will make any difference."

He was almost savage then, wanting to cause her pain for all the hurt she was dealing him. "They'll laugh in your face! They'll scorn your country ways and your country clothes!"

"Please, don't."

He looked helplessly into the soft gray eyes and saw defeat at last. Why couldn't she see that he would only love and cherish her? Why couldn't she see that it was marriage that she needed, not foolish escapades like this? Other women were content enough with their lot, happy to contemplate futures with loving husbands and with children, why couldn't she be as they were? Why did she always seem to be seeking something, he knew not what? Was it because she was half Lexham? Was that why? He wanted to say so much to her, but the words would not come. She was and would always be a mystery to him, and his own nature was such that he would never reach through the puzzle to find the answer. Slowly he stepped back, closing the door and nodding at Charlie, who immediately roused himself and urged the team on down the track.

Richard watched the old vehicle lumber away. Instinct told him that she would never return to Selford to live, not because that was already her secret avowed intention, but because events would overtake her. For a down-to-earth country squire, Richard Marchand had a surprising belief in the power of dreams, and recently he had dreamed that she would stay in London. Now, as the chaise disappeared from sight, that belief was stronger than ever. Somewhere in the capital there was a gentleman who was going to see past her country clothes and inexperience of society ways, who was going to fall in love with her charm and beauty, her vivaciousness, her sense of humor, and her compassion; that gentleman, like Richard Marchand before him, was going to want to keep her forever, but where the squire of Selford had failed, the London gentleman was going to succeed.

Sadly Richard remounted. The wind gusted icily through the combe, bending the trees and momentarily making the sound of the water even louder as it foamed and splashed over the rocks. There was a promise of more snow in the air as Richard turned his horse back up the track to ride home. This new year of 1818 was to have been the year he made Caroline Lexham his bride; instead it was to be the year of losing her.

Chapter 2

As the carriage drew away, Caroline resisted the temptation to look back, for to have done that might have made her falter in her resolve. She did not know what she would do on her return to Selford, merely that somehow she would have to make him understand that she would never marry him. She felt that after escaping to London and having separated herself from the influence of Dartmoor and Selford, she would find it easier to face him with the incontrovertible facts. Maybe then he would at last accept that she would never be his wife. She looked out of the ill-fitting window, watching the gray winter scene slip slowly by. Dartmoor in the spring and summer was very beautiful, but in the middle of winter it was desolate, brooding, and unkind.

The chaise jolted at last from the moorland track onto the main highway between Plymouth in the west and Exeter toward the east, but although she expected to see many more vehicles, it seemed that most travelers had decided to shun the raw cold and the risk of flooding. After half an hour, the only others she saw were a carrier and his wagon, drawn by eight oxen, and a smart yellow curricle driven at breakneck speed by a dashing young blood with golden Apollo curls and a tight-waisted crimson coat. She heard his mocking laughter as he shaved dangerously close to the chaise, earning a blasphemous response from the furious Charlie.

Looking out of the opposite window, away to the south across the valley, she could see a great white house set in a magnificent park. This was Petwell, the estate belonging to the young widow of old Admiral Lord Chaddington. Caroline had never met her, but she had heard a great deal about her. Lady Chaddington was rumored to have married the old man in order to inherit his considerable fortune. Now she was an important and influential society hostess in London, and invitations to Petwell and her house in Berkeley Square were much sought after by the *haut monde*. Said to be a very beautiful woman, she was nevertheless not liked in this part of Devon, for she was harsh and unfeeling with her tenants. On balance, Caroline was glad that she had not moved in the same circles as Lady Chaddington, and she hoped that she would not encounter anyone like her in London.

Thinking about London inevitably made her wonder about her Lexham relatives. She knew little of them, beyond the fact that they were very wealthy, that she had numerous uncles, aunts, and cousins, that the country seat of the senior branch of the family was Watermoor Chase in County Durham, and their London address was the famous Lexham House in Mayfair Street. This town house was said to be one of the most luxurious in London, having recently been completely refurbished. It was said to be so modern and exquisite a mansion that even the Prince Regent envied it. She wondered what it would be like to live in such a house, and then she smiled a little wryly, for it was hardly likely that her proud kinsmen would ever afford her the opportunity of finding out, her cousin Dominic least of all. He was the new Earl of Lexham, the thirteenth of the line, and he seemed to her to be the most arrogant and prideful of the whole family. He it was who had returned her thoughtful letter of condolence on the death of his mother, the twelfth countess, three years earlier. With it he had enclosed a curt note, instructing her never to communicate with the rest of the family again. She would willingly have abided by this had it not been for the letter from her late uncle's lawyer, Mr. Jordan of Maitland Court. It wasn't that she expected a bequest, far from it, it was more that she felt it right that she should attend, right for Philip Lexham's only daughter to be there when his brother's will was read. Absentmindedly she toyed with her grandmother's necklace—her grandmother, the eleventh Countess of Lexham.

The chaise drove on, seeming to take an age to travel the ten miles to the White Boar. The clouds had taken on that yellow-gray hue that heralds snow, and even as she noticed, the first flakes began to dance and spin through the freezing air. Charlie urged the tired team along the deserted highway, glancing in dismay at the worsening weather. The old chaise bumped and swayed alarmingly over the ruts and hidden stones, and as Caroline instinctively reached for something with which to steady herself, there was an ominous splintering sound from somewhere beneath the vehicle. Charlie drew the horses to a standstill and dismounted wearily, cursing to himself, for he recognized the sound and knew that the axle had been damaged. That would mean it would be even longer now before he toasted himself in front of a warm fire!

As he bent to inspect the damage, Caroline leaned out. "What's happened?"

"The axle's almost gone."

"Oh, no!"

"We'll be able to go on," he said, straightening and looking slyly at her, hoping that this would deter her from thought of continuing to the White Boar. "But we'll have to go very slowly indeed."

"How slowly?"

"No more than a snail's pace."

"But I have to meet the mail!"

"I daren't take risks, Miss Lexham, for we could get stranded altogether, and what with the weather closing in and the danger of highwaymen . . ." He allowed his voice to fade meaningfully away, intending to frighten her as much as possible with such dreadful thoughts.

But she knew Charlie Hargreaves and his love of his creature comforts. "Continue as best you can," she said. "For if it is possible to reach the inn in time, then I wish to do so."

He scowled. "Yes, ma'am." Muttering beneath his breath, he remounted and urged the chaise on its way again, but very definitely at the promised snail's pace. The axle made alarming grinding sounds at each jolt, but it did not give completely.

The White Boar was a busy hostelry, used by the mails and stages which regularly plied this route between London and the west country. It was also busy with the considerable trade produced by the posting side of the business, although today it seemed inordinately quiet. It was built in a sheltered combe, protected from the worst of the winter weather by the surrounding heights of Dartmoor and by a copse of large trees. The breeze tore wisps of smoke from the chimneys, and there were lights in the windows in spite of the early hour. The weather had closed in still more and the snow was beginning to fall heavily. Caroline could no longer see the high tors, which were shrouded in mist and cloud.

The chaise passed slowly beneath an arch into a galleried courtyard, where the smell of roast beef hung appetizingly in the air. Ivy twined up toward the roof, the shiny, dark green leaves shivering a little as the wind caught them. The only other vehicles were the yellow curricle that had passed the chaise on the highway, and the Plymouth mail, which was preparing to leave. The guard made a final check, the mailbags were loaded, and the lids slammed. With a loud blast of the post horn, the coach drew away, emerging from the shelter of the inn and turning west into the snowstorm.

Caroline alighted. Few snowflakes found their way down to the cobbles, where wisps of straw lay everywhere, and she stepped hastily out of the way as grooms and ostlers hurried about their tasks. The landlord emerged from the taproom, having perceived the chaise's arrival. His practiced eye took in the shabby vehicle and its only passenger's plain, unremarkable clothes. He trimmed his manner to suit her apparent station, being civil but not too courteous. "Can I be of service?"

"I am hoping to travel on the Exeter mail, am I too late?"

He shrugged. "Hard to say, for the Exeter mail hasn't come through yet, but that's probably because it can't manage the floods between here and Plymouth."

"But the Plymouth mail has just left!"

"There's grave doubts that it will reach its destination. I expect it back here within an hour or so. They're getting through from the east, but as soon as they reach the floods . . . It's been like this since yesterday, that's why there's so little on the roads. You might be lucky and get a stage come through, the Red Glory for instance."

"The stagecoach? When?"

"It should have been through over an hour ago and hasn't

arrived yet. It has two fords to come over, mind, so I reckon it's had to go around the long way to the north. If so, then it won't call here at all.''

"But it might?"

He nodded. "It might."

"I'll wait then."

"As you wish. Will you take some refreshment? We've some very fine roast beef."

"Yes, I think I will."

He nodded at a nearby maidservant and then walked away, considering that he had given enough attention to a traveler who did not look likely to leave a handsome tip.

Leaving Charlie Hargreaves to attend to the repair of the damaged chaise, Caroline followed the maid into the hallway of the inn, where bowls of water had been provided, each with a clean towel. The maid added hot water from a steaming kettle and Caroline took off her gloves. She didn't realize how very cold her fingers were until she sank them into the water and painful feeling began to return. When she had washed and tidied herself a little, she was conducted into the dining room, which was very crowded indeed, many travelers having been stranded by the failure of the mails and stages. There were very few places left at the tables, except at one, which was occupied by one dandified gentleman. As she was led to one of the crowded tables, she recognized him immediately as the man driving the yellow curricle. She made herself as comfortable as possible in the confined space her chair occupied between a fat farmer and an equally enormous man of the cloth, and as she did so she surreptitiously glanced again at the dandy.

His crimson coat looked very gaudy and bright in the flickering light from the fireplace, next to which his table stood. The upturned collar collar of his shirt extended to his ears and his starched muslin cravat was very elaborate indeed. A large bunch of seals was suspended from his fob, and the lower part of his anatomy was attired in a voluminous pair of cossacks, those full trousers made popular by the Czar of Russia and which were pleated at the waist and gathered in with ribbons at the ankles. They were a ridiculous fashion, not made any more attractive by the fact that his upper portion was squeezed into a corset that tightened his already narrow waist and puffed out his chest like that of an angry hen. His cheeks were rouged and his golden hair teased into unnatural Apollo curls, thus completing the destruction of his good looks. With a blanched hand he raised a quizzing glass, inspecting her in that rude, deliberate way so often affected by dandies. His manner offended her and she felt her cheeks coloring with annoyance and embarrassment.

As the maid brought Caroline's plate of roast beef, he rose languidly to his feet, his tasseled ebony cane swinging in his pale fingers as he crossed to her table. Hastily the maid put down the hot plate and then hurried away. Conversation died as everyone looked at Caroline and her unwanted admirer, who began to speak in a lisping drawl that closely resembled a bray.

"I thay, would you care to join me? I vow it would pleathe me immenthely to share my table with you."

"I am quite content where I am, sir," she replied in a tone calculated to spurn him.

"I'm sure you'd pwefer it clother to the fire," he persisted, being importunate enough to place his hand familiarly upon her shoulder.

Icily she moved away. "Thank you, sir, but no."

"Oh, come now," he insisted. "Why ith a pwetty little thing like you twaveling all alone, mm? I'm sure you'd find it much more congenial if you—"

"Would you please leave me alone, sir?" she interrupted angrily. "I have attempted to be polite to you, but you make that impossible. It is hardly gentlemanly to continue to pester a lady who has made her wishes very plain!" Gasps greeted this hot censure, for everyone knew that it was unwise to cross a gentleman of his obvious character and rank.

At last he snatched his hand away, his eyes suddenly sharp. "Obviouthly I wath mithtaken ath to your bweeding, madam," he snapped, "for you are thertainly not fit to join me!" For a moment he remained where he was, thus giving her a last opportunity to see the folly of her ways, but she calmly began to eat, and so he furiously strode away across the red-tiled floor, slamming the door behind him.

The other diners exchanged glances, but it wasn't long before conversation broke out again and Caroline was able to finish her meal in peace. Indeed, when later she emerged from the dining room, her fingers crossed for favorable news of the Red Glory, she had put the odious dandy from her mind.

But the landlord shook his head when she inquired, and he avoided meeting her eyes. "Er—no, there's no sign of it yet, but it could be through at any time."

With a sigh, she went out into the courtyard, which was silent now. Through the rear archway she could see Charlie Hargreaves arguing with the man who was to repair the damage to the chaise, and she could also see the dashing yellow curricle belonging to the man who had so rudely accosted her, but apart from those two vehicles, there was nothing else at all. Seldom could the White Boar have been more quiet. Glancing up at the heavy gray sky, she could see the snowflakes hurrying through the eddying air. They were beginning to find their way into the yard now and a thin layer of white had settled on the wooden steps leading up to the gallery.

Turning back into the passageway, she found herself face-to-face with the dandy. His eyes were mocking and scornful and there was a disagreeable smile on his lips. He didn't say a word to her, but he sketched a derisive bow before turning on his heel and vanishing into the inn. His manner should have warned her that he had not let her escape scot-free, but she thought nothing as she sat down on an uncomfortable chair, resigning herself to either a long wait or to the possibility of having to return to Selford after all.

An hour or more passed as she sat there. Outside the snow still fell and the courtyard was silent. At last she could bear the chair no more, and to stretch her legs she went out into the courtyard again, this time going up the snowy wooden steps to the gallery. Leaning on the rail, she gazed down at the yard. Suddenly, she heard the unmistakable sound of a coach approaching, and she straightened hopefully. It had to be the the Red Glory, it simply *had* to be!

Chapter 3

But the elegant carriage which entered the inn yard was not the awaited stagecoach, it was a very costly private drag. In spite of her disappointment, she could not help gazing down at it in admiration, for it was truly the most magnificent traveling carriage she had ever seen. Drawn by a team of perfectly matched bays, it was attended by gold-liveried footmen, and its similarly clad coachman was obviously one of the very best, for he maneuvered the carriage effortlessly in the enclosed yard, gaining maximum response from the team with the minimum of command.

The coach came to a standstill by the open inn door, its panels gleaming brightly and the heraldic device emblazoned upon it quite easy to see from where she stood. It was a four-headed black swan. She looked at it, her brows drawing together in puzzlement, for somehow that badge was familiar to her. But how could that be so? Her attention was drawn to the occupant of the coach then, for one of the footmen went to open the shining door.

A gentleman alighted. He was arrestingly handsome and was dressed more finely than any man she had ever seen before. He was tall and broad-shouldered, but his hips were slender, and she judged that he was about thirty years old.

His clothes could only have come from London's finest tailor, for the coat fitted his manly figure to perfection and the gray cloth from which it was made must, in her opinion, have cost a fortune. A silk cravat burgeoned discreetly at his throat, a diamond pin nestling in its folds, and his dark green waistcoat struck just the right note of contrast. A heavy Polish greatcoat was flung casually around his shoulders, spurs shone on the heels of his top boots, and his long, well-made legs were encased in breeches that hugged very close indeed. His top hat rested rakishly on his dark hair, and as he glanced around the courtyard, she recognized in him a nonpareil of the first order, a man always to be reckoned with. He needed no rouge to enhance his looks and was the sort of man for whom being immaculate would always come effortlessly. And yet he was not haughty or inordinately grand, for there was no mistaking the glint of wry humor in his hazel eyes as the obsequious landlord came scurrying out, bowing and smiling in a way which contrasted rather too greatly with the greeting he had accorded Caroline earlier.

"Sir Henry! Welcome to my humble hostelry! Welcome to the White Boar!"

Sir Henry! Of course, now she understood the familiarity of the four-headed swan. Her cousin Richard's almost obsessive following of all matters concerning the turf allowed her to recognize the badge as the one worn by jockeys riding Sir Henry Seymour's famous racehorses. Sir Henry was known almost universally by his nickname, Hal, and he was revered throughout the land by every lover of horse racing. He was also well known as a leading light of the *beau monde* and as a close friend of the hero of Waterloo, the Duke of Wellington. Caroline had read much about him, but as she looked down now she thought that what she had read had not done him justice, for he was at least twice as handsome as any journalist had hinted.

The landlord's servile smile was almost unbearable. "May I be of any assistance to you, Sir Henry?"

"You can inform me if Lord Fynehurst has arrived."

"He has indeed, Sir Henry, and he awaits you within."

"Excellent." Hal turned back to the carriage, and it was then that Caroline realized that he was not traveling alone, for he held out his hand and a lady emerged, stepping daintily down to the cobbles.

She was very lovely, although her beauty was marred by a certain hardness. She was dressed very much *à la mode*, for her mauve traveling pelisse was adorned with military epaulets and black frogging, and she wore a miniature of the Iron Duke upon her curving bosom. Her auburn hair was twisted up expertly beneath a little hat bedecked with tassels and braid, and she looked very London, a vision from the engravings in *La Belle Assemblée*. Hal smiled at her. "Your brother has arrived," he said.

Marcia, Lady Chaddington—for it was she if Lord Fynehurst was her brother—did not look well pleased with this information; indeed she was positively disappointed. "What a pity," she murmured a little petulantly, "For I was hoping he would be his usual tardy self so that I could be on my own with you for a little longer."

"I promise I will visit Petwell again soon."

"I still do not understand why you must hurry back to Town. What on earth did that messenger tell you?"

"Come now, Marcia, a lady does not ask such things of a gentleman," he replied teasingly.

"This lady does. Oh, Hal, there cannot be anything *that* pressing, especially as you've only recently returned from rushing off to Brussels and the Duke of Wellington! It cannot be anything to do with your racehorses, or you would have said so, and surely it cannot be that wretched banquet you've somehow become involved with for the duke." She searched his face for a moment. "Dear God, it *is* the banquet, isn't it? Now I feel more miffed than ever with you, for it seems that I must play second fiddle to a mere gastronomic exercise!"

"It is hardly to be spoken of so disparagingly," he protested, laughing.

"I could be even more rude about it if I so chose. I don't understand you, Hal Seymour, for why are you, of *all* men, involved with arranging a banquet. Even if it is on account of the Duke of Wellington, I still find it very mysterious."

"Perhaps I am more of an eccentric than you have hitherto guessed."

"My brother prides himself on being an eccentric, Hal, and you are certainly not even slightly in the same mold."

He smiled. "Then put it down to my desire and willingness to come to the aid of a friend. Reggie Bannister was to have arranged the whole diversion, but now he is ill and has asked me to step in for him.''

She was doubtful. ''That is plausible, I suppose, except that I can think of any number of gentlemen Reggie would have approached before you for such a task.''

''Meaning that you suspect me of fibbing?''

''Meaning that you are not telling the whole truth, which is a different thing entirely. There is obviously a great deal more to this banquet than meets the eye. I don't profess to know yet what it is, but I do know that it is not what it appears to be.''

''It is just a banquet, my dear, no more and no less.''

''That, my dear sir, is rubbish,'' she replied impolitely. ''For the mere fact that you are mixed up in it points to it being anything *but* a simple banquet.''

''How devious you make me sound.''

''Devious? Mysterious, perhaps. There have always been two sides to you, Hal, for you have never been just a privileged man of leisure. You are prepared to live dangerously, you are shrewd and capable, and I wonder greatly about the number of invitations you have to Downing Street.''

''You see mysteries where there are none, Marcia.''

''Do I?'' She spoke very softly, her blue eyes thoughtful as they searched his face.

He smiled, turning to the waiting landlord. ''Please conduct Lady Chaddington to Lord Fynehurst.''

The landlord bowed and smiled, and reluctantly Marcia followed him into the inn. Hal watched them, his expression almost guarded, and it seemed to Caroline that his thoughts were anywhere but upon the White Boar or any of its patrons, even the beautiful Lady Chaddington. Suddenly, as if he sensed the close scrutiny to which he was being subjected, he looked up at the gallery, straight into her horrified eyes.

She was transfixed with dismay at having been detected staring down at him. Her cheeks flamed and her gray eyes widened with embarrassment, but at last she found the wit to step back out of sight.

Amused, he continued to look up at the spot where she had been. One glance had told him immediately that she was not a grand or fashionable lady, but that same glance had also told him that she was breathtakingly lovely—and so bewitchingly mortified at having been caught spying! He wondered who she was. Smiling to himself, he left thoughts of the delightful stranger, and went into the inn to seek Marcia and her brother.

Caroline felt dreadful and was careful to remain well back out of sight from the courtyard. What *must* he be thinking of her? How *could* she have stared down so blatantly?

A maid emerged from a nearby doorway. It was the same one who had shown her into the dining room earlier. Smiling, the girl bobbed a curtsy. "Begging your pardon, ma'am, but should you not be thinking of taking a room for the night? There's only one room left now, and as there won't be any mails or stages through today now—"

"But I was hoping that the Red Glory would be able to get through."

"Oh, no, ma'am, it's been taken off. A rider arrived to say so about five minutes after you sat down to your meal."

Caroline stared at her. "Five minutes after? Are you sure?"

"Yes, ma'am, I distinctly heard him telling Mr. Baldwin—that's the landlord."

Perplexed, Caroline could only look at her. The landlord had known that the stage was not going to arrive and yet had not told her so? Belatedly she remembered how uneasily he had avoided her eyes, and the triumphant scorn upon the dandy's face. Suddenly it was only too clear. Determined to punish her for spurning his attentions, the dandy had made it his business to inquire about her. Making her wait in vain for a stage which was not going to arrive was his revenge, and the landlord had placed more value upon pleasing such a gentleman than upon doing the right thing by a more lowly traveler!

She thanked the maid, who was looking curiously at her, and then went slowly down the slippery, snow-covered steps to the courtyard, but she misjudged her footing, and with a scream tumbled forward—straight into Hal Seymour's arms as he emerged once more from the inn.

Catching her with ease, his arms firm and strong, he held her for a moment before releasing her. Then he smiled into her flushed face, framed so prettily by honey-colored curls. "So," he murmured, "angels do still fall from the heavens."

"F-forgive me, sir."

"What is there to forgive? I am sure you did not fling yourself down on purpose." Still smiling, he bowed and introduced himself. "Sir Henry Seymour of Daneborough, at your service."

Hesitantly she accomplished a reasonable curtsy, robbed of true grace by the fact that she was again covered with confusion. "Miss Lexham," she replied.

The name conveyed nothing to him, for he could hardly be expected to guess that she was first cousin to the new Earl of Lexham and her clothes proclaimed her to be anything but grandly connected. "I trust you are not injured in any way, Miss Lexham," he said.

"I am quite all right. Thank you." She lowered her glance shyly, horribly mindful of having been seen peering down so rudely from the gallery. To her relief, she saw the landlord emerging from the inn, and she made him her excuse to escape from an embarrassing situation.

The landlord turned as she called his name, and once again he looked anything but comfortable. "If it's about the stage, then I'm afraid there's no word—"

"That, sir, is an untruth," she said coldly. "As I believe you know only too well!"

His guilt was written plainly on his face, plainly enough to intrigue Hal, who watched the exchange with growing interest. Now he came to her side. "Is something wrong, Miss Lexham? Perhaps I can be of some assistance."

Before she could reply, the landlord spoke up hastily. "It's nothing, Sir Henry, nothing at all!"

"Allow me to be the judge of that," replied Hal, glancing at Caroline's angry gray eyes.

"I swear it's of no importance," insisted the anxious landlord, wishing that he'd remained safely inside instead of coming out to this possible hornets' nest.

Hal's tone was clipped. "I asked what was going on, and I await an answer."

"It was merely a prank, Sir Henry, nothing serious. The lady was stranded waiting for the Exeter mail and so was hoping to take the Red Glory stagecoach instead. The stage isn't coming through after all, but she was not informed of the fact."

Hal's hazel eyes were bright and hard. "Indeed? And may I ask why not?"

"It wasn't my fault, Sir Henry!" protested the landlord, "for how could I go against Lord Fynehurst?"

Caroline stared at him in sudden dismay. The dandy was Lord Fynehurst? She hardly dared to look at Hal, who was on such intimate terms with Lord Fynehurst's beautiful sister.

For a moment Hal was silent, and then he waved the relieved landlord away. "Very well, I know his lordship's ways only too well." He looked at Caroline. "Unfortunately this hostelry is part of the Petwell estate, which goes a little way toward explaining the landlord's actions, although I do not excuse his conduct. Or the conduct of Lord Fynehurst, for that matter. Miss Lexham, am I to understand that you wish to reach Exeter?"

"Yes, for I am on my way to London, where I have an appointment tomorrow morning."

"Then consider your difficulties to be over, for London is my destination and I too have an important appointment there in the morning. I am on the point of leaving now, if you wish to take me up on my offer."

She was taken aback. "You are offering to convey me all the way to London?"

"Yes, Miss Lexham, that is exactly what I am doing."

"Oh, but I couldn't possibly—"

"Why not? There is more than enough room and it would please me to be of some service to you, especially as the good name of the English gentleman must be redeemed."

She was torn, for she wished to accept his offer, not only because it would mean her timely arrival in London, but also because it would mean being in the company of a man she found more than a little attractive. There was something about his warm hazel eyes and almost teasing smile which quite set her at sixes and sevens, although she hoped that he did not realize the fact. Yes, she wanted to accept, but would such a course be proper? She hardly knew him. Then she remembered Lady Chaddington—surely her presence would put things beyond reproach? She smiled a little shyly at him. "Thank you, Sir Henry, I would be pleased to accept."

He conducted her to the waiting carriage and a footman was dispatched to retrieve her solitary valise from Charlie Hargreaves' chaise, her other belongings having been dispatched a day or so earlier on the mail and thus undoubtedly already at the lawyer's premises in London.

The carriage shook a little as the coachman climbed up to his seat, and Caroline glanced expectantly at the door of the inn, thinking that at any moment Lady Chaddington would emerge. But, to her horror, the carriage door was slammed and the whip cracked. A second later the heavy vehicle was pulling out of the inn and turning east toward Exeter and London! Nervously her fingers crept to her grandmother's necklace, something she frequently did when anxious, and now she had good reason to be anxious, for suddenly the situation had ceased to be at all proper. She was traveling alone all the way to London, a distance of some two hundred miles, with a gentleman she had only just met, and whose intentions might be anything but chivalrous or honorable.

Chapter 4

There was nothing of a snail's pace about the speed with which Hal's coachman urged the team along the snowy highway. The horses moved with seeming effortlessness and Caroline could only compare the comfort in which she now traveled to the undoubted *dis*comfort of Charlie's rickety old chaise. In place of the worn upholstery of earlier there was soft green leather, and it was the fine smell of this that permeated the air, not the unpleasant odor of stale straw. The glass in the windows did not rattle and the springs protected the occupants from the worst of the ruts and potholes. She was comfortable and warm, for there was a hot brick wrapped in cloth by her feet and a woolen rug tucked around her knees.

For a while they traveled in silence, for she was preoccupied with the impropriety of the situation into which she had got herself. Hal, on the other hand, was preoccupied with other things, things which were obviously of great importance. At last she felt she must break the silence and say something to make herself feel a little easier about her predicament.

"It really is most kind of you to convey me to London, Sir Henry."

The faraway look vanished from his eyes and he smiled at

her. "It seemed the obvious and sensible thing to do, Miss Lexham. But tell me, do you make a habit of setting out on such long journeys all by yourself?"

She colored a little. "No."

"I'm relieved to hear it. I know your destination is London, but from where have you come?"

"Selford."

"I confess I have never heard of it."

"It is only a small village on the moor."

"And you have always lived there?"

"Yes."

"So, you are most definitely a country mouse, but I rather warrant you'd make a very fetching town mouse."

Was the compliment simple gallantry? Or was it perhaps the opening move of her seduction? She smiled a little nervously.

"Please do not look so painfully anxious, Miss Lexham, for I assure you I am no Fynehurst."

Her color deepened at his perception. "Oh, I did not for one moment—"

"Oh, yes you did, Miss Country Mouse, oh, yes you did. If you had but seen your face when you realized that Lady Chaddington was not to accompany us after all!"

Her embarrassment was so great that she did not know where to look.

He grinned a little wickedly. "Do I embarrass you?"

"A little."

"Forgive me, I did not mean to."

This reply made her suddenly bold. "Oh, yes you did, Sir Henry, oh, yes you did."

He threw his head back and gave a roar of approving laughter. "*Touché* But your swift riposte is confirmation that you are indeed at heart a town mouse."

She smiled too, feeling inexplicably at ease with him, in spite of her earlier uncertainty. He was so much more worldly-wise than she was, so easily able to make her blush, and yet there was nothing disagreeable about his manner—no unpleasant touch of a Lord Fynehurst. Indeed, there was something disarming about his smile and his willingness to laugh at himself. She was drawn to him and found herself wondering what it would be like to be courted by him, what it would be like to be kissed by him. The color which had seemed to flare so frequently on her cheeks since first she had seen him flushed hotly again now, and she looked quickly out of the window.

He did not seem to notice. "Do you often go to Town, Miss Lexham?"

"I have never been before."

"And you choose this appalling weather to do it for the first time? You must indeed have a pressing reason."

"I go for the reading of my uncle's will."

He did not reply, but his glance moved in puzzlement to her clothing, which did not display one token of mourning.

She felt the need to explain. "I did not once meet my uncle, Sir Henry; indeed his dealings with my part of the family were less than cordial. And before you think my reasons for going to hear his will are purely mercenary, let me assure you that they are anything but."

"You do not need to be so defensive with me, Miss Lexham, for I have not condemned your motives unheard. However, since you have brought the subject up, let me admit that I find it curious that a delightful little country mouse should scuttle off to London when there is no tasty bit of cheese at the end of the journey. I shall, therefore, be impudent enough to inquire what your motives really are."

"It is simply that I have seized the opportunity to see London."

His shrewd hazel eyes seemed to see right into her soul. "Oh, you fibber, Miss Lexham, you fibber."

"I'm not a fibber!" she protested.

"Yes, you are, for there is far more to your flight from Selford than a mere desire to see London."

"Just as there is more to your banquet than a mere banquet?"

His glance was quizzical. "Little mice have large ears, it seems."

"I could not help overhearing."

He grinned at that. "No, from the way you were positively hanging over the edge of the gallery, I can quite believe it!"

"I'm sorry about that."

"I'm not, for if you had not been there, then you would not have fallen into my arms and I would now be traveling to London all alone and without your stimulating conversation to keep boredom at bay. However, we digress, for I believe we were discussing your intriguing reasons for fleeing to

London. Let me see now, what does my vast experience of the world tell me has happened in your case?'' He studied her face for a moment and then nodded. ''I have it. You are fleeing from an importunate suitor.''

She lowered her eyes. ''Yes, I suppose I must concede that you are right.

''Do you wish to talk about it?''

She looked at him again. ''Are you really interested in the goings-on of the Selford mousehole, Sir Henry?''

He smiled. ''If you knew me better, Miss Mouse, you would know that if I was not interested, then I would not have asked. Who is this dastardly fellow? Is he a Lord Rat? A Sir Rat? Or just a Mr. Rat.''

She smiled. ''He is a mister, but he is not a rat at all; he is my cousin Richard and in fact I am very fond of him.'' To her surprise, she found herself telling him all about herself, although she somehow omitted to mention her grand connection with the House of Lexham.

When she had finished, he nodded in approval. ''You are right to escape, even if only for a short while, Miss Lexham, and I applaud your spirit.''

''I would like to believe that, Sir Henry, but I wonder if you would say what you just did if I was—say—your sister, or your cousin? Would you not then condemn me for being willful, obstinate, and opinionated?''

He seemed amused. ''You appear to know me very well all of a sudden. It so happens that if you were my sister, I would still applaud your actions, as indeed I have already proved with my real sister. The many spinster aunts and maiden cousins with which the Seymour family appears to be endowed had set their communal hearts upon matching my unfortunate sister with the dull and elderly Marquis of Wye. She, on the other hand, had set her sights upon the less wealthy but considerably younger and more congenial Lord Carstairs. She told me her wishes and I upheld her. Does that answer your question?''

''Yes, I suppose it does. Forgive me, Sir Henry.''

''Because your cousin is the epitome of unthinking male arrogance, it does not signify that every man has to be colored from the same paintpot.''

''I apologize, Sir Henry.''

"Apology graciously accepted, Miss Lexham." He bowed his head.

"But it is still a fact, is it not, that gentlemen are much more free to decide their own destiny than are ladies."

"Possibly."

"Definitely, Sir Henry. Do you honestly expect me to believe that when you marry you will have to bow to the wishes of others, or even that others will attempt to impose their will upon you in the matter? No, because you will be free to choose whichever bride you wish."

He smiled. "I do not think it is quite as simple as that for the male of the species, Miss Lexham. However, since that is your belief, I put it to you that you are yourself in the process of deciding for yourself about who you marry. Is that not what this precipitate flight to London is all about?"

She had not thought of it quite like that. "Yes, I suppose it is."

"Thank you, Miss Lexham," he said infuriatingly, "that is another apology I will graciously accept." Glancing at her again, he added softly, "I sympathize with the unfortunate Marchand, for his loss is great indeed."

She didn't hear, but instead was looking out of the window once more. There was less snow in the air now, and she could see the trees swaying in the fierce wind, but the well-fitting glass kept out all sound except the rattle of the wheels. When she next spoke, it was on a completely different subject. "Is it true, Sir Henry, that you have sent one of your very best racehorses to America to challenge all comers? Foxleaze is the horse, I believe."

"You are remarkably well informed, Miss Lexham. Yes, it is true. But how do you know about it?"

"My cousin Richard is very interested in horse racing. I believe he must purchase every racing publication in the country."

"I trust he has not lost a fortune on my nags."

"No," she replied, laughing, "but I know that he would never forgive me if he discovered that I had met you and yet had failed to ask for a reliable tip concerning the coming season."

"Deuce take it, madam, you are impudent!" he said, pretending to be stern. "And you are by far too concerned still with pleasing your disagreeable cousin."

"He isn't disagreeable, truly he isn't."

"I say that he is, Miss Lexham, for any man is disagreeable who thinks only of himself and refuses to see the point of view of others. However, as it is you who asks for a tip, and not Mr. Rat himself, then I shall oblige you. I have a nag named Nero which is believed to have excellent prospects for this year's Derby. I warn you, though, that my rivals have put it about that the beast has woodworm in its peg leg, which is a damnable lie, for the wood is perfectly sound."

"How fortunate for the horse."

He smiled. She interested him greatly, for it was not often that one found a young lady with such an impish and irrepressible sense of humor, or one who had come direct from a secluded, restricted country life and yet was prepared to parry words with a man like himself. Initially he had wondered if he would soon regret the impulse of offering to convey her to London, but already he knew that he would not. He studied her as she looked out of the window again. Put her in fine lace and costly silks, and she could be from one of the highest families in the land. There was something mysterious about her. She was cousin to a lowly squire and she dressed accordingly, but there was nothing of the country squire about the quality of the silver and ruby necklace at her throat which she toyed with so frequently. How did she come to possess such a costly piece of jewelry? His idle curiosity prompted him to wonder what her first name was. Had she been of aristocratic birth, undoubtedly she would have been a Georgiana or a Henrietta, but she was not of aristocratic birth and so was most likely a Susan or an Anne. Almost before he realized it, he found himself putting the question into words.

"Forgive my curiosity, Miss Lexham, but what is your first name?"

"Caroline. Why do you ask?"

"Oh, no particular reason." So, she was a Caro, which was as aristocratic a name as any.

"May I ask you a question, Sir Henry?"

"Not if it is inquire what my other names are, for I promise you that wild horses could not drag that embarrassing information from me."

She smiled. "I was merely going to ask you if you could tell me a little about the Duke of Wellington, for I know that you are his friend."

For a fleeting moment she thought his smile seemed to falter. She even imagined she saw a guardedness creep into his eyes, but then it had gone and his former good humor had returned. "And what is it that you wish to know?"

"Everything, I suppose."

"That is too tall an order."

"Just tell me if he is indeed the paragon the newspapers say he is."

"On the whole I have to say that he is, unbelievable as that may seem. He is first and foremost a soldier, of course, and his manner is therefore that of a soldier, but he is also very witty and entertaining company. He is a staunch and loyal friend, and an infuriatingly stubborn fellow when he so feels, especially where his own personal safety is concerned, for he believes that overattention to such things frequently interferes with the performance of his duty. On the field of battle he shows genius and diabolical cunning, which qualities he also shows in the corridors of Westminster. With one glance he can make a man his friend for life, but he can also with one glance quell an army. So you see, Miss Lexham, he is indeed a great man."

"And you admire him very much indeed."

"I admire no one more."

"Is it true that the Bonapartists attempted to murder him in Brussels last summer?"

Again she thought for a moment that she detected a wariness in his manner. "Yes, Miss Lexham," he said after a slight hesitation. "It is true."

"What happened? The newspapers said so very little."

"There was not a great deal to comment upon. Two French journalists lay in wait for the duke in a Brussels park after he had been to a dinner engagement, but purely by chance he took a different route."

She was horrified. "And but for that chance decision, the duke could have been assassinated?"

"I fear that that indeed could have been the case."

"But how was the plot discovered?"

He looked swiftly at her. "You ask a great many questions, Miss Lexham."

"Oh, forgive me, I did not mean to—" She broke off, suddenly flustered.

His eyes softened. "No, you must forgive me, Miss Lexham,

for I should not have addressed you so sharply. You are quite right to wonder how an unsuccessful plot should have been discovered, and the answer—I should imagine—is that governments employ secret agents, spies to infiltrate enemy organizations.''

''Such men must lead very dangerous lives.''

He smiled faintly. ''They do indeed, Miss Lexham.''

''However, at least the duke is safe now.''

''For the moment.''

''What do you mean?''

''You surely do not imagine that the Bonapartists will let the matter rest there?''

''Well, I—''

''They will not, Miss Lexham, they will not cease until they have put an end to the Iron Duke, or until the day Bonaparte himself passes away.''

Something about the way he spoke made her want to shiver. She fell silent, looking out of the window. He smiled to himself. What, he wondered, would the delightful Miss Caro Lexham say if she knew that within the last week in Paris there had been another attempt to assassinate the duke? This latest attack had come perilously close to success, with a shot being fired at the duke's carriage as he returned to his mansion in the Rue Champs-Elysées. The duke had not been hurt and the whole affair was being kept secret for the time being, but there was immense and deep concern in Downing Street. These Bonapartist plots were becoming more daring and more efficient, for to be able to claim the life of the hated Iron Duke would be the greatest of feathers in their evil cap. They would be encouraged as never before and their cause would be given an impetus which could lead to the restoration of Bonaparte upon the throne of France. That was something which could not be contemplated by the victors of Waterloo.

He took out his fob watch. They were making good speed, and if the roads were clear all the way to London, he would be well in time for his appointment with the prime minister. He smiled a little, for Marcia had been right when she guessed that there was more to his recent activities than met the eye; it was this latest attack on the duke's life which had cut short the pleasant dalliance at Petwell.

He glanced out at the Devon countryside, so bleak and forbidding, and thoughts of Marcia faded away as his concentration returned to the matter in hand. The situation was far more serious than anyone in the government wished to admit, for the Bonapartists had now daringly brought their cause across the Channel and were known to be in London itself. Unless they were foiled, and their most ruthless assassin captured, the Duke of Wellington could be murdered in the heart of England's capital.

Chapter 5

They continued to make excellent speed, the roads proving to be as clear as Hal had hoped. He had arranged in advance for fresh horses to be in readiness at a number of inns along the way, as well as another coachman to replace the weary man who had driven so magnificently through the dangerous Devon terrain.

Hal's air of quiet urgency made Caroline wonder greatly about the nature of the appointment he had in London. What could it be about? Whatever it was, it was important enough for no expense to be spared, for the extra horses and coachman must have been costing a great deal. But he gave no intimation of his purpose, and she could not even begin to guess.

The farther east they went, the milder the weather became. There was no snow now and the teams of fresh horses moved swiftly and easily over the broad highways. Their halts were as brief as possible, but toward the end of the afternoon, with Exeter behind them now, they paused at another inn to eat, Hal insisting that she join him at the table. However, such was his desire to press on that they did not remain long at their repast.

Day gave way to night, and now the lamps pierced the

darkness as the carriage sped onward. Caroline's head lolled against the green leather, her eyes closed. Her bonnet lay on the seat beside her and her tousled hair was coming free of its pins. Hal leaned across to tuck the rug around her once more, and as he did so he paused to look at her face. How very lovely she was, and how charmingly unaware of the fact. She was a beguiling, unaffected creature, a challenge, and if she weren't a lady, he would not have refrained from attempting to seduce her. Also, affairs of the heart had no place in his life at the moment.

Drawing the blinds down over the dark windows, he sat back again. He did not feel at all tired, his mind was too active, too preoccupied with the danger surrounding the Duke of Wellington, the hero of Waterloo, his own personal friend, and the man it had become his duty to protect at all costs.

As dawn approached he was still awake, but Caroline slept on, her head rocking very gently to the motion of the carriage and her honey-colored hair tumbling in profusion over her shoulders. Hal glanced outside and saw the pale gray lightening the eastern sky and he felt more relaxed suddenly, for now there could be no doubt that he would be in time for his appointment in Downing Street. With a snap he raised the blinds, and Caroline's sleepy eyes opened.

"Good morning, Miss Lexham."

For a moment she forgot where she was. A stray curl rested against her cheek and she pushed it aside, sitting up swiftly as memory returned and she realized what an untidy, disheveled sight she must be.

He smiled. "Don't look so concerned, for I promise you that even now you look disconcertingly splendid."

"I don't, I look positively dreadful," she replied, returning the smile. "Where are we?" She glanced out at the unfamiliar, flat countryside.

"I don't know precisely, but I do know that London lies not too far ahead now. We should both be in time for our respective appointments."

She took the few remaining pins from her hair and began to swiftly comb it. It was not a ladylike thing to do, but really she did not feel able to sit there without doing something to rectify her appearance. In a matter of minutes she was neat and reasonably tidy again, and as she straightened her grandmother's necklace, she felt much more presentable.

He glanced at the necklace, his curiosity about it returning. "That is a very handsome bauble, Miss Country Mouse."

"It belonged to my grandmother. She was the eleventh countess, I believe."

Her words startled him. "Your grandmother was a *countess*?"

"Yes, she was the Countess of Lexham. The late twelfth earl was my uncle and it is his will I am going to hear."

He was unable to conceal his surprise. "So, you are one of *the* Lexhams?"

She nodded. "Perhaps a great deal would become more clear to you if I explained that my father was Philip Lexham, the late earl's only brother."

"The black sheep of the family. Yes, that does explain a few things, and it certainly accounts for my never having encountered you in society before."

"It also accounts for my unfashionable, plain appearance."

"I did not say that."

"No, Sir Henry," she said with a smile, "but you could not be blamed for thinking it."

"I admit that I did not for one moment imagine you would belong to the exalted Lexhams, for to begin with you are too sweet and charming. Have you ever met any of them?"

"No."

"Then I cannot in all honesty say that you have missed a great deal."

"You do not mince your words, Sir Henry."

"Where the House of Lexham is concerned, I do not, and that is especially so of the new earl, who, I realize now, is your first cousin."

"Dominic? Yes, he is."

"He is a harbinger of mischief, Miss Lexham, and I warn you to be on your guard where he is concerned. He is, without a doubt, the most disagreeable, odious, untrustworthy, and sly insect it has ever been my misfortune to come across. He does everything to excess, whether it be gambling, indulging his considerable appetite for the ladies, lying, cheating, or anything else. In my opinion there is no depth to which he is incapable of sinking. He would, as they say, sell his own grandmother for sixpence."

She was shocked at this blunt assessment of her cousin and his apparent legion of faults. "He cannot be as black as you paint him, Sir Henry."

"He can be and he is, Miss Lexham. Unfortunately, however, his looks are deceiving, for he has the appearance of an angel." He looked at her again. So, the mystery about her was explained. Of *course* she was closely related to Dominic Lexham, how had he failed to note the incredible likeness before? They shared the same honey-colored hair, the same large gray eyes, and the same fine-boned features; but where the new Earl of Lexham was all that was bad, his lovely country cousin was in truth the angel of the family.

She sensed that he was still thinking about her unexpectedly grand connections. "Well, my cousin's character is hardly likely to be of any concern to me, Sir Henry, for I do not expect to have much to do with him during my brief stay in London. But now that you know I am one of *the* Lexhams, would you be very cross with me if I asked if it would be possible for us to drive along Mayfair Street when we reach Town?"

"To see Lexham House? Of course I am not cross, and certainly we may drive along Mayfair Street." He looked outside at the ever-brightening morning. "Miss Lexham, I believe I am hungry enough to eat the proverbial horse. At what time did you say your appointment was?"

"Eleven o'clock."

"Excellent, for my appointment is a little after that, which means that we have more than enough time to partake of a hearty inn breakfast." He lowered the glass to instruct the coachman to pull in at the next suitable hostelry.

She felt that she had already imposed too much upon his generosity, and could not, therefore, enjoy breakfast at his expense too. "Sir Henry—"

"Think nothing of it, Miss Lexham," he interrupted, knowing exactly what was on her mind, "for I have more than enjoyed your company. Besides, I loathe eating alone; it is uncivilized and disagreeable in the extreme. Tell me, in the far recesses of Dartmoor, do you usually enjoy a gargantuan breakfast?"

She smiled. "My cousin does, Sir Henry, but I certainly do not. He likes nothing better than a spread of cold meat, beefsteak pie, cheese, and beer, to say nothing of the more usual bacon and eggs and fresh bread."

"Dear God," he murmured dryly, "the fellow must be

built like Goliath. However, you will be pleased to note that I am a genteel London weakling, and I breakfast accordingly.''

"I'm relieved to hear it," she replied, her tone a clever reproduction of his own.

It was not lost upon him. "Miss Country Mouse, I perceive that you have already begun to metamorphose into a sharp-tongued town rodent.''

"I am told that I have always been thus, Sir Henry," she said, smiling.

"By your overbearing cousin Richard and his clique of hunting, shooting, and fishing friends?''

"Yes.''

"They would naturally say that of you, for such dull fellows have little appreciation of a woman's wit." He smiled.

"I know," she said with a sigh.

"You would make a dreadful lady of Selford Manor, Caro Lexham, you may take my word for that.''

"Is that a compliment?" she asked hesitantly.

"Oh, yes, it most certainly is," he replied softly, his hazel eyes almost lazy as he looked at her.

She colored just a little, for she could not help but be affected by what he said and the way he said it. From the outset she had been drawn to him, sensing that he was a man apart, so singular and different that she would never be able to forget him. Never before had she experienced an emotion so strong and instantaneous; but she knew that it was an emotion she must put firmly from her mind, for she was no Lady Chaddington, and it was to the Lady Chaddingtons of this world that men like Hal Seymour turned, not the Caroline Lexhams.

He watched her, wondering what she was thinking. How easy it was to bring that charming color to her cheeks and to make her look so delightfully confused and uncertain. It would indeed be pleasant to lay siege to her, for the prospect of her eventual sweet surrender was tantamount to the blackmailing of his senses. He smiled wryly to himself, for had she known his present train of thoughts, her illusions about the gallant and gentlemanly Sir Henry Seymour would have been more than a little shattered. Best to speak of other things. Breakfast, perhaps. "I trust we do not have to travel much farther before we find an inn," he said. "And I also trust that when we do find it, it provides an acceptable table.''

''Surely all the inns on such an important road to London would be excellent, Sir Henry.''

''Possibly. Whatever they provide, however, it will not be up to Oxenford standards.''

''Oxenford? I don't understand.''

''The Oxenford is a fashionable hotel in Piccadilly. My sister and I lodge there at the moment while my house in Hanover Square is being refurbished.''

''You lodge in a hotel?'' She was surprised.

''Why yes, is that so strange?'' He was amused at her reaction. ''Hotels like the Oxenford are not like inns, Miss Lexham; they are exclusive and expensive and are fast becoming very fashionable indeed, especially since the Czar of Russia and his sister, the Duchess of Oldenburg, stayed at the Pulteney three years or so ago. Kings and princes find the best London hotels very much to their liking, and that in turn means that it is quite proper for gentlemen to take their wives, sisters, and daughters there too. Ladies do not like to stay at inns, but they find the new hotels very acceptable indeed. And of course, the hotels provide the very best of French cuisine, which is exceeding fashionable. In fact, I would say that French cooking is practically *de rigueur* at the moment, as you will no doubt discover for yourself.''

''Oh, I doubt if I shall be lodging at an establishment as grand as the Oxenford, Sir Henry.''

''Has your uncle's lawyer made arrangements for you?''

''I do not know.''

''Who is he?''

''Mr. Jordan of Maitland Court.''

''Ah, I know him. He is an excellent fellow and you may rely upon him to do right by you, for although he acts for the Lexhams, he is in fact a most honest and upright fellow—as lawyers go, of course.'' He grinned mischievously. ''He also looks after the welfare of his stomach, so I think you will most certainly be sampling French cuisine, Miss Lexham, if Jordan is involved.''

''What is French cooking really like, Sir Henry? Richard says that it is nothing but overrich sauce poured over indifferent ingredients and is not to be in any way compared with good, plain English cooking.''

He laughed. "There is John Bull personified! However, in one thing he is right, and that is that French cooking is in no way to be compared with the English variety, but when I say that, of course, I speak from personal preference. No doubt your cousin would loathe the fare at the Oxenford, and that is his privilege."

"Presumably the Oxenford has a French chef?"

His eyes took on a thoughtful expression, an almost far-away look which she did not think was entirely on account of her innocent question. "Yes," he murmured, "it boasts the services of one of the finest French chefs in England, one Gaspard Duvall, late of Chez Grignon in the Rue Vivienne, Paris."

"He sounds very impressive."

"Oh, he is, Miss Lexham. He is. As a master of his art I believe that he excels Escudier, Ude, Jacquier, and possibly even Carême—although I would be strongly challenged on that last name."

The names meant nothing to her. She lowered her eyes, feeling suddenly very Selford indeed.

They drove on for a mile or so before the carriage turned at last into the yard of a busy inn, where they partook of an excellent breakfast, which while it was obviously not the work of a Gaspard Duvall, was very tasty. The eggs were done just as she liked them, the bacon was perfectly crisped, the bread warm and fresh, and the coffee strong and aromatic. Much fortified and refreshed, they drove on toward London, and with each mile now, Caroline's excitement mounted. For as long as she could remember, she had longed to visit the capital, and at last the moment was almost upon her.

In spite of the smoke and mist which hung in a pall over the city, she was not disappointed in it. It was so immense, so noisy and thronged after the quiet of Dartmoor, and as the carriage passed through Tyburn turnpike, she felt she was entering the heart not only of London, but of the world itself.

Mindful of her wish to see Lexham House, Hal instructed the coachman to take that route for Maitland Court, and so instead of driving on down Oxford Street, the carriage turned south into Park Lane and then east once more into Mayfair. Through tree-lined avenues they drove, and around quiet, gracious squares where the houses were very elegant and exclusive. At last she looked up and saw the name "Mayfair

Street'' engraved high on a wall, and the carriage began to go more slowly as it approached a high brick wall with a pedimented gateway, and it was through this gateway that she caught her first glimpse of the house in which her father had been born.

It was a beautiful mansion, not all that large by London standards, but certainly very handsome indeed. Set at the far end of a cobbled courtyard that was flanked by coach houses, stables, and other offices, the house rose splendidly against a background of evergreen trees in the gardens at the rear. Perfectly symmetrical, it was breathtakingly simple with its tall, rectangular windows, the flight of white marble steps to the plain door, and the grand balcony extending the width of the floor immediately above. She gazed at it, oddly overcome by seeing at last the house from which she would always be excluded. There was something sad about the building, something closed and unused. There was no smoke rising from any of the chimneys and the windows were all shuttered.

The carriage drove on and she sat back. ''What a lovely house it is, Sir Henry.''

''The Duchess of Devonshire considers it to be the prettiest house in Town.''

''I'm sure it must be,'' she declared, ''But tell me, Sir Henry, are my relatives not residing there at the moment? It looks closed.''

''The Lexhams are only in Town for the Season, Miss Country Mouse, and therefore will not officially be in residence until April or thereabouts. They have come up from County Durham because of the old earl's death, but I believe they are staying at the Clarendon in New Bond Street. Opening Lexham House for a stay of such short duration would be prohibitively expensive.''

''I don't know anything at all, do I?'' she asked suddenly, painfully aware of the gulf between the life she knew and the world he moved in.

''But you will learn swiftly enough,'' he replied. ''Have no fear of that.''

They were driving along Piccadilly now, and in a while he pointed out the Oxenford Hotel, with its pink walls and the balconies overlooking Green Park opposite. Liveried footmen paraded up and down the pavement outside the entrance, rushing to greet a gleaming barouche which drew up at the curb. He also pointed out the Pulteney Hotel, which was nearby. It was here that the czar and his sister had greeted the huge crowds from their balcony.

Apart from exclusive hotels, Piccadilly seemed to contain a vast number of coach offices, for the street was thronged with mails and stages, and with countless travelers, either just arrived in Town or just about to embark for the country. Private curricles and cabriolets threaded their way in and out of the crush, the ribbons tooled with great dash by young blades, some of whom reminded her only too much of the unpleasant Lord Fynehurst, for they too were almost ridiculously fashionable and foppish.

Had Caroline not been so excited and enthralled by it all, she would have been overwhelmed. Hal watched in amusement as she gazed almost breathlessly out of the window. There was more Lexham in her than there was Marchand, he thought, for she was a town mouse to her fingertips. If she returned to the wilds of outlandish Dartmoor, it would not only be her loss, it would be London's loss too.

Just as the church clock in Maitland Court struck eleven, the travel-stained carriage drew up outside Mr. Jordan's premises and the footmen jumped down to open the door and carry her valise into the building. Hal alighted and then handed her down to the pavement.

"I believe I have delivered you on time, Miss Lexham."

"I hope that you will not be late for your appointment, Sir Henry."

"There is no fear of that."

"Thank you for your kind assistance, I am truly indebted to you."

"No, Miss Lexham, I am indebted to you," he corrected.

"In what way?"

"Your sweet presence was a delight and certainly brightened a long and lonely journey."

She looked up into his eyes, realizing quite suddenly that this was the moment of parting and she would probably never see him again. The realization came as a shock, and was not without a little pain. "Good-bye, Sir Henry," she said, her voice deceptively light.

Without warning, he pulled her close, kissing her fully on the lips. "Good-bye, Caro Lexham," he murmured. "Please do not cherish too saintly an impression of me, for I have been struggling against very base thoughts concerning your person." Fleetingly his lips brushed hers again, and then he had climbed back into the carriage, which immediately drove swiftly away in the direction of Westminster.

She stood on the pavement, her senses reeling and her lips still tingling from his kiss. Tears pricked her eyelids as the carriage turned the corner of Maitland Court and passed out of sight, out of her life forever. "Good-bye, Hal," she whispered.

Chapter 6

Before going into the chambers, she glanced along the pavement, where several elegant carriages waited at the curb, and on the panels of one she saw the Lexham coat-of-arms. She knew that this was Dominic's carriage. Looking up at the facade of the building, she was suddenly aware of how close she was to the family of which she was part, but which did not want even to acknowledge her existence. A nervousness overtook her; gone was the excitement of seeing London, the sense of having escaped from Selford for a little while; instead there was the uneasy certainty that no pleasant experience awaited her when she entered the building. With a final glance at the corner where last she had seen Hal's carriage, she went up the shallow, worn steps and into the cold hallway.

A clerk hurried up the stairs to inform the lawyer of her arrival, and a moment later Mr. Jordan came down to greet her. He was a short, stout man, and his round face was pink and flustered, as if he was anticipating a disagreeable hour or so at the hands of the Lexhams. His short-queued wig rested uncertainly on his balding head as he bowed over her hand, and she noticed that his black coat appeared to be several inches too small around his ample waist. She tried to bolster her flagging courage by telling herself that before he had

discovered the delights of French cuisine, his coat had probably fit him excellently.

"Good morning, Miss Lexham, I'm so glad that you have
been able to come all this way."

"Good morning, Mr. Jordan."

"I was concerned that you should be present."

"I gained that impression from your letter, Mr. Jordan, but
truly I cannot imagine why you think I should be here, for it
is hardly likely that I am a beneficiary." Still aware of the
need to screw herself up to a certain pitch in order to face her
family, she went on: "Indeed, my only real reason for making the journey was so that I would at last be able to see
London. There, is that not a dreadfully impious admission?"
She laughed nervously.

"Please don't be anxious, Miss Lexham," he said kindly,
"for in me you have a friend. You are Philip Lexham's
daughter, and for me you need no other recommendation."

She stared at him. "But you are my late uncle's lawyer—"

He smiled. "I am a man of business, Miss Lexham, and
perhaps I have not always allowed my heart to rule my head.
Of late, however, as you will soon discover, I have attempted
to correct that fault in my character. Shall we join everyone
else now?"

Slowly she nodded, accepting the arm he offered, and
together they went up the staircase. She heard the low sound
of refined conversation emanating from beyond the door at
the top of the stairs. In spite of her efforts, she could not
dispel her nervousness, and she knew that the hand resting on
the lawyer's black sleeve was trembling as they approached
the door.

A large group of elegantly clad ladies and gentlemen occupied the room. Dressed uniformly in the deepest mourning,
they presented a daunting sight as they turned as one to look
at her. Their eyes were cold and their faces unsmiling, and
the room fell horribly silent. Their icy disdain was almost
tangible, and not one word was uttered by anyone. Her heart
began to pound, for this ordeal was already far worse than
she had imagined. It seemed that she could hear Richard's
warning echoing in her head. *They will never forgive you for
being a living reminder of an episode they would prefer to
sweep under the ancestral carpet. They'll scorn your country*

ways and your country clothes. They've ignored you all your life and they are not about to change now.

A young man stood apart by the window, and she knew immediately that this was her cousin Dominic, the new earl. His honey-colored hair, so like her own, was disheveled and bright in the pale winter sunlight, and his profile was quite perfect as he gazed out, not even glancing at her, although he must have known she was there. He was tall and slender, and dressed very fashionably, although he was no fop. He made no concession at all to his father's death, and in this he was alone among the Lexhams, with the exception of Caroline herself. His coat was dark green and excellent, his breeches a tight-fitting pale gray, and golden spurs gleamed on the heels of his top boots. His cravat was worn in the unstarched style so popular with young gentlemen of fashion, and a large bunch of seals was suspended from his fob. He was very handsome, there could be no disputing that, but there was a chill about him that made her feel instinctively that what Hal had said of him was the truth.

He turned at last and she saw the hard twist of his sensual mouth. For a moment he surveyed her in silence, and then he deliberately crossed to a vacant chair, flung himself impatiently into it, and then glanced at the lawyer. "Get on with this circus, Jordan, I haven't got all day."

His action in seating himself while she remained standing was a calculated insult which only a fool could have failed to note. She lowered her eyes, wishing that her ordeal was over so that she could escape and forget that she was part of this prideful family.

Mr. Jordan hastily conducted her to a chair and then sat at an immense desk. Unlocking a drawer, he took out a rolled, sealed document, which he opened and then set on the green baize before him. Clearing his throat, he began to read, and as he spoke the familiar opening lines, it was evident that everyone expected the will to be merely a formality, but as he progressed, all eyes were suddenly on him, for it was soon obvious that this was no ordinary last will and testament.

. . . I have always been a proud, strict man, conscious of my duty to my family and aware at all times of my rank and position in life. Unlike my foolish, contemptible brother, Philip, I saw to it that I married suitably, into a titled and respected family, thus forming a union which was acceptable

in the eyes of the society of which I was part. My brother's actions brought shame and scorn upon the name of Lexham, but through me it has been restored to the respect and dignity it should always command. Philip was unworthy to bear such a noble and ancient name, and I see it as my duty to make certain that my successor proves to be in my image and not in the image of my brother. I have viewed with some alarm the profligate conduct of my son Dominic, and I have no intention at all of allowing him to fritter away the family fortune which he so fondly imagines is now his to do with as he pleases. In order to curb his many excesses, I have imposed certain strict conditions if he wishes to inherit that which I have chosen to leave him. . . .

For some time an increasing stir had been passing through the gathering, but now an incredulous murmuring broke out. Caroline kept her eyes lowered as she quelled the anger her dead uncle had aroused with his disparaging remarks about her father. Dominic remained motionless and silent, his handsome face very still indeed.

Mr. Jordan glanced uneasily around and then cleared his throat once again. Silence returned, and he continued to read.

For a period of six calendar months from the day upon which this document is read, my son will not receive one penny from my estate. At the end of that period he will receive almost everything, provided he has limited his conduct and proved himself to be reformed. He must be entirely free of debt, both gaming and otherwise, he must no longer keep company with rogues and women of no character, he must have taken a suitable wife, a woman of name and property, and his own name must be free of any ignominy. If he does not do these things, then another period of six calendar months will ensue, and then another, and so on until he bows to my wishes and becomes a man worthy of the title of the thirteenth Earl of Lexham. . . .

At this there was immediate uproar, for no one could believe what they were hearing. Dominic had been listening in stunned silence, but now he leaped to his feet, his eyes diamond bright and his lips thin with fury. "Is this some jest of yours, Jordan? If it is, then I'll have your miserable hide!"

"It is no jest, Lord Lexham," replied the lawyer, raising his voice to be heard above the clamor.

"I'll contest it!" cried Dominic. "I'll take it to every court in the land if need be!"

"You cannot contest it with any hope of success, my lord, for your father was most definitely of sound mind when he made the will. And perhaps I should warn you that he deliberately chose as one of the witnesses a gentleman of such rank and eminence that I do not believe you would wish to offend him by challenging a document to which he had appended his name. I speak of the Prince Regent himself."

Dominic stared at him, and the prince's name was not lost upon the others, who heard it in spite of their disorderly protests. Abruptly the room was quiet again, and everyone looked at Dominic. His face was very pale, and his demeanor chilling as he held the lawyer's nervous gaze. "Correct me if I am wrong, Jordan," he said softly, "but did you not read out that I would inherit *almost* everything?"

"That is indeed what I read out, Lord Lexham." The lawyer was uneasy.

"From which I understand that this damned charade is not yet over."

"I fear not, my lord."

"Then proceed, lawyer." Dominic's voice was almost silky.

"If you w-would please be seated once again, m-my lord," stammered the unfortunate Mr. Jordan, beads of perspiration clearly visible on his glistening forehead.

"I will remain standing."

Mr. Jordan's hand shook as he picked up the will again, and he was obviously very uneasy indeed, just as Dominic intended he should be.

As I believe that my son will think me not to be in earnest about these conditions, I am going to demonstrate my firmness of purpose in a most signal way. I do, therefore, omit from his inheritance a very important part of my estate. That part is Lexham House itself. . . .

The lawyer paused, expecting another angry outburst, but the room was absolutely silent. From where she sat Caroline could see Dominic's face very clearly, and although he did not move a muscle, she could tell that he was immeasurably shocked. But when he spoke, his voice was very calm. "To whom does the house go?"

"It is not quite as simple as that, Lord Lexham; indeed it is very complicated."

"Goddammit, man, will you get to the point!" cried Dominic, his control snapping.

Mr. Jordan flinched as if he had been struck. "Y-yes, my lord, I will c-continue immediately." He took a deep, steadying breath.

That part is Lexham House itself, together with its contents, which are enumerated in the inventory appended to this document. The inventory is necessary in order to prevent anyone from removing any item from the house until such time as my conditions are met. The person I am about to name will be subject to restrictions similar to those pertaining to Dominic's portion of my estate. The house must be lived in for a period of six calendar months, commencing not later than one week after the reading of this will. During those six months the property must be opened up completely, no rooms may remain closed, and no debt must be incurred in order to do this, nor may there be any gift or loan taken out. If the person should wish to marry during this period, then nothing may be received from the new spouse in order to finance the running of the house. The occupancy of the house must be completely respectable, with no hint of scandalous or licentious activity. If at the end of six months these conditions have been complied with in every detail, and provided that the inventory is complete down to the last spoon, then the house will become the full and undisputed property of the person to whom I now leave it. However, if the conditions are not met with, then the house will revert to the rest of the inheritance and will become subject to the conditions I have placed upon my son. I have taken this drastic action in order to convince my son that I mean what I say. He prides himself upon being a gambling man, and so I trust that he appreciates that in these particular stakes, he is still the odds-on favorite, the new owner of the house having in truth little more than an outside chance of success. Indeed, I have entered the new heir simply and solely to goad the favorite, to spur him into doing exactly as I wish. But an outside chance is still a chance, and I fully intend that my son should realize

*this and do all in his power to meet my terms and thus make
sure that the delay before he receives his patrimony should
only involve the first six months. All this having been said, I
now tell you that the person to whom I leave Lexham House
and its contents, is my niece, Caroline Mary Lavinia
Lexham. . . .''*

Chapter 7

It seemed that as one the gathering gave a gasp of horrified disbelief, and Caroline could only look up in swift amazement at hearing her name. One of the gentlemen leaped furiously to his feet, shouting that the whole affair was an outrage and an insult, while the ladies looked at one another in dismay, obviously already concerned with the ridicule the family would be subjected to once the story began to circulate in the drawing rooms of London.

For a moment Dominic seemed stunned, but then he whirled about to face Caroline, his body as taut as a bowstring and his hands clenched so tightly that his knuckles were white. An immediate hush fell over the room and Caroline could hear her own heartbeats as her cousin slowly approached her. Incongruously she found herself remembering Hal Seymour's description of him. *His looks are deceiving, he has the appearance of an angel, but he is a harbinger of mischief and I warn you to be on your guard where he is concerned.* But in spite of his golden, masculine beauty, there was little of the angel about the Earl of Lexham in that moment, for he was in the grip of ugly rage, his gray eyes as hard and unyielding as flint.

54

Before he could speak, she rose to her feet. "My lord, I promise you that I knew nothing of this!"

"No? I think you lie, madam, and I shall make you pay dearly for this incredible impudence. You wish to play the lady, do you? Well, it seems that for six months you may attempt to do just that, but you will never be a lady, coz, for you are nothing, an upstart who thinks she may claw herself up at my expense! You are wrong, so very wrong, for before I am finished with you, my dear, you will wish that you had remained in the safety and obscurity of Devon."

She was trembling. "I swear that I knew nothing," she repeated.

His eyes flickered. "The whole thing is purely academic anyway, is it not? You do indeed have only an outside chance of keeping the house, for in order to live in it as the will instructs, you will need money, which if I am any judge, is the one thing you most certainly do not possess." He allowed his disparaging, contemptuous glance to move slowly over her plain bonnet, the voluminous, concealing mantle, and the laced ankle boots peeping from beneath its hem.

"Please, sir—"

"Save your breath, madam, for you will surely have need of it! But I warn you here and now, that notwithstanding the Prince Regent's involvement, I shall do all in my power to prove the will to be invalid, and I shall also see to it that you find it utterly impossible to meet the conditions. The kid gloves are off, dear coz, and you would do well to glance frequently over your shoulder from this day forth."

Turning, he went to the table where he had left his top hat and gloves, and then he looked for a last time at Mr. Jordan. "You have crossed me, lawyer, and that was very foolish of you."

"My lord, I merely carried out the late earl's wishes."

Dominic smiled just a little, but there was no warmth or humor in him. "You have crossed me," he repeated, and then he had gone. They heard his light, swift steps on the staircase.

For a moment no one else moved, and then the rest of the Lexham family followed in his wake. The gentlemen avoided meeting Caroline's eyes, and the ladies flicked their costly black skirts aside from her as if they feared she might in some way contaminate them.

At last they had all departed, and Mr. Jordan did not disguise his sigh of relief as he sank into his chair, wiping his shining forehead with a large handkerchief. "Forgive me, Miss Lexham, but I fear I have long been dreading this morning, for I knew only too well how that will would be received. I fully expected to lose the Lexham family as my clients, of that you may be sure. However, at least now you understand why I wrote to you asking you to attend if it was at all possible."

She nodded. "It was in fact that phrase, 'if at all possible,' which made me feel that I should make the journey. But in spite of the will, Mr. Jordan, I feel that I can only agree with my cousin, the earl."

"Agree with him?" The lawyer looked taken aback.

"Oh, not with his conduct, merely with his statement that my tenure at Lexham House can only last for the initial six months, for he is quite right, I don't possess sufficient funds."

"That is a grave obstacle," he admitted. "But at the same time I feel I must advise you to think most carefully about the whole matter. Have you any idea of the value of the house and its contents?"

"No."

"Well, the building itself is worth a great deal, for it is a first-class property occupying a prime Mayfair site. The contents comprise many art treasures, paintings by great artists, an irreplaceable collection of jade and Chinese porcelain, magnificent silver and gold plate, furniture from Versailles itself . . . At the end of six months all that would be yours, if you could meet the terms of the will." He held her gaze. "Miss Lexham, you would be a considerable heiress."

She was silent for a moment. "That's as may be, Mr. Jordan, but it will be quite impossible for me to achieve, because my uncle laid his plans with great care. He calls me an outsider, but what he really means is that I have no chance at all. He had no intention at all of allowing me to slip through, for he has effectively tied my hands by imposing conditions which present an insoluble problem. I am cast in the role of goad, no more, and no less, and to judge by my cousin Dominic's reaction, I would say that my uncle chose his goad with admirable skill."

"And so you mean to give up without a fight?"

"I do not have any choice. Besides, if I am honest, I do

not think that I have any right to the property, for in spite of my cousin's odiousness, he is the new earl, the new head of the family, and Lexham House should go to him.''

Mr. Jordan was appalled at this sentiment. "My dear Miss Lexham," he exclaimed, "you have *every* right to the house, for it has been left to you. It does not matter what ulterior motive your uncle may have had, it is an indisputable legal fact that for the next six months at least, Lexham House belongs to you and only to you. And I tell you here and now, that nothing would give me greater pleasure than to see Philip Lexham's daughter as mistress of the house in which he was born and from which he was so cruelly excluded by his own flesh and blood. Of all the Lexhams, he alone was worthy, he alone could really lay claim to the title of gentleman. I know that at the moment it seems impossible that you can win, and indeed I have been putting my legal mind to the problem ever since I knew your uncle's intention and I have been unable to see a way through—but there is still one week left in which to solve matters, and in law I promise you that a week can be a very long time. Your uncle used you heartlessly and deliberately, with no thought of your feelings, but he forgot one cardinal rule in racing, Miss Lexham, and that is that sometimes outsiders romp home by a distance. My advice to you is that you thumb your pretty nose at your disagreeable family, and at the new earl in particular, that you take your deceased uncle on and play him at his own game. Fight for your inheritance if you can, my dear! You owe nothing to any of the Lexhams, except perhaps to yourself and to your father's memory, which has been so cruelly disparaged here today. Don't give up just yet, Miss Lexham, I beg of you.''

"And if I do," she said quietly, "the result will still be the same—the week's grace will pass and still I will not have thought of a solution.''

He rose to his feet, coming around the desk to take her hands. "But you will at least think about it, won't you? You have so very much to gain by trying to meet the conditions, and so very much to lose by throwing in the towel.'' He smiled. "But you will be in Town for a while, won't you? You wish to see the city, and that will allow me time to show you over your inheritance in Mayfair Street.''

"Not if that means any risk of encountering my relatives, sir.''

"The house is closed, I promise you, for they lodge at present at the Clarendon in New Bond Street. The house is in the care of the housekeeper, a Mrs. Hollingsworth. Look at it this way, Miss Lexham, you have an opportunity now of seeing over the house in which your father was born, the house which bears your name. Does that not mean anything?"

She smiled. "It means a very great deal, Mr. Jordan, and so I thank you and will indeed be pleased to see it whenever it is convenient. But my first priority must be to find somewhere to stay."

"You do not need to worry about that, my dear, for it has already been attended to."

She was a little alarmed, fearing that his choice might be expensive and beyond her poor purse. "Mr. Jordan, I do not have a great deal of money. . . ."

He smiled in a way that could only be described as both sleek and satisfied. "Your stay in London will not cost you one penny, Miss Lexham, for it will be paid for by your late uncle's estate."

She stared. "But how can that be?"

"I made it my business to point out to your uncle that if he wished to use you to spur his son, then it would be achieved to greater effect if you were present—which would entail your coming to London and so on. He thought this a capital notion and instructed that a clause be entered. He intended me to install you in the meanest accommodation available, but there was nothing in the wording of the clause to indicate any such thing; I saw to that. I have reserved for you a suite of rooms in one of London's finest hotels, Miss Lexham, the Oxenford in Piccadilly."

She heard the name with something like a jolt. The Oxenford! Her first thought was that she would be seeing Hal Seymour again after all, but such notions were immediately replaced by more sobering considerations. "Mr. Jordan, I thank you for your kindness, but there is no way at all that I may stay at the Oxenford; it is far too exclusive and I am not at all the sort of person they wish to have as their guest. I am traveling without a maid—because I do not possess one—and I am obviously far from fashionable. No, the Oxenford is quite out of the question."

"My dear, you are the first cousin of the Earl of Lexham, whether or not that gentleman appreciates the fact, and you are also the new owner of Lexham House; of *course* you are worthy of the Oxenford. Besides, the apartment has already been paid for and all arrangements made. I am sure you will not regret staying there, for it is acknowledged to be one of the foremost hotels in Town.''

"I know.''

"You do?''

"Yes, although until this morning I had never even heard of it.''

He was puzzled. "But how did you learn of the Oxenford, Miss Lexham?''

"Sir Henry Seymour told me all about it.''

Now he was startled. "You are acquainted with Sir Henry?''

"He was kind enough to convey me to London in his carriage; indeed, but for his kindness, I would probably still be stranded in Devon.''

Mr. Jordan looked at her. "Am I to understand that you traveled all the way to London with Sir Henry Seymour?''

"Yes.''

"There was another lady present, of course.''

She colored a little. "No, I'm rather afraid there wasn't.''

He was appalled. "Oh dear, I do not think that that was at all wise or proper.''

Her color heightened. "It came about quite by accident, sir, for I truly believed Lady Chaddington was to travel with us. By the time I realized my mistake it was too late and we were leaving the inn. But Sir Henry was a perfect gentleman in every way, Mr. Jordan.'' She had to look away, however, for she remembered Hal's last words to her only too clearly, and she could almost feel again the warmth and excitement of his lips over hers.

The lawyer shifted a little uneasily. "Miss Lexham, I know it is none of my concern and you would be perfectly justified if you told me to mind my own business, but I feel a little responsible for you, because you are not only Philip Lexham's child, you are also here simply because of my invitation. Forgive me for saying so, but it was not at all proper for you to have been alone with a gentleman like Sir Henry, especially as you can have had little experience of the ways of such men. Those like Sir Henry can be so very charming, attentive, and amusing; they are rich, intent upon the pleasures of life, and they are only too skilled in the pursuit and flattery of the fair sex. You are a young lady of great loveliness, my dear, and that fact will not have been lost upon Sir Henry, for he is no laggard when it comes to such things, that much I promise you."

Her cheeks were aflame now. "Maybe so, but he was a gentleman toward me, Mr. Jordan."

"Well, perhaps I wrong Sir Henry by implying that he could be otherwise, but you were still very much at risk, for you did not know him at all, did you?"

"No."

"You were alone with a stranger in his carriage, you traveled overnight with him a distance of some two hundred miles, and had he chosen to behave like a blackguard and a libertine, there would have been very little you could have done to defend your honor. Please do not think ill of me for speaking so bluntly, my dear, but I would not feel I had myself behaved with any honor if I had not said something." He smiled then, determined to set such a disagreeable topic aside. "Come now, I do not wish to sound as if I enjoy lecturing, especially as I hope to have the pleasure of dining with you tonight at the Oxenford."

She returned the smile, the uncomfortable flush dying away from her cheeks. "I do not think you are lecturing me, Mr. Jordan, for I know that you are truly concerned about my welfare, and of course I would be delighted to dine with you tonight."

"And you do not still object to the Oxenford?"

"No."

"Excellent."

She briefly lowered her eyes. "Mr. Jordan?"

"Yes?"

"Is Sir Henry to marry Lady Chaddington?"

He looked surprised at the question. "Why, I believe such a betrothal is soon expected, and rumor has it that her ladyship has been endeavoring for some time to win him."

She looked up at him. "What do you know of the banquet he is arranging for the Duke of Wellington?"

He seemed amused. "Why do you ask?"

"Well, I overheard Lady Chaddington express extreme surprise at his involvement in such an affair, and I must confess that I too am most surprised, for he does not seem at all the sort of man to bother with banquets."

He nodded. "It is indeed a strange affair, especially as until recently there was a very curious, although utterly discreet, rumor that Sir Henry was involved in things of grave national importance—grave things."

"What do you mean?"

"I will tell you, but you must remember that it is a rumor and probably has no foundation whatsoever; indeed, I do not see that it can have, in view of Sir Henry's subsequent activities. It was being said that he was working on behalf of the government, involved secretly with matters on the Continent, in Brussels and Paris. There was even one suggestion that he was assigned to guard the Duke of Wellington!" The lawyer chuckled, shaking his head. "Well, if he is guarding the Iron Duke, then he has a very strange way of doing it, for he returned to England, promptly decided that his already excellent town house must be completely refurbished from cellar to attic, and then he and his delightful sister, Miss Seymour, took up residence at the Oxenford, where he took over the arranging of the banquet from poor Reggie Bannister, who is so sadly indisposed with the gout at the moment. Now then, Miss Lexham, does that sound to you like the movements of a man who is involved in life-and-death affairs of state?"

She smiled. "No."

"I agree. Now, however, I will take you to the Oxenford, for you must be tired, and then this evening we will dine together there, and you can sample the exquisite cooking of Mr. Duvall—which, I trust, will prove an unforgettable experience and which is to blame for the immense amount of weight I have put on in recent months."

She smiled again, but then a thought struck her. "Oh, Mr. Jordan, I trust that my baggage has arrived. I took the liberty of sending it ahead to this address, I do hope that that was not too much of a liberty. . . ?" Her voice died away at the look of surprise on his face.

"Baggage? Why no, Miss Lexham, nothing has been delivered here."

"Oh, no!"

"Perhaps it is still at the coach office. I will send a man there immediately. Please do not look so concerned, my dear, for I am sure that all is well."

But his words lacked conviction and they both knew that

her baggage was gone forever. Dismayed, she allowed him to usher her to the door. Things were now even worse, for she was not only going to stay at one of London's most exclusive hotels, she was going to do so with a wardrobe of only two dresses, the one she was wearing and the one in her little valise! Why, oh why had she been so foolish as to dispatch her other things ahead? She had only done so in order to make her determination to go all the more plain to Richard—now she was, as the saying went, hoist with her own petard!

Chapter 8

Caroline's heart thumped nervously as she and Mr. Jordan entered the Oxenford a little later, having crossed London in the lawyer's chariot. Her worst fears about the exclusive nature of the hotel were fast being realized, for even as she alighted from the chariot she had witnessed the exchanged glances of the two liveried footmen parading so importantly up and down on the pavement outside the building. Passing through the discreet doorway into the black-and-white-tiled hall, she was conscious of a rather intimidating hush pervading everything, as if no one dared to speak above a whisper.

Little or no daylight pierced the hall, which was consequently lighted by an immense crystal chandelier suspended from the elegant domed ceiling high above. There were footmen everywhere, and long-aproned waiters hurrying to and from the nearby dining room, where it seemed that the guests were enjoying light luncheons. She felt very provincial indeed in her old mantle and sensible ankle boots, and she was horribly aware of her lack of a maid or lady companion; she was aware too of how glaring were the scratches on her old valise, which the porter had placed so prominently on the floor directly beneath the glowing chandelier. As the porter hurried away in search of Mr. Bassett, who was, so Mr.

Jordan whispered to her, the *maître d'hôtel* or majordomo, she knew already that she would not enjoy staying in this place.

Mr. Algernon Bassett proved to be a very superior being indeed. Wearing a discreet and tasteful coat of the darkest blue cloth, and pantaloons which she thought would be more suitable for evening wear, he approached the two new arrivals, his lofty glance taking barely a second to discern that the Miss Lexham who was to occupy the elegant apartment on the second floor was not at all the sort of person he had been expecting. Like Mr. Baldwin of the White Boar, he too trimmed his courtesy to suit her apparent social standing. His smile of welcome, while not exactly withering, was not warm either, and his pale blue eyes seemed to flicker coldly.

He said very little as he snapped his fingers, calling a black boy dressed as a rajah and instructing him to conduct madam to her apartment. She felt her cheeks flush with embarrassment as the little boy picked up the valise, after first glancing around curiously for the rest of her luggage. After arranging to dine with Mr. Jordan that evening, she followed the little black boy up a very grand staircase, along a carpeted passage, and through an ornate doorway into the magnificent apartment she was to occupy for the next few days.

Never before had she been in such elegance, indeed the rooms were almost palatial. There was a small drawing room, a bedroom with a magnificent four-poster bed, and a little dressing room. All were hung with gray brocade, all had beautiful Axminster carpets on the floor, and all overlooked Piccadilly and Green Park, and the magnificence of nearby Devonshire House. Gold-framed mirrors hung on the walls, candles were placed in girandoles on either side of the white-and-pink marble fireplaces, and the mahogany furniture had been polished until it gleamed.

When the little boy had gone, she walked slowly around the apartment, gazing at everything, touching the lacy curtains, running her fingers over the elegant upholstery of a sofa, and testing the softness of the bed. The noise of Piccadilly was muffled and the lace curtains muted the sunlight. The atmosphere of the hotel seemed to fold inexorably over her. She felt very, very alone.

She slept for most of the afternoon, more tired than she had realized after the long journey and the harrowing experience

of her first meeting with her father's family. Outside it was
dark now and across Green Park she could see the lights of
Buckingham House, while nearby Devonshire House was
brilliant, every room illuminated. A maid came to draw the
curtains and light the candelabra, and it was time for Caroline
to dress for her first London dinner.

With a sigh she opened her valise and took out her only
other gown, the turquoise lawn. She held it up a little
doubtfully, for there was no mistaking the fact that it was a
morning gown, not an evening gown, but then she had packed
it in the valise merely as a standby in case her gray wool
became travel-stained. Now it was to serve for a fashionable
dinner in London! Wryly she smiled a little, for there was no
doubt that even had her baggage been delivered as promised,
the gowns she wore for evenings in Selford would still have
looked dreadfully ordinary here in the Oxenford. Still, there
was no way out of her predicament and she must do the best
she could with the few clothes she had—and at least she had
her grandmother's necklace, which was surely grand enough
for any occasion.

She washed in the porcelain bowl provided in the dressing
room, shivering a little from the cold water, and then she
lightly applied rouge to her cheeks and lips. Her hair proved a
little difficult, for she so wanted to look as modish as possible,
which was not easy when one was not used to such things. It
was one thing to peruse past issues of fashionable publications,
it was quite another to achieve an acceptable imitation of their
engravings.

At last she had finished combing and pinning and she
surveyed the result in the cheval glass. She had twisted the
honey-colored tresses into a creditable knot on the top of her
head, and one long curl hung prettily down over her left
shoulder. At Selford she had always called upon the capable
services of her cook-housekeeper, Mrs. Thompson, who could
dress her hair up with considerable skill, if not in accordance
with each successive whim of fashion, and Caroline had
found it unbelievably difficult to do the job herself, bending
and turning to try to see in the mirror. She patted the length
of matching turquoise ribbon which she had managed to
twine through the knot of hair, and she was pleased with the
way it fluttered a little when she moved.

Next she stepped into the turquoise lawn, puffing out the

little sleeves and arranging the soft folds to fall evenly from the high waistline. She had wondered how well her grand-mother's rubies would look with the turquoise, but she was pleased to see that they went very well indeed, for the rubies were dark and the turquoise was a muted, almost dusty shade. Picking up her plain white shawl and draping it over her bare arms, she surveyed herself in the mirror again. She sighed, for there was no mistaking the fact that she was provincial, a country mouse newly come to Town. Well, there was nothing for it but to brave the dining room, which would in all probability be thronged with the most fashionable, most criti-cal of the *haut monde*!

For a moment her courage almost failed her, until she told herself that Hal Seymour had complimented her upon looking good even when she had just awoken; if such a gentleman could say such a thing and mean it, then she must hold her head high and believe her appearance tonight to be adequate. As she left her apartment she wondered if Hal would be dining at the hotel tonight.

Her shaky courage wavered anew, however, as she de-scended the magnificent grand staircase and a group of ladies and gentlemen in the hallway all turned as one to survey her. Her hand shook upon the gleaming rail and her cheeks be-came very pink as the gentlemen raised their quizzing glasses and the ladies whispered together behind their fans.

To her relief, Mr. Jordan had already arrived, and he came forward immediately to greet her, bowing gallantly over her hand and saying that she looked very fetching indeed. She was very conscious of how exquisite were the gowns of the nearby ladies, so obviously the work of the finest London *couturières*, whereas the turquoise lawn was as obviously the handiwork of Eliza White of Selford. She was so preoccupied with this thought that she hardly heard Mr. Jordan telling her that unfortunately there was no sign at all of her missing luggage; it had indeed gone completely astray somewhere between Selford and London and had probably been stolen.

The dining room of the Oxenford was a very severe chamber, decorated in dull colors and illuminated by so many chande-liers that the light was harsh and glaring. The lower portion of the walls was paneled in dark-gray, while the upper por-tion was hung with silk the color of the sea, which last seemed somehow to drain the warmth from the faces of the seated guests. The white-clothed tables were not large and were partitioned from their neighbors to give a little privacy to the small parties of diners. Candelabra stood upon each table and the gleaming cutlery had been set out with such precision that Caroline felt it would be a crime to actually pick up a knife and use it. Waiters hurried to and from the immense sideboards lining the far wall, their long starched aprons crackling, and the drone of polite conversation and the clatter of knives and forks filled the air.

Caroline glanced swiftly at the other guests, but to her disappointment she saw no sign of Hal Seymour. She and Mr. Jordan descended the shallow flight of steps to the floor of the room and another of the little black boys greeted them, his splendid Indian clothes made of the very finest cloth-of-gold. He beamed at the lawyer, recognizing him immediately. "Good evening, Mr. Jordan, sir."

"Good evening, Hercules."

"Follow me, sir. Madam." Hercules bowed very grandly and conducted them to an empty table, where he drew out Caroline's chair for her and then presented her with the *carte*.

She glanced at it in dismay, for it was entirely in French, for which language Parson Young's careful tuition had not prepared her. She was suddenly very aware of the shortcomings of an education which the folk of Selford had regarded as unfemininely thorough but which here in London seemed very inadequate indeed. A little self-consciously she smiled at the lawyer. "Please order for me, sir, as I am sure your choice will be excellent."

He smiled. "I would be delighted, my dear." After regarding the card for a moment, he gave instructions to Hercules, who nodded several times and then scurried away.

The lawyer sat back, looking pleased with himself. "If I said that I had ordered mere chicken broth, then beefsteak and then apricot tart, no doubt you would be singularly unimpressed, but I promise you that those dishes, when prepared by a chef of such genius as Gaspard Duvall, are in a class of their own."

She smiled, but although she tried to appear at ease, it was almost impossible. Under the glare of the chandeliers she felt more conspicuous than ever and quite out of her depth. On reflection, she did not know if she was sorry or relieved that Hal Seymour was not present, for surely the shortcomings of her background and appearance would be only too evident to him in these surroundings—perhaps he would not even wish to acknowledge her.

In spite of these private thoughts, she still found the dining room very interesting. She watched as the waiters spirited heavy silver dishes to and fro with such dexterity that she did not once see a risk of accident. She saw the superior Mr. Bassett wending his regal way between the tables, smiling sleekly at the influential guests, and qualifying his manner even with them. She pondered that in all probability he had a chart upon the wall of his private room: a prince of the blood would receive a deep, scraping bow and a sickly, servile smile, a duke would merit a slightly less scraping bow and an equally servile smile, and so on. Yes, the more she watched him, the more convinced she became of the existence of such a chart. A waiter called the majordomo to carve at a table occupied by bejeweled dowagers, and he stepped up with great verve, picking up the implements with a flourish and proceeding to give the entire room a display of swordsmanship. Caroline hid a smile, for had he challenged the motionless joint of roast beef with a dashing "On guard!" he could not more have resembled a fencing master. How different such carving was at Selford, where Richard hacked with gusto rather than grace, and where the carving knife and fork were discarded afterward with a loud clatter, not with refined daintiness.

Mr. Jordan drew her attention away from the majordomo. "Tell me, Miss Lexham, are you comfortable in your apartment?"

"Oh yes, indeed, the rooms are most elegant."

"Mr. Bassett assured me that the Earl of Lexham's cousin would be most pleased with that particular apartment. I understand it has a fine prospect over Green Park."

"Yes, it has."

"And what do you think of the Oxenford? Are you not glad now that I took rooms here for you?"

He seemed so anxious that she should be pleased that she had not the heart to be honest and say that she found the Oxenford too intimidating and that she would much have preferred a comfortable room at a good inn. Instead she murmured complimentary things and smiled.

He seemed satisfied with her response, for he sat back once

more, glancing around and nodding. "Yes, indeed, when I think back to the days of my youth, there were no such establishments—certainly nowhere quite as eminently suitable for ladies. Now persons of great rank are content to lodge in these hotels. Why, the Prince Regent has a private suite at Mivart's, so that he may enjoy the cooking of its French chef whenever he pleases, and the King of France recently stayed at Grillion's on his way back to Paris to claim his throne. Jacquier, who keeps the Clarendon, was until recently chef to that same King of France, which makes one wonder if perhaps there was some disagreement, for his majesty must have declined the Clarendon in favor of Grillion's. Yes, the fashion has changed a great deal in recent years, and now one is as likely to find members of the aristocracy taking suites in hotels as purchasing town houses. The most recent development, however, is that a very important society wedding is to take place in a hotel—right here at the Oxenford in fact. I speak of the marriage of Lord Carstairs and Miss Seymour."

Caroline was immediately more interested. "Sir Henry's sister?"

"Yes. A most charming and delightful young lady. She wishes, so I understand, to set a new pace, and that is why she insists upon marrying here instead of at the Seymour country seat at Daneborough in Wiltshire, or indeed at fashionable St. George's in Hanover Square." He smiled. "I believe she will succeed in starting a new mode, for ladies of rank and fashion are very receptive to new ideas. Don't you agree, Miss Lexham?"

"I do indeed, sir."

At that moment a waiter brought the chicken broth the lawyer had ordered and Caroline's attention left the interesting topic of Hal's enterprising sister and turned instead to the matter of French cuisine. She had only taken a spoonful when she knew that this meal was an entirely new experience. The chicken broth was magical and deserved its grand title of *consommé princesse;* the beefsteak was called *tournedos à la béarnaise* and was a succulent dream; and the apricot tart was composed of exquisitely sharp fruit upon a feather-light pastry, and it fully deserved to be known by the more interesting name of *tarte aux abricots*.

Mr. Jordan waited until the meal was at an end before at last inquiring what she thought. She smiled. "It seems small wonder to me, sir, that the French were defeated at Waterloo, for if their army had dined upon such wonderful delicacies, no doubt they were feeling too good to put up too much of a struggle.''

He laughed. "So, you approve of this rage for French cooking?''

"I think I must, sir.''

"Then maybe you will shortly be able to congratulate the chef in person, for I believe he is about to appear among us.'' He glanced behind her and she turned with interest. There was a slight stir among the other guests and then the incredible figure of Monsieur Gaspard Duvall descended the steps to the floor of the room.

She looked at him in utter amazement, for he did not present at all the traditional figure of a cook: there was no white hat and no apron. He must have been about forty years old, although he moved with the sprightliness of a much younger man. He was small and dark, and with his bright brown eyes and animated expression, was very French indeed. His hair was beginning to go gray at the temples, and had he been of greater stature, he would have been pronounced a very handsome fellow. However, it was his choice of attire which was the most startling thing about him, for it was not at all conventional. His hat was a floppy blue beret, worn at a rakish angle over one ear, his waistcoat was a vivid peacock blue, and his trousers were as close fitting as some gentlemen wore their breeches. His tight-waisted, full-skirted coat was aquamarine in color, and altogether his appearance was such that he could not have passed unnoticed in a crowd. Whatever his taste in clothes, however, his smile was infectious, and it was immediately obvious to Caroline that the little Frenchman was liked as much for his good humor as for his eccentricity.

Fascinated, she watched him progress from table to table, exchanging greetings with the gentlemen and bowing gallantly over the hands of all the ladies. At last he approached her table, and Mr. Jordan rose immediately to his feet.

"Ah, Monsieur Jordan!'' exclaimed the chef, recognizing the lawyer, "How pleasant it is to see you here once more.''

"The frequency of my visits are proof of my delight with your brilliant cuisine, monsieur. May I present to you Miss Lexham, a lady who has tonight tasted French cooking for the first time.''

The chef looked quickly at her. "Miss Lexham? Miss Caroline Lexham?"

She was surprised. "Why yes, monsieur. But how—" She broke off, glancing around as she realized that those at nearby tables had heard the chef say her name, and that that name was not unknown to them. She received many curious glances and people leaned together to whisper.

The chef smiled. "You see, you are already famous, mademoiselle. I think everyone in London knows of the amazing Lexham will."

"Oh." She colored, lowering her eyes.

Mr. Jordan was comforting. "Don't look so uneasy, my dear, for the story was bound to get out, and will have circulated through every drawing room in Town by now."

"I didn't think anyone would hear of it."

The lawyer chuckled. "My dear Miss Lexham, I doubt if a single person present at the reading of that will would have been able to keep his or her tongue still about what happened. Discretion was never a Lexham trait, you know."

She smiled at that. "No, I begin to realize that.

Gaspard Duvall still stood at the table. "So, mademoiselle, you have today become an heiress, and you have also sampled French cooking for the first time. This must surely be a momentous day for you."

"It is indeed, monsieur. I cannot with honesty say how I feel about my inheritance, but I can say that I found the cooking to be quite superlative."

"To hear such praise from the lips of one so very beautiful is sweet indeed, mademoiselle," replied the chef, obviously as pleased as he said he was. "And I am all the more delighted since I have been forced to labor in the bowels of the earth."

"I beg your pardon?"

"The kitchens, they are in the cellars. They are, therefore, *odieuse et abominable*." He spoke with considerable feeling as he lapsed into his native tongue. "Such kitchens are not worthy of Duvall," he went on, tossing an almost venomous glance at the unknowing Mr. Bassett, who stood nodding and smiling just out of earshot. "For they are small and dark, their ovens are old-fashioned, and there is no range at all! In Paris I had magnificent kitchens, large enough to serve *twenty* dining rooms, equipped to produce *thirty-four* soups and *one hundred and twelve* fish dishes on one *carte* alone! Here, everything is *abominable*!'' With this, the little chef took his leave of them, moving on to the next table, where he was once again all smiles and charm.

For a little longer Caroline and Mr. Jordan remained at their table, but she was aware of still being the object of much curiosity now that her identity was known, and so at last she asked Mr. Jordan if they could leave. Without hesitation, he agreed, and a minute later they were being shown from the room by little Hercules, into whose upturned turban Mr. Jordan dropped a coin. In the entrance hall, the lawyer took his leave of her, arranging to call upon her at eleven the following morning, when they would drive to Lexham House so that she could see her inheritance.

No sooner had the lawyer departed, however, than the porter was opening the doors again to admit two returning guests, a young lady in delicate lilac muslin, and a tall, distinguished gentleman whom Caroline recognized immediately: Hal Seymour. Her heart almost stopped as she paused at the foot of the grand staircase, and again, as if he sensed her gaze upon him, he turned swiftly in her direction. Their eyes met, and for a moment he seemed surprised, but then he smiled at her. ''Why, Miss Lexham,'' he said, coming toward her. ''What an unexpected pleasure this is.'' He took her hand and raised it to his lips.

Chapter 9

"Good evening, Sir Henry," she replied, wishing that she looked cool and collected, but knowing that a telltale color was flaming on her cheeks.

The young lady he was with now joined them. She was very attractive, with her fluffy dark hair and large, dancing green eyes, and she wore jewelry which was so costly that the precious stones winked and flashed at the slightest movement.

Hal turned to her. "Jennifer, allow me to introduce you to Miss Lexham."

"*The* Miss Lexham?"

"Yes, indeed. Miss Lexham, my sister, Miss Seymour."

Jennifer Seymour smiled, holding out a white-gloved hand. "I am so pleased to meet you, Miss Lexham, for as you will have gathered, I have heard all about you, both from my brother and from the rumors which have today been racing around Town."

Caroline's cheeks continued to burn. "I trust you have heard only good of me, Miss Seymour."

"But of course, for how could there be anything bad about the damsel my brother rescued upon the king's highway, and who has subsequently become Dominic Lexham's *bête noire*!"

"Jennifer!" reproved her brother sternly. "It is not at all

the thing to make one's personal feelings about someone quite so obvious."

"Well, I am being honest, Hal," she replied firmly. "I do not like Dominic Lexham, and I haven't ever since he locked me in that cupboard and left me there for five hours. He was a beastly little boy, and now he's a beastly big boy. I'm glad Miss Lexham is to have that house, and I have no intention of pretending otherwise."

Hal rolled his eyes at the ceiling, smiling. "You see, Miss Lexham? My sister has had a privileged upbringing, an expensive education at one of the very best academies for young ladies, and still she does not know how to conduct herself in public."

"Don't be a disagreeable bear, Hal," went on his irrepressible sister, "for you know that I am only saying what you've said yourself on many an occasion. Dominic Lexham is in sore need of a salutary lesson and I trust that this one will be very salutary indeed. In fact, I hope with all my heart that Miss Lexham will be able to meet all those wretched conditions so that in six months' time she will be the full and undisputed owner of Lexham House." She turned to Caroline then. "Since you will be in Town for some time, I do hope that we may become better acquainted, Miss Lexham, for from what Hal has said of you, I am sure that you and I could become firm friends."

Caroline glanced quizzically at Hal, wondering what it was that he had said, but she had to shake her head at his sister. "I am afraid that I will not be staying in London more than another day or so."

Jennifer looked shocked. "But that cannot be so! You will be living in Lexham House!"

Caroline lowered her eyes. "I do not think that that will be possible."

"But—"

"Jennifer," interposed her brother swiftly. "Do not presume to comment upon something of which you know little or nothing. I think you embarrass Miss Lexham with your rattle."

Jennifer was immediately contrite. "Oh, forgive me, Miss Lexham, for I know that I speak too often and too thoughtlessly."

Caroline smiled, liking her very much. "There is nothing

to forgive, Miss Seymour, for no doubt if I had been in your place I would have said exactly the same thing.''

"I am very sorry that you will not be in Town for long, because I was indeed looking forward to furthering our acquaintance." Her green eyes brightened suddenly. "But I have an idea! Miss Lexham, will you join us in our box at the Italian Opera House tonight? We are to see von Winter's *Il Ratto di Proserpina* and the opera *The Haunted Tower*. It will be excellent fun, and you will be able to meet Lord Carstairs, who is to be my husband. Do say that you will join us.''

Caroline would dearly have liked to accept this kind invitation, but her turquoise gown had barely done service for the Oxenford's dining room, it would not do at all for a venue as glittering as the Italian Opera House. "I would like to accept, Miss Seymour, but—''

"No buts," cried Jennifer delightedly. "You *shall* join us!''

Hal instinctively knew Caroline's dilemma, however, and for the second time he intervened discreetly on her behalf. "Jennifer, I think that Miss Lexham has a prior engagement."

Jennifer's face fell. "Oh, I did not think.''

Caroline was touched at such genuine disappointment, and she liked Hal's lively sister too much to allow her to remain ignorant of the truth. "Miss Seymour, Sir Henry is being very kind and considerate toward me, for he has perceived the true state of things. I cannot join you tonight because I have nothing even remotely suitable to wear, not because I have an engagement elsewhere. My baggage has unfortunately disappeared *en route* to London, and I confess that even had it arrived, my wardrobe would still not have contained a gown elegant enough for the Italian Opera House. Were it not for that, I would most warmly have accepted your generous invitation.''

Jennifer, initially crestfallen, now brightened again. "Oh, Miss Lexham, again you must forgive my lack of tact, for I am truly most thoughtless at times. But since you have been so very honest and forthright with me, perhaps I may be the same toward you. There is a very simple solution to the problem, a solution which I would be only too pleased to be of assistance with if you would let me. I believe that you and I are the same size, and up in my apartment there is an immense wardrobe of togs from which you could choose.''

Caroline did not quite know what to say. "Oh, but I couldn't possibly," was all she could think of.

"Why not?" inquired Jennifer, obviously seeing this as an admirable answer to the problem and dearly hoping to persuade Caroline to take it up.

Hal smiled, looking at Caroline. "For once, Miss Lexham, I believe that my sister has had an excellent idea, and I assure you that I would be delighted to have your company tonight, for you will save me from the ignominious role of gooseberry.''

Jennifer was indignant at this. "You, Hal Seymour, are being a bear again!''

He grinned, but then returned his attention to Caroline. "Please consider my sister's plan, Miss Lexham, for I know that you will enjoy the opera house, and I would be pleased to be your escort.''

To be with him for the whole evening? To be escorted by him? Her pulse was racing as she looked helplessly from one to the other, but at last she capitulated. "I would love to join you. Thank you so much for your kindness.''

Jennifer was triumphant. "Oh, I'm *so* pleased! Come, we will repair to my rooms immediately and see what you would like to wear; it will have to be something very splendid indeed if it is to show off that beautiful necklace, of which I am already green with envy!''

In something of a daze, Caroline allowed the other to spirit her away up the staircase. The unbelievable had happened. She was going to the Italian Opera House, she was going to wear a costly and fashionable gown, and she was to be on the arm of one of England's most handsome and fascinating men!

Jennifer's apartment was very fine indeed, the rooms lofty and elegant, the furniture more classical than that in Caroline's apartment. Fires crackled brightly in the hearths as Jennifer's maid, Simpson, was brought hurrying up to assist her mistress. In the dressing room, the maid flung open the wardrobe doors to reveal a bewildering array of beautiful, extremely expensive, and fashionable garments.

Jennifer was almost apologetic. "I'm afraid that when my brother suddenly announced that we were coming here because our house was to be completely refurbished, I simply could not decide which togs to bring—so I brought absolutely everything.''

"That I can well believe," murmured Caroline, running her fingertips in awe over the shimmering fabrics.

"I shall be wearing this apple-green silk," said Jennifer, taking down a gown which was so soft and light that it seemed to slither over her hands.

"Oh, it's so beautiful," breathed Caroline. "And you will look quite perfect in it; it will go so well with your eyes."

Jennifer was pleased. "That is what I am hoping, for tonight I mean to positively devastate my beloved Charles.''

"Charles?"

"Lord Carstairs." Jennifer removed the glove from her left hand, revealing a betrothal ring of the most dazzling diamonds Caroline had ever seen. "I love him so much," she murmured dreamily, gazing at the ring.

"When is the wedding to be?"

"On the evening of Friday, the twentieth of March, by special license here at the Oxenford, but it is simply *ages* away!"

"It's only a month!"

"Which is a lifetime. It would have been earlier in March but for my brother's odious and incomprehensible decision to move here. The house in Hanover Square is perfectly all right; it doesn't *need* refurbishing. Still, I suppose that coming here does have its advantages, for by having my wedding in a hotel I will surely be starting a new vogue."

"Soon all brides will wish to marry *à la Seymour*," laughed Caroline.

"*À la Carstairs*, you mean! Oh, I shall positively float down that grand staircase in my silver tissue, a wreath of diamonds in my hair, followed by twelve bridesmaids, six in primrose and six in lilac. I shall *glow* with happiness. I know it is not considered the thing to adore one's intended husband, but I love my dearest Charles with all my heart and believe myself to be the most fortunate of creatures for having won him.'' Slowly her smile died away and her green eyes became less happy. "I only wish that a similar happiness lay ahead for my brother."

Caroline received the distinct impression that Jennifer Seymour did not hold out much hope for the granting of this wish, and that this was because she did not like Marcia, Lady

Chaddington, with whom her brother's name was so firmly linked.

Jennifer smiled a little self-consciously. "I know I am foolish to worry so about him, for as he says, he is big enough and ugly enough to do as he sees fit."

"I'm sure he is right."

"I know. I can't help it, though, for he seems set to choose the wrong bride, and what with that and all the danger he seems to involve himself in . . ." She broke off, biting her lip, and it was obvious that she had been at the point of saying something she should not. She smiled again then. "Come, we must hurry and decide upon your togs for the opera house, for if we don't hurry, we will be late."

An hour later, with the final minutes ticking away to the moment they were to depart, they were both ready. Jennifer was attired in the apple-green silk, her hair got up in the style known as *à la Rome*. A golden fillet rested across her pale forehead and a trailing gauze scarf was pinned to the back of her hair, the ends draped elegantly over her bare arms. Emeralds shone at her throat, in her ears, and on the bracelet worn over her long white gloves. Her cashmere shawl put Caroline's plain white one to shame, for it positively glowed with colorful embroidery, and its long silken fringe shivered as Simpson arranged it with great care over her mistress's arms.

After much deliberation and consultation, Caroline had chosen a high-waisted gown of the palest rose muslin, sprigged with tiny silver leaves, and as she looked at herself in the tall cheval glass, she had never dreamed that she would one day wear a gown so modish and beautiful. Its low, revealing neckline displayed her flawless skin and set off her grandmother's silver and ruby necklace to perfection. Its hem was heavy with little pink satin bows, and similar bows adorned the long, diaphanous sleeves which were gathered in at the wrists, the resultant frills spilling over to hide most of her hands. Her toes, peeping from beneath the gown, were clad in white silk stockings and pink bottines tied on with ribbons. She gazed in wonderment at her reflection. Gone was the countrified cousin of the squire of Selford, and in her place was a fashionable lady, the Earl of Lexham's cousin.

Jennifer smiled. "I vow that that necklace enhances the gown more than any I have. Goodness, is that the time? We will have to go down now. Oh, don't forget the fan I gave you, for the opera house is always suffocatingly hot, even in the middle of February!" Tweaking her shawl to make it hang more satisfactorily, she hurried to the door, which Simpson hastened to open. Jennifer laughed as she and Caroline walked along the passageway toward the staircase. "I do hope that tonight's performance goes as well as last night's was reported to have done."

"What do you mean?"

"I have been informed that the rowdier elements in the gods so disliked the performance of *The Haunted Tower* that a positive hail of missiles was rained down upon the stage!"

"At the *opera house*?" gasped Caroline, startled.

"Oh yes, it is quite usual," replied Jennifer as they reached the head of the staircase. There she paused, gazing down. "Oh, I can just imagine sweeping elegantly down here in my wedding gown! Never will a bride have made a more impressive entrance!"

Hal was waiting in the entrance hall, looking very distinguished in his black velvet evening coat. The coat was very fitted and had ruffles at the cuffs, and he wore a complicated white cravat which looked very startling against the coat's somber velvet. His white waistcoat was unbuttoned to reveal the frill of the shirt beneath, and his knee breeches sported handsome golden buckles. A sword swung at his side and a tricorn hat was tucked under his arm, two formal items of apparel which were *de rigueur* for gentlemen attending the opera house. He was donning white kid gloves as the two women approached, and he turned to greet them.

Jennifer put an apologetic hand upon his arm. "Are we very late, Hal?"

"Surprisingly enough," he replied dryly, "you are not late at all, which for you, my dear sister, is little short of a miracle."

"Don't be facetious," she retorted. "Besides, if I *had* been late, I would have had excellent excuse, for there was Miss Lexham's apparel to decide upon."

"So there was," he remarked, allowing his glance to move slowly over Caroline, taking in every last detail of her appearance. His eyes met hers then and she saw in them that lazy warmth which almost bordered on the cynical, but did not quite. Had he said again those last words of their parting outside Mr. Jordan's premises, they could not have hovered more audibly in the air in that moment. She was aware of a heightening color on her cheeks and a trembling in her breast which had no place at all in the makeup of a proper young lady and everything to do with the senses of a woman in the presence of a man to whom she was irresistibly attracted.

He smiled. "You look exquisite, Miss Lexham, but then I would expect that of you."

"Thank you, Sir Henry." Oh, please don't let him guess how much he was affecting her!

"You should always be clad in such elegant togs, for as I said before, you were fashioned for London, not for the provinces. Such beauty as yours should be displayed to the discerning eyes of gentlemen such as myself, and not to the cloddish glances of inconsequential country squirelings." There was a continued amusement in his eyes and she did not know if he only teased her or if he meant what he said.

The porter announced that the landau was waiting at the door, and they left the Oxenford, emerging from the warmth of the hotel into the ice-cold February night. She sat back on the cool gray velvet seat, glancing out of the small window in the hood. Her borrowed gown felt gossamer light, too flimsy for a winter occasion, but the silver sprigging shone and the satin bows looked frivolous and lighthearted. Renewed excitement swept through her as the carriage drew away from the curb.

Chapter 10

The Italian Opera House, which was also known as the King's Theater, stood on the corner of the Haymarket and Pall Mall. It was a large, classical building, its base surrounded by an arcade illuminated by beautiful wrought-iron lamps and by the windows of the little shops which formed part of the ground floor. Caroline noticed immediately that this arcade appeared to be the haunt of ladies of dubious character, who openly approached any unattached gentleman alighting from the throng of elegant carriages drawing up outside the opera house.

As Hal's landau halted at last, Caroline thought fleetingly of her distant home and of Richard Marchand. Selford Village would be so dark and quiet now, the only sound being the moaning of the wind sweeping down over the moor. What would Richard be doing? Would he be seated at his estate ledgers? Or would he be seated comfortably before the fire reading Captain Flint's informative treatise on the breeding, training, and management of horses? She smiled as she gazed out at the glittering scene before her, for no doubt Richard would be poring over Captain Flint again, a pastime he found much more congenial and satisfying than the humdrum of estate ledgers. But then all thought of Richard Marchand fled

from her mind as the carriage door was opened and Hal
Seymour's fingers closed over hers as he handed her down
into a night that was loud with the sound of hooves and
carriage wheels, of laughter and conversation.

Her first glimpse of the immense auditorium took her
breath away, for it was a splendid vista of red and gold. The
horseshoe-shaped pit was encircled by tiers of red-curtained
boxes, and there was a very large and spectacular chandelier
above the gallery, its brilliant light making that part of the
opera house very bright indeed. Everywhere there was the
sparkle of jewels and the tremble of ostrich feathers, the
subtle shades of dark velvet coats and the flash of military
orders upon crimson uniforms. It was a scene never to be
forgotten, and as she paused for a moment before taking her
seat in the box, she committed every detail to memory, so
that for the rest of her life she would be able to recall the
breathless excitement of this incredible night. Looking up
toward that area of the auditorium known as the gods, she
saw a sea of faces peering down, and she wondered if there
would indeed be a disturbance such as there had been the
night before. The orchestra was tuning up, the sound almost
drowned by the babble of voices, and she leaned forward a
little to watch the musicians. Behind them the drop curtain
shielding the stage moved a little as someone brushed against
it, and she was conscious of a surge of anticipation, for it
would not be long now before that curtain rose and the
performance began.

Down in the pit, the fashionable young men were on
display in their elegant clothes. They lounged gracefully on
their seats, affecting to be in the grip of an ennui which was
only to be dispelled when an interesting new arrival in one of
the boxes required a closer inspection with the aid of their quizzing glasses.

At last Caroline sat down, suddenly realizing that until she
did so Hal must remain politely standing. A swift blush
warmed her cheeks as she smiled apologetically at him, her
borrowed fan wafting busily to and fro before her hot face.

Jennifer, who had obviously attended the opera house on
countless previous occasions, was quite uninterested in the
magnificence of her surroundings; she was occupied with
wondering what had happened to Lord Carstairs, who had yet
to join them. Then, barely a minute before the curtain was

due to rise, he arrived, explaining that he had been forced to walk due to the crush of carriages. He smiled, bowing lovingly over his bride-to-be's hand.

Charles, Lord Carstairs, was of medium height and rather slender. His hair was dark, his complexion pale, and his eyes were soft and brown. He dressed fashionably and yet without that effortless elegance which was Hal's stamp. There was something very appealing and romantic about him and Caroline could well understand how he had won the heart of his vivacious future wife.

He exchanged a friendly greeting with Hal, who then introduced him to Caroline. He smiled warmly as he bowed over her hand and she realized that he knew all about the notorious Lexham will and that he agreed with Jennifer that it was a long overdue lesson for Dominic. As he took his seat next to Jennifer, there was some cheering from the gods, and Caroline turned her full attention upon the brightly lit stage.

Il Ratto di Proserpina was obviously an established favorite, for the audience sang its opening melody, but as the opera progressed, the noise gradually ceased. Caroline enjoyed every moment, for the company gave a creditable performance, and when the final notes were played, there was lengthy and appreciative applause.

It was during the intermission that she first became aware that she was attracting many glances, and that the cause of the interest lay in the presence in the pit of a group of gentlemen who had dined earlier at the Oxenford and who had heard Gaspard Duvall mention her name. These gentlemen pointed out the intriguing Miss Lexham to their friends, who then spread the interesting information to others, and so on, until the whole auditorium seemed to be aware of her identity. This was bad enough, but then things were made suddenly much worse by the arrival in an opposite box of the new Earl of Lexham himself. He too soon perceived that he was the object of much unwelcome whispering, and when he realized why, his handsome face became cold and angry, his eyes flashing when he looked across at Caroline.

She lowered her eyes, toying with the tassels of her fan, and Hal leaned a little closer to her. "You do not seem to appreciate your newfound glory, Miss Lexham."

"It is hardly glory, sir, especially when in spite of my

cousin's unpleasant nature, I find myself in sympathy with him.''

Hal looked at her. "I do believe you mean what you say, and that is very much to your credit, but your sympathy is sadly misplaced.''

"He has every right to resent me, for after all, who am I to interfere in his life?''

"You are the new owner of Lexham House, that is who you are, and you must not forget that.''

She smiled a little. "But I am afraid that I will have to forget it, Sir Henry, and soon.''

The second half of the concert began, the curtain rising for *The Haunted Tower,* which against Caroline's expectation, proved to be a comedy. She forgot about Dominic for a while as she laughed at the performance, but she was suddenly very rudely reminded of her aristocratic cousin when one of the players, a Mr. Braham, stepped forward to sing a ballad entitled "Come tell me where the maid is found.'' Immediately there was an exceedingly loud and raucous shout from the gods. "She's in the box opposite my lord of Lexham! The one togged in pink!''

This was greeted with a burst of laughter from the audience, and she saw Dominic rise furiously to his feet.

The voice was merciless. "Can't you see her, my lord earl?''

Caroline felt quite dreadful, the flush returning to her cheeks as she kept her glance lowered. Hal leaned close again, putting his hand reassuringly over hers, but it did little to make her feel better, for the audience was quite set upon bringing the performance to a halt now.

On the stage, the unfortunate Mr. Braham endeavored to continue, but even his splendid voice was drowned by the mirth that followed Dominic's precipitate departure from his box. The atmosphere of the evening was ruined for the company of singers, but undeterred, Mr. Braham drew himself up for another song, having decided to move on, but his choice proved even more unhappy. "Slow broke the light,'' he began, but he got no further, for at that moment another member of the company knocked over a tall candelabrum, which fell with a clatter. The humor of this coincidence was too much for the audience, which dissolved into delighted laughter. This uproarious mirth was the signal for the unruly elements in the gods to begin pelting the stage with a barrage of orange peel, apple cores, and nutshells. The performance came to an abrupt halt, the curtain beginning to fall, only to become stuck with barely a yard to go, so that only the performers' feet could be seen.

Caroline had been staring openmouthed at all the mayhem, but the sight of those feet scuttling around behind the curtain was so funny that she too began to laugh, her earlier mortification disappearing completely. Tears streamed down her cheeks as the curtain gave a shudder and then collapsed completely, trapping the hapless Mr. Braham, who struggled valiantly beneath it, arms waving feebly under the considerable weight.

Jennifer and Lord Carstairs were helpless with laughter, Jennifer holding her aching sides. Hal rose to his feet, trying to hide his own mirth. *"Eh bien, mes enfants,"* he said. "I think it time we removed ourselves from his unseemly melee."

Still laughing, they emerged at last from the opera house, and were soon being conveyed back to the Oxenford. There, Jennifer and Lord Carstairs elected to enjoy one of the suppers for which Gaspard Duvall was becoming famous, but Caroline was too excited to even begin to think of eating. She smiled a little apologetically. "I fear I would not be able to do justice to a supper, Miss Seymour, and so will retire to my bed instead."

"Oh, what a shame," replied Jennifer disappointedly. "But maybe there will be another time."

"I do hope so. Thank you all so much for this evening. I truly enjoyed it."

Jennifer smiled. "As we enjoyed your company, Miss Lexham. Perhaps you and I could spend tomorrow morning together?"

"Tomorrow morning I am to go to Lexham House with Mr. Jordan."

"Perhaps the afternoon instead?"

Caroline smiled. "That would be most agreeable and I shall look forward to it. Good night, Miss Seymour. Lord Carstairs." She was about to say her farewell to Hal too when he smiled at her and offered her his arm once more.

"I will escort you to your apartment, Miss Lexham."

"There is no need, Sir Henry," she began, but he would not hear of anything else.

Jennifer was anxious to go into the dining room. "Shall we order for you, Hal?"

"No, not tonight, Jennifer, for I shall not be able to join you."

A swift anxiety came into his sister's eyes. "Why?"

He hesitated. "I have to see someone."

There was no mistaking Jennifer's alarm. "Hal?"

He drew her hand gently to his lips. "There is no need for you to worry, my dearest, I promise you."

Her fingers closed over his. "You do promise it, don't you?"

He smiled. "Yes."

Caroline watched this little exchange in surprise, remembering Jennifer's reference earlier to the danger in which Hal involved himself and remembering too the rumors of which Mr. Jordan had spoken. The realization that Hal was not joining them because he had an appointment to see someone had caused Jennifer too much anxiety, and Caroline could only wonder if perhaps there was some truth in Mr. Jordan's rumors after all; perhaps Hal Seymour *was* involved in matters of the gravest national importance.

She and Hal left Jennifer and Lord Carstairs then, and Hal walked with her to the door of her apartment, but he did not leave her immediately.

"Miss Lexham, you spoke earlier of having to soon forget your inheritance."

"Yes."

"My advice to you is that you consider very carefully indeed before coming to any decision."

"That is also Mr. Jordan's advice, Sir Henry, but even though I would dearly like to keep the house, I really don't think there is any way in which I may do so. My uncle's conditions are really intended to prevent me from any permanent enjoyment of my inheritance."

"Thwart his intentions and you would be a very wealthy woman."

"I know."

"And so you will instead merely return to Selford, and the dull, frustrating existence you have just escaped from?"

She looked away. "Yes."

He put his hand to her chin and turned her face toward him again. "Will such a life suit you ever again?"

"It will have to, Sir Henry."

He smiled a little wryly. "Selford will *never* satisfy you again, Caro Lexham, for you have tasted London now. I watched you when first you looked out on the streets of this city, and I watched you tonight at the opera house. I told you earlier that you were fashioned for London, and never have I said anything truer. You came home today, which I believe you realize only too well."

She lowered her eyes, very conscious of how close he was and how warm his fingers were against her skin. "And if you are right," she said at last, "what good will it do me to acknowledge my happiness here? I may be fashioned for London, but fate intends me to live my days in Selford."

"Does it?" he murmured, searching her gray eyes.

"Yes, Sir Henry, it does."

For a moment longer he continued to look at her, then he lowered his hand. She sensed a subtle change in him, a withdrawal which was as tangible as it was inexplicable. "Perhaps you are right," he said then, taking out his fob watch and flicking it open. "I fear I must leave you now, Miss Lexham, but no doubt we will encounter each other again before you depart. Good night." He inclined his head in a way that could only be described as cool, and then he left her.

Her eyes filled with tears. "Good night, Sir Henry," she whispered after him. Why had he changed? Had she said something wrong? If she had, she did not know in what way she was guilty, which made his abrupt withdrawal all the more hurtful. And yet what did she expect of him? He was kind and courteous toward her when the occasion demanded it; he had treated her most cordially and with consideration. He conducted himself in a perfectly gentlemanly way toward a woman who meant nothing to him, but who had been thrust into his company. She watched him walk away, and a tear wended its slow way down her cheek. She meant nothing to him, but he meant everything to her, for tonight she knew that she had fallen in love with him.

Chapter 11

Sleep proved elusive that night, for she had too much on her mind and there seemed to be so many different sounds to disturb the silence of her bedchamber. Outside there was a constant rattle of carriages passing along Piccadilly, while inside there were the noises of the hotel itself, from the distant clatter of plates in the basement kitchens to the soft, hurrying footsteps of a pageboy conveying a late order to a nearby apartment. She heard a group of noisy, rather tipsy gentlemen returning from a successful night at a gaming club, and she heard a woman's low, teasing laugh as she spurned the hopeful advances of the gallant who had escorted her to her door.

Caroline lay there, gazing up at the shadowy patterns on the canopy of the bed, and it seemed that sleep would never come, but come it did, for she was awoken at dawn by the low humming of the bootblack as he collected the footwear left outside the door of a gentleman who was temporarily without the services of his valet. For a moment she forgot where she was, but then she remembered everything and sat up, shivering a little as she slipped from the bed and her bare feet touched the cold floor. Her breath stood out in a silvery cloud as she went to the window, flinging back the heavy curtains and unfastening the shutters.

Outside everything was frozen. The eastern sky was a pale primrose and a low mist clung beneath the trees of Green Park. There were lamps burning in the windows of a nearby house, and wisps of smoke rose from its chimneys. She knew that the Oxenford possessed gardens at the rear, and on impulse she decided to walk in them while everything was deserted and quiet.

She donned her gray woolen gown and mantle, pulling a face as she looked at her reflection in the cheval glass this morning. She was herself again; gone was the fine London lady of the previous evening. She had done her best with her travel-worn clothes when putting them away, but somehow they still looked in dire need of laundering. She had not dared to call upon the services of the Oxenford, first because she did not possess an abundance of money with which to reward such labors, and second because she shrank from sending such lowly garments to servants accustomed to handling the clothes of the wealthy. She could well imagine the disdain with which her poor mantle would have been received, and so she had endeavored to do what she could herself, but it had been to little effect. With a resigned smile, she twisted her hair up into a tidy knot, put on her bonnet, and tied the ribbons firmly beneath her chin.

She encountered no one as she slipped down through the hotel, and she soon found her way out into the gardens, where the bitter cold caught her breath. The mist had frozen the trees, which loomed frosty and white in the dawn light. As she strolled along a path, she noticed the snowdrops on the lawn, and beneath a hedge the waxy blooms of the last of the Christmas roses. Beyond the confines of the garden, London was beginning to stir. She heard a milkmaid calling in the mews lane, and a boy selling freshly made toffee began to shout his wares at the top of his lungs. In the distance a church bell began to ring, followed by another and then another until the air seemed to vibrate with the noise. Never before had she heard so many, for she was used to the gentler tones of Selford church's solitary toll.

As the bells stopped, she heard voices close at hand, and saw some shadowy figures coming from the direction of the mews. There were two men, followed by three small boys pushing barrows, which appeared to be laden with meat, fish, fruit, and vegetables. One of the two men was Gaspard Duvall, and she realized that the little procession had been to all the various markets to choose the choicest items for the tables at the Oxenford. There was no sign this morning of the chef's sprightly joviality, for he was engaged in a low, urgent conversation with the other man, who appeared to be another Frenchman. Something was obviously wrong, for even allowing for a certain Gallic tendency to gesticulate excitedly, the chef's manner could only be described as exceedingly agitated. He argued heatedly with his more taciturn countryman, whose attitude was one of muted but determined disagreement. It was this dark-haired, thickset second man who suddenly saw Caroline standing in their path. With a sharp word of warning, he nudged the chef, who immediately fell into a confused silence, seeming to find it difficult to collect himself sufficiently to manage one of his usual smiles of greeting.

"Wh-why, Mademoiselle Lexham, how early you are out," he said at last.

"Good morning, monsieur," she replied, glancing curiously at the other man, who now retreated to join the kitchen boys waiting obediently with their heavily laden barrows.

The chef followed her glance and seemed to think he should explain who his companion was. "That is Boisville, mademoiselle, he is my *entremettier*."

"My French is very poor, monsieur, and I am afraid you will have to explain."

He appeared relieved that she had not understood anything earlier, and he beamed. "Ah, forgive me, mademoiselle, and of course I will explain. An *entremettier* has charge of preparing the soups, the vegetables, and the desserts, whereas I am the *chef de cuisine*, and I am in charge of everything. I am call the *gros bonnet*, which in English means the 'big hat,' because chefs wear tall white hats. Do you understand?"

"Yes." She was surprised, however, to learn that Boisville was Duvall's subordinate, for his manner before he had realized she observed them had been anything but subordinate; indeed, it had been the very opposite!

Boisville bowed then, smiling, although it was not a smile

she particularly liked, and murmuring in excellent English
that he would, with the chef's permission, proceed to the
kitchens with the boys. Duvall nodded his agreement and the
little group moved on toward the hotel, vanishing into the
swathes of mist.

She smiled at the chef. "Please don't let me detain you,
monsieur, for I know you must have a great deal to do."

"But it is a pleasure to be detained by so lovely a lady,"
he replied, his bright eyes dancing with his usual gaiety.
"Besides which, I welcome any diversion which keeps me
from those *odieuse* kitchens!"

"Are they really as bad as you say?"

"They are worse!" he cried with feeling. "And today I
shall inform Monsieur Bassett as much. I shall complain and
I shall demand improvements."

She wondered what the superior majordomo would make
of such animated and impassioned criticisms, for the chef was
evidently determined to carry out his threat.

He gestured angrily toward the hotel. "I must make do
with old-fashioned ovens and open fires, when in Paris I had
closed ranges. But here they expect me to create the most
recherché of banquets, the most exquisite of wedding feasts!
I am the *gros bonnet*, I have the best *brigade de cuisine*—that
is the kitchen team," he added almost as an aside. "And yet
I must work in the most *odieuse* of kitchens! It will not do,
and today I will say so."

"I wish you well, monsieur."

He smiled, drawing her hand to his lips. "I thank you,
mademoiselle. But now, I fear, I have to go and see that the
brigade carries out its tasks correctly. They may be the finest
team in the world, but they do not always do things the way I
like. *Au revoir, mademoiselle.*"

"Good-bye, monsieur."

With light, swift steps, he hurried away into the mist, and
as she watched him she thought again of Boisville's curious
attitude. The *entremettier* had not conducted himself as if
Duvall had been his superior, and there was no mistaking the
fact.

She walked alone for a little while longer, thinking of other
things, and then she decided to return to the hotel to write a
letter to Richard before taking breakfast. Inside she inquired

of the porter where she might find writing implements, and she was directed to the library, where she found an escritoire. A housemaid was attending to the fire, but she hurried out immediately when Caroline entered. Sitting at the escritoire, she took a sheet of the Oxenford's superior parchment and settled down to write.

Oxenford Hotel, Piccadilly. Before breakfast. She smiled, for it was so very grand. Dipping the quill in the ink again, she continued writing. She knew that Richard would be very anxious about her, in spite of his anger at her insistence upon going, and so she wrote in great detail about everything that had happened, even describing the evening gown she had borrowed from Jennifer Seymour. She worded the letter with great care, for she wished it to strike just the right note of affection, neither seeming to encourage him to hope she had changed her mind about marriage or seeming to rebuff him too much, for that would have been hurtful. She wanted him to know that she thought of him, that she loved him still, but that he must not hope she would return to become his bride. She was glad now that she had thought of asking Hal Seymour for a racing tip, for that gave her the perfect ending for her letter. *I was exceeding impudent on your behalf,* she wrote, *for when I traveled with Sir Henry I shamelessly pumped him for some inside information about the turf. He was good enough to tell me that he sets great store by a horse named Nero for this year's Derby—that is surely as good as from the horse's mouth and will make you a very knowing one with your cronies. I will end now, but I promise to write again before I return to Selford. Your affectionate cousin, Caroline.*

After sanding the letter, she folded it, melted some sealing wax against the flames of the crackling, smoking fire, and a moment later the letter was ready to be posted. But as she went toward the door to take it down to the porter, the door was thrust open and she halted in shocked dismay as she saw Lord Fynehurst standing there.

The pale morning light from the window fell coldly on his Apollo curls, making them seem more contrived than ever. He was dressed from head to toe in pale blue, and he held a lace-edged handkerchief lightly between the thumb and first finger of his left hand. His eyes flickered unpleasantly, and he stepped aside, and Caroline realized that he was accompanied by his sister, Marcia, Lady Chaddington.

She advanced slowly into the room, and Caroline instinctively backed away from her. Marcia was clad in chestnut velvet, the same color as her lovely hair, and there was deep fur trimming at her throat, cuffs, and hem. She wore a beaver hat at a rakish angle, and her hands were plunged into the largest fur muff Caroline had ever seen. She was a vision of modish style, but there was something malevolent about her as she halted before Caroline. Lord Fynehurst slowly closed the library door, leaning back against it to prevent anyone from entering unexpectedly.

"Well," murmured Marcia quietly. "You have looks enough, I suppose, but in other ways you are rather drab, are you not?"

Caroline said nothing, swiftly gathering her skirts to hurry to the door, but Lord Fynehurst wagged a reproachful finger at her. "Not yet, dearetht, not yet."

"I wish to leave, sir, please allow me to pass!"

Marcia turned. "I have not done with you yet, miss."

"What do you wish of me?"

"I have come to issue a warning."

"A warning? About what?"

"About interfering with that which does not concern you."

"I'm afraid that I don't understand," replied Caroline, but she sensed that it was because of Hal Seymour. It could be nothing else.

A cool, contemptuous smile played about Marcia's lips. "You don't understand? Come now, don't let us pretend, for you are a scheming, conniving jade and you know full well why I have felt it necessary to come here like this."

"No, my lady, I do *not* know."

"I note that you appear to know who I am."

"Yes."

"Then you must also know in what way you have transgressed."

"No."

"What a vulgar, little creature you are, to be sure, for your conduct has been that of a *demimondaine* of the meanest order."

"A *demimondaine*?" gasped Caroline, her gray eyes widening with shock and anger.

Marcia's rich hem swung as she walked slowly along the tall shelves of books, an elegant gloved finger dragging along the embossed spines. "What else are you but a common Cyprian? Only such a creature would stoop to the level you stooped to in order to gain a place in Sir Henry's carriage. You flaunted yourself quite outrageously, or so he tells me."

Caroline felt as if she had been struck. Hal had said that of her? Her trembling fingers crept to her grandmother's necklace, moving nervously over the chased silver.

Marcia turned to face her, her eyes cold and filled with loathing. "You are an adventuress, Miss Lexham, and your purpose is quite plain to one and all. Why, you even went to the length of taking rooms in this very hotel!"

"I didn't reserve the apartment here; Mr. Jordan, the lawyer, did."

"At your instruction, no doubt."

"No!"

"It doesn't matter, for you will not succeed. You will not succeed in this and you will not succeed in retaining your hold upon Lexham House. I mean to be rid of you, my dear, and quickly."

"I do not wish to hear any more of this, Lady Chaddington. Please allow me to leave."

"In a moment. First I warn you that I mean what I say. I intend to be rid of you, and soon you will have proof of how determined I am and how powerful is my influence. Take my advice, Miss Lexham, forget your notions of grandeur and forget Sir Henry Seymour, whose derision you have already earned. Take yourself back to the remotenesses of Devon, where you belong. Now, I will bid you good day, and I trust good-bye as well. Be sensible and remove yourself from Town as swiftly as possible. Be tardy or obstinate, and it will be the worst for you. I am an implacable enemy, I promise you that."

Her rich skirts rustling, Marcia swept out, followed by her mean-hearted brother. Caroline leaned weakly against the escritoire. She was shaking, her emotions swinging between anger at being so unjustly threatened and abused and a dreadful humiliation that Hal should have expressed such an opinion of her. To her face he had been charming and courteous; behind her back he was false and contemptuous. Furiously she blinked back the hot tears, forcing them away as she strove to retain her poise. Then, her head held high, she emerged from the library into the deserted passageway.

Chapter 12

Such was her mortification at finding out what Hal had said of her that the thought of perhaps seeing him at breakfast was quite dreadful. To her immeasurable relief, however, neither he nor his sister appeared in the dining room. She did not enjoy her first fashionable breakfast, for she was too distressed after her confrontation with Lady Chaddington. She sat almost alone in the elegant dining room, for most of the guests had yet to rise. Although it was now bright and sunny outside, the room was gloomy and depressing, for its windows did not catch the morning sun, and she was glad enough to escape into the lighter hallway to await Mr. Jordan's arrival.

The hall was very busy now, the porter was always rising from his chair to open the door, and a constant stream of waiters, their long aprons crackling, hurried up and down the grand staircase with trays, or in and out of the dining room, which was beginning to attract more guests now. Mr. Basset occupied a prominent position on the tiled floor, smiling obsequiously at the more exalted guests, and outside she could see the liveried footmen parading importantly up and down, exchanging disdainful glances with their opposite numbers outside the nearby Pulteney.

Sitting on one of the elegant sofas, Caroline watched everything, and she was surprised that she found something with which she could most certainly find fault. A door opposite stood open, and she could see that the room beyond was the coffee room. It was sun-filled and bright, with many white-clothed tables, and it was a much more welcoming proposition for breakfast than the dark dining room. Had she been in the majordomo's place, she would have seen to it that breakfast was served in the sunny coffee room, of that she had no doubt.

As she dwelt upon this, a carriage was pulling up at the curb, and its arrival was greeted with immediate service by the footmen, who hurried to open the door, which was adorned with an aristocratic coat-of-arms. A young gentleman with honey-colored hair alighted and entered the hotel, his expression dark, and he had advanced to where she was sitting before she sensed his presence and looked up sharply into those gray eyes which so mirrored her own.

"My lord earl!"

Dominic's lips were thin and cruel. "I would have words with you, madam. In private."

"I am sure that whatever you have to say can be said here," she began, a little apprehensively.

"In private," he repeated, the tip of his ebony cane indicating the open door of the deserted coffee room.

Seeing that they were attracting the interest of both the porter and Mr. Bassett, she decided against her better judgment to do as he wished, and in the coffee room she turned nervously to face him.

The sunlight streamed over his elegant figure, burnishing the brown of his coat and flashing upon the jeweled pin in his cravat. He did not deign to remove his top hat. His whole being exuded utter contempt and disdain for her. He did not pretend to be polite, for he regarded her as an inferior creature without any right to civility. "I think, madam," he said in a chilling tone, "that I have been foolish to allow this charade to progress this far. I speak of your unwelcome presence in Town and your impudent pretensions to my property."

"The impudence was not mine, sirrah," she replied coldly, her anger aroused. "It was your father's for bringing me into his will."

"Don't think to be clever with me, missy!"

"I'm not being clever, I merely repay you in kind for your arrogant rudeness."

His gray eyes flashed furiously. "Be careful, I warn you. Besides, it is immaterial what you think or say, it is what you do which concerns me—and I intend that you shall leave London immediately and that you will renounce any spurious claim you may have to Lexham House." He gave a brief, mirthless laugh. "You fancy yourself to be a fine lady all of a sudden, don't you? You languish in one of the best hotels in Town, flaunt yourself in an opera box in borrowed fripperies, and believe yourself to be very much the Lexham! But you are only a vulgar little Marchand, and your posturings are laughable."

"Really? I did not notice you laughing last night, my lord."

His control snapped at this sarcastic defiance, this unwanted reminder of the humiliation he had suffered because of her presence at the opera house. With an oath, he seized her roughly by the arms, shaking her with a savagery that frightened her. She began to struggle, wanting to shout for help but somehow unable to do so. Her efforts were in vain against his furious strength, but then she was saved by the sudden opening of the door as a maid came in with a pile of freshly laundered napkins.

Dominic released her immediately, turning away with an air of apparent nonchalance, and needing no prompting, Caroline gathered her skirts and hurried out past the startled maid.

To her immense relief, she saw Mr. Jordan waiting for her in the hall, and she slowed to a sedate walk, composing herself as she approached him. She would not say anything of what had just taken place, for there was no point, and it was probably better left untold. She smiled. "Good morning, Mr. Jordan."

"Good morning, Miss Lexham." His shrewd eyes took in her flustered appearance and noted the emergence of the new Earl of Lexham from the doorway behind her. Dominic walked past without a word, and Caroline lowered her eyes as the lawyer looked at her again. "Another unpleasant confrontation with your kinsman, my dear?"

"Yes."

He waited, but she did not elaborate, and so he offered her his arm. "Shall we go?"

"By all means, Mr. Jordan."

Dominic's carriage had gone when at last Mr. Jordan's chariot drew away from the curb and proceeded west along Piccadilly before turning north into Mayfair. The lawyer glanced at her, wondering what had passed between the two cousins, for whatever it was she was greatly upset by it, he could see that by the way her hands trembled. To break the silence, he spoke of the housekeeper at Lexham House, Mrs. Hollingsworth.

"She is expecting us and will conduct you over the house, which I fear is very cold, having been closed since last autumn. She has been under some difficulty since the late earl's demise, for she has hardly any staff, barely sufficient even for an unoccupied house."

"Why is that?"

He cleared his throat. "I—er—believe they were reluctant to fall under the jurisdiction of the new earl."

"I can sympathize with their dilemma," she replied shortly.

They drove on toward Mayfair Street in silence, and he began to wonder if her quiet mood was caused solely by her disagreeable interview with her cousin. The more he considered it, the more the lawyer sensed that there was something else of concern to her, and he hoped for her sake that it had nothing to do with the handsome, charming Sir Henry Seymour, in whose company she had apparently spent a great part of the previous evening.

The chariot turned into Mayfair Street, and Caroline sat forward, putting aside her problems and thinking instead of the house which was so briefly to be hers. She was aware of holding her breath as the carriage rattled beneath the pedimented gateway and entered the wide, cobbled court before the house. She saw again the flanking wings of stables, coach houses, and kitchens, but it was at Lexham House itself that she gazed as the sound of the carriage's approach echoed all around.

It was a handsome, red-brick building, symmetrical and harmonious. The ground-floor windows were arched, while those on the two floors above were rectangular, and the raised double front doors were approached by a magnificent flight of seven white marble steps. Above this regal entrance was a long balcony stretching across the front of the house, offering a commanding view of the court, over the wall, and into Mayfair Street itself.

They alighted at the steps, and Caroline looked up at the house where her father had been born and where, but for fate, she too might have been born. It was a strange feeling to be looking at this building which carried her family name, and she was suddenly glad that for six months at least it would belong to her.

Mr. Jordan glanced approvingly around. "It is indeed a handsome place. It was designed by Sir William Chambers— Mr. Chambers as he then was—in 1771 and was built on the site of an older house, which had been purchased by your grandfather, the eleventh earl, for the princely sum of sixteen thousand five hundred pounds." He gave a wry laugh. "It is worth considerably more than that now, I promsie you."

She did not reply, for at that moment the double front doors of the house were opened and a woman appeared at the top of the steps. She was about fifteen years Caroline's senior and was handsome in an austere, almost forbidding way. Her dark hair was swept up severely beneath a crisp white mobcap, and she wore a plain brown wool gown and a starched apron. A large bunch of keys was suspended on a chain from her waist, and those keys immediately proclaimed her to be the housekeeper, Mrs. Hollingsworth. With a silent curtsy, the woman stood aside to admit them, and slowly Caroline and the lawyer mounted the wide, white steps.

Inside the echoing vestibule it was ice cold, the chill emphasized by the pale blue walls and black-and-white-checkered marble flags on the floor. Some sofas were hidden beneath dust sheets, and the chandeliers above were wrapped in ugly brown holland bags. To one side there were rolled carpets, lying limp and colorless against the wall. Caroline gazed around, her glance carried from the vestibule and into the heart of the house by a vista of arches opening on to the inner hall where rose a truly magnificent black marble staircase, more impressive even than that at the Oxenford.

Her first impression was one of vastness, but that was because her eye was deceived, as the architect had intended. As London mansions went, this house was not very large at all; there were many others which were more than twice its size. Her second impression was that the house, like its housekeeper, was austere and forbidding, and this feeling was reinforced by the dull, echoing thud with which the housekeeper closed the outer doors. The sound reverberated through the empty rooms and corridors, and Caroline felt the urge to shiver.

Chapter 13

Mrs. Hollingsworth's keys chink-chinked as she came to where they stood. "Shall I conduct you on a circuit of the house, madam? Sir?"

Mr. Jordan hastily declined, declaring that he had taken circuits enough when compiling the inventory, and turning back the dustcover on the nearest sofa, he prepared to sit down the moment the two ladies had left him.

Caroline turned a little apprehensively toward the house-keeper. "I would like to see the house, Mrs. Hollingsworth."

"If you will come this way, madam." The keys chinked together again as the woman crossed the vestibule to an impressive doorway above which was fixed a coat-of-arms emblazoned in the bright green, white and gold of the Earls of Lexham.

The door opened onto the private apartments, formerly occupied by the late earl and countess. The rooms were in darkness, for the curtains were drawn and the shutters closed, but in a moment Mrs. Hollingsworth had opened everything up to allow the sunlight to stream in. The light revealed still more ghostly dustcovers, more brown holland over the chandeliers, and more rolled-up carpets. The paintings on the walls were covered with brown paper, and the only item of furniture which did not appear to have been protected in some way was the immense canopied bed with its carvings and heraldic devices.

From the private apartments they proceeded into the library, which was once again in darkness, its furniture covered. The opening of the tall bay windows revealed a prospect over the extensive gardens to the rear of the house; it also revealed a magnificent painted ceiling which was dazzlingly colorful and depicted mythical scenes. Caroline gazed up at it in admiration.

Mrs. Hollingsworth spoke with some pride. "It was painted by Cipriani, madam, the Florentine master."

"It's very beautiful."

"Everything in the house is beautiful," replied the housekeeper, her voice catching unexpectedly. To hide this display of emotion, the woman hurried across the library to the great pedimented doors opening onto the red saloon beyond.

The same cold, desolate atmosphere pervaded this handsome chamber. The opened shutters revealed dull crimson brocade walls and elegant French furniture stacked to one side. Their steps echoed in the carpetless floor as they proceeded quickly through to the next room, which was the dining room and which occupied the opposite corner to the library.

Immense Sheraton sideboards were ranged down one wall, but they were bare now of the gleaming plate which would set them off to such advantage. Indeed, as Caroline glanced at them, she realized that she had seen no porcelain, silver, or gold, none of the treasures Mr. Jordan had mentioned, except the paintings, all of which were so carefully covered by brown paper. The dining room was dominated by the long mahogany table which stretched almost from the window bay to the low Ionic colonnade screening the entrance to the butler's pantry, the kitchens, and other offices forming the one flanking wing of the courtyard.

Mrs. Hollingsworth did not conduct Caroline to these lowly places; instead she led her out of the dining room to the inner hall and then up the grand black marble staircase to the next floor. Here the rooms were smaller in size but more in number, and like their counterparts below they were all shuttered and in darkness, their paintings concealed and their furniture covered. There was something so very sad about these unused chambers with their cold, yawning fireplaces and musty, closed atmosphere, for this was a house which cried out to be occupied again and needed to be warm and lively.

Before ascending yet another flight of stairs to the next floor, they emerged briefly onto the balcony overlooking the courtyard. It was a magnificent vantage point and afforded a view as far as Piccadilly, the chimneys of Devonshire House, and the trees of Green Park. Down below, Mr. Jordan's chariot waited, the stamping and snorting of the impatient horses echoing around the empty stables and coach houses and the long dormitories above them where the male servants normally slept.

The circuit of the next floor was completed more swiftly, and they spent little time in the attics, which comprised storerooms and small bedchambers for the lower female servants. Descending the grand staircase to the ground floor once more, Mrs. Hollingsworth inquired if Caroline would like to see the cellars, where all the valuables were stored, as well as a considerable stock of wines and other such beverages.

Lighting a candle and shielding the weak flame with her hand, the housekeeper unlocked the door and led the way down into the icy darkness, where the raw cold was such that it took Caroline's breath away.

Mrs. Hollingsworth heard her gasp and turned with a smile that quite transformed her stern face and told Caroline that the housekeeper was not as unamiable as she had at first appeared. "I'm afraid that these cellars are said to be the coldest in London, madam."

"That I can well believe!"

"But such cold does have a singular advantage for a fashionable household."

"It does?"

"Such low temperatures ensure that ice placed here in the winter endures almost through the hottest summer." The housekeeper indicated a deep hole in the floor, where by the candlelight Caroline could just make out the straw that would be packed around the ice to insulate it. "The late earl regularly purchased large quantities of ice from the Icelandic suppliers; indeed I recall one memorable summer when Messieurs Gunter, the confectioners of Berkeley Square, had to come to him for ice when their own supply was exhausted. He charged them handsomely for the privilege."

They walked a little farther into the cellars, past casks and barrels, racks of wine, and boxes of expensive candles. There were numerous crates packed carefully with the porcelain, plate, and Chinese jade Mr. Jordan had spoken of, and finally they reached the coal cellar, which was filled almost to capacity with enough fuel to warm the house for several months. It was here that Caroline halted, for she detected a strange gurgling sound.

"Whatever is that?"

"The Tyburn, madam."

Caroline stared. "Do you mean the river?"

"Yes, madam, it flows directly beneath the house."

"What an unpleasant thought," replied Caroline, moving away with a shiver.

The housekeeper smiled. "It passes beneath several Mayfair houses, and I know for certain that it flows beneath the Pulteney Hotel in Piccadilly before disappearing somewhere in Green Park. They do say that it is because of the invisible waters of the Tyburn that that part of Piccadilly is so often enveloped in mist."

Caroline was not sorry to emerge again from the sepulchral cellars. Mrs. Hollingsworth carefully extinguished the candle and then locked the cellar door again. The sound of her keys echoed through the house. The housekeeper turned to Caroline again then. "Apart from the grounds and the kitchens, madam, you have now seen the entire house."

"I would like to see the kitchens, if you please."

The woman could not conceal her astonishment. "You would?"

Caroline had to smile a little. "It will not have escaped your notice that there can be little hope of my becoming the permanent mistress of this house, Mrs. Hollingsworth, which naturally means that soon I must return to my home in Devon. That home contains a stout country cook by the name of Mrs. Thompson, and she would never speak to me again if I failed to examine the kitchens of a great London mansion. She will hear of my visit here and she will fully expect to be regaled with every last detail, especially the kitchens."

Mrs. Hollingsworth smiled, and again it was a genuinely warm smile which revealed a kinder nature than one would have expected. "I see that you are truly Master Philip's daughter, madam, for it was your father I heard in your voice then. Of all the Lexhams, he alone was kind and concerned about the servants, just as you are about your Mrs. Thompson."

"You knew my father?"

"I was a very young parlor maid then, and like all the other servants, I thought the world of him because he was so natural with us. He did not give himself airs and graces, he laughed with us and he sympathized with us. He was sorely missed when he left." The woman looked away for a moment, as if afraid to say fully what was on her mind, but then she looked at Caroline once more, taking a deep breath. "It is this house's great misfortune that Master Dominic does not more resemble his uncle Philip, madam, for all those who had places here have looked elsewhere for employment rather than exist under the new earl's tyranny. Apart from myself and three others, everyone has gone, finding the hazard of seeking positions elsewhere preferable to the thought of your cousin as master. Forgive me for speaking out of turn, madam, but I thought you would understand."

"I do, Mrs. Hollingsworth, for I too have made my cousin's acquaintance now. But tell me, why do you remain here?"

"Because I was paid for one year only last August, just before the old earl closed the house and went back to County Durham for the winter. I am an honest woman, madam, and when I undertook to serve in this house for one year from that date, I considered myself bound by honor so to do, even if Master Dominic had succeeded to the title." The housekeeper smiled a little. "When first Mr. Jordan told me that you were the new owner of Lexham House, I confess that I was overjoyed, for I knew in my heart that the daughter of Master Philip could only be a good and kind woman, but my joy was short-lived, for Mr. Jordan pointed out that it was unlikely that you would be able to keep the house. But I tell you this, madam, if you were to retain this house, I would regard it as an honor to serve you."

"I wish too that I could keep the house, Mrs. Hollingsworth, but as Mr. Jordan told you, I am afraid it will be impossible. Come, shall we look at the kitchens now?"

Mrs. Hollingsworth nodded, leading Caroline back into the dining room, beneath the Ionic colonnade and into the butler's pantry, with its special repository for the most valuable plate. Before conducting her to the kitchens proper, the housekeeper showed Caroline her own little rooms, comprising a parlor, bedroom, and tiny storeroom. There were other such rooms for the upper servants, such privacy being regarded as a necessary acknowledgment of their superior position.

The kitchens were bright, warm, and welcoming after the main house, for the fires were lit, the windows unshuttered, and there was a delicious smell from the joint of mutton turning slowly on a spit. The walls were a gleaming white, their lower portion tiled in the same color, and against them stood enormous dressers laden with crockery for everyday use. On their tops were the largest of the numerous saucepans, while smaller utensils occupied rows of shelves next to one of the immense fireplaces. Copper shone around the hearths and the flames reflected warmly in the burnished metal. At the windows were sheets of fine metal gauze to exclude insects when the casements were open, and the walls that were free of dressers or shelves were hung with countless implements, the uses of which Caroline could only begin to guess.

There were ovens and larders, cupboards and washrooms, pantries and laundry rooms, and in the main kitchen there was even a miraculous supply of hot water from a tap protruding above a stone sink, supplied, Caroline was told, by a heated boiler in the adjacent airing room. In this same large chamber the rafters were laden with cages, baskets, and hooks from which were suspended bunches of herbs, muslin-wrapped hams, and dried mushrooms. Meat and bread occupied their respective cradles, and there was one of the largest sugarloaf cages Caroline had ever seen. She gazed around in wonderment, for never before had she seen such modern, well-equipped kitchens, and she was sure she would not be able to remember even half of it to tell Mrs. Thompson.

There was one marvel she had yet to see, however, and now Mrs. Hollingsworth proudly led her to a curious, low, red-brick construction about the height of a table, occupying the center of the flagstoned floor. This was, announced the housekeeper, the famous set of closed ranges designed scientifically by Baron Rumford, Fellow of the Royal Society and creator of the much lauded kitchens of the Royal Institute in Albemarle Street. These ranges were a very modern invention, a brilliant advance in cleanliness and convenience for the cook. Special long-handled pans nestled in the holes provided for them in the flat top, and Mrs. Hollingsworth pointed out that it was a simple and swift exercise either to damp down the heat or to bring it up to full strength. There were few houses in London which possessed such magnificent closed ranges, and none which possessed finer examples, and Mrs. Hollingsworth took immense pride in telling Caroline all she knew about them.

Caroline could only wonder what Mrs. Thompson would make of such an innovation—or indeed what Gaspard Duvall would say of these kitchens, which were everything he desired and everything the Oxenford's *odieuse* offices were not!

When she had seen all there was to see, she was conducted briefly into the servants' hall where waited the only three remaining members of the staff: the woman cook, an underbutler, and a kitchen boy. Then Mrs. Hollingsworth prepared to conduct Caroline around the grounds, but Caroline thanked her and said that she would prefer to walk alone. The housekeeper quite understood and showed her to the little door opening onto the kitchen garden.

She emerged into the surprisingly warm February sunshine, went through a wicket gate and onto lawns studded with fruit trees that would soon be in blossom. She sat on a wrought-iron seat by an ornamental pool, gazing across the lawns at the house, its red bricks bright in the sun. She no longer felt that the house was austere or forbidding, for now that she had been all over it, she felt a strange affinity with it. Her gaze moved from window to window, from the library with its Cipriani ceiling to the crimson-walled saloon, from the dining room with its Sheraton sideboards to the low roof of the kitchen wing, just visible from where she sat. What would those elegant, sumptuous rooms be like if they were opened up again and filled with all those treasures hidden away in the safety of the cellars? She could imagine the gleaming chandeliers, free of their ugly holland bags, the paintings without brown paper to hide them, the carpets rolled out once more to cover the floors with beautiful designs and colors. And then there was the staircase. Oh, *what* a staircase! It was far more regal and beautiful than that boasted by the Oxenford, and she smiled a little, thinking to what advantage Jennifer Seymour would appear in her silver tissue and wreath of diamonds descending the Lexham House staircase; and also thinking what a wedding feast Gaspard Duvall would be able to prepare in the magnificent kitchens, which were everything the Oxenford's were not.

Suddenly, and quite without any warning at all, an impossible thought entered her head. It was a ridiculous thought, but it would not go away, it insisted upon being considered. Her eyes became pensive as she stared at the house, and then slowly she stood. The thought was improbable, nonsensical even, but with a sudden excited gasp, she gathered her skirts and hurried back to the house, calling Mr. Jordan's name.

The lawyer came running into the kitchens as a startled Mrs. Hollingsworth inquired if something was wrong. Caroline's eyes shone and she shook her head. "No, Mrs. Hollingsworth, indeed I believe the very opposite may be the case." She looked at Mr. Jordan's alarmed face. "I think I have thought of a solution, a way to defeat my uncle's conditions."

The housekeeper gasped hopefully and Mr. Jordan stared at her. "You have?" he asked in amazement.

She smiled. "What would you say if I told you I intended turning Lexham House into an exclusive hotel?"

Her words fell onto a stunned silence.

Chapter 14

Mrs. Hollingsworth's lips parted in astonishment, and the other servants looked askance at one another and then at Caroline. Mr. Jordan was rendered speechless for a moment, but then he recovered. "You cannot possibly be serious, Miss Jordan! You mean to turn this great house into a—a *hotel*?"

"I am perfectly serious, sir."

"It's quite out of the question."

"Why? Does it contravene the terms of the will?"

"Not as far as I can say on the spur of the moment, but it is by far too risky a venture!"

"But I have nothing to lose, Mr. Jordan, as you yourself have pointed out. You told me to play my uncle at his own game, and that is exactly what I am doing. Until this morning I still had sympathy with my cousin Dominic's dilemma, but after his conduct at the Oxenford I no longer have any sympathy for him whatsoever. I believe I have thought of an admirable solution to my predicament, and if I possibly can, I will go ahead with it."

"But to turn this princely residence into a hotel . . ." he began.

"A hotel such as I envisage is very respectable, sir, for who can find fault with establishments considered suitable for

110

the Czar of Russia and his sister, for occasions like the Duke
of Wellington's banquet, and for the solemnization of important society marriages, like that of Miss Seymour and Lord
Carstairs? The terms of the will demand that I live here for
six months, that I open up the entire house, and that I do all
this without incurring any debt whatsoever. As a hotel, I must
hope that the house will pay for its own upkeep—and there is
nothing in the will to say that I may not do that.''

Mr. Jordan clearly thought she had taken leave of her
senses. "But you are a lady, and ladies do not involve
themselves in commercial enterprises of *any* kind!''

"Except when the devil drives, sir, and as far as I am
concerned, he most certainly holds the reins at the moment.''

"And I do not believe,'' he continued as if she had not
spoken, "that society would accept such a wild venture! Not
in Mayfair!''

"Because this has been until now the town residence of the
Earls of Lexham?''

"Yes.''

"But what was the Oxenford originally if not a private
residence? And the Clarendon, the Pulteney, Mivart's, or
Grillion's? Were not they also private and exclusive houses?''

"Maybe they were, but now they are in male hands, Miss
Lexham, owned or managed by men who were formerly great
chefs, experienced and knowledgeable house stewards or
butlers. You know nothing of such things, you are a young
lady, fresh from the country, and green as to the ways of high
society.''

"Do you tell me, sir, that these men know more about the
running of a great house than a woman like Mrs. Hollingsworth?
I cannot agree that there is some mystery about running a
hotel, a mystery known only to the male of the species and
which a more than competent housekeeper cannot hope to
solve. Running a private residence with many titled and
wealthy houseguests must be the same as running a hotel,
with similar guests—what do you say, Mrs. Hollingsworth?''

The housekeeper was startled at being asked to express an
opinion. "I—er—agree with you, madam, there cannot be a
great deal to choose between the two situations.''

Mr. Jordan was appalled that the sensible and practical
housekeeper was apparently allying herself with the lunatic

plan. "Mrs. Hollingsworth," he exlaimed, "I am surprised at you!"

"But I must agree with Miss Lexham," explained the housekeeper, "for her idea is *not* as wild and impossible as it at first appears."

Caroline was triumphant. "There!"

Mr. Jordan took a cross breath. "I still say the whole thing is harebrained, for you have not considered anything in detail. In order to throw open the doors of this house to guests you will have to employ a full complement of staff; staff must be paid, Miss Lexham. You will also need to heat the whole house, for it is a long time until the warmth of late spring and summer, and you will need to illuminate it, which will require a great deal of fuel and candles. And then we come to the not insignificant matter of food and drink. Guests of consequence expect fine French cooking and excellent wines; they also expect their own servants to be fed and accommodated. No, Miss Lexham, your idea is out of the question, it simply cannot be done."

Caroline was not defeated yet, for she had found an ally in the housekeeper, and she detected a crack or two in the lawyer's argument. "Sir, it seems to me that you are guilty of a faulty memory."

"Faulty? In what way?"

"You declined earlier to accompany me on a circuit of the house because you had done several circuits when compiling the inventory. During those circuits you are bound to have seen the stocks of wines, candles, and coal in the cellars, stocks which I do not believe are entered in the inventory. Am I right?"

He colored just a little. "You are right, Miss Lexham."

"So, we will take your other arguments. Staff can soon be hired, and even I know that they are not paid for the first three months of their employment, nor are the tradesmen who supply food and so on. I'll warrant that reluctance to immediately pay bills applies more in London than it does in Selford! As to any other consideration, well, the house contains everything in the way of accommodation for both guests and servants, it has immense supplies of crockery, cutlery, bedding, and other such things, because it has *always* had to provide for large parties of guests and their servants. There will be no difference whatsoever, Mr. Jordan, except that from now on those guests will pay for the privilege of lodging here.''

"And the small matter of providing French cuisine? No hotel worth its salt would dare to open its doors to the *haut ton* without being able to boast the services of a French chef.''

"Chefs are surely not impossible to find.''

"My dear Miss Lexham, you dismiss this culinary matter too lightly. Last night at the Oxenford you saw how important Duvall is. Society *expects* the finest cuisine, they *expect* to pay four guineas for such meals, for that is what the Oxenford charges, and they *expect* to enjoy for their money the work of a Duvall, a Carême, an Escudier, or an Ude. Such men do not come two a penny. Have you any idea how much they may command?''

"No,'' she confessed.

"I happen to know that the Earl of Sefton pays Ude three hundred pounds a year, that sum being supplemented by the promise of two hundred guineas for life when Ude retires. The sum offered to Carême by the Prince Regent was astronomical and far in excess of that. You cannot possibly contemplate opening this house as a hotel unless you have such a chef, Miss Lexham, and in order to lure one here you will need money—which I need not remind you is the one thing you do not have.''

She was silent for a long moment. All eyes were upon her, but she was still resolute. Her plan was possible, it gave her a chance to meet the terms of her uncle's will, and she would never be able to forgive herself if she turned her back on it. Slowly she reached up and unfastened her grandmother's necklace, laying it gently on the surface of the table before her. The sunlight pouring in through the windows flashed blood red on the rubies and made the chased silver gleam with an almost blue light.

Mr. Jordan stared at it and then slowly raised his eyes to her serious face. "I beg you reconsider,'' he said gently. "For it is my belief that you are about to cast this precious, beloved item away, and to no purpose.''

"I am set upon my course, Mr. Jordan, and as I will need money, the necklace must be sold.''

"It will not finance you for six months.''

"No, but it will give me the finance to begin. I trust that the hotel would soon begin to support itself."

He looked helplessly at her, seeing the determination in her eyes and feeling in his heart that the idea was doomed from the outset. "Miss Lexham, you speak as if you regard success as a matter of fact!"

"I don't, sir, I promise you that."

Still he could not give up. "And what of your cousin the earl? He is hardly likely to stand by and let this happen to his house—"

"*My* town house," she interrupted calmly. "For the next six months, anyway."

A glimmer of humor touched his eyes at this, for he recognized his own words. "Very well, *your* town house. It matters not, for in the end it comes to the same: the Earl of Lexham will not let you proceed."

"Can he stop me?"

"Not legally, but I doubt very much if he is a man to let such niceties stand in his way."

"Then his interference is something to be coped with if and when it occurs. Oh, Mr. Jordan, don't you see that I *have* to do this now I've thought of it? Now that I've been in this house, it means far more to me than I would have dreamed possible, and if I give up without a struggle, I will regret it for the rest of my life. And there is more; Sir Henry Seymour said to me last night that when I came to London, I came home, and that is very true. I don't want to go back to Selford; I loathe it there. I want to stay here; this is where I feel I belong. I must do everything I can to keep this house; it may be the only chance I ever have of changing the course of my life. Please, at least say you understand."

He saw there there was no point in further argument, for she did indeed mean to go ahead with her plan, her commercial enterprise. "And is there nothing at all I can say to instill wisdom into your pretty head?"

She smiled. "Nothing whatsoever."

He nodded heavily. "Very well, I capitulate. I have grave doubts and reservations, but I will do all I can to help you."

"You will? Oh, *dear* Mr. Jordan!" she cried in delight, forgetting both herself and his dignity by flinging her arms around his neck.

The servants' eyes widened at this uninhibited display, but

Mrs. Hollingsworth saw it as still more evidence that Philip Lexham's warm, open, and genuine nature had been passed on to his daughter.

Caroline turned to the housekeeper then. "You will help me too, won't you?"

"Oh yes, Miss Lexham, have no fear about that."

Caroline smiled, biting her lip a little ruefully. "Mr. Jordan was right about one thing; I certainly do not know the first thing about the running of hotels or great houses."

"I believe I know all that is necessary. We will begin by engaging staff. Advertisements must be placed in the correct publications and the various tradesmen informed. Tradesmen are very useful for such purposes, for they put word about in the hope of benefiting in the form of orders."

Mr. Jordan cleared his throat. "Miss Lexham, nothing can be done until the necklace is sold, for until then you will have no money at all."

She picked it up and pressed it into his hands. "Will you sell it for me?" She smiled a little wickedly then. "I am sure a lady should not participate in anything so mercenary and vulgar!"

He laughed. "You are incorrigible, Miss Lexham, quite incorrigible."

A short while later, Caroline was being conveyed back to the Oxenford in the lawyer's chariot. She was still in a state bordering on elation; it seemed that her plan could not fail, for it had only to succeed for six months! She had arranged with Mrs. Hollingsworth that she would return to Lexham House that very day, cutting short the duration of her stay at the Oxenford, and she did this in part to avoid any further meetings with Hal Seymour. She tried to push all thought of him from her mind, but that was impossible, for in a very short time he had stolen her heart completely, which made the pain of knowing what he had said of her all the more distressing.

Mr. Jordan had placed his chariot at her disposal for the rest of the day, and so she instructed the coachman to wait for her outside the Oxenford as she did not intend to be long. As she entered the quiet vestibule, however, the porter informed her that Mr. Bassett wished to see her immediately. There was something in the porter's manner which told her that her meeting with the majordomo was not going to be pleasant, and she went apprehensively to the dining room, where she was told she would find him.

The dining room was deserted, and so she heard the sound of raised voices before she entered and recognized them as belonging to Mr. Bassett and Gaspard Duvall.

The little chef was obviously very angry. "The kitchens are *not* satisfactory, monsieur!"

"And I say that they must suffice!" replied the equally cross majordomo.

"I am a master, a *genius,* not a slave! A banquet of the size and importance as that for the Duc de Wellington requires finer facilities than those you provide here!"

Mr. Bassett endeavored to take a little of the heat out of the argument. "I agree with you, monsieur," he said in almost conciliatory tones. "And I understand your predicament, but in order to meet your demands it would be necessary to close the hotel completely while the kitchens are rebuilt. That is simply not possible, for how can we close our doors when we have accepted many functions such as the banquet and Miss Seymour's wedding. Be reasonable, monsieur—"

"Reasonable? *Reasonable?*" cried the infuriated chef, obviously quivering from the tip of his floppy beret to the toes of his elegant shoes.

"Please, monsieur," pleaded the anxious majordomo, who was beginning to fear that the chef would resign, which would be a devastating blow to the Oxenford.

Caroline peeped into the room and saw the little Frenchman hesitating. She too believed he must resign, but incredibly he did not; he turned on his heel and walked swiftly toward the door, muttering darkly to himself as he pushed past without seeming to see her. He was so unlike the man she had last spoken to in the garden that she could only stare after him in surprise. After a moment she looked into the room again and, seeing Mr. Bassett wiping his brow with a handkerchief, judged that it would be all right for her to approach him to discover what it was he wished to say to her.

He turned as he heard her approach, and he stiffened visibly. "Ah, Miss Lexham."

"You wished to speak to me?" She could not help noticing that he did not offer her the courtesy of a seat.

"It will not take long, madam, for I merely wish to inform you that your presence is no longer required at the Oxenford."

She was completely taken aback. "I beg your pardon?"

"You will be expected to leave immediately," he went on coldly. "And the sum paid for your stay will be reimbursed to the proper party. That is all."

Her indignation flashed into light. "It most certainly is *not* all!" she said icily. "I expect to be told why this disgraceful request is being made."

"I am not compelled to give you any details, madam, but will say that we have received complaints about your presence."

"From whom?" But even as she asked, she dreaded that she would hear him say Hal's name.

"The identity of anyone concerned is not your business, madam," he replied, his tone very superior as he looked down his pointed nose at her.

"On the contrary, sir, it is very much my business."

He saw the light of angry, determined defiance in her gray eyes and decided that telling her would remove such misplaced impudence and would almost certainly hasten her departure from the premises. "Very well, Miss Lexham, I will tell you. I have this morning received strong complaints from three persons of rank and consequence: Lady Chaddington, Lord Fynehurst, and the Earl of Lexham, your kinsman. All three objected to your presence in this respectable establishment as you are not a person of either quality or good character, and they informed me that unless you were ejected forthwith, they would see to it that they and their friends and acquaintances did not patronize the Oxenford again."

Not a person of either quality or good character? Her eyes darkened with anger at such an appalling insult, but she was glad that at least Hal and his sister had not joined in this exhibition of petty and unnecessary spite. Hal may not have been as open and genuine as he had made out, but she was sure that Jennifer had meant every kind word and action the night before.

The majordomo drew himself up importantly. "I trust that the situation is now perfectly clear, madam. Such persons as I have mentioned cannot be ignored, and I therefore have no choice but to—"

"On the contrary, sir, you have every choice, but you have decided that although their complaints are unwarranted and untrue, and although I am innocent and very much the injured party, I am not of sufficient consequence to warrant consideration. You, sirrah, are as despicable as they!''

Giving him a glance of proud disgust, she turned and walked away, her head held high, but as she hurried up the grand staircase, her eyes brimmed with hot tears and her cheeks flamed with the humiliation and injustice of being treated in such an unkind and disgraceful way.

At the top of the staircase, she halted to look back down at the elegant vestibule with its gracious furniture and attentive page boys and footmen. Defiance stirred her then. She would not allow them to treat her as if she did not matter! She would show them! She would show the Marcia Chaddingtons, Dominic Lexhams, and Oxenfords of this world that she was a person to be reckoned with after all! She would not scuttle out of London because they wanted her to; she would stay and she would make a success of what Mr. Jordan called her ''commercial enterprise'' and soon all London would be talking of the new Lexham Hotel and its unusual owner!

Chapter 15

But her moment of bravado began to shrink to a more timorous apprehension as she packed her few belongings into her valise. Glancing around at her magnificent apartment, the enormity of what she was contemplating began to truly dawn upon her; indeed, the sheer audacity of it made her wonder if perhaps Mr. Jordan was right after all and she *had* taken leave of her senses. Why, only a day or so before she had had qualms about setting off for London at all, and now here she was, determining to embark upon turning a great London mansion into an exclusive hotel.

She had almost completed packing when there was a knock at the door, and before she could say anything it opened and Miss Seymour entered in a rustle of red-and-white-checkered silk, the fresh ribbons in her little day bonnet bouncing prettily beneath her chin. For a moment Caroline froze warily, able to think only of what Hal had said to Marcia Chaddington. What if Jennifer shared her brother's views after all? But the warmth of her smile and her obvious dismay when she saw Caroline's packed valise soon dispelled such fears.

"Oh, Miss Lexham, surely you are not leaving already?"

"I fear that I must."

"But I was so looking forward to your company, and you

promised that we would see each other today. Has something happened that you must return to Devon so soon?''

"I-I'm not going back to Devon."

"But where are you going then?"

"I am going to Lexham House."

Jennifer stared at her, and then her eyes brightened. "You are going to fight the will after all? Oh, how wonderful! How excellent! And how gladdening, for this means that I will be able to see you often." She paused for a moment. "Do you really have to leave the Oxenford so quickly? I mean, Hal and I were hoping that you would join us for dinner tonight. . . ."

Caroline secretly doubted very much that Hal joined his sister in any such hope, but at least Jennifer's enthusiasm and warmth proved that he had not shared with her his true opinion of the upstart and disreputable Miss Lexham.

"You will join us, won't you?" inquired Jennifer, thus placing Caroline in the unenviable position of having to admit that she was now *persona non grata* at the Oxenford.

"I would have loved to have joined you, Miss Seymour, but I am afraid that it will not be possible, for I have been requested by Mr. Bassett to leave the hotel immediately."

Jennifer was incredulous. "Surely there is some mistake!"

"There is no mistake; he was most definite."

"But why?"

"Because he has received complaints about my presence here." Caroline spoke carefully, hoping that she would not be asked to name any names.

"But who would complain about you?" demanded Jennifer, her eyes flashing with anger that such a thing could have happened. "I suppose it was that odious cousin of yours. I saw him leaving earlier this morning!"

"Yes, it was my cousin," admitted Caroline, determined to say nothing about Marcia Chaddington or Lord Fynehurst, for it would have placed Jennifer in an invidious position to mention Hal's future bride and brother-in-law in such a context.

Jennifer was indignant on Caroline's behalf. "How infamous and despicable your cousin is! And how monstrous it is that this hotel could do this to you! I think them all odious and disagreeable in the extreme. And I feel insulted."

"*You* feel insulted?" asked Caroline, a little taken aback.

"Naturally, for you are my friend, as you are Hal's, and

you were our guest last night at the opera house. To treat you in this demeaning and cavalier fashion is tantamount to an insult to us too!''

"Oh, please do not feel like that . . ." began Caroline anxiously.

"I will not remain in this dreadful place a moment longer," declared the other suddenly. "And when I tell Hal, I am sure that he wil feel exactly the same way."

"Please don't do anything because of me!" begged Caroline, not wanting to stir things up to such an extent and wishing with all her heart that she had somehow managed to avoid all mention of being asked to leave the Oxenford.

Jennifer took her hands. "I like you immensely, Miss Lexham, for in you I feel I have found a true and constant friend, and it simply is not possible for me to allow you to be treated so abominably without showing in some way how much I abhor what has been done. Nothing on this earth would prevail upon me to remain here after this! Come, we will go immediately to tell Hal."

"Oh, no!" cried Caroline, but to no avail, for Jennifer was carried along by her indignation on her new friend's behalf, and Caroline found herself being hurried through the hotel to Hal's apartment.

He had not long returned from riding. His top hat, gloves, and riding crop lay on a table and his green riding coat was unbuttoned. He stood by the immense fireplace of the drawing room, which like Caroline's, overlooked Piccadilly and the green expanse of the park opposite. His valet was just pouring him a small glass of cognac as his sister entered, followed very reluctantly by Caroline, who had no wish to face him, and certainly no wish to see him being informed of events he almost certainly already knew about.

The discreet and efficient valet conveyed the cognac into his master's hand and then spirited the top hat, gloves, and riding crop from the room, closing the door softly behind him.

Jennifer hurried immediately to her brother, her whole body quivering with indignation. "Hal, I have something most dreadful to tell you!"

Caroline could not bring herself to even look at him. She kept her eyes firmly on the Kidderminster carpet, and Marcia Chaddington's scornful, taunting voice seemed to ring in her ears. *You flaunted yourself quite outrageously, or so he tells me. Forget your notions of grandeur, and forget Sir Henry Seymour, whose derision you have already earned.*

Hal glanced momentarily at Caroline's quiet, bowed head, and then took his agitated sister by the hand. "It must indeed be dreadful to bring you bursting in so unceremoniously. What has happened?"

"Miss Lexham has been told she must leave this hotel, and all because her wretched and contemptible cousin complained about her! Is that not awful, Hal? I am so upset about it, so insulted and angry, that nothing will do but that we leave this horrid place too!"

Hal seemed quite nonplussed for a moment, and to Caroline his initial silence was proof enough that he knew precisely what had happened and whose influence lay behind it. Her cheeks flushed miserably and she didn't raise her eyes to look at him. At last he spoke, "Jennifer, I can quite understand how you feel, and indeed I share your indignation, which is more than justified, but I think that to talk of quitting the Oxenford is to go a little too far."

Caroline looked up then, for although he spoke of sharing his sister's feelings, it was obvious that in truth he did no such thing. He had no intention of making any grand gesture on behalf of a woman he held in contempt. Jennifer, however, was visibly shocked and dismayed by his apparently lackluster reaction to something she regarded as of the utmost importance. "Hal! You cannot understand what has been done. This hotel has gravely insulted our friend, it has dealt appallingly with someone we have openly acknowledged to be agreeable and acceptable to us. By doing that, it has insulted us too."

He swirled his cognac for a moment, saying nothing, and Caroline wondered what was passing through his head. "I repeat," he said then, "that although I can understand your considerable displeasure at what has been done, I do *not* share your belief that we should quit this hotel." He glanced at Caroline. "Forgive me, Miss Lexham, for I do not wish to sound as if I in any way condone what has happened."

She held his gaze and said nothing in reply, but inside she felt an immeasurable hurt.

Jennifer was totally astounded. "Hal! You surely do not mean to remain here."

"Yes, that is exactly what I mean to do."

"I cannot believe that I hear you correctly," she replied, withdrawing her hand from his. "Indeed, I think you behave as odiously as the Oxenford and the Earl of Lexham."

Caroline spoke up quickly. "Please, Miss Seymour, don't say any more, for I do not wish to be the cause of any disagreement between Sir Henry and yourself."

But Jennifer did not seem to hear, for she still stared up disbelievingly into her brother's hazel eyes. "You may not think this thing to be of any importance, Hal, but I most certainly do! I will not remain another night under this discredited roof!"

"Jennifer—" he began.

"My mind is made up," she interrupted. "To remain here would be to ignore what has been done, and it would also mean allowing the arrangements for my marriage to go ahead. Nothing would make me celebrate my marriage here now, *nothing*!"

"Jennifer!" he said sharply, his eyes bright with something, Caroline could not gauge exactly what. "I wish you to stop right now and reconsider!"

"No!" His sister's chin was raised stubbornly.

"I have excellent reason to ask you to remain here."

"I know, and that reason is your own convenience. No, Hal Seymour, I will not stay here, I will leave immediately, and nothing you say can stop me."

"I do not think it would be wise to test the veracity of that statement, Jennifer," he replied quietly. "As head of the family, I think you will find that my powers extend considerably further than you appear to think."

"So, you will force me to do as you wish!" she cried, trembling with anger and frustration.

"I have never *forced* you to do anything in your life, and it ill becomes you to suggest that I am capable of such conduct. I merely said that my powers are extensive enough for me to stop you leaving. I did *not* say that I was about to employ those powers. If you insist upon going elsewhere, then you may do so, provided you choose an address which is acceptable. Where do you intend going? Mivart's? Grillion's?"

"I don't know yet," she replied.

"Perhaps you intend to be the new Lexham Hotel's first guest," he said quietly, glancing at Caroline's astonished

face. "Oh, yes, Miss Lexham, news does indeed travel with
bewildering speed in this capital of ours."

Jennifer stared at him in puzzlement and then turned
toward Caroline. "What does he mean?"

Hal spoke again. "When I was returning from my ride in
Hyde Park, I encountered Mr. Jordan, the lawyer, and he
informed me that Miss Lexham has a notion to turn Lexham
House into a hotel, thus defeating the terms of the will."

"Is this true?" asked Jennifer in astonishment.

"Yes," answered Caroline.

For a moment Jennifer seemed at a loss, but then her green
eyes began to dance with delight. "What a splendid thing!
What a brave and wonderful plan! Oh, I wish I had half the
spirit." She turned triumphantly to her brother once more.
"Yes, Hal Seymour, I *do* intend to be the new Lexham
Hotel's first guest. I shall take great delight in telling that
horrible Mr. Bassett what I think of him, and if I see Dominic
Lexham I shall tell him too. I shall make a great deal of noise
about leaving this place, and about canceling my wedding
here and holding it at the new hotel instead."

Caroline gave a start, her breath catching. "Miss Seymour!
You cannot possibly!"

"Why not?" inquired the other, smiling almost archly. "I
think it is a capital notion, for it does everything I wish it to
do: it strikes back at the Oxenford and at Dominic Lexham,
and it goes a considerable way toward setting your admirable
enterprise up. It also makes my brother's reprehensible inac-
tion look all the more obvious, which is no more or less than
he deserves!"

Hal said nothing to this and his face was expressionless.

"But Miss Seymour," said Caroline, "Lexham House is
closed, the rooms are not aired and—"

"But you are about to go there, aren't you?"

"Yes, but—"

"If it is good enough for you, then it is good enough for
me—unless—perhaps you do not wish me to go there?" There
was a sudden hurt in the green eyes.

"Oh, no," replied Caroline swiftly. "Please do not think
that, for it is not so. Of course I would love to have you join
me; it's just that I don't want you to do anything you may
regret. All your wedding arrangements are made, you have
told me how delighted you are at the prospect of having

Monsieur Duvall prepare the feast, and how advantageous will be your appearance on the grand staircase!''

Jennifer had to smile. ''As I recall, the staircase at Lexham House is *far* more grand, which must mean I will appear to even greater advantage there. As to the feast, well before Hal decided we must uproot and come to this horrid place, I was quite content for Messieurs Gunter to do the feast. The feast is not important, Miss Seymour, but my gesture in leaving the Oxenford and going to the new Lexham most certainly is. My mind is made up and I shall have Simpson begin packing immediately.'' With a final defiant glance at her silent brother and a flick of her red-and-white skirts, she turned on her heel and hurried from the room, calling for the maid in the adjoining apartment.

Caroline hesitated, not knowing quite what to say to Hal, for there was no trace now of the ease she had once felt in his company. She could not shrug off the sense of hurt and betrayal she felt at what he had said about her and she knew a deep pain at his silent complicity in what had been done to her. In spite of this, however, as she looked into his unfathomable hazel eyes, she knew that she still loved him.

''I don't think there is anything more to be said, Miss Lexham,'' he said then. ''So do not let me detain you any longer.''

Without a word, she left the apartment.

Chapter 16

That first evening at Lexham House was very strange indeed, for Caroline and Jennifer shared Mrs. Hollingsworth's little rooms, that lady declaring that on no account could she permit ladies of such delicate constitution to sleep in the damp, cold house. For Jennifer, the housekeeper's rooms were a novel experience, but Caroline found them very similar to some of the rooms at Selford and would, therefore, have felt quite at home in them had it not been for her awareness all the time of the echoing vastness of the main house close by.

Caroline had half expected Jennifer's rush of loyal enthusiasm to fade quickly away once she realized how very uncomfortable Lexham House was going to be for a while, but she was soon proved wrong, for Jennifer entered with great relish into the spirit of things. One thing was soon apparent, and that was that Hal Seymour's vivacious and unpredictable sister was nothing if not adventurous, and she certainly had scant regard for what she regarded as foolish and overfastidious rules of etiquette, which she took considerable delight in flouting at the first opportunity. Naturally, she never went too far in this, which was part of her charm, and which was also probably why she seemed to get away with what others would deem to be horrendous sins.

It was quickly decided that Jennifer would have Mrs. Hollingsworth's bed, the housekeeper refusing to hear of anything else and preparing for herself a bed of sorts on the floor of the storeroom where she kept her jars of pickles and preserves. Caroline was provided with a spare mattress in a corner of the parlor, and when everything had been made ready, the unlikely trio sat before the fire to discuss what must be done next to put Caroline's momentous plans into action. There was something very unreal about the situation, and Caroline almost expected to wake up soon and find herself back in her bed at Selford, but when she pinched herself she knew she was very much awake and that this was all really happening.

She glanced approvingly around the parlor, which was an inviting room with a red-tiled floor and whitewashed walls. There were colorful chintz curtains at the window and matching cushions on the dark wooden chairs, and against one wall stood a dresser displaying the housekeeper's prized crockery and the silver-gilt candlestick presented to her by Caroline's grandmother, that same countess who had once owned the necklace which was to finance the first weeks of the great commercial enterprise.

Occasionally they heard bursts of laughter from the servants' hall, where Jennifer's maid, Simpson, was very much the center of interest. Outside, the wind had risen and rattled the panes of glass from time to time. Each gust drew a draft down the chimney, making the fire glow very red, which in turn burnished the fur of the large, gray cat curled up before the hearth. Mrs. Hollingsworth sat on a low stool in front of the fire, toasting bread on a long-handled fork, and the smell was very appetizing indeed, prompting Jennifer to remark that not even Monsieur Duvall could create such a delicacy. This made them all smile, and Caroline found herself thinking what a very strange, ill-assorted trio they were: a lady of wealth and fashion, a housekeeper, and an unlikely heiress, all seated around a fire sharing toast together! Indeed, it was all so improbable that she wanted to laugh, but after all, it *was* said that the truth was often much more strange than fiction. But as she sat there, thinking about the situation in which she now found herself, she was aware more and more that she was flying in the face of adversity, defying influential enemies, and risking all on a venture which many would have been generous to call madcap.

Mrs. Hollingsworth saw her pensive expression, and judged it correctly. "It will be all right, madam, I know that it will."

"I wish I could be so certain, but somehow the whole idea suddenly seems impossible, conceived when the moon was full."

"I recall my mother saying that notions taken at such times were frequently the best notions of all, and far from being moonstruck. We'll set to work here in the morning, we'll open up the house and light the fires, and you'll soon begin to feel better then. I will see to it that suitable staff are found, and I promise you that in a week or so you'll see a complete transformation. Once you see Lexham House as it was meant to be, you will know that your idea of defeating your uncle's will by this plan is a stroke of genius and not to be spoken of as mere moon madness. The Lexham Hotel will become one of London's finest and most exclusive establishments, you mark my words, and Miss Seymour's wedding will be spoken of for seasons to come."

Caroline wanted so much to take comfort from the housekeeper's words, but she couldn't. It seemed that with the coming of darkness, her buoyant optimism had all but completely gone, leaving her feeling very vulnerable and unsure.

Jennifer leaned over to put a reassuring hand on her arm. "Mrs. Hollingsworth is right, you simply cannot fail, for there will be enough talk and interest to carry you through those all-important six months."

"Maybe. Or maybe the whole thing will prove to be a nine days' wonder. We all know that a hotel is nothing at the moment unless it offers the finest in French cuisine; the Lexham cannot do that."

"Yet," replied Jennifer firmly.

"I will need to find another Gaspard Duvall. And not only for the everyday cooking—what of your wedding? At the moment, it seems inevitable that we will have to approach Gunter's, and that will mean providing exactly the same feast as countless other fashionable weddings. There will not be anything memorable about that, will there? So, when the nine days of wonder are over, the Lexham will be judged on its own merits, and will be found wanting.''

Mrs. Hollingsworth inspected the toast and then held it to the fire again. ''Your hotel will only be found wanting in that one respect, in all the others it will be superlative, of that you may be quite sure. It will offer the most elegant accommodation, the most exclusive address, and the finest service—I will personally see to the latter. As to using Gunter's, well I agree that it is not ideal, but they are caterers of the highest quality and can be as French as need be—which should certainly be the case as they charge five guineas for the services of one of their man cooks and one guinea each for his eight attendants. I know these figures because the late earl employed them from time to time.'' The housekeeper paused for a moment, her expression suddenly very thoughtful, and then she lowered the toasting fork, looking directly at Caroline. ''This Mr. Duvall is the finest French chef in London, is he not?''

''So I believe.''

''And he is dissatisfied at the Oxenford on account of the kitchens?''

''Yes.''

''Lure him here then.''

Caroline stared.

Mrs. Hollingsworth smiled. ''I'll warrant this house boasts the very best kitchens in England—excepting the Pavilion in Brighton, perhaps. Steal him from the Oxenford, Miss Lexham, for you owe that establishment nothing.''

Caroline was nonplussed. ''Are you serious?''

''Never more so in my life.''

''I would dearly like to think I *could* lure him here, but I cannot. He may be dissatisfied at the Oxenford, but he is at least very well paid there. I can't offer him anything but an uncertain future and the finest kitchens in Town. Indeed,'' she added almost as an aside, ''I can't afford to do anything at all unless Mr. Jordan manages to sell my necklace.''

Mrs. Hollingsworth was not to be defeated. ''Perhaps it will not be necessary to offer him grand sums of money, Miss Lexham. If your enterprise is a success, at the end of six months this house and its contents will be yours. You could offer Mr. Duvall a valuable item from the house in lieu of payment; and if he has an eye for a good bargain, he'll see the benefit of such an arrangement. In my experience, madam, those who get to such eminent positions as he has reached do not do so without being shrewd men of business as well as masters of their chosen field.''

Jennifer had been listening with great interest, and now she smiled approvingly. "Mrs. Hollingsworth is right, and you must at least try. And just *think* what a sweet revenge it would be upon that horrid Mr. Bassett!''

Caroline looked from one to the other, and then slowly she smiled. "Very well, I will approach Monsieur Duvall.''

At that moment they heard a loud knocking echoing through from the front doors of the main house, and all three fell silent with surprise. Mrs. Hollingsworth got up and went to the window, peering out into the darkness, and then she smiled. "It's Mr. Jordan, I recognize his chariot!'' She hurried out and a moment later ushered the lawyer into the little parlor.

He bowed immediately to both Caroline and Jennifer. "Good evening, Miss Lexham. Miss Seymour.''

Jennifer smiled. "You do not seem surprised to see me here, sir.''

"That is because I already knew what had happened, Miss Seymour. Word of your actions has begun to spread already, and there is quite an upset at the Oxenford, as you can well imagine, for your—er—defection is not good for its reputation.''

"Excellent.''

He smiled a little. "My sentiments precisely. However, I will not beat about the bush and will come directly to the point of my visit. Miss Lexham, I have sold your necklace.''

Caroline stared. "Already?''

"It was most fortunate. This afternoon a gentleman from Scotland had an appointment with me, and he happened to see the necklace. On learning that its owner wished to sell it, he immediately offered me a most handsome price, saying that it was just the thing to present to his future wife. The transaction was completed there and then.'' He placed some documents in her hands. "I took the liberty of depositing the money in a very reputable bank, that of Messieurs Coutts, and now you may conduct your business through them, using their checks—a much safer proposition than keeping too much money in the house. There are so many rogues and thieves about, Miss Lexham, and it would not do at all for you to lose anything at this delicate stage.''

She gazed in wonder at the very handsome price her necklace had fetched. ''Did he really pay this?''

''Certainly.''

''But who was he?''

For a moment the lawyer hesitated. ''Oh, no one you know, my dear, and perhaps it would be best to leave him as a stranger, for the necklace meant a very great deal to you.''

''Yes, I suppose you are right. Oh, Mr. Jordan, I can hardly believe all this is really happening.''

''No,'' he said with some feeling. ''Nor can I.''

She smiled. ''You must forgive me for so unsettling you, Mr. Jordan.''

''My dear Miss Lexham, you haven't merely unsettled me, I fear you have quite taken my breath away. However, no doubt the novelty of it all will do me good. Now I must leave you, for I have a dinner to attend and shall barely be in time for the final speech. Good night, ladies.''

''Good night.''

Mrs. Hollingsworth showed him out, and Jennifer turned to Caroline. ''There is something I have been meaning to mention to you.''

''Yes?''

''When I departed from the Oxenford today, Mr. Bassett went to great lengths to dissuade me, imploring that it was not his fault, that he had been in no position to defy *three* such eminent persons when they were intent upon having you removed.''

''Oh.''

''You let me believe that the Earl of Lexham was the only person involved, but I now know that Lady Chaddington and her brother were too.''

''Yes.''

''Why?''

''I believe you know why.''

''Because she is to marry Hal?''

''Yes.''

Jennifer lowered her eyes. ''I have always loathed Marcia Chaddington, and now I loathe her more than ever. She is everything that is wrong for my brother, and yet he does not seem able to see it. She will make him very unhappy, and I cannot bear the thought, for I love him very dearly. I will tell him what she did to you, for he should know the depths to which she is capable of sinking.''

"Please, don't."

"Why?"

Caroline couldn't answer, for she could hardly say that she thought Hal already knew full well what Marcia had done, and more, that he approved.

Jennifer was firm. "I mean to tell him. It isn't as if I am breaking a confidence, for Mr. Bassett informed me, did he not?"

"I would still rather you said nothing."

"His happiness is too important to me. I feel I must do all I can to make him see sense about her. Forgive me."

Caroline smiled. "There is nothing to forgive, Miss Seymour."

"Please call me Jennifer; after all we can hardly remain so formal when we are about to share slices of toast which resemble doorsteps!"

Caroline laughed then. "Very well, provided you call me Caroline."

"Naturally."

Chapter 17

Nearly two weeks passed and February gave way to March. Preparations at Lexham House went on apace, but although Caroline expected some sign of further action on the part of her enemies, nothing happened. She learned that Dominic had been called away suddenly to his County Durham estate, which explained his silence, but Marcia Chaddington and her brother were very much in Town, and yet they appeared to be ignoring her continued presence. She had written a brief note to Gaspard Duvall, asking him to call upon her at his earliest convenience, but as yet she had not received a reply. In the meantime she and Mrs. Hollingsworth had searched in vain for another chef, but as Mr. Jordan had said, such persons were not two a penny. The matter of a chef caused Caroline more and more anxiety as time went on, for the hotel was set to open in one week's time, on the ill-starred Friday, the thirteenth of March. She had thought twice about tempting providence by choosing this particular date, but to wait another week would have clashed a little with Jennifer's wedding, and to bring the date forward would have meant opening before the house was completely ready. So, with her fingers crossed, she had set the date for the thirteenth.

When she had taken up residence in the house, she had

immediately met the first condition of her uncle's will, and
the second condition was met when the army of nearly thirty
servants Mrs. Hollingsworth engaged opened up the rooms
and lit fires in all the hearths.

It was good to be in the house when it was warm and
welcoming. The dust sheets had been removed from the
furniture, the brown paper taken down from the paintings, the
carpets unrolled and put in their allotted places, and the
crystal chandeliers glittered brilliantly on being released from
their dull holland prisons. Plate gleamed on the dining room's
handsome sideboards, and the mahogany table was a highly
polished mirror in which shone perfect reflections of the
silver-gilt candelabra standing upon it. The red saloon was
also magnificent again, its beautiful furniture and paintings
showing up to perfect advantage in the fresh spring sunlight
which daily poured in through the tall windows. Throughout
the house the story was the same, and in the grounds gardeners tended the lawns and flower beds where daffodils were
now in bud. The greenhouses had been put to full use again,
and evergreen shrubs had been purchased, complete with
terra-cotta pots, to place at various points where their foliage
added a welcome contrast of color against the red brick of the
house. They looked especially well upon the grand balcony
overlooking the courtyard, as Caroline noted with approval
each time she returned to the house after an expedition to the
shops of Oxford Street or to the inexpensive dressmaker Mrs.
Hollingsworth had found for her. Caroline knew that she was
in dire need of new clothes, for the mistress of the Lexham
House could hardly appear alternately in gray wool or turquoise lawn. The thought of paying for such apparel, however,
seemed dreadful, for it drained her resources, but so far her
expenses had been minimal.

Jennifer now occupied gracious apartments at the front of
the house, and she declared herself to be very well pleased,
especially as it was so much more peaceful there than it had
been at the Oxenford, where the noise of Piccadilly had
intruded until well into the night.

After much deliberation, Caroline had been persuaded to
take the private apartments on the ground floor. Her first
instinct had been to take some rooms at the top of the house,
but both Mrs. Hollingsworth and Jennifer had been appalled
at such a suggestion, pointing out that already society was

talking about the new venture, and about Caroline in particular—she would be expected to conduct herself as the mistress of the house, and would therefore have to play the part to the full. Eventually she was persuaded, but she felt ill at ease in rooms which had until fairly recently been occupied by her uncle, and she hated climbing at nights into the huge, canopied bed.

As preparations continued in Mayfair Street, society discussed the piquancy of the situation, for the Lexham will had intrigued many people. Dominic's absence from Town caused a little disappointment, but the appearance one morning of an item in *The Times* assured onlookers of his imminent and furious return. The article detailed the goings-on at Lexham House, and was worded in such a way as to fan the flames of the family feud which had glowed steadily since the very day Philip Lexham had run away to marry Catherine Marchand. Caroline had read the newspaper that morning too, and she could well imagine the effect its appearance at the breakfast table would be having upon her prideful, vengeful cousin. That edition of *The Times* would appear on the table at Selford too, which prompted her to sit down and write a lengthy letter of explanation to Richard, who was bound to be most alarmed when he realized what she was doing. She intended her letter to soothe his worries if at all possible, but when she read it through afterward, it seemed to show up the faults and hazards of her plan rather than conceal them. There was nothing for it but to dispatch the letter, however, and trust that it would serve the purpose for which it was intended.

Of Hal Seymour Lexham House saw nothing. He had remained firmly entrenched at the Oxenford, much to the annoyance of his sister, who was determined to show her disapproval by staying away from him. She wanted him to call upon her, but as yet he had not shown any inclination so to do. Unlike his future brother-in-law, Lord Carstairs upheld Jennifer on every count, declaring himself to be appalled at the conduct of the Oxenford, Dominic Lexham *et al,* and to be totally mystified by Hal's refusal to join in the condemnation.

Hal appeared to be supremely unconcerned, continuing as if nothing had happened. He supervised the arrangements for the banquet, dined every night at the Oxenford, inspected the progress on his house in Hanover Square, and was seen

absolutely everywhere with Marcia Chaddington on his arm.
As far as Caroline was concerned, he could not have expressed himself more clearly had he placed a notice in a
newspaper, but she hid her feelings so well that no one could
have guessed that Sir Henry Seymour even crossed her mind.

As the day of the opening approached, Caroline wondered
what she would have done without the help of Mrs. Hollingsworth. Having decided that Caroline's plan for Lexham House
offered it salvation from Dominic, the housekeeper did all in
her power to help. She seemed to have an endless capacity
for seeing simple solutions to problems that seemed enormous
to Caroline. Every hotel should have two footmen to parade
up and down outside, but that meant livery. Caroline could
hardly array her footmen in Dominic's livery, but to provide
them with entirely new clothes would have been exorbitantly
expensive. The housekeeper produced some black braiding
from a trunk in an attic room and set some housemaids to
remove the silver lace and rosettes from the dark red coats
and tricorn hats, replacing both with the braiding. The result
was a transformation which Dominic would not be able to
complain about with any justification. The housekeeper also
solved the less important matter of the lack of hair powder for
the footmen, advising the use of ordinary household flour
instead. Thus, the two handsome fellows were all ready for
their first day of duty on the pavement of Mayfair Street.

If Caroline felt indebted to the housekeeper, she was similarly obliged to Jennifer, for there was no doubting the considerable fillip the forthcoming wedding was giving to the new
hotel's fortunes. The mere fact that Jennifer and her future
husband were staunchly in favor of marrying at the Lexham
had already produced several tentative inquiries from people
who wished to hold functions there, from a reunion of old
soldiers to a fund-raising subscription dinner for the widows
of Trafalgar. But in spite of her delight at these signs of
society's interest, Caroline was horribly aware of the Lexham
Hotel's one great failing: its lack of a French chef.

This problem had still not been solved when one morning
Hal Seymour paid his first call upon his sister. Wearing a
wine-red coat, his full cravat ruffled by the breeze, he drove
smartly up to the door in his cabriolet. As he drew the vehicle
to a standstill, the tiger jumped down from his perch behind
and took the reins from his master, who alighted and then

paused to tip his top hat back on his dark hair for a moment. He gazed around the elegant courtyard, his expression thoughtful, and then he ascended the steps to the door, which was opened immediately by the vigilant porter.

Caroline was in the vestibule, but she was unaware of his arrival, for she was supervising the surprisingly difficult task of arranging the various sofas and tables to best advantage. The men moving the furniture were becoming harassed, and she was confounded by the seeming impossibility of achieving a suitably balanced and elegant arrangement.

Hal handed his hat and gloves to the porter, watched her for a moment more and then approached, smiling a little. "It would seem to me, Miss Lexham, that everything looks quite well as it now is."

She whirled about. "Sir Henry!"

"The same." He bowed.

It was a shock to see him again so unexpectedly, and his smile confused her, for when they had last faced each other he had been anything but smiling and friendly. "You startled me," was all she could think of saying, and it sounded very lame.

"So it seems," he replied. "Which is a dreadful admission from the chatelaine of such an establishment. You are not permitted to be anything but alert and imperturbable from now on, Miss Lexham."

"I will be sure to remember that in future."

He smiled again, but there was something in his glance that told her he was aware of the reserve of her manner. "You would be wise to do just that, for I fear you may soon receive a very unwelcome visit from a certain titled gentleman."

"My cousin?"

"He returned to Town yesterday, brought hot-foot by what he had read in *The Times*. He then spent a considerable time with his new lawyer, a very sly fellow who knows more about the curves of the law than the straight lines, after which he took himself to Watier's where he lost a considerable fortune. So far your cousin has done nothing whatever to meet the terms of his father's will, in fact he has not curbed his extravagance in the slightest. He now begins to see that you, on the other hand, are prepared to do a great deal, and that is something he will find unendurable. I feel I should warn you most earnestly to be on your guard from now on."

"I will be. Thank you for your warning, Sir Henry." She meant what she said, but her voice sounded stilted. She could not help it, for although he sounded so concerned, she could only contrast his present manner with his actions over the past two weeks. She was anxious to escape from him suddenly, and with a weak smile prepared to conduct him to Jennifer's apartment. "I am sure you did not come here to discuss my family problems, sir, so I will take you to Miss Seymour straight away."

For a moment his shrewd gaze seemed to read her thoughts, but he merely nodded, following as she led him beneath the arch and into the inner hall, where they began to ascend the grand staircase.

"I trust my sister is keeping well, Miss Lexham."

"Yes. Although—"

"Yes?" He halted. "Is something wrong?"

"No, I was only going to say that she is feeling a little low today, so perhaps a visit from you will do her good."

"I trust it is nothing—"

"Oh, I think it is probably just the understandable apprehension of a bride almost on the eve of her wedding." Caroline continued on up the staircase, and after a moment he followed her, but as she approached Jennifer's door, she wondered if her explanation for Jennifer's mood had been entirely truthful. Jennifer had breakfasted with her that morning, and she had been in high spirits, laughing at the morning paper's sly jibes at the Prince Regent, but then the next moment she had suddenly folded the paper and put it to one side. Her smile and humor had gone and she had been quiet and withdrawn for the rest of the meal.

Jennifer was seated by the fire in her apartment, reading Mrs. Edgeworth's *Tales from Fashionable Life,* but she set the volume aside immediately when Caroline showed Hal into the room. Hesitantly she rose to her feet, obviously undecided about how to greet him, but when he smiled and held out his hands to her, she forgot her crossness and hurried gladly to him.

He caught her close, hugging her. "And what is this I hear about you being a little low today?"

"Oh, it's nothing."

He put his hand to her chin and raised her face, searching

her eyes for a moment. "That is not so, sweeting. Tell me what is wrong."

Caroline judged that the time had come for her to leave them alone, but as she began to make her excuses, Jennifer immediately begged her to stay. "No, don't go, Caroline, I would like you to sit with us for a while."

"I am sure Sir Henry has much he wishes to say to you without me being there.'

He smiled. "Nothing which would not be made more pleasant by your presence, I assure you. I would be glad if you joined us."

She did not want to sit in the same room with him, but she had little choice, and so she allowed him to conduct her to the sofa. The moment they were all seated, however, Jennifer revealed that she had an ulterior motive for desiring the presence of a third party. Sitting on the very edge of her chair, she faced her brother, her whole manner urgent and anxious. "Hal, you wished to know what is wrong—now I will tell you. I read in the newspaper this morning that the Duke of Wellington is about to return to London for a little while. Is this so?"

His eyes had become very wary and he glanced momentarily at Caroline before replying. "Why do you ask?"

"I think you know why, Hal."

"I hardly think this is a suitable time to discuss it, for I am sure we will only bore Miss Lexham."

"Caroline is not bored, and I am sure that this is an excellent time to discuss it," replied Jennifer, her tone little short of defiant. "*Is* the Duke returning from Paris?"

"He is."

"For how long?"

"Possibly about three days."

"Will you be with him throughout?"

"You begin to sound like an interrogator, Jennifer. Yes, I will be with him."

His sister's eyes filled with tears then. "Why has it always to be you? Why can't they find someone else after all this time?"

"Please, Jennifer," he began, again glancing uneasily at Caroline.

"You've only just returned from attending him in Brussels, and I know you were in danger there. I think it heartless and unkind of the duke to expect so much of you!'' Jennifer's hands twisted miserably in her lap and large tears welled up in her eyes.

He went to her, gently taking her shaking hands. "The duke expects nothing of me, my love, and you wrong him by saying that he does. Come now, these tears are not necessary.''

"They are, Hal! I worry so about you, and with good reason, for you are so often in great danger!''

He bowed his head for a moment. "Please, Jennifer, I think you've said more than enough already.''

"I want to say much, much more!''

A little self-consciously, Caroline rose to her feet. "Perhaps it would be better if I left, Sir Henry, for I have no wish to hear anything which is not my business.''

He smiled at that. "My dear, discreet Miss Lexham, I think that that would indeed be like closing the stable door after the departure of the horse. My sister has achieved her aim, knowing full well that your presence prevents me from being the bear I should be with her.''

Jennifer had the grace to look ashamed. "He is right, Caroline, I have used you most abominably for my own purposes. Please forgive me.''

"I am sure there is nothing to forgive,'' replied Caroline.

"So please do not go now,'' went on Jennifer. "For if you do, I will fear that you are cross with me after all. I could not bear to have you cross with me as well as Hal.''

"Oh, I'm sure Sir Henry isn't cross,'' said Caroline quickly.

"He most certainly is,'' he interposed. "And with justification. Please sit down again, Miss Lexham, for you may as well hear whatever it is my sister has on her mind.''

Caroline obeyed as Jennifer looked anxiously at her brother again. "I'm truly sorry for being so devious, Hal, but the moment I saw that notice in the newspaper I knew I had to speak to you. If you had not come here today, then I would have sent Simpson to you, asking you to call on me.''

"You have no need to worry about me, Jennifer.''

"Would you swear that on the Bible?''

He did not reply.

"You see? I am right to be anxious for your safety!''

"I could not swear on the Bible that I will return safely to the Oxenford, Jennifer—swearing such things is not sensible.''

"You are playing with words, Hal Seymour. I am talking

about the danger you get into because of your involvement in perilous intrigues concerning the Duke of Wellington. I want to be a happy bride, Hal, with my adored brother to give me away. I don't want to be in mourning for that brother instead."

He smiled, putting his hand softly to her pale cheeks. "What a very depressing thought. I promise you that you will indeed be a happy bride, for this brief visit of the duke's will not endanger me in any way."

"I wish that you no longer had anything to do with the duke's safety."

"I do what I do gladly, Jennifer. Nothing will change that."

"I know."

He squeezed her fingers again and then returned to his seat. "I think we should talk of something more pleasant—your wedding, perhaps."

Jennifer smiled, struggling to push away her gloom. "Oh, things are going on handsomely, Hal."

He glanced at Caroline. "I've no doubt they are."

"I still mean to set new standards of brilliance. I mean to make it the thing to be married in a hotel, to go away to Venice, and to receive invitations to the home of Lord and Lady Carstairs."

"Society is obviously about to be shaken by the scruff of the neck."

Jennifer's low spirits were evaporating. "I went to Gunter's yesterday to see the cake. Oh, Hal, they're doing it so well. It is surely the most handsome of confections and will look magnificent reposing in the center of the table with its ribbons and flowers. If they do the whole feast as well as they have done the cake—"

"They are to do the whole feast?" he inquired, looking surprised.

"We hope not," replied Jennifer, before Caroline could say anything. "For we hope that soon the Lexham will have a very celebrated chef of it own."

"Oh? Who have you found?"

Jennifer was almost gleeful. "Monsieur Duvall! Is it not splendid?"

Hal stared at his sister, his smile fixed for a briefest of seconds before he recovered from his obvious shock at this revelation. "Duvall is to do your wedding feast? But he is surely not leaving the Oxenford?"

"I certainly hope that he is," said Jennifer triumphantly. "Which will leave you with dull English fare again, Hal Seymour, and serve you right."

"You only *hope* he is? Does this mean nothing has been settled?"

Caroline spoke up quickly. "I have communicated with Monsieur Duvall, Sir Henry, but as yet I have not received a reply. I am not as sanguine as Miss Seymour that he will leave the Oxenford in favor of the Lexham."

"He will," insisted Jennifer. "I just *know* that he will."

Hal glanced again at Caroline before replying. "I fear that I agree with you, Miss Lexham, and I do not think you should rely at all upon gaining Duvall's services."

Jennifer sat back and sniffed. "We will see. However, we've talked about *my* wedding, perhaps it is time to speak of yours."

"Mine?" He looked surprised. "I have no wedding to discuss."

"I doubt if Marcia Chaddington would agree."

"I cannot speak for her, of course."

"Does that mean that you haven't asked her to marry you yet?"

"It most certainly does."

"Good, and I trust that that situation will continue indefinitely."

"I had no idea you disliked her quite that much," he replied dryly.

"I like her less and less with each passing day, as you would too if you knew the whole truth about her."

Caroline could see what was coming and she was alarmed. "Please, Jennifer! Don't say anything more!"

"I shall say what I please," retorted Jennifer determinedly. "He should be told what a horrid creature she is."

He glanced from one to the other. "And what, precisely, should I be told?"

Jennifer faced him. "That Marcia Chaddington and her brother also complained to Mr. Bassett at the Oxenford about Caroline's presence there. They demanded that she should be told to leave. Marcia is extremely odious, Hal Seymour, and you will be the biggest fool of all time if you take her as your wife!"

Hal looked silently at his sister for a moment. "And why would Marcia do that?" he asked softly. "What possible reason could she have?"

For the third and final time Caroline determined to leave the room. Her cheeks were aflame with embarrassment, and she gathered her skirts to hurry to the door. "I-I have a lot to do," she said. "So I beg that you excuse me."

Chapter 18

On the eve of the opening, Caroline and Mrs. Hollingsworth worked very hard indeed, checking and rechecking that everything was in readiness for the following morning when the doors of the Lexham Hotel would at last be opened and when some of the huge stock of champagne from the late earl's cellar would be served, chilled by ice from the large block purchased from an Icelandic supplier who had advertised in the newspaper earlier in the week. Notices concerning the opening had been placed in various publications, and now it was only a matter of hours before Caroline would see if all the interest stirred by the novelty and audacity of her actions would bring the required result. She went to her bed at midnight, but she was so nervous about a number of minor details that she doubted if she would be able to sleep. Within minutes, however, she sank into a deep, exhausted slumber.

It was very dark when the noise of hammering at the front doors awakened her. With a gasp she sat up, glancing around the shadowy room. Her night-light had gone out, leaving only the vague glow from the dying embers in the hearth to illuminate the chamber. The hammering echoed urgently through the house again, and as she slipped anxiously from the bed, reaching for her shawl, she heard the porter open the door. An authoritative male voice demanded Miss Lexham's immediate presence, and she paused in surprise, for she knew that voice: it belonged to Jennifer's betrothed, Lord Carstairs. But why come at such an hour and when Jennifer wasn't present? In her nightgown and holding her shawl around her shoulders, she hurried out to the vestibule, where she saw that it was indeed Lord Carstairs, but he was accompanied by several officers of the watch, and they looked very much as if they were present in their official capacity.

Lord Carstairs looked a little uncomfortable as she approached, and he removed his tall hat. "Forgive this intrusion, Miss Lexham, but I fear that I am here on a matter which I find unpleasant."

"Unpleasant?" She stared at him.

"I am here not as your personal acquaintance, but as a magistrate."

"But what has happened?"

"We have been informed that certain rooms in this house are being used by—er, ladies of ill repute."

Caroline's lips parted in amazement. "You have been wrongly informed, my lord."

He looked uncomfortable. "I trust that that is indeed so."

"I don't understand, my lord, why you and these gentlemen have come here. Even if this house were being used by every Cyprian in London, I do not see why a magistrate should come in the middle of the night to—"

"I come because I have been requested so to do by the Earl of Lexham. Forgive me, Miss Lexham, for I would infinitely have preferred someone else to have come in my stead, but the earl was most specific that *I* should undertake this search of these premises. He wishes the matter to be officially investigated as he is anxious to see that the terms of his father's will are not being violated. You must understand, Miss Lexham, that if we do indeed find anything untoward during our search, then we will have to report that we have discovered the house being used for purposes which are other than respectable."

She nodded. So, at last Dominic had made a move against her—and how neat to decide upon Lord Carstairs as his instrument. As she accompanied her visitors up the grand staircase, she knew in her heart that they would indeed discover what they had come to search for: Dominic would have seen to that. She was glad of one thing: Jennifer was staying overnight with friends.

The sound of laughter was faint at first, but it grew louder as they reached the first landing. As one they glanced up to the floor above, Lord Carstairs gave a reluctant nod, and the officers of the watch led the way up the next flight of steps. The noise was much louder now; Caroline could discern that the laughter was a mixture of both male and female, and that it was not at all discreet. Her heart began to rush with anger and dismay as they followed the sound to a remote apartment at the rear of the house, an apartment Caroline knew had never been occupied since her arrival at the house.

One of the watch rapped once upon the door with his staff and then opened it. The dazzling light of the chandeliers leaped out onto the shadowy passageway, and with it came the heavy smell of Spanish cigars. Caroline felt numb as she gazed at the scene now revealed before her. There were three young gentlemen and three ladies, if ladies they could be called, for their muslin gowns were of the sheerest stuff imaginable, their bosoms were almost bared, and their faces were painted in a most brazen way.

Silence fell, and knowing, triumphant glances were exchanged as Lord Carstairs turned unhappily to Caroline. "Are these ladies and gentlemen guests here, Miss Lexham?"

"No."

One of the women approached then, her lips pursed provocatively and her whole figure swaying in a way that reminded Caroline of the courtesans flaunting themselves beneath the arcade at the Italian Opera House. "Of course we're guests here," she said. "As you know full well, dearie, for you met us at the door. There's no point trying to deny it, you took a chance and it didn't work. Cut your losses, we all have to at some time or other."

"I have never seen you before in my life and you are not here with my knowledge or permission," replied Caroline, glancing then at Lord Carstairs. "My lord, I swear that I know nothing about this."

The courtesan laughed. "Oh, that's rich! You took our money gladly enough, and now suddenly you're all prim and proper. You opened your front door to us, you showed us up here, and now suddenly you don't know anything about us." The other occupants of the room burst into laughter at this, and Caroline looked helplessly at them. How could she prove that she was telling the truth?

Lord Carstairs gave a heavy sigh. He had not enjoyed his duties this night in the slightest. "I'm sorry, Miss Lexham, but I will have to report what I have witnessed here tonight."

Another voice interrupted at that point. "Then you will have to report that the whole thing is an artifice, Charles, and was dreamed up by Dominic Lexham for his own foul purposes."

With a gasp Caroline whirled about to see Hal approaching along the passage. His cane swung lightly in his white-gloved hand and his top hat was tipped nonchalantly back on his dark hair. The sapphire pin in his cravat sparkled brilliantly as he paused within the arc of light from the chandeliers.

"Hal?" Lord Carstairs looked dumbfounded. "What are you saying?"

"I am saying that these persons did not enter this house with Miss Lexham's knowledge. They certainly did not receive a greeting at the front door from her, nor did she show them up to this apartment; indeed they entered *after* she had retired to her bed."

"And how do you know this?" asked Lord Carstairs.

"Because I made it my business to find out. They entered illegally from the gardens, breaking a window in order to do so. I think it safe to say that Miss Lexham is innocent of any complicity in this plot."

"And Dominic Lexham is behind it, you say?" inquired Lord Carstairs.

"Don't be tiresome, Charles, of *course* he is!" replied Hal, a little irritated. "He has to be implicated if he was the one who reported things in the first place! Now then, you have done your duty, and you can report your findings—which can only be that Miss Lexham has done nothing to contravene the terms of her uncle's will."

Lord Carstairs cleared his throat uncomfortably, his cheeks coloring a little at the hint of sarcasm in Hal's reply. "Yes, well perhaps you are right. As for you, ladies and gentlemen," he went on, turning to face the six culprits, who were no longer as slyly clever as they had been, "I think it would be best if you left immediately, unless Miss Lexham wishes to press charges against you."

Caroline hastily shook her head. "No, I don't, I just want them to leave and never return."

The six needed no urging, and within a minute they had vacated the apartment and were being shown out through the front door by the porter. The gentlemen of the watch descended to the vestibule, where they waited for Lord Carstairs, who stood for a moment to offer his apologies to Caroline. "Again I must ask your forgiveness, Miss Lexham, for I did not gladly undertake this night's work, but in my capacity as magistrate I truly had no choice."

"I quite understand, my lord."

He drew her hand to his lips. "I pray that that is indeed so, for it would grieve me to think that I had alienated myself from your friendship by my actions." He looked a little shamefaced. "The truth of the matter is that I was anxious because of Jennifer. If there had been anything untoward here tonight—which there would have been but for Sir Henry's intervention—her character might in some way have suffered. I do trust that you understand and forgive my anxiety on her behalf."

"Of course I do."

Still a little embarrassed at the whole affair, he glanced at Hal. "My carriage is outside, can I convey you anywhere?"

"Yes, that would be agreeable, Charles. I will join you in a moment, after I have spoken with Miss Lexham."

Charles nodded and left them, and Caroline looked at Hal. "I must thank you, Sir Henry, for if you had not come when you did . . ." She hesitated. "Why *did* you come here tonight?"

"As I said, Miss Lexham, I made it my business to find out what was happening."

"Because of Jennifer?"

He smiled a little. "Certes, Miss Lexham. Because of Jennifer."

Although she knew she should not wish to hear him say more, she was still inestimably hurt by this fresh evidence of his disinterest in her, but she managed to return the smile. "Then I am indeed most fortunate that your brotherly concern has saved me from my cousin's spite."

"Most fortunate. However, my intervention has only saved you on this occasion, Miss Lexham, for I have no doubt that your odious and disagreeable kinsman will try again. He has not been idle; both he and your other relatives have busied themselves since learning of your activities by spreading word among their friends and acquaintances that the entire Lexham family will be displeased if any sign of favor is shown to the Lexham Hotel.''

She lowered her eyes, wondering if Marcia and Lord Fynehurst had also been thus busying themselves against her—and if they had, did Hal know of it? Slowly she raised her eyes to his face once more, inevitably wondering whether he would do anything to aid her if he knew about Marcia and her brother. It was one thing to thwart the plans of the Earl of Lexham; it was quite another to move against the actions and wishes of the woman he would soon make his bride.

He smiled again, his glance sweeping over her, taking in her cloud of honey-colored hair, the little bare toes peeping from beneath the voluminous nightgown, and the way she clutched her plain white shawl about her. "Sometimes you are still a little country mouse, are you not? Tonight you stood in need of assistance from this wicked town rat in order to be kept safe from the vile plots of other town rats.''

"It seems I am destined to be always in your debt, Sir Henry.''

"Then tomorrow you may thank me properly.''

"Properly?''

"Tomorrow is the occasion of the grand opening, is it not? I understand my sister intends to return here by hook or by crook in order to celebrate with you.''

"Yes, at least that is what she said.''

"If she said it, Miss Lexham, then you may count upon her doing it. You may also count upon me calling upon you, for I shall make time in order so to do. Oh, by the way—''

"Yes?''

"Did you receive a reply from Gaspard Duvall?''

She was a little surprised. "No, I'm very much afraid I did not.''

His eyes seemed to clear, although until that moment she had not realized that a veil had descended over them. "So, you are still without your *chef de cuisine*.''

"Unfortunately that is indeed the case, although I still hope that somehow I will find another chef—certainly in time for your sister's wedding.''

''I am sure that she will be quite content with what Gunter's can offer.''

''That isn't really the point, is it?''

He searched her face for a moment. ''No,'' he said softly, ''I don't suppose that for you it is. However, I am sure that all will be well in the end.''

''I hope so, Sir Henry.''

''Until tomorrow then, when I trust you will see fit to broach a bottle of old Lexham's finest champagne with me, for I believe I will have something of interest to celebrate.''

''Something of interest?'' She could only think that he was referring to his betrothal to Marcia.

''All will be revealed, Miss Lexham. Good night to you.''

''Good night, Sir Henry.''

She remained where she was as he walked away.

Chapter 19

She slept poorly for the rest of the night, rising especially early the next morning in order to attend to the remaining arrangements before the opening at eleven o'clock. After Dominic's attempt to destroy her careful plans, she felt more uneasy than ever about having chosen Friday the thirteenth, but it was too late to change her mind now.

The morning was dull and wet, gusts of wind carrying the low, gray clouds swiftly over the heavens. It was the very worst kind of spring morning, not at all the sort of weather she would have wished for. She stood by the window of her apartment with a cup of black coffee, gazing out over the forlorn courtyard, where the rain lashed the puddles that had already collected in the dips. As she looked out, wondering how many of the *beau monde* would choose to stay at home rather than sally forth to inspect London's newest hotel in such conditions, a very bright and gaudy yellow chaise drew into the courtyard from Mayfair Street. It passed the Lexham's two footmen, who, although well trained and used to the ways of the wealthy, were nevertheless startled enough to gape after it. They stared even more as it halted by the hotel's entrance and two men alighted. One was the strange, eccentric Gaspard Duvall; the other was his dark, discomfiting *entremettier*, Boisville.

Never one to shun bright colors, the chef wore a purple frock coat, beige trousers, a loosely tied black satin cravat, and a floppy green beret which rested jauntily over his left ear. He advanced to the door with swift, light steps, rapping upon it with his gold-tasseled cane. He was followed at a respectful distance by the more soberly clad Boisville, whose gloomy presence Caroline believed would have cast a shadow over the sunniest of days, let alone one as dismal as this. But the mere fact of the chef's arrival at the hotel was gladdening enough for her to set aside any thought of the strange *entremettier*. Putting down her cup and crossing her fingers for luck, she hurried into the vestibule to greet Duvall.

Mrs. Hollingsworth had been supervising the setting out of the glasses in the dining room, and she emerged just as Caroline reached the two Frenchmen. The housekeeper remained discreetly beneath one of the arches which led to the inner hall, watching as Duvall took Caroline's hand and drew it gallantly to his lips.

"Ah, Mademoiselle Lexham, how good it is to see you once more. I trust that we have not called too early, but I knew that later you would be very busy."

"Of course it isn't too early, monsieur, and I'm so glad that you have called."

"Forgive me that I did not come more swiftly, but there has been so much to do." His dark eyes moved briefly to Boisville's stern, unsmiling face. Then he caught sight of Mrs. Hollingsworth, and he looked at her with obvious and immediate interest, admiration shining in his dark brown eyes. Caroline looked at him with some surprise, and then was more surprised to see that Mrs. Hollingsworth's reaction to him was scarcely less obvious. The housekeeper's cheeks flushed with pretty color and she lowered her glance as coyly as any young girl.

He looked at Caroline again. "Who is the lady in brown?" he asked softly.

"She is my housekeeper, Mrs. Hollingsworth. Allow me to introduce you." Caroline conducted him to the arches. "Monsieur Duvall, allow me to present you to Mrs. Hollingsworth. Mrs. Hollingsworth, Monsieur Gaspard Duvall of the Oxenford."

The chef took the housekeeper's hand, drawing it warmly and slowly to his lips. "*Enchanté, madame*. Mr. Hollingsworth is a very fortunate man to have so beautiful a wife."

Mrs. Hollingsworth's cheeks were aflame now and she was covered with confusion as she drew her hand away. "Mr. Hollingsworth is dead, monsieur."

He said no more, but his eyes were very eloquent as he smiled at her.

Caroline was aware of Boisville, who watched everything without uttering a word and without even the slightest smile touching his straight lips. She spoke again to the chef. "Monsieur, I wonder if you could advise me about the kitchens here?"

"The kitchens? Ah, mademoiselle, there is no one in the world who can better advise you than I, Gaspard Duvall." With another smile at Mrs. Hollingsworth, he offered Caroline his arm, and together they went through into the dining room, through the butler's pantry, the safes of which were filled now with valuable plate, and into the kitchens. Mrs. Hollingsworth followed, walking beside Boisville, who glanced at her but still said nothing.

Caroline and Mrs. Hollingsworth stood watching as the chef, accompanied by the *entremettier,* inspected every inch of the Lexham's wonderful kitchens. Nothing slipped Duvall's attention, and his admiration was complete. He could not have been more impressed by Baron Rumford's magnificent closed ranges, and he spent a considerable time upon them before at last returning to where the two women stood.

"Mademoiselle Lexham, you wished for my advice, but I see nothing upon which I may advise you, for everything seems to be in the most perfect of order."

She felt uncomfortable, for Boisville's shrewd eyes rested coldly upon her face, as if he knew full well what she was about to say and as if he knew also exactly what Duvall's reply would be. She didn't want to ask the chef in front of his oppressive companion, but she did not have any choice. "Monsieur, I have not been entirely honest with you; it is not your advice I would like, it is your presence here, at the Lexham Hotel. Monsieur Duvall, I would very much like to offer you the position of *chef de cuisine* here."

Many emotions seemed to pass through his bright eyes. He glanced very briefly at Boisville's cold face and then turned back to Caroline. "Forgive me, mademoiselle," he said quietly, "but I fear I must refuse your so kind invitation. There is nothing I would like more than to leave the kitchens of the Oxenford and take charge of these magnificent offices instead, but I regret that it is impossible."

She stared at him in the utmost dismay, for somehow she had convinced herself that he would accept. She saw an unpleasant gleam in Boisville's eyes, and she could not help wondering if the chef might have accepted had it not be for the presence of this subtly insubordinate subordinate.

Duvall took her hand and raised it to his lips again. "I am most honored that you should have offered this prize to me, and I am truly sorry that it is not in my power to accept." He looked for a moment at Mrs. Hollingsworth. "Believe me, madame, if it was possible for me to come here, I would come."

A short while afterward, Caroline stood on the steps of the house with the housekeeper, watching as the gaudy yellow chaise swayed away across the windswept courtyard. "Why did he refuse, Mrs. Hollingsworth?"

"I don't know, and that's a fact. I was so sure that he would accept; he was so interested in the ranges." She paused for a moment. "I did not care for that Boisville fellow."

"No, in fact I dislike him somewhat, although he has never said or done anything to make me so feel." Caroline turned to walk slowly back into the vestibule. "So, it is to be Gunter's for Miss Seymour's wedding after all."

"They will do it handsomely," reassured the other quickly, sensing Caroline's dampened spirits.

"As they do for everyone else. The feast will not be a novelty, Mrs. Hollingsworth, and I think that Miss Seymour is disappointed, even though she hasn't said so to me." She turned to the housekeeper. "I am afraid that her kindness and loyalty to me is to cost her the sort of wedding she wished for, and I feel very badly about it." Gathering her skirts, she hurried off to her private apartments, and Mrs. Hollingsworth looked sadly after her.

At eleven o'clock precisely, the first carriage rolled across the courtyard, and at the same moment Caroline positioned herself in the vestibule to receive the Lexham Hotel's first guests. She wore her turquoise lawn, the dressmaker not having completed her other gowns, and she wished that she still possessed her grandmother's necklace, not only because she loved it so, but also because it set off the gown's plain but pretty neckline so well. She felt a little drab, but then as Mrs. Hollingsworth pointed out, the visiting ladies would not wish to find themselves being challenged by the mistress of the house.

As the carriage came to a halt at the foot of the hotel steps, the rain stopped and the sun shone through a break in the clouds. The ladies and gentlemen occupying the carriage were laughing and chattering as they alighted, and the porter threw open the doors as they came up the steps. Her heart thundering, Caroline stepped forward to greet them. This was the all important moment, for she was only too conscious that a great deal of the interest in the hotel centered upon her. Did she strike just the right note as far as they were concerned? Did she look acceptably London? Or was she hopelessly provincial still? Smiling, she sank into a curtsy. "Good morning, ladies and gentlemen. Welcome to the Lexham Hotel."

The gentlemen bowed and inclined their heads graciously, while the ladies gave her that minute examination which only ladies can manage in a glance of a second's duration, decided she was tolerably pretty but in no way to be placed on their level, and were therefore pleased to accord her their smiles of approval. The dreaded moment was over, and with a secret sigh of relief, Caroline escorted them into the dining room, where the long mahogany table was laden with numerous ice buckets containing bottles of champagne, with tray after tray of crystal glasses, and with silver-gilt dishes of Gunter's very finest wafers and comfits. In an affable mood, the ladies and gentlemen accepted their first glasses of the late earl's champagne, sipped them, and murmured favorably. They then strolled through the house, admiring the magnificence of the red saloon and recalling various incidents that had happened there during the late earl's lifetime before going on to inspect the countless books in the library. They proceeded through the entire building, taking note of everything with their critical, knowing eyes.

And so it went, as London's *beau monde* sallied forth to Mayfair Street to survey the unexpected enterprise of a young woman whose name had been on every tongue in every drawing room since her arrival in Town such a very short

time before. They all made leisurely circuits of the house,
pronouncing themselves to be much impressed and to be
beginning to understand why that clever Miss Seymour had
deserted the Oxenford and wished to marry here instead. The
ubiquitous Mrs. Hollingsworth was able to report with great
delight that she had heard several parties compare the comforts of the Lexham favorably with those provided by the
Oxenford, the Pulteney, and Mivart's.

As she had promised, Jennifer returned some time after
midday, and was pleased to be able to tell Caroline that such
was the crush of carriages in nearby streets that she had
almost forsaken her landau in favor of walking. Glancing
around at the crowded room and recognizing many important
faces, she told Caroline that the grand opening could only be
described as a success—Dominic and the Lexhams had been
put to rout.

Glancing around too, Caroline knew that for the moment
this was indeed so. But if Dominic had failed, there were
others who might still succeed, and they had actually chosen
to honor the Lexham's grand opening with their presence.
She had known a feeling of great dismay and wariness when
Marcia and her brother had alighted from a carriage, together
with a number of their friends. Caroline's smile of greeting
was very guarded as they approached. Marcia looked very
beautiful in lemon-yellow muslin, a particularly dazzling silk
shawl trailing along the floor behind her. She leaned elegantly on her brother's arm, and she paid hardly any attention
to Caroline. Indeed, as they passed on into the dining room,
Caroline distinctly heard Marcia's purring tone as she ex-
tolled the countless virtues of the hotel which was so soon to
be the scene of "dearest Jennifer's" wedding.

Bearing in mind the unpleasant threats these two had issued
to her at the Oxenford, Caroline took this new behavior very
much with a pinch of salt. They were up to something—but
what was it? Nervously she watched their progress around the
house, but everywhere they were sweetness and light, pointing out things which pleased them and always being sure to
bring the Seymour name into the conversation if they possibly
could. A reluctant Jennifer was inveigled into joining them,
and Marcia made a great point of linking arms with her, as if
they were sisters by marriage already.

An hour or more of this passed, and still nothing had

happened, and Caroline began to think they were not planning anything after all, for they were all gathered in the vestibule waiting for their carriages. But then it happened, and Caroline was quite unable to prevent disaster from striking.

With a sudden squeal of disgust and horror, Marcia pointed a quivering finger toward the shadowy inner hall. "Look! There's a rat! Oh, Perry, do you see it?" She clutched her brother's arm fearfully.

The other ladies gasped and moved closer together, staring in the direction she pointed, but no one could see anything—except Lord Fynehurst, of course. "By Gad, yeth!" he cried. "Yeth, I do thee it!"

The ladies squeaked a little and everyone else within hearing had suddenly fallen silent. Caroline stared in dismay, for there was no rat, she knew that quite well, but how to convince everyone else that Marcia and her loathsome brother were "mistaken"?

Lord Fynehurst held a perfumed handkerchief to his nose. "I thay, what a bad show," he murmured, all but shuddering. "One don't expect to find vermin in plateth like thith! Jennifer, m'dear, you can't pothibly still be thinking of marryin' here! No, 'pon me thoul, you can't!"

Jennifer was at a loss for words, glancing unhappily in Caroline's direction, but at that moment a smiling Mrs. Hollingsworth emerged from the inner hall, her large gray cat in her arms. "I'm so sorry Tibby startled you, my lady," she said to a stony-faced Marcia. "The naughty creature slipped past me and he knows that he should not! Large and gray he may be, but he's certainly no rat, I assure you." She smiled, stroking the purring cat.

The ladies relaxed quite visibly, some of them laughing a little, and the gentlemen exchanged knowing glances; how typical of a woman, those glances said, taking to the vapors over an imagined rat!

Marcia gave the housekeeper a positively poisonous glance. "Do you expect me to believe I mistook that great animal for a rat?"

"It was only the cat, my lady," replied Mrs. Hollingsworth. "And from a distance he probably does look a little—"

"I saw a rat," repeated Marcia, two specks of high color touching her pale cheeks.

Lord Fynehurst thought the whole thing was better left.

"Come now, Marthia," he murmured uncomfortably. "It wath the wretched cat."

Jennifer smiled brightly then. "Of course it was, Marcia, you don't imagine I could have lived here for some weeks now and failed to notice if the place was infested with rats."

Several chuckles greeted this, and Marcia knew that she had lost the moment. Without another word, she took her brother's arm and swept out of the hotel, but at the door she paused to glance back spitefully at Caroline. The future Lady Seymour had not finished with the Lexham Hotel and its mistress yet.

Only one thing more happened to mar the day, and it had nothing to do with the Lexham Hotel; it concerned the contents of a specially printed late edition of a newspaper. It seemed that in Paris at the beginning of February, almost a month earlier, there had been another attempt on the life of the Duke of Wellington, several shots being fired at his carriage. The government had decided to keep the whole thing suppressed, and would have had an indiscreet individual not shown a private letter from someone in Paris to an interested London newspaper.

Jennifer became very pale and upset at the news, although she strove to conceal the fact from everyone, but Caroline realized only too well how Hal's sister had received the story. Caroline also realized now what lay behind his urgent journey back to London, the journey which had brought him into her life. He had known about the assassination attempt within days. Glancing at Jennifer again, Caroline knew that Jennifer had guessed this to be the case as well, his efforts to soothe his sister's anxieties about the duke's forthcoming visit to London were now in vain. Catching Caroline's eyes, Jennifer smiled wanly, but she could not conceal her fears for her brother's life. Hal had not seen fit to mention this attempt on the duke's life—what else might he not have seen fit to mention?

Chapter 20

The rest of the day passed without incident—and also without the promised visit from Hal, which inevitably led Caroline to wonder if he was engaged upon something connected with the news now revealed.

It was past midnight before the last of the guests had departed, and for the Lexham Hotel at least the day had been an unmitigated triumph. Even to Caroline's cautious heart it seemed that the enterprise must go from strength to strength, for not only could it now boast Jennifer's wedding, it could also boast reservations for several anniversary dinners and a large reunion of officers who had served under Nelson. A number of rooms and two apartments had been reserved, and apart from the sabotage attempt by Marcia and her brother, not a single word of criticism had been uttered against the hotel throughout the day. But then, as Caroline realized only too well, not a great many people were aware yet that the Lexham could not offer French cuisine; that discovery might put a different complexion upon the whole venture. Somehow she must find another chef; she and Mrs. Hollingsworth would redouble their efforts in the morning and keep their fingers crossed.

As the clocks struck half past midnight, Caroline sat at the escritoire in her private apartment, going over the arrangements for the wedding. Gunter's was to provide the cake, the whole of the feast, and was to send a man known as a *glacier* to carve decorations from the solid block of ice reposing in the cellar. Among these decorations would be vases of the flowers and ferns ordered from the flower market at Covent Garden. From the same ice would come the nests for the butter, and the sorbets and cream ices which would be made by Gunter's main cook and his eight attendants. The wedding over, the bride and her new husband would go away in a white, flower-garlanded landau, drawn by four cream horses with rosettes and white satin bows on their harness, driven by a postilion clad entirely in white. This magical departure for distant Venice would be the perfect ending to a fairytale day—but for Caroline at least, it would be spoiled if she could not provide for Jennifer the same sort of magnificent feast Gaspard Duvall would have prepared for her at the Oxenford.

Pushing the papers away, Caroline leaned back in her chair. Jennifer had gone out of her way to try to reassure her that it did not matter that Gunter's was to do the catering, but Caroline still felt that it *did* matter. There was no point in regretting it, though, for the wedding must go ahead. Thinking about Jennifer brought Caroline to ponder the day's news again. She hoped that Hal had managed to charm his way around his worried sister with whom he was dining at Lord Fynehurst's.

Getting wearily to her feet, Caroline decided that she had pored over lists and figures from Messieurs Coutts, the bankers, for long enough. It had been a long and tiring day, and it was now well past time to retire to her bed. Even as the thought entered her head, however, she heard a loud noise from the vestibule. Someone was shouting! Her eyes widened as she heard steps approaching her door, then the porter called out in warning, "Miss Lexham! Miss Lexham! He's coming in, I can't stop him!"

At this the door opened, and Dominic pushed his way in. His face was flushed, he was a little unsteady, and she perceived immediately that he was the worse for drink. "Good evening, *cousin!*" he said, sweeping a scornful bow.

The anxious porter appeared in the doorway behind him. "I tried to prevent him, Miss Lexham—"

"It will be all right, you may go," she said, still looking warily at her cousin.

"Very well, Miss Lexham, but I'll be within hearing if you need me."

"Thank you."

The porter went out, being careful to leave the door open. Dominic gave her a contemptuous glance. "My, my, aren't we the fine lady now?"

"Did you have something of importance to say to me, sir?"

"Oh, yes, sweetheart, a great deal."

"Please say it, and then leave."

"You seem to forget, my dear, that you were the one who was supposed to leave—but you are still here, aren't you?"

"I see no reason to do your bidding, my lord earl, or to bow to your wicked plots against me."

His eyes darkened. "Guard your tongue!"

"Nor do I have to stand here and listen to your abuse, sir. You obviously have nothing of consequence to say, so I ask you to leave."

He gave a cold laugh. "Leave my own house?"

"It isn't your house, sirrah, not yet."

"You've been very clever, haven't you? Somehow you've dreamed up this way of complying with my father's will—but have you done so legally, eh? That is the question."

"What do you mean?"

His smile was chilling. "How have you financed this little enterprise? Has Seymour filled your purse? And if he has, what manner of payment did he receive? Has he enjoyed your favors, my dear coz?"

She was shaking with fury. "Get out of here, sirrah!"

"You haven't answered my question," he said, coming closer.

"Nor do I intend to. Leave this house immediately, my lord, or I will have you thrown out."

"I think not," he murmured softly, his eyes glittering in the candlelight.

A third voice broke into the silence. "On the contrary, Lexham, I think your ejection from these premises is imminent." It was Hal, who not for the first time had arrived at a very opportune moment.

Dominic whirled about with an oath. "Seymour! Am I to

presume that you have *carte blanche* to enter these private apartments?''

Toying with the frill protruding from his cuff, Hal came a little nearer, his hazel eyes very cold. ''Keep a civil tongue in your fool head, Lexham, for I am not in the best of moods and I can be very touchy when slurs are cast upon the characters of ladies.''

Dominic swallowed but held his ground. ''By what right do you play the master in this house, Seymour?''

''I merely act upon the wishes of the mistress of the house.''

''Mistress?'' Dominic gave a laugh which was almost a sneer. ''Perhaps that is the perfect word to describe my fair cousin!''

With a swiftness that left Dominic breathless, Hal seized him by the lapels and then thrust him disdainfully away. ''I will spare you this time, my maraschino lordling, but only because you are in drink. However, be warned that if you cause Miss Lexham one more moment of distress, you will answer to me. Is that quite clear?''

Dominic clutched at a table to steady himself. ''You will regret this, Seymour!''

''I doubt that very much,'' replied Hal coolly. ''Now, get out.''

For a moment Dominic considered defying this command, but then discretion had the better part of valor, and he strode from the room with as much dignity as he could muster, pushing between the porter and the footmen who waited there.

The door closed, and Hal turned to Caroline. ''Are you all right?''

''Yes,'' she replied, but her voice was a little shaky.

''Come and sit down,'' he said quickly, leading her to a chair by the fire.

She smiled. ''It seems to be my lot in life to be continually indebted to you, Sir Henry.''

''Maybe it is my good fortune to be so often able to come to your rescue,'' he replied.

''Why did you come here?''

''I was under the impression that you expected me.''

''At this hour?''

He smiled. "I would have come earlier, but—er, something came up."

"Sir Henry, it came up in Paris at the beginning of last month."

"So it did," he murmured, lounging back on the sofa opposite her. A half smile touched his fine lips as he surveyed her. "Very well, I will be honest with you. I called here at this hour because a little bird whispered to me at Fynehurst's that Lexham was in his cups at Watier's and threatening to call upon you. I deemed it the honorable thing for me to once again become St. George and dash to the rescue of the fair damsel who was undoubtedly about to become distressed."

She smiled a little. "I am truly grateful, Sir Henry, and I am very sorry that my affairs have interfered with your enjoyment of your dinner."

"Say rather that your affairs *saved* me from that dinner, which was far from being up to Duvall's standards."

"Shall you dine at the Oxenford instead then?"

"I begin to think you believe me to be operated entirely by the moods of my stomach, Miss Lexham."

"Oh, I did not mean—"

He smiled again. "I know. However, I must forgo Duvall's genius as well, for he is most unwell tonight—or so I am told."

"I trust it is nothing serious."

His tone was bland. "No, nothing serious. A headache, I believe. I understand that there are times when he is prey to such indispositions."

"I am sorry to hear that, for he is such a charming man."

His eyes were half closed as he looked at her. "Charming, but disconcertingly attached to the Oxenford. Jennifer told me what happened."

She didn't reply, for she was thinking suddenly that Gaspard Duvall was not the only man who was disconcertingly attached to the Oxenford. The thought made her feel suddenly uncomfortable, for it reminded her of what Marcia had said—of what Hal had said to his future wife about the woman he had conveyed so kindly to London in his carriage. Nervously she stood. "I will not detain you any longer, Sir Henry, for I am sure you have much to do—"

He seemed amused. "First Lexham is ejected, and now it is my turn?"

"I did not mean to sound as if I were ejecting you, Sir Henry," she replied quickly.

"I sincerely hope not, especially as I was expecting to share a bottle of champagne with you. Or had you forgotten?"

She stared at him. "N-no, of course I hadn't forgotten."

"Excellent, then you had best send someone to bring it, had you not?"

Not knowing quite what to make of him, she picked up the little bell, and in a moment one of the footmen appeared. She instructed him to bring champagne and two glasses.

Hal leaned back. "Congratulations are in order I believe, Miss Lexham."

"Congratulations?" Her heart sank.

"Why yes. I must congratulate you upon the success of your grand opening, and you must congratulate me upon the success of my horse."

She could only look at him, quite taken aback. "Your horse?"

"Foxleaze. Come now, Miss Lexham, you surely recall Foxleaze! As I remember, you asked me about the wretched nag during our journey from Devon. I heard a whisper yesterday that the beast had won a famous victory in America, and today I had that news officially confirmed in a letter."

"Oh!" She could not help the way her eyes brightened. "Why, of course I congratulate you, Sir Henry."

"What did you think I was going to refer to, Miss Lexham?"

She colored a little. "I don't really know, Sir Henry."

The footman returned with the champagne, and when he had gone Hal poured out two glasses, pushing one into her hand and then raising his own. "To the success of the Lexham Hotel—and to the continuing success of my nag."

"To the success of both."

He nodded appreciatively at the champagne. "One thing old Lexham could be counted on for was his excellent taste in things alcoholic, especially champagne. Jennifer told me that things went decidedly well today, with many a rosy glow imparted by this same beverage."

"I hope things went well because this hotel deserved its praise too, Sir Henry."

"No doubt that was mostly the case," he replied, smiling at her. "All the effort you went to deserved to be rewarded."

"How is Jennifer tonight?"

He lowered his glass. "Why do you ask?"

"I think you know why, Sir Henry."

"Are you on the point of quizzing me, Caro Lexham?"

"Yes, Sir Henry, I do believe I am."

"You can be most disconcerting at times."

"Don't try to avoid the subject."

He smiled. "How tenacious you are. Very well, I do know why you ask, and Jennifer is now quite at ease again. Will that do for an answer?"

"Partly."

"And what does that mean?"

"It means that I am still concerned for Jennifer. She worries a great deal about you, Sir Henry, and I want you to tell me that her fears are unjustified."

His hazel eyes were almost lazy as they studied her. "And if I decline to answer?"

"That will be answer enough in itself, Sir Henry."

He laughed a little. "So it will."

"I don't wish to be disagreeable or difficult, Sir Henry, but I regard your sister as my dearest friend, and if there is anything I can do to help her, to make things easier for her, then I will do it gladly. Forgive me if I speak out of turn, but you are on your own admission involved in the welfare of the Duke of Wellington, and I believe that you were in full possession of the facts concerning this latest attempt on his life almost as soon as it happened. She realizes that as well as I do, and it is only natural now that she should be concerned about what might happen when the duke visits London soon. Is she right to be so concerned?"

"I will say this. There is no reason to suppose that this forthcoming visit will offer any danger to me. Will that suffice?"

"It is no more or less than you said before, Sir Henry. You, sir, should be a politician, for you are certainly master of the art of appearing to say something important when in actual fact you have said nothing at all."

"What a waspish tongue you have at times, Miss Lexham."

"It is no more than your answer deserves."

He smiled. "Very well, I will try again. What makes you

think there will be any danger? This is London, not Brussels or Paris, and it is on the other side of the Channel that the wicked Bonapartists lie.''

''I am sure they are as capable of crossing the Channel as you are, Sir Henry.''

''But why would they bother?''

''We can fence like this forever, Sir Henry, but in the end it will come to the same. You *will* be in danger because of the Bonapartists' avowed intent of killing the Duke of Wellington, and that killing could quite easily take place here in London, couldn't it?''

He smiled a little, resting his hand against her cheek for a moment. ''You are too clever by half, Caro Lexham. But one thing I ask of you.''

''What is it?''

''That you do not let my sister realize anything.''

''You wrong me to think that I ever would, Sir Henry.''

He nodded. ''Yes, perhaps I do, and for that you must forgive me.''

''When does the duke come to London?''

He smiled a little ruefully then. ''He sails for Dover before dawn today.''

Her eyes widened. ''Sir Henry? You will take care . . .'' How lame the words sounded, but they were all she could think of. He had not discounted what she had said about the Bonapartists crossing the Channel, which to her meant that it was indeed what he expected to happen. He would be in danger, and that danger was imminent. She was afraid for him, more afraid than she could ever begin to tell without conveying the truth of how much she loved him.

He took her hand. ''My dearest Caro, I think you may count upon me doing my very best to preserve my elegant hide. I must leave you now, but I thank you from the bottom of my heart for your concern about my sister. It gladdens me to know that I may count upon you to do all you can to set her mind at ease. She is very dear to me and I do not wish to cause her any unhappiness, especially at this time.''

She knew suddenly that he did not want her ever to mention the matter again. ''I promise to do what I can, Sir Henry.'' *Because I love you.* The sentence was completed only in her thoughts.

Slowly he turned her palm to his lips. ''I am glad that this

Friday the thirteenth was not an unlucky day for you, Caro Lexham. Good night.''

"Good night, Sir Henry."

When he had gone, she sat down, gazing into the glowing heart of the fire. Her gray eyes were luminous in the half-light. Tonight he had trusted her; he had admitted more to her than he had to Jennifer, or even to Marcia. A ghost of a smile played upon her lips. He may once have thought badly of her, but he did not do so now, she knew that beyond a doubt.

Chapter 21

At breakfast the next morning, Caroline had her first opportunity to carry out her word to Hal about soothing Jennifer's worries. The few guests who had already taken rooms at the hotel had not stirred when Jennifer came down to take breakfast alone with Caroline in her private apartment. The future Lady Carstairs looked particularly fresh and pretty in a cream muslin morning gown, with lace at her throat and cuffs and a crimson sash at her waist. At first she was determined to set aside the anxieties of the previous day and talk instead about the dinner party at Lord Fynehurst's.

Pouring herself some more coffee, she grinned impishly. "There was one moment last night which I would not have missed for the world."

"And what moment was that?"

"When Hal announced that he was coming back here to see that you were all right. You should have seen Marcia's face! She was absolutely *furious*! I do believe she was jealous."

"I assure you she has no cause," said Caroline hastily, coloring a little.

"What a pity."

"How unkind you are."

"She's horrid and I wish with all my heart that Hal would

168

see her for what she is. She may soon be my sister-in-law, but I will never like her, and I will never forgive her for what she has done to you, Caroline. First there was that dreadful business at the Oxenford, and then yesterday that imaginary rat! Really, it was too bad of her.''

One of the footmen came in with a tray upon which lay the morning newspaper and a letter for Caroline. The letter was from Richard Marchand, but before Caroline could break the seal she heard Jennifer's gasp of dismay.

''What is it?'' she asked quickly, seeing how pale Jennifer's face had gone.

''The newspaper—''

Caroline looked at it where it lay upon the snowy tablecloth, and she saw immediately what had upset Jennifer. The headlines announced further intelligence about the attempt on the life of the Duke of Wellington.

''Will you read it, Caroline? I don't think I could bear to.''

Caroline picked the newspaper up and glanced swiftly at the relevant columns. ''It says that the Paris police have made several arrests, although they have not caught the actual assassin yet. The man they seek is said to be a man of extraordinary strength and ferocious temper, and they believe they are well on his trail and will soon have him successfully under lock and key.''

''He sounds perfectly horrible.''

''He does rather.'' Caroline smiled lightly, setting the newspaper aside.

''I dread to think of Hal being involved with such men.''

''This fellow is in France, not England, and Sir Henry told you that he was not in any danger. You must believe him.''

Jennifer's eyes were very large. ''Do you believe him, Caroline?''

''Yes, of course I do. Now then, drink your coffee before it gets cold, and don't think anything more about the wretched newspaper.''

For a moment Jennifer seemed inclined to continue with the subject, but then she smiled. ''You are right. I must be more sensible. Who is your letter from?''

''My cousin.''

''The earl?'' Jennifer was taken aback.

''No, my *Selford* cousin.''

''The one who wishes to marry you?''

"Yes." Caroline broke the seal and read the rather brief communication.

"Is it bad news?"

"No, not exactly. He merely says that he intends to visit me soon."

"You do not look very pleased. Is he disagreeable?"

Caroline smiled. "No, he isn't disagreeable; he just doesn't understand, that's all."

"Well, to do him justice, I suppose *any* country squire would find it difficult to understand a woman who on the spur of a moment decided to turn her back on all she had ever known and set up in business in London as mistress of a hotel! The only kind of man who would understand *that* kind of spirit would be a man from London society, someone like Charles, or Hal. They are not narrow in their outlook, they admire a woman who shows she is not merely a cipher, and they accept that she has as much right as they to her opinions and dreams. Hal is right about you, Caroline, you could never be happy in a place like Selford, and you would be wretched and miserable if you made the mistake of marrying Mr. Marchand. London is where you belong, where you should have been all along." Jennifer smiled then. "There, was that not a profound and instructive speech?"

"It was indeed."

"You see? I am not always a scatterbrained creature."

"No, you are the dearest, kindest, and most loyal friend I have ever had, Jennifer Seymour, and I love you as much as I would a sister."

"That is how I feel about you, Caroline Lexham, and it gives me great pleasure to be able to say that, because I have never said it before in my life. Oh, I've had many friends, but no one to whom I have felt so instantly close. It's funny, but I feel as if I've known you all my life, and yet it has been such a very short time. Goodness! Is that the time? I should have been at my *couturière* five minutes ago!"

Caroline couldn't help laughing. "So, the time for profundity is past, and the scatterbrain is to the fore once again!"

"You, Caroline Lexham, are a positive beast!" Jennifer laughed as she got up.

Caroline settled back to enjoy a final cup of coffee before she too would have to attend to her daily tasks; it would be so different today, because this was the hotel's first real day.

The footman returned and she looked up. "Yes? What is it?"

"Lady Chaddington has called, madam, and she wishes to see you."

Caroline's heart sank. "Very well, please show her in here."

Marcia entered, the ostrich plume in her hat trembling and the fur-trimmed hem of her elegant pelisse swinging. She was clad entirely in virginal white and her hands were thrust deep into a muff. She looked as breathtakingly lovely as ever, and as brittle. She halted, surveying Caroline, an expression of disdain on her face. "Oh dear, the turquoise lawn again. How very repetitive."

"You wished to see me, Lady Chaddington?"

"No, I do not *wish* to see you; in fact the very opposite is the case. However, since you have chosen to defy me, I find this disagreeable visit forced upon me. I am not well pleased with you, Miss Lexham, but I am a civilized person, and so I shall endeavor to rid myself of you in a civilized way."

"You surprise me," replied Caroline. "I did not think there was anything civilized about imagined rats."

Marcia flushed angrily, but refused to be drawn. She glanced around the room. "You have indeed begun to do well for yourself, haven't you? Some say this house is the prettiest in London, which would make you very fortunate indeed if you managed to keep your country claws upon it."

"Why did you come here?"

"To make you an offer you would be foolish to refuse."

"I don't think I wish to hear—"

"I am capable of destroying you, Miss Lexham, you may count upon that. But such a course would maybe take a little time, time during which I would be irritated by your continued presence. You may think you are set to succeed here, but it will all come to nought. I will see that it does. I will wreck Jennifer Seymour's wedding, Miss Lexham, and that is no mere threat, it is a promise."

Caroline stared at her. "But she is to be your sister-in-law! How could you think of doing such a thing?"

"It is Hal Seymour I shall be marrying, my dear, not his vapid little sister. Now then, we can all be spared any unpleasantness if you cut your losses now and accept a substantial sum of money from me before leaving Town forever."

Caroline was trembling. "I refuse your offer, Lady Chaddington."

"What a fool you are."

"Please leave, my lady, and take your 'civilized' methods with you."

Marcia's lip curled with anger. "Your days of glory in this house are numbered, just as are the days when you may count upon a courteous word from Hal Seymour and his sister. Soon you will not even receive a nod from them, they will cut you, as will all London society. You and your high-flying plans are about to take a tumble, Miss Lexham, and I shall take supreme delight in being the instrument of your downfall. You've given yourself airs and graces, queening it in this great house, glorying in your important friends. You think you are very grand, don't you? Well, you are nothing at all, as you will shortly discover to your cost. I will not cease until I have trodden you into the ground, and even then I may not relent." With this, she turned and walked from the room, leaving the door open so that Caroline heard her light steps crossing the tiled floor of the vestibule. The outer door closed and a moment later came the sound of a carriage moving away across the cobbled courtyard.

Still trembling, Caroline rose from her chair and went to look out of the window. She saw Marcia's carriage leaving beneath the pedimented gateway into Mayfair Street. She had meant every word of her threat; she would indeed try to destroy Jennifer's wedding. But how? What would she do? And should Jennifer be warned? No, no, that would not do at all, for it would cause her too much distress. This was something Caroline had to face alone.

It was an hour or so later that an anxious Mrs. Hollingsworth came looking for her. Thoughts of Marcia came immediately to the fore. "Is something wrong?"

"I'm afraid there might be. A gentleman from Gunter's has called and says he must speak urgently with you."

"Did he say why he called?"

"He said that there had been a regrettable oversight of which you must be told immediately."

The wedding, it could only be the wedding! Slowly Caroline went into the vestibule, her turquoise skirts rustling and her little shoes making hardly a sound.

The gentleman from Gunter's was perched nervously on

the edge of one of the sofas, turning his hat in his hands. He was plump and balding and did not look happy in his almost formal coat and pantaloons. He leaped to his feet as she approached, and she knew that he was loathing every moment of his unwelcome errand.

"M-miss Lexham?"

"Sir."

"My n-name is Johnson, Archibald Johnson, and I am here on behalf of Messieurs Gunter."

"What may I do for you, Mr. Johnson?"

"I f-fear that I am the bearer of unfortunate t-tidings."

She waited, but she knew already what he was going to say.

"There has b-been a m-most dreadful and regrettable oversight, M-miss Lexham, and I fear that w-we will not after all be able to cater for Miss Seymour's nuptials."

It was what she had feared, but even so it came as a dreadful shock. She paused for a moment, steadying herself. "May I ask why, sir?"

"A p-prior booking." He looked thoroughly wretched.

"Indeed? What booking?"

"I'm afraid th-that I am n-not at liberty to divulge—"

"Whose booking, sir? I demand to know, and I believe I have the right to know."

"Lord and Lady Stapleton."

She looked away. Their daughter, the Honorable Georgiana Stapleton, was soon to be betrothed to Marcia's brother, Lord Fynehurst. "Mr. Johnson," she said at last, "I put it to you that this other booking is fictitious, or at the very least has been made since you were approached concerning Miss Seymour's wedding."

"Oh, no, Miss L-lexham!"

"But yes, Mr. Johnson, and you know it as well as I do, which is why you are so uncomfortable about the whole thing!"

"The other booking was overlooked."

"You, sir, are fibbing."

"Miss Lexham!" he protested, "I swear—"

"You are not telling the truth, sir, but there is little I can do about it, is there?"

He fell silent.

"I find it quite intolerable that a firm of such standing

should lend itself to such petty and disgraceful vindictiveness and be party to something which injures an innocent person. I promise you that this hotel will never again patronize you. Good day, Mr. Johnson.''

''Miss Lexham—''

''Good day, sir!''

Without another word he almost scuttled to the door, escaping gladly from the justified accusation in her gray eyes. But the moment he had gone, Caroline's bravado deserted her and she turned helplessly to Mrs. Hollingsworth. ''What am I to do? What can I say to Miss Seymour?''

The housekeeper put a gentle but firm hand on her arm. ''Don't despair yet, Miss Lexham, for there is another caterer who may be able to help.''

''Who?''

''Messieurs Owen of Bond Street.''

''We will go there immediately, for I must engage someone!'' But even as she spoke, she knew that Mrs. Hollingsworth's suggestion offered little hope. Marcia's hand lay behind Gunter's defection, and she would not have left any obvious loophole; she was too thorough and too clever for that.

Chapter 22

At Messieurs Owen it was immediately obvious to Caroline that Marcia had been at work. The prinked young gentleman who dealt with them had that same rather uncomfortable look worn earlier by the hapless Mr. Johnson, although he brazened things out a little more successfully than had the representative from Messieurs Gunter. The end result was the same, however, and that was that Caroline and the Lexham Hotel were still without a fashionable caterer to do Jennifer's wedding feast, and as she and Mrs. Hollingsworth emerged onto Bond Street, her spirits were very low indeed.

She had reached an impasse that would leave Marcia—and through her, Dominic—the victor, for failure to cater satisfactorily for the wedding would mean the collapse of society's faith in the new venture; she knew this as surely as she knew night followed day. She would lose Lexham House because she would not be able to meet the terms of her uncle's will after all. This she could have borne, for she had come to London with nothing, and she would leave in the same way, but she could not so easily bear having failed Jennifer, whose warm friendship she valued so very much. Tears stung her eyes as she and Mrs. Hollingsworth walked south along Bond Street toward Piccadilly. The housekeeper walked in silent sympathy, knowing the thoughts going through the other's bowed head and sharing the agony of despair at what seemed inevitable disaster.

It was Mrs. Hollingsworth who saw the group of fashionable young gentlemen standing by a handsome landau drawn up at the curb; recognizing one of them, she put a warning hand on Caroline's arm. "Miss Lexham, your cousin the earl is over there."

As she spoke, Dominic turned and saw them. For a dreadful moment the two Lexham cousins looked at each other, and then, unbelievably, a warm smile curved his fine lips. Bowing a little to his surprised companions, he left them and approached the two women. He looked very elegant indeed, clad in a dark gray coat and beige trousers, his honey-colored hair very bright in the March sunlight as he removed his tall hat and sketched a very handsome bow to them.

"Good morning, cousin."

Caroline stiffened, very much on her guard at this unexpected and rather doubtful transformation. "Good morning, my lord."

His gray eyes bore an expression that seemed contrite. "I am glad that I have encountered you, cousin, for now I may attempt to make amends for my odious and unworthy conduct."

She could not trust him. "I don't think we have anything to say to each other, sir."

"Please, can you not take pity upon this poor penitent? Beneath this coat I assure you I wear a hair shirt of the most tortuous nature." He smiled a little.

"Forgive me, sir, if I find the thought of your penitence a little hard to believe."

"I swear that I am truly repentant, cousin, for in the cold, sober light of day I have come to realize that I have behaved atrociously and now the onus is upon me to raise myself in your estimation. We are first cousins, tied by blood, and we should not be at odds." He gave her an almost boyish smile then. "Perhaps I should correct that, for you were never at odds with me, were you? The fault lies entirely with me, and I can only abjectly beg your forgiveness."

Caroline stared at him, for he sounded so genuine, but her every nerve was alive with mistrust. Those eyes, which were so sad and guilty now, had been so cold and full of loathing only the night before; and that mouth, which smiled in hope now, had curled with contempt and venom when last she had spoken with him.

He took her hand then, raising it to his lips. "I know that I do not deserve your kindness, cousin, but I do mean every word I say now. Please, let us take this as our first meeting, and forget all that has passed before."

She withdrew her hand, still unable to credit this new Dominic. "Why should I believe you, sir? Why should I agree to do as you ask? You have indeed behaved odiously toward me, and although you say you are sorry, I see no reason why you should have undergone this miraculous change of heart since last night."

He caught her hand again, as if he feared to release her. "Can you not see that I am ashamed of myself? Dear God, I am not blackhearted, I *know* that what I have done is appalling, but now that I realize in full how much I have sinned against you, I can only come in abject remorse to beg your forgiveness. You are the mistress of Lexham House, but it is entirely my own fault that this situation has arisen. I know that you are not to blame, and yet I have behaved in a way which shames me to my very soul. Forgive me now, cousin, look into my eyes and know that I am speaking the truth."

Still holding her hand, he came a little closer, clasping that hand in both his and looking down into her face. She did not know what to say or do, for his behavior now quite took her breath away. She was aware of his companions watching with great curiosity, and although she still mistrusted him in her heart, she knew that under the circumstances she had little choice but to say she forgave him. A rather tremulous and uneasy smile touched her lips as for a second time she withdrew her hand. "Of course I forgive you, my lord, and I would be glad to take our acquaintance as beginning from this moment."

He smiled then, his handsome face lightening. "Thank you, cousin, you are more kind than I deserve." Before she knew what was happening, he bent his head and in full view of everyone kissed her upon the cheek. Her face immediately flamed with color, but the thing was done now. Smiling and bowing once more, he replaced his tall hat on his bright hair and then took his leave.

She watched him rejoin his companions, and a moment

later they had climbed into the landau, which drew away and disappeared in the throng of traffic on Bond Street.

Mrs. Hollingsworth was skeptical. "Don't trust him, Miss Lexham—he may say that he isn't blackhearted, but he is, through and through."

"I didn't have much choice but to say I forgave him."

"He's up to something."

"You are probably right, but I really do not care what he says or does, for I have too many problems of my own to worry greatly about him. What am I to tell Miss Seymour when next I see her? She will return to the hotel in such high spirits and happiness after having the final fitting of her wedding gown, and I will have to tell her that I have no one to do the catering. Oh, Mrs. Hollingsworth, I feel so wretched about it."

"It isn't your fault," said the housekeeper, putting a comforting hand on her arm. "You have done everything in your power to see that the wedding arrangements are as excellent as she would wish."

"And I have failed."

"Not yet, there is still time."

Caroline wanted to take comfort from this, but she could not. They had time, true enough, but only a matter of days; wedding feasts took weeks of preparation. . . . Slowly she walked on down toward Piccadilly, Dominic's strange new conduct very far from her thoughts.

As they reached the corner of Bond Street and Piccadilly, they became aware of a large gathering outside the premises of Messieurs Hoby, the fashionable bootmakers on an opposite corner, where St. James's Street began. There appeared to be a large traveling carriage drawn up at the curb outside, and it was surrounded by an excited crowd, who were all interested in something going on inside the bootmaker's shop.

"What is happening, do you think?" asked Caroline, stretching up onto tiptoes in the hope of seeing more.

'Well, if it was a print shop, I could understand the excitement," replied the housekeeper. "But what on earth can be of such interest in a *bootmaker's*?"

"Shall we be very vulgar and go and see?"

With a smile, the housekeeper nodded, and they threaded their way across the busy thoroughfare to join the crowd. At first they were afforded no opening, but by chance a way

opened up and in a moment they found themselves right next
to the window. Inside they could see the polished oak counter
and behind it the dark shelves with pairs of boots and shoes
awaiting collection. It was very superior and discreet, and at
first Caroline could see nothing that might cause such a
crowd to collect, but then she made out the shapes of two
gentlemen standing by the counter in the darkest corner of the
shop, inspecting a pair of top boots which had been brought
by a very nervous, wide-eyed assistant. One gentleman Caroline felt looked vaguely familiar, although she could not place
him, but the other she knew only too well. It was Hal
Seymour! With a gasp, she stepped back from the window,
dreading that at any moment he might turn and see her
peering in. Seizing Mrs. Hollingsworth by the arm, she began
to push back through the pressing crowd, anxious to escape at
all costs before he realized she had been there. How dreadful
it would be if he caught a glimpse of her staring in so
vulgarly!

They had hardly emerged from the crowd, however, when
she heard the stir as the door of the bootmaker's shop opened.
Hal called after her. Dismayed, she halted, turning slowly
toward him. She felt too mortified to be aware of the interest
she was receiving from the crowd.

Smiling, he approached her. "I trust you were not about to
depart on anything urgent."

"No. I, er—"

"Excellent, for that means you have time to meet someone
who has expressed a desire to meet you."

"To meet *me*?" She was quite taken aback.

"Please come inside," he said, drawing her hand through
his arm and nodding at the housekeeper to signify that she too
was included in the invitation. Caroline became increasingly
aware of the buzz of envy spreading through the crowd as she
and Mrs. Hollingsworth were led back to the bootmaker's
shop.

The doorbell tinkled pleasantly as they entered the cool,
dark premises, and the smell of leather seemed to close over
them. After the brightness of the day, she was unable to see
much at first, but gradually her eyes became accustomed to
the gloom and she found herself being presented to the other
gentleman by the counter.

He was, she guessed, somewhere in his forties, although

he had the figure of a younger man. His appearance was imposing; he seemed much taller than his five feet nine inches. He was very handsome, with an aquiline nose and a surprisingly youthful and fresh complexion. His brown hair was cropped very short, his eyes were an arresting, far-seeing blue, and although he wore a plain, somber, dark blue coat, he was nevertheless a figure of great presence and authority. To Caroline he still seemed vaguely familiar, although she knew full well that she had never seen him before. He smiled as Hal introduced her.

"Miss Lexham, allow me to present you to His Grace, the Duke of Wellington. Your Grace, this is Miss Lexham, of whom you have heard so much."

She was dumbstruck, her gray eyes huge, and from just behind her she heard Mrs. Hollingsworth's astonished and delighted gasp.

The duke chuckled, pleased at the effect he had upon them both. "Would to God I'd been able to stop Boney in his tracks with such ease—eh, Seymour?"

Hal grinned. "It would have saved a great deal of time and trouble."

The duke looked at Caroline again. "Forgive me, m'dear, but when Seymour glimpsed you passing by, I told him I wished to meet you. I have indeed heard a great deal about you."

Hastily she gathered her scattered wits. "You've heard about me, Your Grace? I cannot believe that that can be the case."

"M'dear, even Paris drawing rooms ring with your name, for you are such a very interesting subject and such a delightful diversion from the more mundane aspects of life. And if I may say so, m'dear, you are also very beautiful indeed, which adds greatly to the piquancy of the situation."

"Y-your Grace is too kind," she murmured, knowing that she should say more but fast finding herself overwhelmed by the great honor not only of being in the presence of such a great man but also of being paid gallant compliments by him. She must say something else—but what? Inspiration came at last. "Your Grace, I congratulate you upon your fortunate escape from the attempt on your life. I trust the villain will soon be apprehended."

"Why, thank you, Miss Lexham. I am reliably informed

by the Paris police that they hope to arrest their man soon."
He glanced at Hal, and then smiled at Caroline again. "But
enough of me, it is of you that I wish to speak, m'dear."

"Me? But I am not—"

"But you are, Miss Lexham, you are. I confess that when
first whispers reached me about you, I could not believe what
I heard. No *lady,* thought I, would have the audacity and
spirit to do such things; but the whispers persisted and soon I
had to believe them. You are indeed a lady of great spirit,
m'dear, and I admire that more than anything else."

She colored. "You are being too kind again, Your Grace."

"Nonsense!" He gave an unexpected whoop of laughter.
"I am merely an admiring male, m'dear, for even the Iron
Duke has human frailty! I wish you well of your enterprise,
Miss Lexham, and I trust that your audacity and acumen
shakes the very devil out of establishments like the Oxenford,
the recent conduct of which I find totally abhorrent."

Uneasily she glanced at Hal, but his face was inscrutable.
She smiled then as she thanked the duke for his kind thoughts,
but she refrained from adding that she doubted if her audacity
and acumen were about to avail her of anything, for Marcia's
interference with Gunter's and similar caterers had closed the
last door upon the Lexham Hotel's ability to provide the sort
of cuisine the *haut ton* of London sought.

The duke detected her reticence, but misread it. "I agree
that your rivals should be held in contempt, m'dear; in fact I
too wish to show my contempt for them." He shot a meaning-
ful glance at Hal, who immediately stiffened warily. "What
say you, Seymour?"

"Your Grace—"

"I have decided," interrupted the duke, almost with an air
of relish, "that I do not wish my banquet to be held at the
Oxenford."

"But, Your Grace, all the arrangements are made."

"Unmake them."

Hal struggled to conceal the anger this caprice had aroused.
"That is more easily said than done," he replied, and Caroline could have sworn she detected a note of warning in his
voice.

"Nevertheless, Seymour, my mind is made up. In fact, I
will go further and say that the banquet must now be held at
the Lexham Hotel instead."

Behind the counter the assistant's eyes were as round as saucers. Caroline started with shock and Mrs. Hollingsworth's sharp intake of breath was clearly audible in the ensuing silence. Then Hal spoke again, his voice tight with anger. "Your Grace, I must protest! You put me in an impossible position!"

"In my experience," replied the duke infuriatingly, "that is when a man is at his best."

"With all due respect, sir, I think you are forgetting certain—"

"I forget nothing!" the duke interposed sharply. "Indeed, I think *you* forget, Seymour! I have no time for all these careful plots and plans, and endure them under sufferance!"

"Ditto!" was the sharp rejoinder, Hal making clear his complete disapproval and, in so doing, showing that he was fully prepared to brave the ducal wrath.

For a moment the duke's blue eyes flashed, but then he grinned, clapping the other on the shoulder. "Point taken, my dear fellow, but I cannot help it if in this particular instance I think you are totally wrong and that you persistently bark up the wrong tree."

"But what if it is the right tree after all?"

"It isn't."

Hal gave a faint smile. "It would not be the first time Bonaparte has humbugged you."

Again the duke's eyes flashed, more angrily this time. "You are probably the only man alive to whom I would allow such liberties, Seymour."

"And you, sir, are the only man for whom I would take such risks."

The duke looked away for a moment. "I still believe you are wrong, and as far as I am concerned that is the end of it. I will not have my reputation and valor celebrated in the Oxenford. The matter is finished." Straightening a little, he turned suddenly to Caroline, taking her hand and raising it to his lips. "Forgive our ill-mannered asides, m'dear, we have been boors to exclude you from our conversation for so long. It is settled; the banquet must be removed to your establishment. My honor will not permit any other course."

"But, Your Grace," she began hastily, seeing how stormy Hal's face was and being anyway only too aware of the

Lexham's inability to cope with such a grand and important function.

"No buts, m'dear, and you shall not rush to Seymour's aid because he is prettier than I am." The duke grinned roguishly at Hal's continued expression of dark anger.

Caroline looked helplessly at the duke. "Your Grace does not understand—"

"I understand perfectly, my dear, and still will not change my mind. Come now, to have a good business head is surely little different from being a good commander on the field of battle. Tactics must be swift and sure if advantage is to be seized. I offer you considerable advantage now, m'dear, and I shall be very disappointed in you if you fail to snatch it up immediately."

"But, Your Grace—" she said again, wanting to tell him of the predicament which prevented her from taking the advantage he so gallantly pressed upon her, but he did not wish to hear her protests.

"I must leave you now, I am afraid, for I have one thousand and one matters to attend to before returning to Paris in a day or so's time. I look forward to our next meeting, m'dear, when I trust you will greet me in person at the door of the Lexham Hotel, on the occasion of the banquet. Seymour here will call upon you to attend to the details— won't you, Seymour?"

Hal nodded stiffly, but he looked anything but pleased, which fact Caroline was finding increasingly hurtful, for it brought with it echoes of other occasions when he had shown himself to be completely uninterested in the success of her plans.

The duke grinned and then drew her hand to his lips once more. "Good-bye, Miss Lexham."

"Good-bye, Your Grace."

He glanced then at the openmouthed assistant, who had been paying great attention throughout. "The boots'll do, fellow, but I promise you that you will hear from me if I experience so much as a single twinge!"

"Y-yes, Your Grace."

With that the duke donned his tall hat and strode from the shop, the crowd immediately breaking into cheers as he pushed his way toward his waiting carriage.

Caroline turned swiftly to Hal, but he was about to leave

too. He smiled a little, his whole manner stiff with reserve. "I will indeed call upon you, Miss Lexham."

"I am so sorry that all your careful arrangements have been disturbed, Sir Henry."

"There is little I can do about that, for the duke's wish is very much my command."

"But there is something you should know—"

"I cannot delay now; he is waiting for me." Inclining his head, he withdrew, leaving her to watch as he joined the duke in the carriage. The crowd pressed around, and it was some time before the carriage could move away. When it did, the crowd surged in its wake, and the whole concourse passed noisily along Piccadilly.

Caroline stood in the silent shop. She should have been dancing on air, but instead she was in the depths of despair. The duke had talked of tactics and advantage, but on her field of battle the opposing commander had closed all avenues. Marcia was still the victor, in spite of the Duke of Wellington's good intentions on behalf of the Lexham Hotel.

Slowly Caroline walked from the bootmaker's, and her heart was heavy as she and Mrs. Hollingsworth proceeded along the pavement to Mayfair Street. Jennifer would probably be waiting there by now, and she would be devastated by what had happened with Gunter's.

Mrs. Hollingsworth put a gentle hand on her arm. "We'll think of something," she said soothingly.

"Will we?" Caroline's eyes stung with salt tears as she walked on, for on top of all her anxiety about the hotel, she knew the certain anguish of having once more seen evidence of Hal Seymour's indifference.

Chapter 23

The dreadful moment of having to confess failure to Jennifer was to be postponed, however, for when they returned to the hotel they found her maid, Simpson, waiting for them with a message that her mistress had encountered some distant cousins and would be spending the rest of the day with them. Thus Jennifer remained unaware of the catastrophe that had befallen the wedding arrangements.

Mrs. Hollingsworth did all in her power to find a solution, resolutely sending out the footmen to other, lesser caterers. That all was at such short notice did little to help, but even so the results of the inquiries were abysmally discouraging. One caterer could provide some of the desserts, another a small selection of cold fish dishes, while a third was eager to positively deluge the guests with countless meat pies. No one seemed able to undertake the complete feast, and Caroline was justifiably wary of engaging the services of so many cooks, for the broth would undoubtedly have been spoiled beyond redemption. Tentatively they discussed the possibility of preparing the entire feast in the hotel's own kitchens, although of course this would necessarily mean very plain fare indeed; but the merest hint of such a thing had immediately reduced the cook to hysteria, and the idea had been hastily abandoned. The day wore on, and Caroline knew she must accept that all was lost.

Meanwhile the duke's decision about the banquet had been fanned around London like a forest fire, the story being carried initially by the excited assistant at Hoby's, and then by the guests in the dining room at the Oxenford when Hal had imparted the tidings to the horrified Mr. Bassett. Within hours of the duke's announcement to Caroline, it seemed that the whole of London knew about it. It was at this point, with the short March afternoon drawing to a close, that Mr. Jordan called upon Caroline, delighted at having heard about the banquet's removal to the Lexham. He had been conversing with an associate at his club when he had overheard some others talking about what had happened at Hoby's and subsequently at the Oxenford. It seemed that when Hal had informed the unfortunate Mr. Bassett of the news, Gaspard Duvall himself had been nearby and had heard every word. The chef had been so staggered by what he had heard that he had halted in his tracks, causing the waiter who had been following him to drop the tureen of consommé he had been carrying. For a while there had been pandemonium in the usually superior and discreet dining room, and the chef had once again taken to his bed with a headache!

Mr. Jordan repaired immediately to tell Caroline what he had heard, and he chuckled as he related the tale. His smile faded, however, when he perceived that far from being overjoyed at her triumph, she was pale and wan. "My dear, whatever is wrong? Here I am, because of the most wonderful news imaginable, and you look more miserable than I have ever seen you before!"

"I have reason to be unhappy, Mr. Jordan," she replied, gesturing to him to sit in a comfortable chair close to the fireplace in her drawing room.

"I don't understand. Did the duke or did he not say that he wished the banquet to take place here instead of the Oxenford?"

"Oh, that is true enough."

"Then why are you not dancing a jig?"

"Because I will not be able to hold the banquet here, or hold anything else for that matter."

"You jest, surely."

She explained in detail all that had happened. "So you see, Mr. Jordan," she finished, "the banquet is quite out of the

question. Lady Chaddington has seen to that. I tried to tell the
duke and Sir Henry, but neither of them would listen. Now I
must tell Miss Seymour that she has no wedding feast, and I
must face the fact that my high-flying plans for this house
will come to nought.''

He listened in growing dismay. "Oh, my dear Miss Lexham,
I'm so sorry. But surely something can be done to save
things? I am certain that Miss Seymour would be agreeable to
a plain feast if she was to be acquainted with the facts—''

"Oh, of course she would, Mr. Jordan, but I would not be.
I could not and would not ask her to put up with anything less
than perfection for her wedding. She deserves the very best,
for she is truly an angel; I can no longer offer her anything
approaching the best, and that is the end of it.''

"I did not mean to offend you, my dear,'' he said gently.

She smiled. "I know.''

"It grieves me very much to think that your fine venture
will come to nothing after all. Oh, I admit that in the beginning I was less than enthusiastic, but I had truly come to
believe that you would make a resounding success of it all.
But for the machinations of a jealous, spiteful woman, you
would have done it, wouldn't you?''

"You are a very dear friend, Mr. Jordan.''

At that moment they both heard swift, excited steps approaching the door, and Caroline detected the chink-chink of
Mrs. Hollingsworth's keys. It was quite out of character for
the housekeeper to run anywhere, and even more out of
character for her to burst unceremoniously into Caroline's
private apartments, but this is what now happened.

"Whatever is it, Mrs. Hollingsworth?'' cried Caroline,
getting up in alarm.

"Oh, madam, such wonderful news!''

'News?'' Caroline's tentative fingers crept to touch the
vanished necklace.

"We have a chef after all!'' Mrs. Hollingsworth's eyes
danced with delight and her smile made her whole face glow.

"We do? Who is he?''

"*The* chef, madam!'' Pink with pleasure, the housekeeper
stood aside, beckoning to someone waiting in the antechamber.

Caroline stared as two men entered; it was Gaspard Duvall
and his dour *entremettier,* Boisville!

The chef advanced, his step as light and bouncy as ever,

and he seemed to have fully recovered from his headache. His mustard-colored coat was oddly bright in the dying rays of the afternoon sun, and he removed his beret with a flourish as he bowed over her hand. "Good evening, Mademoiselle Lexham. Forgive me for calling so unexpectedly, but it gives me great pleasure to be able to say that I can now accept your kind offer and I am immediately at your disposal."

She continued to stare, totally taken aback by this latest development. At last she found her voice. "You-you mean you wish to be *chef de cuisine* here after all?"

He smiled, glancing fleetingly at his silent, unsmiling companion. "*Mais oui, mademoiselle,* but then I always wished to come here. Unfortunately it was not immediately possible."

She did not know what had happened to change that state of affairs, she only knew that by some miracle all her problems had been solved. "Oh, Monsieur Duvall, you have no idea how overjoyed I am to hear you say this!" She could almost have run to hug the beaming little chef.

Mr. Jordan was delighted. "Providence has smiled upon you, my dear Miss Lexham, and no one could be more pleased than I!"

Mrs. Hollingsworth was scarcely less enthusiastic. "Now Miss Seymour will have the finest feast imaginable after all, and then there will be the banquet! Oh, madam, I'm so pleased for you!"

Caroline smiled too, but she could not help noticing how surly and silent Boisville remained. Not once did a smile or any other emotion touch his motionless lips, and such lack of expression was somehow chilling.

Gaspard Duvall spread his hands and smiled quizzically at her. "It is settled then, mademoiselle? I am your *chef de cuisine*?"

"Of course you are, monsieur."

"Then I and my entire *brigade de cuisine* will commence first thing tomorrow, and I will immediately put my mind to the *carte* for Miss Seymour's wedding feast. The dishes I had in mind before will not do now, for there is no time to acquire the necessary ingredients, but I promise to produce a feast which will be worthy both of the occasion and of my good name. After that, I will turn my thoughts to the banquet, *oui*?" He cleared his throat a little and then smiled once again.

"Welcome to the Lexham Hotel, Monsieur Duvall," said Caroline, "And you, Monsieur Boisville." She inclined her head at Gaspard's assistant, but she felt uneasy as she did so. There was something about the *entremettier* which she could not like in the slightest.

His response was toneless. *"Merci, mademoiselle."*

It was with some relief that she turned to the chef once more. "I think we have much to discuss, monsieur, so if you would please be seated?" She indicated a vacant chair.

Mr. Jordan immediately made his excuses and departed, after congratulating her once more upon this excellent turn of events, and soon Caroline was seated with the chef, Boisville, and Mrs. Hollingsworth while matters of the size of his *brigade de cuisine* and their accommodation and so on were gone over in a little more detail. Gaspard pronounced himself quite willing to forgo the usual method of payment for his services, and instead to take something of value from the house at the end of six months. He brushed aside any other difficulties that seemed to offer themselves, quite determined to take charge of the Lexham's fine kitchens.

Boisville sat stiffly and did not speak once. His presence was oppressive and Caroline detected Mrs. Hollingsworth glancing uncomfortably in his direction. Caroline was at a loss to understand why a man as lighthearted and cheerful as Gaspard Duvall should want such a gloomy and disagreeable person at his right hand. There was something else she found disturbing, and that was the distinct impression she received that whenever Gaspard was required to make a decision, no matter how small, he first secretly sought Boisville's silent consent. When she first received this impression, she told herself she imagined it, but it persisted until she knew she was not mistaken. She was reminded of the first occasion she had seen the two men together, in the garden at the Oxenford. She had thought then that Boisville seemed more the master than the subordinate; now she thought it even more.

At last the discussion came to an end and the two Frenchmen departed, leaving a very different atmosphere behind them than had existed before their arrival. Mrs. Hollingsworth stood with Caroline at the window, watching the chef's bright yellow carriage roll away across the courtyard, its color visible even though darkness had almost completely fallen now. "I'm so glad things have turned out this way, Miss Lexham."

Caroline smiled. "I'll warrant you are. You positively glowed the entire time he was here."

The housekeeper blushed a little. "I will not pretend that I don't find him the most charming of gentlemen. Nor will I pretend that I don't find his sour companion Boisville decidedly unpleasant."

"He certainly isn't full of the joys of spring," agreed Caroline, closing the shutters and drawing the curtains.

Mrs. Hollingsworth smiled again. "So, Lady Chaddington hasn't won after all. She'll be positively pinched with rage when she hears what has happened now."

Caroline looked swiftly at the housekeeper. "Miss Seymour is not to learn of Lady Chaddington's intriguing."

"I understand, madam, for she is to marry Sir Henry."

"Yes, so it would not do at all for anything to be said. We will just let her know that Monsieur Duvall is to come here after all, and we will say nothing concerning Gunter's."

The housekeeper nodded and prepared to leave to go about her tasks, but at the door she paused. "Miss Lexham? Why do you think the chef changed his mind?"

"I don't really know."

Mrs. Hollingsworth grinned then. "And nor do you care?"

"Something like that, for I'm only too glad that he is to come here after all. His reasons simply do not matter."

Not long afterward Jennifer returned to the hotel, accompanied by her brother. Caroline happened to be in the vestibule at the time, and so was able impart the good news immediately.

"Oh, Jennifer," she cried, hurrying forward in a rustle of turquoise lawn. "I have something very exciting to tell you We have a chef after all and so you will have your feast à la français as you've always wanted!"

Jennifer had been a little withdrawn, but now her eyes brightened with delight and she clasped Caroline's hands. "Oh, can it truly be so? After what Marcia told me about Gunter's, I was fearing dreadful news would be awaiting me, and instead it was all untrue!"

"Untrue?" Caroline still smiled, but she stiffened inside.

"Yes, she was most distraught, she told me that she had heard that Gunter's could not do the feast after all because of a prior booking. She said that she was so upset for me that she personally went to all the reputable caterers to see if one of them could take the feast on, as a special favor to her, but none of them could. There, I *knew* she was fibbing to be spiteful!'' Jennifer cast a knowing, arch look at Hal.

Caroline spoke up quickly. ''Well, perhaps in part it is true, for Gunter's did indeed back out of the arrangement, and I was very worried indeed, but now all is resolved and the problem at an end.''

Jennifer smiled. ''Tell me, who is the chef? Will I have heard of him?''

''Oh, yes, you certainly have heard of him,'' replied Caroline. ''He is none other than Gaspard Duvall himself.''

Jennifer gasped with instant delight, but Hal's reaction was more puzzling. For a moment he seeemed almost stunned, until he realized that his silence was mystifying his sister, at which he smiled and congratulated her upon getting what she wanted once more and Caroline upon this welcome reversal of fate. His words were spoken warmly enough, but there was something behind them, something Caroline did not understand. For an incredible moment she wondered if, as in the past, he was fully aware of everything Marcia had done, but then she immediately discarded such thoughts, for Hal would never, never have been party to anything that would have brought such chaos to his sister's wedding plans. No, on this occasion Marcia had worked alone and had gone to considerable lengths to conceal her tracks, for her plotting struck a little too close to the Seymours for comfort. This being so, whatever it was that lay behind Hal's reaction now, it was not that he had known what Marcia had done. What was it then?

Jennifer hugged him. ''Oh, I'm so happy again! Only one thing spoils it all for me.''

''And what is that?'' he asked, smiling at her.

''That you persist in remaining at the Oxenford. I have asked you to come here and now I ask you again, Hal. You are my only brother, you are to give me away at my wedding—I want you here, close to me, not beleaguered in that odious place!''

''If that is truly what you want,'' he replied suddenly, ''then with Miss Lexham's permission, I will do as you request.''

Caroline could not help staring at him as he said this, for

with a sudden clear insight into his thoughts, she knew that this decision had nothing to do with his desire to please his sister. Unlike the trusting, ingenuous Jennifer, Caroline knew that his actions were brought about by the removal of the banquet to the Lexham—and from that, she deduced that it had something to do with Gaspard Duvall. Stunned at this realization, she did not at first hear him when he addressed her.

"Miss Lexham?"

"I beg your pardon?" She brought her thoughts back with a jolt. "Did you say something?"

He seemed faintly amused. "I asked you if you would be able to tolerate my presence beneath your roof."

"You are always welcome here, Sir Henry."

He sensed something in her manner, but he said nothing more, turning back to his sister and kissing her farewell. "I have to go now."

"Go? But I thought you were going to take supper with me."

"I forgot that I have an appointment, but I am sure Miss Lexham would be pleased to sit with you and listen to your interminable rattle."

Jennifer pretended to be cross. "You are a beast, Henry Seymour, and I hate you."

He smiled and tweaked her cheek. "Good night, kitten."

"Good night."

He looked at Caroline. "Good night, Miss Lexham."

She inclined her head. "Sir Henry."

For a moment his shrewd glance rested thoughtfully upon her, but then he hurried out to the courtyard where his carriage had not yet departed.

"Oh, dear," said Jennifer suddenly, "I forgot to ask him."

"Ask him what?"

"If he would apologize to Marcia for me."

"Apologize?"

"When she came to me about Gunter's and the wedding feast, I wasn't exactly forthcoming; in fact I was decidedly cool. Now it seems that she was telling the truth, and I have a conscience. If I misjudged her about this, perhaps I have misjudged her about other things—oh, not about the way she has behaved toward you, for that was unforgivable, but I didn't care for her before you came to Town."

Caroline said nothing to this, for Jennifer's original assessment of Marcia, Lady Chaddington, was the more accurate.

Jennifer linked arms with her. "So, Monsieur Duvall is to come here after all. How splendid! I insist that you join me for supper, Caroline, and we will celebrate with some iced champagne."

Chapter 24

The speed with which all recent events had taken place at the Lexham was the talking point of society, and the following day, the day Gaspard Duvall and his entire *brigade de cuisine* removed themselves from the Oxenford, saw a constant to-ing and fro-ing of elegant carriages as ladies and gentlemen came in the hope of enjoying luncheon, and later dinner, at the new hotel. After the desolation and uncertainty of the day before, for Caroline it was like a dream come true. She felt like the legendary King Midas, for everything she touched did indeed appear to somehow turn to gold—and consequently she had great reservations about such luck, for things had not gone well for King Midas. . . .

Gaspard's arrival in the Lexham's kitchens had an immediate and electrifying effect upon everyone at the hotel. Such was his genius that he was straightaway able to create a dazzling menu from the ingredients already available; such was his immense charm that he drew a warm response from everyone, even the meanest kitchen boy, and everyone did his utmost to please him. He was one of those rare beings, a man of acknowledged brilliance, feted and adored by society and yet totally unspoiled, and therefore swiftly worshiped by all those over whom he held sway. Within an hour of his arrival, he had the kitchens running exactly as he wished, and he was delightedly experimenting with the wondrous Rumford closed ranges. He sang as he worked, which at first astonished the more staid British, but they soon accepted this French eccentricity, and even came to join in occasionally. Watching him, Caroline began to wonder if maybe she had been wrong to believe Hal's decision to come to the Lexham had something to do with the chef, something sinister.

Gaspard's influence was not only felt in the kitchens; he swiftly offered his advice to Caroline where the dining room itself was concerned. Having come from Paris, city of the world's finest cafés, a place where it was second nature to flatter women, he shook his head disapprovingly at the glare created by the glittering chandeliers. Such a harsh light was not kind to the ladies, he said, and instead the room should be illuminated only by candles, which would throw a soft glow in which even the most elderly of matrons could appear to advantage. This, he pointed out, would also be to the Lexham's advantage, for the ladies were all influential. If they were pleased, then so also were the gentlemen—such things did not work in reverse, for what pleased gentlemen very rarely appeared to please their respectable womenfolk.

He also advised Caroline to have places at the table marked as being reserved, for in this way unwanted persons could be denied entry. If one wished to have respectable ladies as guests, one could not risk them being exposed to the presence of Cyprians. It was a simple matter for the notices to be removed from the places if suitable persons wished to dine, and thus all risk of doubtful respectability was eliminated. This ruse worked excellently in Paris, and must therefore work equally well in London, and was especially advisable in an establishment which was in its infancy and therefore had a reputation to create. She took his advice, bearing in mind Dominic's recent scheming, for respectability was all important if she was to meet the terms of her uncle's will.

True to his word, Hal had quitted the Oxenford and taken an apartment at the Lexham. His arrival, however, inevitably meant frequent visits from Marcia, who swept in every morning, issuing orders and generally behaving as if she were the lady of the house. She played her cards with great care, making all she could of Jennifer's guilty conscience. No one could have been sweeter or more patient than Lady Chaddington, no one could have been more willing to be of assistance to the bride during the frequent rehearsals which now took place. Each day the bridesmaids came, and the bridal procession was to be seen practicing descending the grand staircase, and Marcia was to be seen at the foot of the steps, advising and instructing as if she had all the time in the world. Caroline found her conduct contemptible after her attempt to ruin the wedding arrangements by interfering with Gunter's. But Marcia was a consummate actress, and no one could have guessed the truth about her as she smiled at Jennifer or leaned adoringly on Hal's arm. She was so very credible, superbly beautiful, and every inch a lady of rank and fashion; to Hal she obviously appeared to be the perfect bride, and if the way he glanced at her was anything to go by, that was exactly what he intended her to be. Toward Caroline her conduct was publicly impeccable, containing just the correct degree of courtesy one would have expected considering Jennifer's frequent statements that Caroline was her very dearest friend. Marcia had to gauge her behavior very precisely, according Caroline neither too little nor too much in the way of condescension. Caroline's position was a difficult one to define as far as society was concerned, for she was well connected, being so closely related to the Earl of Lexham, and she was acknowledged to be socially acceptable by both the Seymours and Lord Carstairs, but at the same time she was mistress of a commercial enterprise, which was hardly a ladylike pursuit. All in all, Marcia had to tread very carefully, which feat she achieved superbly well in public—in private it was quite another matter. Only once did the two women encounter each other when no one else was present, and then Marcia made no pretense whatsoever. Her eyes were incredibly cold and her face dangerously still, and she spoke very softly indeed. "I have not done with you yet, of that you may be sure."

But guarding against Marcia was only one of Caroline's worries on the eve of the wedding day. The last guest went up to his room, holding aloft the candlestick he had been handed by the footman in the vestibule. The quivering light threw monstrous shadows over the walls as Mrs. Hollingsworth said good night to Caroline and then proceeded to her little parlor, where no doubt the ardent and attentive Gaspard would be waiting to take supper *à deux* with his unlikely quarry. Caroline smiled as she watched the housekeeper hurry away, her keys chinking busily. Unlikely indeed, for who would have thought that the dapper, excitable Frenchman would have been so inexorably drawn to the prim, correct housekeeper? And who would have expected this feeling to be reciprocated? There was no doubt that this was the case, for Mrs. Hollingsworth had rather too swiftly succumbed to his wish to take his meals alone with her, something Caroline had certainly never expected. Now he was nearly always to be found in her parlor when he was not in the kitchens, and it was here that he seemed to be at his happiest.

He was a creature of sudden moods, lapsing into unexpected and dark silences which only the housekeeper appeared able to laugh him out of, and this she could do with ease. Soon he would be smiling and singing again, and glancing adoringly at his beloved Madame H.

Caroline would have been very happy for Mrs. Hollingsworth, of whom she was very fond, had it not been for her own nagging suspicions that Hal's activities were in some way connected with Gaspard—which led inevitably to the possibility that the chef was involved with the Bonapartist plots against the Duke of Wellington. When Gaspard was happy and smiling, these suspicions seemed unbelievable, but when he was quiet and withdrawn, or when he was with the unpleasant Boisville, then those suspicions did not seem quite as wild. She wanted to ask Hal about it, but somehow she knew that she could not, for when she had given him her word that she would do all she could to ease Jennifer's mind, it had somehow been implicit that she would never again mention the subject. She did not know exactly why she felt this, but she did, and she knew that her instinct was correct; it would not be the thing at all to say anything more.

The housekeeper disappeared toward her parlor, and Caroline returned to her own apartments, intent upon going over the arrangements for the wedding one last time before retiring. Wearily she sat at the escritoire by the light of a candle, taking out all the papers on which she had written seemingly endless lists and notes. One by one she ticked off the items. The white coach had been attended to, the flowers ordered from Covent Garden—including the extra ferns and garlands Gaspard had advised for the dining room—and the cake had been delivered from Gunter's, that establishment being anxious not to find itself left with a specially ordered item

decorated with the heraldic emblems of the Seymour and
Carstairs families. Jennifer's silver tissue wedding gown had
been delivered from her *couturière*, together with the primrose and lilac gowns to be worn by her many bridesmaids,
and on the same day Caroline's new gowns had also been
delivered, although they had not arrived in so grand a style,
being brought to the rear of the house. But at least she could
appear in something other than gray wool or turquoise lawn,
and as she sat in the candlelight, her new white muslin gown
was blushed to the palest of pinks.

"How very pleasing you look in white, Caro."

She turned with a gasp to see Hal leaning against the
doorjamb. He had returned from an evening engagement and
was dressed formally in a black velvet coat and silk breeches.
His waistcoat was of white satin and his cravat edged with
lace. His dark hair was a little ruffled, and this added an
attractively casual note to his otherwise distinguished appearance. He smiled, coming further into the room, dropping his
gloves and tricorn hat upon a table.

"Good evening, Sir Henry."

"Good evening, Caro."

She wondered why he had chosen to come to see her, and
at such an hour. "Is there something—"

"I have merely come to wish you well for tomorrow. Since
I have lodged here I have taken the opportunity of observing
you, Caro Lexham, and what I have seen has impressed me
greatly. You have taken to the running of this house as if you
have known no other life. In short, you appear to have been
born to be the mistress of a great London mansion."

"I think that most of the praise should go to Mrs.
Hollingsworth, for without her I could not—"

"Nonsense, you fully deserve the praise. Mrs. Hollingsworth
is no doubt extremely efficient, but she can only respond to
the lady of the house, and in your case that lady is very
significant."

"I think you are too kind, Sir Henry."

He shook his head. "No, Caro, that is one thing I am not.
In fact, I have not been at all kind, a lamentable lapse on my
part."

"I don't know what you mean."

His hazel eyes moved over her face in the candlelight.
"No, I don't suppose you do, and in a way I hope you never

understand, for that would be a welcome solution." He smiled then. "Forgive me, I think I may have enjoyed a rather too convivial evening."

"Perhaps."

"Don't know me too well, Caro, a fellow likes to retain a little mystery."

She smiled.

"I came here tonight not only to wish you well, but also to thank you."

"Thank me?"

He nodded. "For all you have done for Jennifer. I know that you have toiled as much because you love her as because you need to make a success of this venture. Whatever happens tomorrow, you will have done all you possibly can to make my sister's wedding day the most splendid occasion."

She lowered her eyes then, unable to help wondering if he would still be thanking her at this time the next day, for by then there was no doubt that Marcia would have made some move against her. "I—I just hope that all goes well, Sir Henry," she said at last, raising her gaze slowly to his face.

"Oh, I don't think anything will go drastically wrong," he said softly. "Of that you can be sure."

Could she be so sure? She doubted it very much.

Something in her glance drew him a little closer suddenly, and he put his hand to her chin, stroking her skin gently with his thumb. "How very vulnerable you are at times, Caro, which fact I find quite irresistible—and at this very moment I do not feel inclined to restrain my baser instincts." He slipped his arm around her waist, pulling her toward him and kissing her on the lips, his fingers moving in the warm hair at the nape of her neck. A wild, warm desire coursed through her, a desire to which she momentarily yielded, but then she drew firmly away. He did not mean the kiss, it was merely a passing fancy which would be forgotten within a moment.

"Why, Sir Henry," she said lightly, endeavoring to sound merely amused. "You must indeed have enjoyed a convivial evening."

"I did indeed, and for the sweetest of moments I cherished a hope that it was about to continue."

"That would not be at all the thing, sir."

"So it seems. Pray forgive the trespass."

"Forgive it? Why, I have already forgotten it, Sir Henry."

He raised an eyebrow at that, smiling a little. "Have you, be damned? I must be losing my touch."

"Good night, Sir Henry."

A light passed through his eyes and he gave a low laugh. "Good night, Caro."

Chapter 25

It seemed that she had barely fallen asleep before it was time to rise again. Mrs. Hollingsworth brought her a silver pot of freshly made coffee and, as she set it down, announced that the menu cards, which had had to be hastily reordered when Gaspard came to the hotel, had not been delivered as promised. Nor had the flowers arrived from Covent Garden.

With a groan, Caroline slipped quickly from the bed. Mrs. Hollingsworth hurried away to do her own tasks, and Caroline washed and dressed as swiftly as possible, for if those two vital items had not been delivered by the time she left her apartment, she would have to go out to see what had happened to them.

As she stole a moment or two to enjoy the excellent coffee, the lower servants, who had risen at five to commence their work, were just finishing their early tasks. In the main reception room the fires had been raked out and laid anew, and damp sand had been scattered on the carpets to settle the dust before brushing. Everything was attended to in silence, so that not a single guest was disturbed by all the activity.

In the kitchens Gaspard and his *brigade* had commenced the preparation of the wedding feast, which work would go on at the same time as the guests' breakfasts were begun. So, while truffles were being cleaned and ortolans stuffed, so also were being made ready the bacon and eggs, kidneys, omelettes, and kedgeree which would soon grace the tables of the dining room and private apartments. Everyone worked swiftly and efficiently, with only Boisville apparently having little to do for the time being. Mrs. Hollingsworth was curious about this, until Gaspard pointed out that in the absence of a glacier from Gunter's, it would be Boisville's task to do the ice carving, at which art he was very skilled indeed. She accepted this explanation, but she could not help thinking that Boisville was apparently a very dispensable *entremettier*! The housekeeper had come to dislike Boisville intensely, for she had swiftly realized that it was after speaking with him that Gaspard frequently fell into his quiet, withdrawn moods. However, this morning Boisville had not approached Gaspard, who was fully occupied with all the preparations, and who was enjoying the hard work so much that he sang to himself as he inspected the freshly delivered Severn salmon.

Her coffee finished, Caroline soon ascertained that neither the menu cards nor the flowers had arrived in the meantime, and so, as the rest of the staff sat down in the servants' hall to a well-earned breakfast, she set off to Piccadilly to find a hackney carriage. It would not have done at all to be seen traveling in such a lowly vehicle, and so she went about it as discreetly as possible, trusting that no one saw the mistress of the Lexham Hotel engaged in such an exercise!

The menu cards were ready and so she easily accomplished the first part of her errand, then went on to Covent Garden. The market had been busy for many hours already and the noise and bustle was considerable as porters with baskets on their heads jostled and shouted, as prices were argued, and as wagons and carts struggled to pass through narrow ways. The little single-story shops and open-fronted booths were doing a brisk trade and such was the crush that it was impossible for the hackney to proceed further. Bidding the coachman to wait for her, she alighted and went on foot into the flower market. She stepped carefully over the dirty cobbles where rotting fruit and vegetables had been carelessly thrown, and at last she approached the man who had undertaken to provide the flowers, ferns, and garlands for the wedding.

He was a portly fellow with a bulbous nose and a battered top hat which could have done with a good brushing, but he

was surrounded by the most beautiful flowers in the whole
market. Buckets filled with daffodils, narcissi, and tulips
cluttered the cobbles, together with bowls of roses and carnations from the market garden hothouses upriver from the city
at Chelsea. To the rear of the booth, the man's assistants
were employed making garlands, their bowed figures almost
concealed by large wooden pails of ferns and other greenery.

Caroline hardly dared to ask him about the delivery for the
Lexham Hotel, for a dreadful thought had occurred to her:
had Marcia chosen this way for her next move? But to her
overwhelming relief, the man immediately assured her that
the flowers had been sent off barely ten minutes before, the
delay having been beyond his control as he had not received
his own order until late, the market gardeners having had
some difficulty owing to awkward tides and so on. Caroline
gladly accepted his explanation, for all that mattered to her
was that the order was *en route* for Mayfair Street.

She retraced her steps to the hackney, but when she got
there she halted in dismay, for there was no sign of it. She
glanced swiftly around, thinking that she had mistaken the
place, but no, the hackney had simply gone! Desperately she
cast around for another, for she must return as quickly as
possible. As if to emphasize her predicament, the church
bells chose that moment to chime the half hour; it was already
half past nine and she was stranded on the opposite side of
London!

She did not see the smart red curricle emerge slowly from a
side street, its high-stepping team of bright chestnuts driven
with great skill by the young gentleman at the ribbons. He
was fashionably dressed and wore his top hat tipped back on
his honey-colored hair. He seemed to be searching the busy
street, and then he saw her. "Cousin Caroline?" It was Dominic.

She turned in surprise, hearing his voice above the noise.
What a strange coincidence it was that he should happen to
drive along this very street at the time that she was there. She
greeted him warily. "Good morning, my lord."

He halted the curricle in the middle of the street, ignoring
the angry shouts from the other vehicles which could not now
pass by. "So cool still, cousin? I had hoped we were friends
now. Why are you alone here at this hour?"

The complaints were becoming angrier as he waited deliberately for her to reply, and she glanced uncomfortably at the other vehicles. "Had you not better clear the way, my lord?"

"When you have answered my question. You should not be in this disreputable neighborhood on your own, Caroline, it is hardly advisable."

"I had to come because the flowers had not been delivered for the wedding."

"Ah, then your error is understood and forgiven. I trust that you did not walk all the way, but the apparent absence of any vehicle suggests that that has to be the case."

She was suspicious suddenly, sensing that he knew about the hackney. "I did not walk, my lord, I hired a carriage."

He smiled a little, still ignoring the shouts and waved fists. "Is that a delicate way of admitting that you committed the heinous sin of traveling in a hackney? Tut, tut, my dear Caroline, that is not at all the *ton*. However, I am pleased to be at your disposal and would be honored to convey you back to Mayfair Street. Will you accept my offer?"

She looked up at him, knowing that this was a charade he had deliberately staged. He must have seen her alight from the hackney and he had dismissed it, fully intending to just happen along. But why?

He held out an elegantly gloved hand. "Come on, this is hardly the time to demur, cousin; you are in need of transport and I can provide it."

He was right and she knew it, and so she accepted his hand. He drew her easily up to the seat beside him, flicking the whip so that the red curricle leaped away at a spanking pace. She clung fearfully to the seat as he negotiated a corner.

He laughed. "I haven't lost a passenger yet, coz! I assure you that I always drive like this; our present speed is not, therefore, part of a dastardly plot to dispose of you."

She did not know whether to smile or not, for had anyone else made the remark it would have been amusing, but it simply wasn't when uttered by Dominic Lexham.

He glanced at her. "Your silence is ominous, cousin. Does it mean that you still harbor a grudge against me?"

"A grudge? No."

"Then please treat me as if you now regard me as a friend, for I assure you that I am." He reached over to put his hand over hers, and the curricle flew along a wide thoroughfare.

Straightening once more, he urged the team faster, cracking the whip so that the vehicle dashed across a junction, ignoring the traffic passing in the other direction, and entered Piccadilly at what seemed to her to be breakneck speed. Almost in a blur she saw the window of Hoby's, she saw Green Park and the Pulteney and Oxenford hotels before the curricle turned at last into the quiet streets and squares of Mayfair.

She knew a great sense of relief when they passed beneath the pedimented gateway and slowly crossed the courtyard to the main entrance of the hotel. She wondered what he was thinking in that moment, but she could read nothing in his handsome, expressionless face.

The flower wagon was just departing and some maids were carrying the last garlands into the vestibule as the curricle came to a standstill by the steps and Dominic alighted to help Caroline down. Holding her hand, he smiled into her eyes. "There, cousin, I have delivered you safe and sound, and more swiftly I am sure than your phantom hackney."

"I am most grateful to you."

"I assure you that the pleasure was all mine." His glance was so warm that she felt suddenly embarrassed, especially as some guests emerged from the hotel at that very moment. She began to withdraw her hand, but his fingers tightened over hers. "Until we meet again, Caroline," he said softly, bending his head and kissing her fully on the lips.

With a horrified gasp, she stepped back from him. Still smiling, he climbed lightly back onto the curricle and with a swift crack of the whip jerked the team into action once more.

She was horribly conscious of the guests' curious glances, and her face was the color of flame as she gathered her skirts to hurry swiftly into the house, politely murmuring her greeting as she passed. The ladies smiled and nodded, but exchanged quizzical glances; the gentlemen doffed their hats, their eyes lowered to catch a glimpse of her pretty ankles.

As the door closed behind her, the departing guests strolled slowly on down the steps and across the courtyard. They glanced back at the entrance, their heads together as they discussed the intriguing little scene they had just witnessed, commenting that the two Lexham cousins appeared to have become very intimate indeed.

*   *   *

Caroline had no time to consider Dominic's strange conduct, for in spite of the fact that the wedding itself was not to take place until early evening, there still seemed to be a mountain of work before all was in readiness. In advance there had seemed to be sufficient time to do everything, but now the day was upon them there did not appear to be sufficient minutes in each hour. The everyday life of the hotel had to proceed, the needs of the guests attended to, and thus while the servants labored to decorate the red saloon, the dining room, and the vestibules, there was a constant throng of guests and visitors to make their task even more arduous.

As the day wore on, however, the rooms set aside for the wedding took on an entirely new and fairy-tale appearance. Swathes of flowers and greenery turned them into sylvan bowers, with garlands twined around columns, through the banisters of the grand staircase, along pelmets and around doorjambs. White satin bows were pinned to furnishings, and great bowls of bright spring flowers stood everywhere, filling the air with their delicate perfume, so fresh and full of promise. In the vestibule stood the pretty baskets of wedding favors, the knots of white ribbon and posies of primroses, which would be handed to each guest on arrival.

But it was in the dining room that the greatest transformation took place, for it was here that the fashionable gathering could congregate after the ceremony in order to sample the magnificent feast Gaspard and his *brigade* had prepared. In this room had been created a leafy bower in which one could almost have expected to find Titania lying asleep. Ferns and blossoms had been arranged in huge bowls, garlands were draped everywhere, especially around the white-clothed table, and immense épergnes full of flowers, moss, and fruit stood at intervals along its great length. There were silver bowls of melons, pineapples, peaches, pears, and grapes, and dozens of shaded candles to give that muted light which was at once so romantic and flattering. The light shone on gleaming cutlery and cut crystal, and the menu cards stood elegantly in little silver-gilt stands. The Sheraton sideboards were a vision of splendor with the dazzling Lexham plate displayed in all its considerable glory, and in one corner of the room splashed a little fountain, the mechanics of which were a mystery to

Caroline but which were fully understood by the experienced Mrs. Hollingsworth.

In the cellar, Boisville worked away at carving the ice, and had already finished swans and eagles, the emblems of the Seymour and Carstairs families, and had now begun the very delicate vases in which would soon sparkle the more feathery ferns.

Darkness fell at last and the guests began to arrive, and in her private apartment, Caroline put the finishing touches to her appearance. To achieve a singularly fashionable and elegant effect when funds were at a premium was no simple matter, and she had consulted for a long time with her diligent dressmaker. This astute lady had in her possession a particularly splendid ruff, made to closely resemble those worn in Tudor times, and so it had been decided to create a gown to suit this item. The result was a vision of sixteenth-century fashion, with elaborate, puckered sleeves stitched with hundreds of tiny pearls, but made very modish indeed by the use of a very fine rose-pink Indian muslin. The hem was high enough to reveal her ankles, and was emphasized by stiff *rouleaux* to make the skirt stand out a little, and the long sleeves ended in cuffs of lace which almost completely concealed her hands. Her hair was dressed high and back from her face, as she had seen in portraits of Elizabethan ladies, and was twined with little strings of pearls. These pearls had been pressed upon her for the occasion by a very insistent Jennifer, who perceived that they would be the very thing.

Standing in front of the cheval glass now, Caroline surveyed herself from head to toe. Would she do? She touched the stiff ruff which sprang out so splendidly around the neckline of the gown, revealing her pale, bare throat. Oh, how excellent her grandmother's necklace would have looked now! But there was no point in yearning for what had been lost forever; the necklace had gone and she would never wear it again.

Only one thing remained now, and that was the tiny velvet cap which was to be pinned at the back of her head, and as she bent to pick it up, Mrs. Hollingworth came in, her discreet dark gray skirts rustling and her keys chinking in a familiar way Caroline found suddenly very comforting. As the housekeeper helped her with the cap, Caroline went over and over the final arrangements. Surely they had not forgotten something of vital importance?

"Has everything been attended to, Mrs. Hollingsworth?"

"Everything, madam. The maids finished the ribbons from the cake over an hour ago. We can do no more."

"How do I look?"

"Very lovely."

"Does it show that I have not been to a *couturière*?"

"No, Miss Lexham, it does not." Smiling reassuringly, the housekeeper took Caroline's shawl and draped it carefully over her ruched sleeves. "There, now you are ready to be this day's most important London hostess."

"Oh, don't say that, for it fills me with terror."

"You will carry it off splendidly, I know that you will."

"Not if Lady Chaddington can help it."

"We will be sure to watch her very closely, madam, of that you may be sure."

"I wish I could guess what she will do, but I cannot. She is so unscrupulous that it could be just about anything!"

"You must not think about it, Miss Lexham; you must just carry on as if all is well—which it probably will be, for I cannot think that she will do anything to the actual wedding of her future sister-in-law."

"No? Well I think she is quite capable of doing that, Mrs. Hollingsworth, because as far as she is concerned tonight I am at my most vulnerable. Destroy tonight's celebration, and she has destroyed me; the fact that she will also have ruined Jennifer's wedding day will not really enter into it at all. However, you are right, it will do no good to worry about it, for until whatever it is actually happens, there doesn't appear to be very much we can do about it." She paused for a moment, suddenly very nervous. "Wish me luck, Mrs. Hollingsworth."

In reply the housekeeper made so bold as to suddenly hug her. "Of course I wish you luck, my dearest Miss Lexham."

Smiling gratefully at this warm display of affection, Caroline took a deep breath and left the apartment to go out into the vestibule to greet the wedding guests.

The crystal chandeliers glittered above bare shoulders and jeweled hair, and tall ostrich plumes trembled richly in the warmth from the glowing fire in the hallway. The gentlemen wore coats of velvet, dark green, dark blue, and black, and brass or silver buttons shone elegantly on the rich, somber material. The air was filled with the sounds of refined conversation and laughter, and outside more and more carriages turned into the courtyard, their lamps casting arcs of light in the gloom and their wheels and the hooves of their teams clattering above the cobbles. The Lexham Hotel was ablaze with lights, not a single shutter or curtain being closed and every room being illuminated for this most important of social occasions. To Caroline, as she moved among the crush of distinguished guests, it seemed that the whole of the *beau monde* was assembled here tonight—the whole of the *beau monde* to witness either her triumph, or her ignominious defeat at the hands of Marcia, Lady Chaddington.

Marcia had arrived early on the arm of her popinjay brother, and she looked very elegant indeed, clad in a low-necked slip of the palest lime-green sarcenet with an overgown of silver patent net. Fabulous emeralds lay at her throat and hung from her ears, and frothy ostrich plumes quivered above her magnificently dressed auburn hair. Beside her, clad in pale-blue from Apollo-curled head to slippered toe, Lord Fynehurst looked almost as splendid, but decidedly unmanly, and his braying tones could be heard at frequent intervals above the noise of conversation.

A small orchestra had been hired for the occasion, and they played in the background in the red saloon. The vicar of fashionable St. George's, Hanover Square, sipped champagne with the other guests as he waited for the commencement of the ceremony. A very nervous Lord Carstairs, his slender figure very handsome in an embroidered velvet coat of the richest wine red, moved among the guests, and several times she saw him bid the groom's man, his long-suffering brother, to check again that the wedding ring was safely in his pocket.

At last the appointed hour came and everyone pushed into the red saloon, where the chairs and sofas had been placed around the walls to allow as many as possible to witness the actual ceremony. An expectant hush fell over the gathering, and all eyes were turned on the open doorway, through which could be seen the fine rise of the grand staircase.

The first guests to see the wedding party appear at the top of the steps gave gasps of admiration and Caroline smiled as she saw Jennifer make the magnificent entrance she had so wanted. And what an entrance it was, for she looked so very beautiful and glowing with happiness, and she was the center of attention as she slowly descended on Hal's arm. Her silver tissue wedding gown was adorned with two broad flounces of Brussels point lace, edged with shell trimming, and was fastened at its tiny waist by a beautiful diamond clasp. A breathtaking wreath of more diamonds flashed and glittered in her fluffy dark hair, and there was an air of such joy about her that she outshone every other woman present and was truly the most beautiful and enchanting of brides. Behind her came the twelve bridesmaids, six clad in primrose and six in lilac, and they carried little ribboned posies of sweet-smelling heartsease, with more of these flowers pinned in their hair.

Hal wore a coat of indigo with silver buttons, and his shirt frills and cravat were edged with fine lace. He looked very handsome and dashing, and very proud as he escorted his lovely sister, his hand resting protectively over hers. His eyes met Caroline's for a moment as they passed, and he smiled at her. It was a smile that almost turned her heart over with love for him, and she lowered her glance to hide the effect it had had upon her. Then the procession reached the little floral dais on which the ceremony itself was to take place, and Jennifer at last saw her beloved Charles, who had watched her approach with such adoration that there could be no doubt at all that this was a love match of the first order.

Caroline watched the service with tears in her eyes, for she was so very happy for her friend, and as the ring was slipped onto the bride's finger, nothing could have been further from Caroline's thoughts than the schemes of Lady Chaddington. At last the ceremony was over and Jennifer turned into her new husband's arms as he bent to kiss her, and a loud cheer went up that would have been totally out of place in a church.

Now at last was the time to adjourn to the dining room, which had been closed to conceal the beautiful decorations from view until the last moment. The two footmen, wedding favors pinned to their liveried shoulders, flung open the connecting doors from the red saloon, and the wedding gathering proceeded into the feast, led by the bride and groom, and followed immediately by Hal, with Marcia on his arm.

Gasps of delight greeted the first glimpse of the fairy bower, and more gasps the magnificent table with its épergnes and garlands, and above all the cake. Gunter's had indeed surpassed themselves and had created a confection which

dominated the snowy table. Crisp, dainty ribbons extended
from the cake to the four corners of the ceiling, and in these
corners there were wedding wreaths, adorned with more knots
and trailers of satin ribbon. Boisville's splendid ice carvings
glistened on silver trays, and cool, soft ferns trembled with
each movement of air as the guests proceeded around the
table, seeking their allotted places.

The feast commenced, and it was soon evident that society's
feting of Gaspard Duvall was well justified, for the dishes
that proceeded from the kitchens were delicate, mouth watering,
and well worthy of his reputation. The *potages* were declared
to be quite magnificent, the *brochettes d' ortolans* to be quite
the most delicious dish of those small birds yet tasted, and the
salmon *soufflé* to be the lightest and most flavorsome
imaginable. Platter after platter was offered to the delighted
guests, from dainty slices of chicken breasts on *pâté de foie
gras* to a variety of dishes served with expensive and rare
truffles.

From a discreet position beneath the Ionic colonnade at the
rear of the room, Caroline watched the feast progress. How
different an affair it was from a wedding feast in Selford!
She smiled to herself, pondering the incredible changes
that had taken place in her life in such a short while. Her gaze
moved over the dazzling gathering, the cream of London's
society, and she was amazed anew that all this should be
happening simply because of a sudden, impossible thought
that had occurred to her while sitting briefly in the gardens to
look at the house where her father had been born.

Seeing Jennifer's happy, smiling face as she raised her
glass to share a toast with her new husband, Caroline found
herself suddenly looking at Marcia, who had been so oddly
quiet thus far. There was a look about her now which suddenly made Caroline very wary. Something was about to
happen; Caroline knew it. Every nerve stiffened as she invol-
untarily stepped forward, one hand reaching out to touch the
cool marble of a garland-entwined column. She was deaf to
the noise in the room; it was as if she was alone with her
enemy. Across the assembly, Marcia's cool, contemptuous
glance met hers, and Caroline became aware of the sound of
her own heartbeats. Marcia was about to deliver her *coup de
grace*, and she would do it alone.

From behind Caroline, a footman appeared, bearing aloft

Gaspard's *pièce de résistance,* a magnificent silver platter
bearing an especially created salmon dish, *saumon Jennifer,*
named in honor of the bride. Deliciously garnished, and
decorated with peacock feathers, the dish's appearance was
greeted with admiring claps as the footman bore it deftly to
the head of the table, intending to serve the bride and groom
first. With bated breath, Caroline watched Marcia, whose
whole attitude now was one of confident, gloating anticipation.

From Jennifer and Lord Carstairs, the footman proceeded
to Hal, and then to Marcia, but as he flourishingly placed a
spoonful of the salmon upon her plate, she gave a sudden
scream and rose shakily to her feet. A shocked silence descended instantly over the gathering and all eyes swung toward
her in astonishment. Shuddering with disgust, and somehow
contriving to look genuinely ill, she pointed a quivering
finger at the offending plate. There, reposing horridly in
the midst of the delicious salmon, was a very large, very
dead cockroach.

Chapter 26

Caroline found herself hurrying forward, and many of the guests gave shudders and hastily put down their cutlery, pushing their plates away as if all the food might contain similar insects. An uneasy and questioning stir passed around the elegant table, and Jennifer's happy smile faltered, her eyes filling with tears at what seemed the complete destruction of her wedding feast. The unfortunate footman didn't quite know what to do, and he looked toward Caroline for instruction, but she could not think of anything to say. There the cockroach lay for all to see, and as far as the guests were concerned, it could only have come from the kitchens. Were those kitchens then crawling with such vermin? Was the whole establishment perhaps similarly afflicted? Had they all made a dreadful mistake in honoring these premises with their patronage. Caroline could sense their thoughts, and she could not blame them; how were they to know that Marcia was the culprit?

The moments of shocked silence passed on leaden feet, and Marcia managed to squeeze remorseful tears which coursed wretchedly down her cheeks as she turned to apologize to Jennifer for having been the unwitting cause of the feast's ruination. But it was this final touch that was to prove her undoing, for as she turned, she dislodged her reticule from the edge of the table and it fell to the floor, the contents spilling everywhere. There, among the trinkets and scent phials, lay several more cockroaches.

The guests who were close enough to see gave shocked gasps, and Marcia's face drained of color as she hastily bent to push the guilty items back into the reticule. She was forestalled, however, for Hal was the more agile, picking everything up and dropping it coldly and pointedly upon the tablecloth before her.

"Your belongings, I believe, madam," he said softly, his eyes filled with disgust.

Marcia couldn't speak; she cast around desperately for a friendly face, but by now everyone was aware of what she had done. A sea of offended, appalled faces looked back at her. Even her brother could not ally himself with her, deliberately keeping his gaze lowered to his plate. At last Marcia's haunted eyes returned to Hal, but she saw that she had lost him forever. With a stifled sob, she gathered her skirts and ran from the room, the sound of her footsteps carrying clearly to them all as she fled to the outer doors.

Immediately a buzz of comment broke out, turning as much upon Hal's conduct as upon Marcia's, for he did not appear to be in any way upset that the woman who was to have been his bride should have stooped to such a detestable trick, and at his beloved sister's wedding! A great many interested glances followed him now as he swept the reticule onto a plate and beckoned to a waiter, who immediately spirited it away. Hal then turned to Caroline, who had been standing close by all the while, and with a smile he raised her hand gallantly to his lips, which gesture met with much approbation from the assembly.

Jennifer and Lord Carstairs were all smiles again and the feast proceeded, the conversation dwelling almost solely on the intriguing subject of Marcia's dreadful behavior and Hal's reaction to it. Lord Fynehurst remained uncomfortably where he was for as long as he could, but in the end he uneasily took his leave, only too conscious that the ignominy touching his sister's name was inevitably touching his own, for the guests knew him well enough to realize that he had probably been fully aware of what she planned to do.

Caroline retreated to her position beneath the colonnade, endeavoring to look calm and unconcerned, but in reality feeling the very opposite. If it had not been for the accidental knocking to the floor of the reticule, Marcia's cunning trick would have worked, the wedding feast would have been disrupted beyond redemption, the reputation of the new Lexham Hotel would have suffered irreparable harm, and the odium would in the end have fallen upon Caroline herself. She trembled a little with delayed shock, hardly realizing that she had not only witnessed the biter being bitten, but also the severing of Marcia's relationship with Hal.

Mrs. Hollingsworth, as soothing and reliable as ever, appeared as if by magic at her side, pressing a glass of champagne into her hand. "It's all over now, my dear, and she didn't succeed in her wickedness. Smile now and drink this, and think only that in spite of her efforts, this wedding celebration has been a wonderful success."

Caroline smiled. "Thank you, Mrs. Hollingsworth, there are times when I truly do not know what I would do without you."

The housekeeper gently patted her arm and then slipped away to the kitchens once more.

Jennifer was much relieved that from imminent disaster, the feast was now proceeding excellently once more, and she now took the opportunity of quizzing her brother as he took his place beside her once more. "Hal, you do not appear to be much put out by what Marcia did."

"That depends upon what you mean by put out. If you mean angry, then I do not appear to be gripped by rage because I am doing all in my power to hide it. If she had been a man, I would call her out for what she did. On the other hand, if by 'put out' you mean heartbroken, then that is because I am not."

"But I thought—"

"You thought incorrectly, my dear sister, as indeed did Marcia herself. I may for a brief while have entertained a notion of marrying her, but my sojourn at Petwell soon relieved me of that foolishness. Marcia may be an excellent bedfellow, but she would make a tyrannical wife!"

"Hal!" cried his shocked sister. "Don't be so improper!"

"I have only provided you with a fact you have been itching to know for some time," he replied infuriatingly.

She flushed. "Well, I admit that I *did* wonder if she was your mistress."

"Now you know."

"You might at least have admitted earlier that you weren't intending to marry her, for I've been worrying so about you," she scolded. "I *knew* she would make you unhappy!"

"If I had told you, Jennifer, you would not have believed me."

"That is your own fault, for you have too frequently in the recent past deliberately told me untruths or simply omitted to tell me things altogether."

"My sins are evidently legion," he remarked dryly, smiling at her.

"They certainly are." Jennifer lowered her eyes for a moment. "Hal, Marcia did that dreadful thing today in order to hurt Caroline, which means that she was jealous of Caroline. Do you agree?"

His smile revealed nothing. "To agree would suggest that I am *au fait* with the workings of the female mind, which I am not. Now then, are you going to be a good little thing and eat up your dinner, or must I spoon-feed you?"

She studied his face for a moment and then accepted that he was not going to be any more forthcoming. "You attempt to spoon-feed me, Henry Seymour, and I'll kick you on the shins, as I remember doing when you were a beastly little boy."

For another hour or more after that the feast continued, but then it was time for the bride and groom to prepare to leave on the first part of their lengthy journey to Venice. They were to stay at some undisclosed address in Kent on their first night, crossing to France from Dover on the next morning's tide. Walking with her husband on one side and her brother on the other, and followed by the twelve bridesmaids, Jennifer left the dining room to go up to her apartment to change.

Hal did not accompany them up the grand staircase, but waited at the foot of the steps until the bridal party had passed from his sight, then he turned to go back to the feast, but instead found himself face-to-face with an old friend from his school days. "Digby! How good it is to see you again! I caught a glimpse of you earlier on and could hardly believe my eyes! How did you contrive to get yourself invited, you old reprobate?"

The other smiled. "By nefarious means, how else?" He was a tall, blond man, dressed in unrelieved black, and his rather aquiline nose had become red as the evening wore on and he enjoyed more and more of the excellent champagne. "I believe I must congratulate you upon this evening's celebrations. I'll warrant this particular wedding will be very much the thing for some time to come."

"My sister sincerely hopes so," replied Hal, grinning. "But I cannot take the credit for any of the arrangements. That must go entirely to Miss Lexham."

"Ah, yes, the intriguing Miss Lexham. What a beauty, eh? By Gad, I can understand Marcia Chaddington's green-eyed jealousy. Quite an armful, eh, Seymour?"

Hal's smile faded just a little. "Don't tread further along that particular path, my friend, for you are entirely wrong."

"You mean, there ain't anything between you and the beauteous *chatelaine*?" The other could not conceal his surprise.

"Nothing whatever."

"Well, damn me, if that don't stagger me! One thing's for sure, though, and that is that Marcia certainly thought there was."

"Possibly."

"You're very reticent about the whole thing, if you don't mind my saying so."

"Perhaps that is because I don't consider it to be any of your business—old friend."

Digby pursed his lips. "Don't get on your high horse, I don't mean any harm. Besides, perhaps it's as well you are not interested in the lady of the house, for from all accounts there's another with a rather surprising involvement."

"Another?"

Digby nodded, glancing across the crowded vestibule to the doorway, where Caroline was saying farewell to several guests who had to depart rather earlier than expected. "Yes," he murmured, "I am told that there was a very pretty scene outside first thing this morning, a fond farewell between Lexham and Lexham."

Hal's face was very still. "I beg your pardon?"

"I confess to being surprised that Marcia Chaddington attempted anything to harm Miss Lexham, for from all accounts until very recently the likely perpetrator of such a trick would have been the Earl of Lexham. Now it seems that

Lexham and his lovely cousin are far from at odds with one another.''

"Digby, if you don't come to the point, I swear I will wring your scrawny neck!''

"All right, dear boy, have patience. It seems that the two were seen embracing, and enjoying a kiss which was far from being a cousinly peck on the cheek. Far from it. That would be a turn-up, would it not? After all the furor caused by the will, Lexham does a complete turnabout and falls in love with the lady!''

Hal did not reply for a moment, but his eyes narrowed a little as he glanced at Caroline's smiling face as she moved among the guests. "Yes," he murmured, "it would indeed be a turnabout.''

"Still,'' said Digby, smiling a sleek smile, "it is of no concern to you, is it?''

"None whatever.''

"By the way, no doubt you've been too preoccupied today to have heard the latest news from Paris.''

"News?''

"It seems they've caught the assassin—a fellow named Cantillon. They don't know anything more from him, however, for he's keeping a still tongue in his head. They reckon that this means he still has accomplices on the loose.''

"Probably.'' Hal's expression was thoughtful.

"Ah, I see old Fennimore over there. I must have a word with him. Good-bye, Hal.''

"Good-bye, Digby.''

At that moment Gaspard Duvall made an appearance among the guests, a number of them having sent requests to the kitchens. He was greatly applauded and congratulated upon having prepared the most sumptuous of wedding feasts, and his bright eyes danced with pleasure and pride. Hal watched him, his face still unsmiling and pensive.

Caroline found herself at his side. "Is something wrong, Sir Henry?" she inquired, seeing his stern expression.

"Wrong, Miss Lexham?" he replied coldly. "Why, nothing at all.''

"Sir Henry?'' She was shaken by the change in him. He was almost a stranger, and there was no warmth in him at all.

"You must excuse me, madam, if I find it hard to accept that you would not only be so foolish and misguided, but also so brazen and improper as to indulge in fond and intimate embraces with your cousin in public!'' With a stiff nod of his head, he left her.

Stunned, she remained where she was.

She did not see him again to speak to throughout the evening. The bride and groom departed in their white landau, waved off by their happy friends and relatives, and after that the gathering began to thin. The celebrations continued until well into the night, and it was two in the morning before Caroline could at last take herself wearily to her bed.

There she found that before going away, Jennifer had stolen into her apartment and left a little piece of the wedding cake, together with a traditional little verse, written in her own hand.

> *But, madam, as a present take*
> *This little portion of bride-cake;*
> *Fast any Friday in the year,*
> *When Venus mounts the starry sphere,*
> *Thrust this at night beneath pillow clear;*
> *In morning slumber you will seem*
> *To enjoy your lover in a dream.*

Slowly her fingers closed over the paper, crumpling it, and she closed her eyes as the hot tears of misery and renewed heartbreak stung her lids.

She cried herself to sleep, curled up in the vast bed, her face hidden even from the darkness.

ill terrified, she nodded her head. Slowly he removed his

, jerking his head again to indicate that she had to get out

Chapter 27

The rough hand closed over her mouth in the faint gray light of dawn. Terrified she struggled, but his strength was too great and he merely tightened his grip, his uncouth fingers digging painfully into her flesh.

"Be still, wench, or it'll be the worse for you!"

His voice was unrefined and his breath smelled of ale. She knew that he meant the threat and she lay still, her eyes huge with fear as she stared up at him. The dawn was but minutes old and the light so muted that he was barely discernible. He was dirty and unshaven, wearing a battered boxcoat and wide-brimmed hat pulled low on his forehead. As she watched, he turned to jerk his head at someone she could not see.

"Got the letter, Ben?"

" 'Course I've got the ruddy letter!" growled the other, his voice as coarse as the first man's. "Where's it to be put?"

"Shove it on the mantel shelf, and be quick about it!"

She was aware of a shadowy figure moving silently across the room, just on the edge of her vision. It stretched up and left something small, oblong, and white against a candlestick.

Her captor returned his attention to her then, shaking her a little to show that he meant business. "Now then, my pretty,

f you know what's good for you, you'll come with us nice
and quiet. One squeak, and it'll be the last sound you ever
make? Got me?"

Still terrified, she nodded her head. Slowly he removed his
hand, jerking his head again to indicate that she had to get out
of the bed. His eyes rested leeringly on her bare legs, and she
sought in vain to conceal them with the folds of her nightgown.

"Don't worry, my lovely," he said coarsely. "It ain't for
the likes of Ben and me to gaze upon you. It's for a certain
gentleman to do that."

"Gentleman?"

In reply he reached forward, and even in the half-light, she
saw the glint of a metal blade. The knife pressed against her
throat. "I said no sound, sweetheart, and that means no
questions either. Here, get this shawl around you and then
come quietly; we don't want to wake anyone from their
beauty sleep now, do we?" The blade's tip pressed a little
more against her skin and then was removed.

With a trembling hand, she took the proffered shawl,
wrapping it tightly around her shoulders. He pushed her
roughly toward the door and she stumbled a little, crying out.
With an oath he seized her, twisting one arm up sharply
behind her back.

"I'll break every bone in your lily-white body if you open
your mouth again!" he breathed, keeping his grip upon her
and nodding at Ben, who softly opened the door and slipped
out into the dark, deserted vestibule.

The painful twist of her arm brought tears to her eyes as
she was propelled across the cold, tiled floor, her bare feet
soft and silent. The dark light robbed the wedding flowers
and garlands of their color and made the white ribbon knots
pinned to the sofas look ghostly. Gone now was the joyous
atmosphere of the marriage celebrations, and instead her fear
lent a menace to even the most homely of items. The arches
leading to the inner vestibule appeared to open onto a
mysterious unknown, the statues in the wall niches seemed to
move just a little, and the crystal droplets of the chandeliers
jingled very softly in the draft of cold air sweeping in from
the open front door.

She wanted to scream out for help, but she was too afraid.
She did not know who was abducting her or why they were
doing it; she did not know who the unknown gentleman was

to whom they were evidently taking her. As she was pushed out into the cold March dawn, she looked desperately back at the shadowy vestibule, willing someone to appear and see what was happening, but no one did.

Tendrils of mist rose from the cobbles where an unmarked carriage stood waiting at the foot of the steps. Its blinds were down, its wheels were muffled, and the team's hooves were wrapped in sacking. It had not made a sound as it arrived, and it would not make a sound when it left again. . . .

Her legs felt suddenly weak as she was half dragged down the steps to the carriage, and she struggled as the door swung silently open to admit her. Sensing that she was about to scream in spite of her fear, her assailant swiftly put his dirty hand over her mouth again, heaving her bodily up into the carriage, where other hands caught her. Another man's hand was put over her mouth, a softer hand with several rings upon its fingers. Desperately she squirmed and wriggled, and she was only vaguely aware of her new captor's sudden gasp and the loosening of his grip upon her. Shaken, but alert enough to seize her opportunity, she twisted wildly away from him, scrambling to the doorway and out of the carriage, tumbling helplessly onto the cold, damp cobbles, where she lay for a moment, winded. Almost in tears, she waited for rough hands to seize her once more, but when someone touched her, it was with gentle concern.

"Are you all right, Caro?"

An overwhelming surge of relief swept weakeningly over her as she gazed up into Hal's eyes as he crouched momentarily beside her. She could only nod, watching as he straightened once more, and it was then that she saw he had a pistol in his hand and was leveling it at the occupant of the carriage. There was no sign of the two men who had abducted her, and she was vaguely aware of their footsteps as they fled into the murky dawn.

The barrel of the pistol motioned to whoever was in the carriage to climb down, and she got slowly to her feet, staring as Dominic reluctantly alighted. He did not even glance at her, his attention was fully upon Hal, whose eyes were as cold and hard as flint. "My lord of Lexham," he murmured, "I believe a word or two of explanation is required."

"I have nothing to say to you, Seymour."

"Oh, but you have, you have a great deal to say, my fine lordling, for kidnapping is not a pretty crime. Well?"

"What a bad penny you are, Seymour, continually turning up when you are least expected and least wanted."

"How unfortunate for you, Lexham, but then my activities would not be of any concern to you if you did not have such foul crimes to conceal." The pistol moved threateningly. "Your explanation, there's a good fellow."

Dominic's fearful eyes followed the pistol, but he said nothing.

"Very well, I shall furnish a likely interpretation myself," said Hal, his tone almost conversational. "If I have to guess why the Earl of Lexham would want to abduct his cousin, I would say that it is because he has perceived a rather neat way of circumventing his father's will, the terms of which state that within six months he is not only to prove himself to be a good boy, he is also to have taken for himself a wife, a lady of name and property." A shrewd smile played about Hal's lips as he saw how Dominic's eyes slid guiltily away. "What better name could that wife have than Lexham? And what more desirable property could she possess than Lexham House? You could not afford to wait for those six months to pass, could you? You saw that she was going to make a success of her venture and so you resorted to this extreme length in order to prevent her from keeping the house forever. Oh, you were cunning enough, I suppose, deciding to be all charm and honor toward the unfortunate lady, making certain that whispers sprang up about the apparent intimacy which had begun to flourish between two former enemies. Her abduction would not then arouse the hue and cry it might otherwise have done, especially as it could be made to appear like a romantic elopement, brought about by true love and encouraged by the happiness and atmosphere of my sister's wedding. There, is that not the truth of it, Lexham?"

Caroline had listened in silence, and as Hal's explanation unfolded, she knew that it was the truth. Now she understood Dominic's sudden *volte-face*, she realized now why he had suddenly been so friendly and charming when encountering her with Mrs. Hollingsworth in Bond Street, why he had appeared so miraculously when she was stranded in Covent Garden market. It had all been part of a careful plan to lull her into unguardedness and to convince society that the bitter

feud was ended, and in its place was a romantic involvement.
How easily it might have come off, for everyone knew how
narrow was the border between love and hate, how closely
those two intense emotions marched together. No one would
have truly believed her when she protested that she was
abducted against her will, and Dominic would have been free
to dispose of his detested cousin as and when he pleased. . . .
She shivered a little, knowing that tonight she probably owed
Hal Seymour her very life.

The pistol motioned again. "Is that not the truth of it,
Lexham?" repeated Hal.

"How clever you are, Seymour, so sharp that with luck
you will one day deal yourself a mortal wound."

"If I do, Lexham, you will not be around to rejoice about
it." Hal raised the pistol a little, seeming to take aim.

Caroline's eyes widened with shock and Dominic gave a
start of fear, pressing back against the carriage. The coachman stared down from his perch, believing that he was about
to witness a cold-blooded murder.

Hal gave a contemptuous laugh then, lowering the pistol.
"Not so brave now, eh? It is one thing to play the bully with
a helpless woman, but quite another to face another man. It
would give me great pleasure to put an end to you, but to
indulge myself in such a way would not assist Miss Lexham,
who would inevitably become the center of a scandal—which
in turn might put her tenure of the house at some risk. Get out
of here, Lexham, but I warn you that if you so much as come
near this house again, or if you make one move against Miss
Lexham, then you will hear from me—and I promise you that
when I catch you, there will be no one around to see what
fate befalls you."

For a moment Dominic was rooted to the spot with terror,
but then he scrambled back into the carriage, shouting to the
stunned coachman to drive on, and with as much speed as
possible. The whip cracked and the team strained forward,
but their efforts were eerily silent, their muffled hooves making no sound. Quietly the dark carriage drew away, its wheels
turning secretly. Only the jingle of the harness broke the
illusion that some phantom was abroad in London. . . .

The moment the carriage had turned into Mayfair Street,
Hal checked that the pistol was not cocked before concealing
it in a hidden pocket inside his coat.

In spite of the shock of what had so nearly befallen her, Caroline still sensed his withdrawal, which was so deliberate that it was almost as if he had walked away from her. Her lips trembled a little as she drew her shawl more closely around herself. "S-sir Henry, I am so m-much in your debt, that I don't know how I may thank you," she began.

"I do not require your thanks, Miss Lexham," he replied abruptly. "Let us just leave it that I happened to be in a position to again be of assistance to you."

"I cannot leave it simply at that, Sir Henry, for I do not know what dreadful fate might have befallen me had you not been here tonight."

He smiled coolly. "That fate, my dear Miss Lexham, would in some ways have been little more than your recent behavior has deserved."

Her breath caught and she flinched as if he had struck her. "How can you say that?" she whispered.

"I can say it, madam, because whatever your cousin may have done, he found it extraordinarily easy to win your favors. I gave you my protection tonight, because it was no more or less than any gentleman of honor would have done, but do not imagine that any word or gesture on my part indicates a softening of my contempt for you. You appear to be a woman of little virtue, Miss Lexham, and therefore my advice to you is that you curb your immodest conduct or you will after all forfeit Lexham House."

She felt quite numb, and the hurt was so great that it became a physical pain, sharp and deep. "If that is truly what you think, Sir Henry," she said at last, "I honestly do not know why you bothered to save me. You are entirely wrong about me, but I shall not attempt to defend myself before your unjust condemnation. I thank you again for rescuing me, and I do not think you will be able to find fault in my future conduct, for I will at all times be polite toward you—which in spite of my indebtedness to you, you certainly do not deserve." Pride made her face him in that moment, for nothing would have allowed her to reveal the infinite suffering he caused her. Her head held high, she turned to go back up the steps, not looking back once as she entered the still-silent vestibule.

But as she reached the safety and shelter of her own apartment, she could not stem the tears. Her whole body shook with anguish, but she did not make a sound. Leaning her head back against the closed door, she closed her eyes as she wept.

The sun had risen in a clear sky when Mrs. Hollingsworth brought her her coffee. Caroline was seated in the window, wearing a plain blue gown, her hair dressed neatly beneath her little day bonnet. She had restored a little color to her pale cheeks with rouge, but she could not hide the marks of weeping around her large, dark eyes. The letter her two abductors had so carefully left upon the mantelpiece now lay in ashes in the fireplace. She had read it once, and it confirmed everything Hal had said of Dominic; it purported to be a brief note from her, explaining her absence as an elopement with her "dearest Dominic."

Mrs. Hollingsworth perceived at once that something was wrong, but for the moment she said nothing. Instead she rattled on about how quiet a day it would be after all the excitement of the wedding—and that peace and quiet would be a blessing for poor Gaspard, who had had something of a fright during the night when returning to his room after taking a walk in the fresh air with Boisville to dispel a headache. "An intruder had been searching his room and can only have left a moment before my poor Gaspard entered!"

Caroline was immediately roused from her lethargy, looking up sharply. "At what time was this?"

"Just as dawn was breaking, I believe."

Thoughtfully, Caroline stirred her coffee. An intruder in Gaspard's room? And at that particular time? Could it have been Hal, who had been so fortuitously abroad at precisely that moment and who had taken the unusual precaution of taking a pistol with him?

Mrs. Hollingsworth looked out of the window, noticing nothing in Caroline's reaction. "What a lovely day it is. I believe it is even more fine than yesterday. I wonder if Lord and Lady Carstairs have sailed for France yet?"

"No, I believe they intend leaving Dover later in the day."

The housekeeper smiled. "How wonderful it must be to be going on honeymoon to Venice. I know that it is considered a little vulgar to use that word, but honeymoon is so much more romantic and descriptive than merely going away. Oh, well, I cannot stand here daydreaming about such things. I have work to do. And today I must convince Gaspard that he must be more careful about locking his window properly. I've told him time and time again that there are more thieves in Mayfair than anywhere else, for it's here that they find the houses containing most valuables.'' She went to the door.

"I will not be long," Caroline called after her.

The housekeeper looked gently at her. "Take all the time in the world; my dear, and if you feel like remaining quietly in here, then you do so."

Caroline smiled. "Thank you, but it will do me more good to find something to do."

"I don't know what has upset you, my dear, but if there is anything I can do to—''

"There isn't anything, Mrs. Hollingsworth, but thank you all the same.''

When the housekeeper had gone, Caroline sipped her coffee, thinking again about the mysterious intruder in Gaspard's room. Of course it had been Hal; that was the obvious explanation for him being out and about at the very time when Dominic's henchmen had come to seize her. Hal had been searching for something in Gaspard's room, but what? Evidence of a Bonapartist plot here in London? Evidence of a connection between the chef and the arrested assassin, Cantillon? The thoughts milled urgently around in her head, and at last she got to her feet. She would have to ask Hal about her suspicions; she would have to confront him and risk his displeasure and continued contempt.

Chapter 28

It was to be well into the afternoon before she found an opportunity of speaking to him, for he had come down very late for breakfast and had then gone out. As he had descended the grand staircase, Caroline had been greeting some newly arrived guests. Her eyes had met his, and he had accorded her the coolest of greetings, which coolness her response matched. He could have known nothing of the truth from her expressionless face. Several people noticed the chill exchange and wondered greatly what had happened to give rise to such a remarkable contrast.

He returned to the hotel in the early afternoon, and after writing a number of letters in the library, he went for a stroll in the gardens, where the daffodils were now in full bloom and the blossom trees were bright with pink and white. It was here that at last she confronted him.

"Sir Henry?"

He turned toward her. "I don't think we have anything to say to each other, Miss Lexham."

"You may think not, but I happen to think differently, sir," she replied. "It concerns the intruder in Monsieur Duvall's room last night."

228

His eyes narrowed and she saw the veiled expression close over his face. "Intruder?"

"I believe you know full well to whom I am referring, Sir Henry."

"Miss Lexham," he said a little testily, "I have no desire to discuss this or anything else with you."

"I am sorry to hear it, sir, for I have every intention of doing just that," she retorted, an edge to her voice. "Although you may think it is none of my concern, I happen to think that it is very much my concern as it is taking place on property which for the moment at least belongs to me!"

An angry brightness flashed in his eyes at her defiance, but he saw that a lady and gentleman strolling nearby were glancing a little curiously at them, and so he suddenly changed his manner, even forcing a smile as he offered her his arm. "Very well, Miss Lexham, what is it you wish to say to me?"

They walked side by side, but although her hand rested on his sleeve, it was as if a chasm gaped between them. They were complete strangers, with none of the easy rapport that had once distinguished their relationship.

"I am waiting, Miss Lexham."

"I believe that you were the intruder, Sir Henry."

"You certainly have come straight to the point, haven't you?"

"I have little reason to do otherwise, sir."

"So it seems. I do not admit to anything, Miss Lexham."

"Does that include the possibility of Bonapartists in this hotel?"

He halted, turning to look at her. "What a very quaint notion, Miss Lexham."

"Is it? Correct me if I am wrong, but I strongly suspect that your brief to guard the Duke of Wellington has led you to Monsieur Duvall, and that that was the reason why you so suddenly decided to have your town house refurbished and why you took up residence at the Oxenford. I further suspect that the forthcoming banquet is expected to flush out any conspiracy, and that that is why you have arranged it and why you are so closely involved in it. The duke's sudden decision to remove the banquet to the Lexham is the reason for Monsieur Duvall's change of heart, and therefore the reason for a similar change in you, Sir Henry. If I am correct, and I am sure that I am, then I would like you to tell me so, for I believe that I have the right to know if my hotel is to be the scene of an attempt to assassinate the duke."

For a moment he was silent. "You have evidently given the matter a great deal of thought, Miss Lexham."

"In between my various improper activities, sir, I have obviously had little else to do," she replied coldly.

A faint humor gleamed momentarily in his hazel eyes.

"I am waiting, Sir Henry."

"Very well, I admit that up to a certain point you are correct, Miss Lexham, that is indeed why I am involved in the banquet, it is indeed why I left the Oxenford. That is where it all ends, however, for there has been reliable intelligence from France that if there had been a conspiracy here, it was no longer to be put into operation."

"But you are still at the Lexham, Sir Henry."

"So I am, to be sure. That is because it has been deemed a wise precaution, no more and no less. In the past there have been very definite connections between Gaspard Duvall and certain Bonapartist extremists."

She stared at him. "But that simply does not seem possible, not of Monsieur Duvall!"

"Come now, Miss Lexham, do not be naive. He is a Frenchman."

"But—"

"Even a chef is allowed his political views and his patriotism, madam; surely you will agree with that?"

"Yes."

"Duvall supported Bonaparte and this political leaning brought him into contact with some of those we now know to have conspired to assassinate the duke. My brief, as you describe it, was to keep an eye upon him, which is precisely what I have been doing, to the best of my ability. It is now firmly believed that there is no danger to the duke on this side of the Channel, but, with your permission, of course, I intend to remain here at the Lexham at least until after the banquet."

"As a precaution?"

"Yes, Miss Lexham, as a precaution."

"And was your intrusion into his room last night also merely a precaution?"

His eyes were opaque. "Yes. You need not concern yourself that your premises are to be the scene of a historic murder, Miss Lexham. The name of your hotel will not go down in the annals of time as the place where the hero of Waterloo met his doom. Have I allayed your fears?"

"I suppose so." But as she spoke she knew that she was not entirely happy.

"Excellent," he said with some asperity. "Now we may terminate this disagreeable discussion. Good day to you, Miss Lexham." He stepped away, inclining his head with an outward appearance of courtesy for the benefit of anyone who might be looking, but in reality the gesture was insulting.

She fought back the tears as she watched him walk away across the flowery lawn.

Meanwhile a new arrival was approaching the doors of the Lexham Hotel, his rather battered and lowly hackney coach being greeted with curious and astonished glances by the two footmen as it turned into the wide courtyard. Weary and aching after his two-hundred-mile journey from Selford, Richard Marchand gazed out at the great house, unable to conceal the amazement he felt on seeing how splendid was his cousin Caroline's inheritance. Dismay followed closely upon the amazement, for if this was the life she now knew, what possible hope could he have of persuading her to return to Selford with him?

He alighted heavily at the steps, nodding at the porter, who tentatively inquired if he could be of any service. "Yes, you may inform Miss Lexham that Mr. Marchand is here."

"Very well, sir. If you will please take a seat?" The porter ushered him into the vestibule and indicated one of the comfortable sofas.

Richard sank wearily onto the sofa nearest the fireplace, glancing around unhappily at the elegant furnishings, the efficient waiters, and the little page boy who was searching for one of the guests, his high-pitched voice ringing out clearly.

Only seconds passed before Richard became suddenly and sharply aware of the conversation of two gentlemen seated nearby.

"And I tell you," said one, "that you would lose your wager. The lady has succumbed. She's Seymour's mistress, right enough. I knew that when I spoke to him about her yesterday at his sister's wedding. He was doing his damnedest to appear disinterested in her activities, but the opposite was obviously the case.''

''So you appear to think. I'm not so certain,'' replied his companion. ''I don't believe Caroline Lexham has succumbed to anyone—except maybe to her cousin, the earl, who incidentally, has suddenly rushed off out of Town again.''

''Forget Lexham,'' insisted the first man. ''It's Seymour whose name will come out of the hat, you mark my words.''

''I've followed your bright guesses before, Digby, and look where it's got me!'' grumbled the second man.

''This is no guess, my dear fellow, it's fact. Why else has he come rushing here? Why else does he pretend their friendship is platonic?''

''I don't follow—''

''The terms of the will, dear fellow! If she does anything slightly doubtful, then she loses this pile of bricks and mortar. *Ergo*, they make it appear that they mean nothing to each other.''

''Ah, I begin to see what you mean—''

''At this very moment they are out walking in the gardens together, and yet they would have us believe that they practically loathe each other. It's quite clear to me, dear fellow, that Caroline Lexham is Hal Seymour's mistress, which is what poor Marcia Chaddington must have known as well, hence her foolish prank at the wedding yesterday. If you still believe the contrary, then I suggest you put your money where your mouth is.''

''Oh, no, Digby, I won't rise to that. I admit defeat. I've come round to your way of thinking: the lady has indeed succumbed.''

At that moment Caroline herself came hurrying into the vestibule, her plain blue skirts rustling. ''Richard?'' Smiling, she came toward him, her hands extended.

Slowly he rose from his seat. ''Caroline?''

Digby and his companion looked uneasily at each other, wondering how much of their indiscreet conversation he had overheard, and therefore how much of it would be relayed to Caroline, who was evidently a very close friend.

She smiled. ''I trust your journey was not too wearisome.''

''It was as one would expect.''

''Is something wrong?''

"I think it is, Caroline, very wrong. I believe we should speak somewhere in private."

She stared up into his stern blue eyes. "Very well, if you will come this way." She led him to her private apartment, where she turned to face him, her hands clasped neatly before her. "Well?"

"It does not please me at all when the first thing I hear discussed on my arrival here is whether or not you are Sir Henry Seymour's mistress."

"I beg your pardon?" she asked faintly, her eyes widening.

"I am sure you heard me well enough, for poor hearing was never one of your afflictions, Caroline. Are you his mistress?"

"No!"

"But he is something to you, isn't he?"

"No." She looked away.

"Don't lie to me, Caroline, for that I find supremely insulting. I love you very much, too much to enjoy having to question you like this, but it simply isn't on to find that your name is being tossed around in wagers concerning chastity!"

"Don't be so pompous, Richard."

"Forgive me, but I fear I am not well versed in how one behaves in such circumstances."

"And don't be sarcastic either, for it does not suit you. I cannot help it if people make such wagers. All I can say is that I am not Sir Henry's mistress; indeed, I believe you will find that he loathes my very name."

"Yes, I understand that that is what the world is supposed to think."

"I am not telling you fibs, Richard," she said quietly, containing her anger because she knew his anxiety was indeed born of his love for her.

"What is Seymour to you?"

"Nothing."

"That is not so, and we both know it. I know you too well in some ways, Caroline, certainly well enough to know when you are attempting to pull the wool over my eyes."

She turned away with a sigh. "It isn't your eyes I attempt to draw the wool over," she said softly. "I believe it is my own. You want the absolute truth? Very well, you shall have it. I love Hal Seymour with all my heart, but he does not like or even respect me. He is not interested in me, Richard, and

certainly would not wish to take me as his mistress. I tell yo
this, though, were he to crook his little finger, then I woul
run to him. I would be glad to be his mistress, Richard, glad
There, is that enough honesty for you?'' She looked at hin
again, her gray eyes very dark.

Slowly he nodded. ''Yes, it is enough.''

''I'm sorry, Richard, I don't want to hurt you—''

''I know.''

She went to him, taking his hands. ''I would have mad
you very unhappy, for I would have been always dissatisfied
always craving something you could not give me.''

His fingers closed around hers. ''Instead, you will mak
yourself unhappy, craving something you will never have.''

She lowered her eyes. ''At least only I will be responsible
for my unhappiness, and not also for yours. You will ge
over me, Richard, and you will marry someone like Jose-
phine Leyburn.''

''I cannot bear the creature.''

''She is just the sort of wife you need, Richard Marchand.
Now then, we've said enough of all this, so let us begin ou
conversation again. Why, Richard, how good it is to see you
again! I trust you had a not too wearisome journey!''

He was forced to laugh. ''You are incorrigible, Caroline
Lexham, and I wonder if I will ever get over you, for as they
say in the theater, you will be a very difficult act to follow!''

She pretended to look aghast. ''Why, Squire Marchand,
what would you be knowing about such wicked places as
theaters? What *would* Parson Aylesbury say? And should
Goodwife Whittaker so much as learn one word, why the
whole of Dartmoor woud soon learn of it!''

Still smiling, he pulled her close, his cheek resting against
her little day bonnet. But she did not see how his smile
slowly and thoughtfully faded. He loved her too much to be
satisfied with accepting what she said; nothing would do but
that he spoke with Sir Henry Seymour and learned for himself
how things were.

''Sir Henry?''

Hal looked up from writing to see a tall, fair-haired young
man dressed in good, but hardly fashionable attire. ''Sir?''

''Richard Marchand, squire of Selford. Your servant, sir.''

"Marchand? Ah, yes, Miss Lexham's cousin." Hal rose politely to his feet.

"I trust you will forgive this intrusion upon your privacy, Sir Henry, but I wished to thank you for having assisted my cousin on her journey to London."

"Think nothing of it, Mr. Marchand, for I did but do what any gentleman would have done." He felt he should say a little more. "Are you in Town for long?"

"A day or so, I merely came to see how she was."

"She appears to be very well, and certainly is making a success of her venture." Hal's hand indicated the surroundings. "You—you are a guest, Sir Henry?"

Ah, so that was it. "Yes, Mr. Marchand, but through no actual choice, for I have charge of the forthcoming banquet, which the Duke of Wellington has decided must take place here now, instead of at the Oxenford. I shall be quitting the Lexham directly after the banquet, when I trust my house in Hanover Square will be ready."

Richard was perceptibly easier. "I trust the banquet will be a truly memorable occasion, Sir Henry."

Hal smiled just a little. "Not too memorable," he said softly. "That would not do at all."

Richard withdrew then, feeling satisfied that what Caroline had said was true, for whatever her feelings were, Sir Henry Seymour's were equally as plain: he did not care at all for her. Her honor and good name were not at risk.

Hal sat down again, picking up his pen, but after a moment he cast it down again, the force of the action spattering ink over the page. Would to God the banquet was over and done with and he could quit this damned house!

Caroline waited in her apartment. A table had been laid for two, but Richard was very late. Anxiously she stood by the window, looking out into the darkness of the spring night. Mrs. Hollingsworth had said that Richard was closeted in the library with Hal, and now she could only wait in dread to learn what had been said. Would Hal inform Richard of his true opinion of her? Would he relate to him the tale of her dealings with Dominic? Or worse, would Richard reveal to Hal the truth about her love for him? In an agony of suspense, she could only wait. Then she heard his step approaching.

He entered, smiling quickly at her. "Forgive me, Caroline. I know I am late."

Relief swept through her on seeing that smile. "You are forgiven, sir, especially as I have something to confess."

"Confess?"

"You are not to enjoy your favorite roast beef after all."

"Oh, Caroline! I especially asked—"

"Monsieur Duvall, the chef, threw back his hands in horror at the very suggestion that he should prepare such a plain English dish, and instead he has created something especially for tonight."

"Something French and covered in sauce," grumbled Richard.

"Don't be disagreeable and biased," she reproved. "For until you have tried French cooking, how can you possibly express an opinion. Sit down now, and behave yourself, Squire Marchand."

But as Gaspard personally carried in the first course, it was not of the dinner that she thought, it was of her overwhelming gladness that nothing had been said between Hal and Richard that would have any repercussions. Hal remained in ignorance of her love for him, and Richard had not been regaled with the tale of her apparently disreputable conduct. Her eyes were very bright as she raised her glass of wine, smiling across the table at her cousin.

Chapter 29

Richard remained at the Lexham for two more days and then he returned to Selford, and he and Caroline parted very amicably; indeed their friendship now at last appeared to be on the sort of footing she had always wanted, with him accepting once and for all that she would never take him as her husband. She still did not know what had passed between the two men, but she knew that somehow what Hal had said had put Richard's mind at rest. She knew she would never learn the truth from either man, for Richard behaved as if they had barely exchanged two words, and Hal was as remote and disdainful as he had so suddenly become on the night of the wedding.

Richard was not the only person to quit London that day; so also did Marcia, Lady Chaddington. Having attempted to destroy Caroline in front of witnesses, her failure had inevitably been as public, and by the day after the wedding, the story of what had happened was all over Town. She had become the laughingstock of the *beau monde* and her humiliation was made complete by the fact that Hal had rejected her. The dazzling, successful hostess, the beauty who had reigned for several Seasons and who could have expected to reign for several more, was by her own actions the butt of society's scorn, and she could not bear it. With the Season about to get into full swing, Lady Chaddington closed her beautiful Berkeley Square house and left London in an anonymous carriage, while her brother, feeling that a little too much of the ignominy had brushed off upon him, decided that it would be prudent to return to his own estates for a while.

Dominic's defeat was not so public a thing, but nevertheless he too had immediately removed himself from Town for a while, journeying back to County Durham to attend to "urgent" business there. His departure left Caroline free of her enemies for the first time since she had come to London, but she found no joy in the situation. The Lexham Hotel went from strength to strength as the days passed, providing the most luxurious and exclusive accommodation in Town, as well as the finest cuisine. The distinguished guests and visitors found the new enterprise to be everything they could have wished, and the other important hotels found that the rival they had scorned was a very worthy rival indeed. It seemed to Caroline that nothing could now prevent her from meeting the terms of her uncle's will so that when the allotted period of six months had passed, Lexham House would be hers and she would be a very wealthy woman. But it was a hollow glory, for she was more desperately unhappy than she had ever been in her life. Hal Seymour lodged beneath her roof, she saw him every day, and she endured the contempt in his eyes. She did not approach him, nor he her; it was as if they had never before met, never spoken, and certainly never laughed together. There were many nights when her misery was too great and she cried herself to sleep, her face hidden in the softness of her pillow.

One thing provided her with a welcome release from the pain, and that was the immense amount of preparation required for the great banquet. This might have caused her more distress, for by rights she should have dealt directly with Hal, but she chose instead to delegate this considerable responsibility to Mrs. Hollingsworth. The housekeeper had wondered greatly about this, but had begun to realize now that Hal Seymour was the cause of Caroline's unhappiness. And so each day Mrs. Hollingsworth consulted with him about the banquet, and each evening she sat with Caroline to discuss what had been said.

The banquet was set to be a much more dazzling and

important function than Jennifer's wedding had been, and glancing through the guest list, Caroline saw the names of nearly every gentleman of importance in the land, including several dukes. She realized with quite a jolt that the duke's request that she greet him on his arrival at the hotel meant that she would be the only woman present. Glancing through the guest list again, this time with even greater apprehension, she noticed a name she had missed before: Dominic would be present.

Gaspard was, naturally enough, of supreme importance where the banquet was concerned, and he and Caroline spent long hours discussing the complicated and immense menu called for by the importance of the occasion. She found it difficult to treat him exactly as she had before, for she could not forget what she now knew, but somehow it was hard to believe that there was anything sinister about him. He displayed no unease or secretiveness when speaking of the banquet or the Duke of Wellington, and in fact he seemed to be more jovial than usual, not having been indisposed with a headache or even the smallest of black moods for some time now. He enjoyed creating the menu, and his enthusiasm was quite infectious.

The menu was bewildering, and appeared to offer so many different dishes that no one could possibly sample them all without being decidedly ill for a week. There were to be four soups, two thick and two clear, hot *hors d'oeuvres* and cold *hors d'oeuvres,* intermediate fish courses, intermediate meat, poultry and game courses, and a variety of very splendid *entrées.* There were to be hot *rôts* and cold *rôts,* and last but not least, a seemingly endless list of delicious *entremets,* from *bombes, mousses,* and *sorbets* to cream flans, fruit tarts, jellies, and molds. And the *pièce de résistance,* Gaspard's *pièce montée* was to be a splendid confection called *gâteau Wellington,* which was to depict the moment of victory at Waterloo. He had prepared a rough drawing of this magnificent creation, which was to have cannon made of cake, chocolate barrels, standards fashioned from spun sugar and rice paper, and a statue of the Iron Duke himself, mounted on his charger Copenhagen, made entirely from sugar. Inside this *gâteau* was to be a filling of cherry ice with grapes and currants, and the whole thing was to be carried shoulder high to the table toward the end of the banquet and set down on a bed of crushed ice before the duke himself. This was to be the crowning glory of the banquet, and Caroline had to agree with the excited, pleased chef that it would indeed provide the whole evening with a fitting conclusion.

It was an unusually humid, close day for late March and the windows of Caroline's apartment were open as she and the chef discussed the details of the banquet menu. Outside not a leaf stirred on the trees, and sounds seemed to carry much further than usual. At last the whole menu had been discussed in depth and she agreed to all the chef's suggestions, including the *gâteau Wellington*, trusting as she did so that her account with Messieurs Coutts would not suffer too cataclysmic a shock.

Gaspard departed from her apartment in high spirits, determined to set about ordering some of the more particular ingredients immediately. The Severn salmon would come live from the supplier in Gloucester, the mullet from Harper's. The other fish would come only from McDonald's, the *foie gras* and truffles from Rimell's, and so on, each specific item coming from the tradesman who specialized in it. The orders had to be placed swiftly, for with the banquet set to take place in two weeks' time, the chef and his *brigade* had to be sure all the agreed-upon dishes could be provided.

Throughout the day everyone commented upon the unusually close weather, applying the word "thundery" even though there had been no rumble from the cloudy skies, no drop of heavy rain. In the evening the windows of the dining room stood open and the ladies busily employed their fans. Caroline was glad for once of the fashion for wearing the flimsiest lawn, silk, or muslin even in the depths of winter, for tonight such light materials were the very thing.

A group of young gentlemen had taken a private room for a dinner party, intent upon celebrating a handsome win by one of their number at the tables of a nearby gaming hell. Boisterous and a little merry, they insisted upon Caroline joining them, which eventually she did, for in spite of their being just a little the worse for drink, they were chivalrous and agreeable, toasting her health and making no unwelcome advances. The noisy little party had broken up at last at two in the morning, and Mrs. Hollingsworth joined Caroline to hand each gentleman a lighted candlestick. Laughing and shushing, the tipsy guests wended their unsteady way up to their rooms, and after a minute or two silence reigned throughout the house.

Caroline smiled at the housekeeper. "And so to our beds too, and I for one will sleep like the proverbial log." She saw the other's slightly withdrawn face. "Is something wrong, Mrs. Hollingsworth?"

"No. At least, not really—"

"Please tell me, for maybe I can help."

"It's nothing like that, it's simply that Gaspard is not himself at all tonight. In fact I think he is quite unwell."

Caroline stared. "Unwell? But when I discussed the banquet menu with him he seemed in excellent spirits."

"So he was, but that was before something very silly upset him."

"What?"

The housekeeper looked a little embarrassed. "It was so foolish, and the girl meant no harm—"

"Please explain, Mrs. Hollingsworth."

"Earlier tonight there was a flower woman in Mayfair Street and one of the footmen, who is stepping out with one of the parlor maids, bought a posy of violets for his sweetheart. She pinned them to her bodice and came into the kitchens. Gaspard took one look and became so upset and angry about it that he reduced the unfortunate girl to tears. Really, Miss Lexham, it was so unlike him that I fear he must be ill, especially as he then promptly retired to his bed with another headache."

"He has been working very hard, and today has been very close and humid. Perhaps that is all there was to it. He will be himself again by the morning, and he will probably be so kind to the poor maid in order to make up that he will reduce her to tears all over again. Now then, don't you worry anymore tonight."

Mrs. Hollingsworth smiled. "Thank you. I feel foolish for worrying now. Well, I suppose we should all retire to our beds now, for it is very late indeed, and I rather fancy that for that party of young gentlemen, there will be headaches of another sort come the morning."

Caroline laughed. "There will indeed, for it was not only the quantity that they celebrated with, it was the mixture. Good night, Mrs. Hollingsworth, and don't worry anymore about Gaspard."

"Good night, Miss Lexham."

Caroline watched the housekeeper hurry away in the direction of the butler's pantry entrance, and her smile faded a little unhappily. She could not help wishing that the housekeeper's heart was not so engaged by Gaspard Duvall. As she walked toward her own apartment, she hoped that her unease about the chef, caused simply and solely by what she had learned from Hal, was not well founded; in fact, she hoped that Hal was totally wrong about his past.

She lay awake in her bed, the draperies still tied back and the window open just a little to allow a small draft of air from outside. Her hair was brushed loose and not enclosed in a night bonnet, and she lay there, gazing up at the bed's immense canopy. She heard a nearby church clock sound half past two, and then three, and she heard the watch patrolling Mayfair Street, calling out that all was well. She was very tired, but sleep was elusive. A low, distant rumble of thunder heralded the approach at last of the promised storm, and a movement of air stirred the trees in the avenues and squares, creeping into her room and moving the curtains just a little.

Her eyes began to close. The sound of breaking glass or china carried clearly to her ears from somewhere in the house, and her eyes flew open again immediately. Alert now, she listened carefully, but there was only silence. She considered trying to sleep again, but something about the noise she had heard made her get out of the bed, pulling her shawl around her shoulders. Someone was moving about in the house, and there should not have been anyone at this hour. Maybe it was a guest, perhaps one of the drunken revelers, in which case she would see if she could be of some assistance; or maybe it was someone who had no right to be there at all, someone like a thief. . . .

She slipped stealthily from her apartment, crossing the deserted, shadowy vestibule like a white ghost in her nightgown. Silently she entered the red saloon, but all was quiet and undisturbed, as was the library and the dining room. Not an ornament was out of place. She was about to go back to her apartment when her glance fell upon the fragments of porcelain on the floor beneath the Ionic colonnade at the rear of the dining room. Swiftly she bent to inspect them, recognizing them as once having been a comfit dish which had been kept upon the Sheraton sideboard next to the entrance to the butler's pantry and the offices beyond.

Puzzled, she straightened once more, glancing nervously around. Someone had knocked the dish to the floor and that was what had disturbed her; but who could it have been? And where was he or she now? She stood motionless, gazing carefully at the inky shadows, but there was no movement, no sign of anything. Then, very softly, came the sound of a door opening somewhere in the kitchens, and she whirled about with a gasp. There was definitely someone in there! Her heart began to beat more swiftly as with one hand she gathered the thick folds of her nightgown and with the other eased open the door of the butler's pantry. Outside the storm was nearer, a clap of thunder breaking loudly overhead and reverberating eerily through the house.

Raindrops spattered against the window as she passed through the silent kitchens, where in the daytime all was bustle and noise, and she gave a stifled gasp as a sudden jagged flash of lightning pierced the darkness. For a moment she thought of calling out to Mrs. Hollingsworth, whose rooms lay nearby, but something kept her silent. The seconds passed and she gradually became aware of voices, French voices raised in anger. Recognizing one as Gaspard's, she slipped through the laundry rooms toward the quiet, rather isolated room the chef had elected to occupy. The nearer she came to his room, the more she realized that the other raised voice belonged to Boisville, the strangely insubordinate subordinate who thought nothing of stating his disagreement with his superior. She reached the small passage where the chef's room lay. Candlelight shone from beneath the door. Abruptly she halted, her breath catching silently in her throat, for by that faint light she could distinctly see the figure of a man pressed against the wall, an eavesdropper whom she recognized very clearly indeed. It was Hal. He was so intent upon listening to what was being said that he was not aware of her. For a moment she could not move; she could only stare at him in dismay. He had not told her the truth that day in the garden, there *was* still some suspicion about the chef.

At that moment the argument seemed to come to an end and there was the sound of a chair scraping against the stone floor. The candlelight swayed as one of the men inside picked up the candlestick, and in that split second she knew that Hal would have to retreat from his place, and when he did so he would see her. Even as she turned to flee, he caught a glimpse of a phantomlike figure in white, its honey-colored hair easy to recognize.

With a smothered curse, he pursued her, moving with such speed that he had quitted the small passageway before the door opened and the chef and Boisville emerged. Caroline had reached the dining room before Hal caught her, and her breath was stopped with a jerk as he seized her by the hand and swung her roughly back into his arms, folding her in an embrace and pressing his lips urgently over hers. He held her body close to his, his fingers coiling in the soft warm hair at the nape of her neck, and there was nothing she could do to struggle free, nothing she could do to even move, so strong was he. Helplessly she pushed her hands against his chest, but to no avail. She heard the two Frenchmen approach, obviously meaning to clear away the porcelain from the broken comfit dish. The candlelight flickered, became still as they halted in surprise upon seeing what was apparently a lovers' tryst, and then flickered again, becoming more faint as they retreated.

For a long moment Hal continued to hold her in that ardent, but hollow embrace, and then slowly he released her. Furiously she made to strike his face, but he caught her wrist.

"Now is neither the time nor the place, Caro."

"Don't you presume to call me that!" she breathed. "And how *dare* you lay hands upon me in this way!"

"Don't be irritatingly difficult," he snapped, his tone low and urgent. "I could do without any more problems." Glancing in the direction of the butler's pantry, he took her wrist again, drawing her out of the dining room toward her own private apartment, thrusting her inside, and closing the door firmly behind them both.

"Now you may say your piece, madam," he said. "And I trust that it will be brief and to the point."

"Oh, it will!" she replied angrily. "And it will be in the form of a question. Why did you lie to me?"

"Lie?"

"About suspicion falling upon Gaspard."

"For God's sake, will you lower your tone. We may be private here, but not that private."

"Very well," she said more restrainedly. "Why did you fob me off in the garden?"

"I didn't fob you off."

"Then why are you creeping around at night, eavesdropping upon him and then laying rough hands upon me in order to silence me about your activities?"

"You have the answer to the last in your own question," he said coldly. "It was done in order to keep you quiet."

She flushed. "A word would have sufficed to achieve that, sir."

"The action I took seemed more certain of success."

Her body stiffened. "And what might that remark be taken to mean, Sir Henry?"

"Merely that in order to be absolutely sure that you did not utter an unwise word at a very inopportune moment, I chose to prevent all chance by kissing you. That is all." His hazel eyes rested on her. "Which brings me to wonder why you were abroad at such a time."

"I heard the comfit dish break and came to investigate."

He gave a short laugh. "The damned cat did it."

"The cat?"

He nodded. "Marcia's rat. It seems that Duvall is in the habit of letting the wretched creature back in when it has been put out for the night. He gives it a dish of milk and lets it remain in his room. Tonight it slipped through from the kitchens, jumped onto the sideboard, and knocked the dish over. Duvall and Boisville chased after it, saw what had happened, and went to get something to clear up the bits, and it was then that they fell to arguing." Again he gave a short laugh. "Arguing about a damned cake."

"Cake?"

"A *pièce montée* apparently."

"The *gâteau Wellington*?"

"I believe so. They disagreed about when it should be served, who should help to carry it, where exactly it should be placed upon the table and so on. A blasted culinary discussion! If I'd known that, I could have remained in my bed in comfort."

"Which brings me back to my original question, Sir Henry. Why did you lie to me?"

"I did not lie to you, Miss Lexham."

"You did, sir, for you told me that there was no longer any suspicion where my chef was concerned."

"I said that in the past he had had doubtful connections, but that reliable intelligence had been received that there was no longer a conspiracy here. I also said that I intended to remain here until after the banquet, which inevitably means, Miss Lexham, that I will continue to keep a weather eye open. Tonight was merely another wise precaution, one of many I take. I saw the light in Duvall's window at past three in the morning and thought it worthy of investigation. The rest you know."

She fell silent, for his words had the ring of truth about them.

"I trust that you are satisfied now, madam."

"With your explanation? Yes, Sir Henry."

"Do I detect a qualification in your voice?"

"Yes, sir, you do." She faced him, her anger still burning strongly. "How could I be otherwise satisfied with you, Sir Henry, when I know that you hold an opinion of me which is entirely wrong? I am totally innocent of the immodest behavior of which you accuse me, and of which you still silently accuse me with each cold glance and each contemptuous word. I am no more guilty of having encouraged my cousin to embrace me than I was of encouraging you—or will you now say that I welcomed your attentions tonight, indeed that I responded to them? You have tried and condemned me without a hearing, sir, and with the true arrogance of your sex, which believes itself to be above reproach and believes womankind to be weak and untrustworthy. I will be glad when you leave this house, Sir Henry Seymour, more glad than you will ever know, for at the moment I find your presence both unwelcome and insulting. Now, if you please, I wish you to leave this apartment. Good night, sir."

For a moment he looked at her, his expression impenetrable. "Good night, Caro."

"You do not have my permission to ever address me again by that name."

His inclined his head and withdrew, leaving her standing there alone in the center of the unlit room. Through the slightly open window she could hear the rain falling, and in the distance the thunderstorm, following the course of the Thames. She did not cry this time; she felt unable to weep anymore. But her heart wept with love for Hal Seymour, a love that would never die and would never be returned.

Chapter 30

The evening of the banquet approached with almost alarming rapidity, and the last-minute preparations made life at the hotel very hectic indeed. Now it became impossible for Caroline to deal only indirectly with Hal, for there were simply too many details to be finalized, but she carried these painful meetings off by being always strictly correct, observing every tiny rule of etiquette, and seeming to deliberately distance herself from him. But if that was the outward impression her conduct gave, inside the story was still sadly unchanged. Each time she saw him she wanted to reach out to him, she wanted to tell him how much she loved him, she wanted to feel his arms around her and his lips over hers; but all these things were forever denied her and so she hid the truth behind a facade of cool indifference. His manner toward her remained more or less the same as it had been since the night his sister had married. He was polite, but not warm, he afforded her all the necessary courtesies, but he did not smile at her—and never once did he call her Caro.

In this strained atmosphere, they dealt successfully with all the details, their discussions covering every minute of the evening, from the moment the duke's carriage and its escort of light dragoons arrived, to the moment they departed again in the small hours.

The duke's small procession would inevitably be followed into the courtyard by a considerable crowd. There would be servants carrying *flambeaux*, and the flanking buildings would be bedecked with colored lanterns. The house itself would be ablaze with lights, and the grand balcony would be swathed in patriotic red, white, and blue silk and made bright with more lanterns. From this vantage point young girls would scatter rose petals down upon the duke as he alighted at the steps below, ascending to the doorway on a carpet of flowers and leaves to be greeted by Caroline. They would then proceed through the vestibules between an avenue of orange trees, surrounded by walls decorated with military standards and union jacks, and all the while an orchestra would be playing "Rule Britannia."

It had been agreed with the duke that to satisfy the demands of the adoring crowd in the courtyard, he would make an appearance on the grand balcony. After this, he would descend once more to enter the dining room, once again to triumphant music from the orchestra.

The dining room would be a vision of splendor, its walls draped with scarlet and gold velvet, adorned with military standards and laurel wreaths. There would be flowers everywhere, white carnations, scarlet roses, and blue hyacinths, and on the three long tables that replaced the single one of mahogany, there would be snowy-white cloths and countless tall wax tapers in silver-gilt stands. On a dais opposite the Ionic colonnade and the entrance to the butler's pantry would be the table where the guests-of-honor would sit. Their backs would be to the windows, and the great curtains would be tightly closed, forming a perfect background to the magnificent canopy that would be above the duke's seat. This canopy had been retrieved from the cellars, where it had lain almost forgotten for many years, having originally been made for an entertainment for the Prince of Wales given by Caroline's late uncle. Made of gold-fringed crimson velvet, it was to be adorned with the badges of the duke's favorite regiments, and would make a splendid setting for the hero of Waterloo and the Peninsular War.

When all the guests were seated at their laurel-garlanded tables, the banquet would commence, proceeding through the elaborate menu, to end with the triumphant carrying in of the *pièce montée,* the huge *gâteau Wellington* which promised to be the highlight of the whole evening. It would be borne in by four men and placed before the duke, and there it would be revealed that it was no ordinary *gâteau* but a display of miniature illuminations. At the touch of a lighted spill carried by Gaspard himself, various little candles would cast living light over the confectionery cannon and the equestrian statue of the duke, thus creating the effect of those final moments of victory at Waterloo. This moment was bound to bring rapturous and appreciative applause from a gathering which would have enjoyed a most memorable feast and which had drunk toast after toast with the late Earl of Lexham's diminishing supply of champagne, and it would bring to an end an occasion that should earn the efforts of the Lexham Hotel the acclaim its staff richly deserved.

For Caroline, however, there was a constant and unsettling feeling of apprehension, born not only from the importance of the occasion and the eminence of the many guests, but also of her knowledge of Hal's secret duty. She could not entirely shake off the fear that the conspirators had carried off a successful deception, that something dreadful was to take place at the banquet after all. She felt this when she saw Gaspard and knew that his dark mood had not entirely left him, and she felt it when Hal questioned her very closely about the *pièce montée,* having become very interested suddenly on learning that it was to be lighted. He did not say anything, but she knew that his inevitable suspicion was that it contained more than mere candles; it would not have been the first time that an enemy had chosen to annihilate an opponent in an explosion. These things made her nervous, and she knew that she would not be able to breathe easily again until she saw the duke's carriage leaving through the gateway into Mayfair Street.

This unease was with her on the day of the banquet, when everything was in readiness and she was dressing in her apartment. Outside the lanterns had been lighted and the courtyard was bathed with lights of different colors. It was a fine, clear evening, without any wind and of just the right amount of coolness. Lowering the curtain into place once more, she turned to look at her reflection in the cheval glass. Her gown was made of delicate white muslin, sprigged with a

delicate design of tiny golden stitches. Its waistline was ver
high beneath her breasts and was drawn in by a golden string
The neckline was low but not immodest, and the sleeves wer
very full and diaphanous, gathered in tightly at her wrists
She wore no jewelry, for she had none, and the only adorn
ment was in her hair, where she had pinned a few red roses
stolen from the flowers ordered for the banquet. She surveye
herself in the mirror for a little longer and then picked up th
shawl. She just had time to visit the kitchens and see that al
was well before the guests were due to arrive.

She crossed the vestibule with its walls of standards an
union jacks, the scent of the foliage of the orange trees fillin
the air, and made her way toward the kitchens, where th
bustle was immense as final garnishes were placed upon th
cold dishes and where the ingredients were being prepared fo
the hot dishes that had to be cooked at the very last moment
The smell of cooking was quite delicious as Caroline ap
proached along a passage lined with narrow tables upo
which stood domed silver dishes waiting to be borne into th
banquet.

In the kitchens everyone went efficiently about their allot
ted tasks, and Gaspard, looking pale and tense, gave brie
orders which were instantly and unquestioningly carried out
Boisville, as the *entremettier,* was overseeing the assistant
who were preparing the soups, and he hardly glanced up a
Caroline entered. She had barely stepped into the room
however, when there was a knocking at the garden door, an
Mrs. Hollingsworth hurried to see who it was. Caroline coul
see her at the door, although she could not see who wa
there, and noticing the housekeeper's puzzled expression an
shaking head, she went to discover what was going on.

"What is it, Mrs. Hollingsworth?"

"This fellow is from Covent Garden market; he says he'
delivering our last-minute order."

"But there is no last-minute order," said Caroline, lookin
curiously at the redheaded young man who stood there,
covered basket at his feet, his cap twisting nervously in hi
hands. "What order is it supposed to be?"

"Violets, ma'am, twenty-five posies." He removed th
cloth from the basket and she saw the neat little bunches o
purple flowers.

"We did not order them; there has been some mistake."

"No mistake, ma'am, the man said we was to deliver twenty-five posies of violets to the Lexham Hotel before the banquet tonight. This is the Lexham Hotel, ain't it?"

"Yes, but—"

"Then I've done what I was sent to do. Here you are." He picked up the basket and thrust it into Caroline's hands, then before she could say anything more, he turned on his heel and hurried away across the kitchen garden, through the wicket gate, and on toward the mews lane, soon vanishing from sight among the shadows between the lanterns in the trees.

"Well!" declared Mrs. Hollingsworth crossly. "Did you ever see the like of it? We did not place this order and we certainly will not be paying for it; I'll see to that!"

"We'd better take the basket inside," said Caroline, turning back into the busy kitchen, where she placed it upon the floor in a relatively quiet corner. She saw Boisville turn, his glance going swiftly to the contents of the basket and then immediately toward Gaspard. The chef had paused in the middle of chopping some herbs. His face had drained of what little color it had and he was staring at the innocuous violets as if they were venomous snakes.

"Gaspard?" asked Mrs. Hollingsworth quickly, hurrying toward him. "Whatever is the matter? You look quite dreadful."

The chef did not reply. His eyes were haunted as he dragged them away from the basket at last and looked straight at Boisville. His hand trembled as he put the herb chopper slowly down.

The kitchens had become very quiet suddenly as everyone looked at the chef. The only sound was the bubbling of the pans upon the ranges and the sizzling of the various joints upon the slowly turning spits.

Mrs. Hollingsworth became alarmed. "Gaspard? Are you unwell?"

Still the chef did not say anything, but he seemed filled with dread. Boisville stepped forward then. "I fear, madam, that Monsieur Duvall is—how do you say?—superstitious?"

"Superstitious?" asked Caroline. "About what?"

"Violets, mademoiselle."

"But that is nonsense," she replied firmly.

"Nevertheless, mademoiselle, to him they are an omen o great ill."

"They are only flowers," she said, turning to Gaspard "Monsieur?"

At last he spoke. "F-forgive me, mademoiselle, but cannot help . . ." Again his hollow eyes moved towar Boisville's cold, unsmiling face.

"I will have the violets removed," she said then, her ton brisk, but as she turned to do just that, Gaspard shook h head.

"They have come into the house, mademoiselle, their tas is done."

"Task? What task? What are you talking about?"

He made a great effort to recover, picking up the her chopper again and managing a small smile. "It is of n matter." But his tone lacked all conviction and both Carolin and Mrs. Hollingsworth knew that it mattered very muc indeed. Caroline looked swiftly at Boisville, who silentl returned to his own duties, and as Gaspard brought the chop per down upon the herbs, the whole kitchen began to g about its tasks once more.

Caroline and Mrs. Hollingsworth exchanged glances, an Caroline knew that the housekeeper was wondering exactl the same as she was: who had ordered the violets, and wh had they done so? For a moment she considered the possibil ity that this was the work of one of her enemies—perhaps final effort from Marcia, or maybe it could be Dominic—bu somehow she knew that it had nothing to do with them Whoever had sent the violets had done so for an entirel different motive. But what?

She had no time to think more on the problem, for footman came looking for her at that moment to tell her tha the guests were beginning to arrive. Swiftly she told Mrs Hollingsworth to remove the basket of violets from Gaspard' sight, and with a final despairing glance at his ashen, agitate face, she left the kitchens to take up her position in th vestibule. The great banquet was about to begin.

Chapter 31

The distinguished guests had all taken their places and awaited the arrival of the duke. The light of hundreds of tall wax tapers glittered on military orders, glowed on the scarlet uniforms of generals and the dark blue of admirals, shone upon the somber garb of bishops, and showed up to perfection the elegant clothes of earls, lords, and dukes. The orchestra played softly in the background and the dining room hummed with the low sound of male conversation.

Quivering with apprehension and toying nervously with her reticule, Caroline waited in the outer vestibule, her heart beating more swiftly as she distinctly heard the sound of distant cheering from the darkness outside. Nodding her head at the porter, she watched as the doors were opened, revealing the brightly lit courtyard and the smoking *flambeaux* of the servants lining the path the duke's carriage and escort would take.

At last she heard the clatter of hooves and the splendidly uniformed light dragoons rode beneath the pedimented gateway, followed by the landau drawn by four black horses, and behind this poured the excited crowd, shouting and cheering their hero. With only Hal at his side, the duke glanced neither to the right nor the left as the carriage rolled across the courtyard toward the flower-strewn steps of the hotel.

Caroline turned once, sensing Mrs. Hollingsworth's presence. Her eyes met the housekeeper's a little questioningly, but Mrs. Hollingsworth shook her head, thus conveying to Caroline the unwelcome news that all was not well in the kitchens. Caroline's pulse quickened and she took a deep breath to steady herself, forcing a smile to her lips as the carriage came to a halt and she stepped forward to greet the duke, as he had asked.

From the balcony above, the young girls showered the duke and Hal with rose petals, and the pressing, excited crowd cheered again. As before, the duke looked taller than he was, and tonight he also looked very dignified in navy blue velvet, with a sapphire-blue sash across his breast and a magnificent silver star pinned over his heart. Beside him, Hal wore discreet black, the diamond pin in his lace-edged cravat not in any way vying with the duke's decoration.

The two men mounted the flowery steps and Caroline sank into a deep curtsy, one which she had been practicing time after time in the cheval glass in her apartment. She avoided looking at Hal.

"Welcome to the Lexham Hotel, Your Grace."

Smiling, the duke bent to raise her, drawing her hand to his lips. "By Gad, Miss Lexham, you look dazzling. What say you, Seymour, eh?"

"Quite dazzling," was the cool response.

Momentarily her eyes met his, and then she looked deliberately away again, not revealing by so much as a flicker the easy hurt he inflicted with that bland indifference.

The duke drew her hand through his arm, glancing with approval at the embellishments of the vestibule. "You've done me proud, m'dear, I thank 'e."

Her whole body quivered invisibly as she proceeded between the avenue of orange trees on the duke's arm, the strains of "Rule Britannia" echoing all around. They went slowly up the grand staircase and out onto the balcony, where an immediate delighted roar went up from the huge throng pressed into the courtyard. Hats were thrown into the air, arms waved and coats were shaken aloft, and the duke stood impassively accepting the adulation. He smiled just a little, inclining his head several times, and he certainly did not strain himself greatly to win their rapturous applause, but for all that there was something singularly dramatic and inspiring about him. He commanded them all simply by being there, just as he had done on many a field of battle. He won confidence, loyalty, and reverence, and he did so just by being himself.

Caroline stood nervously behind him, thinking how very vulnerable he was and how he might have done better to have taken Hal's advice and forgone this public appearance where he was so easy a target from anywhere in the milling crowd. Glancing at Hal, she saw how alert he was, how his glance moved constantly over the sea of faces below, watchful for anything which might offer that final danger to the duke. She sensed his relief as the duke withdrew at last into the greater safety of the hotel.

"Damn me," remarked the duke lightly. "I thought this banquet was to be private."

Hal smiled. "You are not permitted to be private, Your Grace."

"Not yet," was the dry reply. "But there'll be a time soon enough when the shine wears off me reputation. Everyone loves a soldier when there's war, but they'll kick him in the pants when peace returns." He glanced out through the closed windows once again. "By Gad," he murmured, "I felt decidedly exposed out there, Seymour, and I began to feel your warnings should have been heeded. Still, it went off handsomely, eh?"

"Yes, Your Grace."

"You'll have heard, of course, that that rascal Cantillon refuses to say a word."

"Yes, but then he wouldn't if he had accomplices still free, would he?"

The duke nodded sagely. "That's only too correct, but in spite of that I believe he will soon go free."

Caroline was unable to smother her gasp of astonishment. "Go free?" she asked in amazement. "But how could that possibly be?"

"Because, m'dear, to convict him we need evidence, and although everyone knows he's as guilty as hell itself, no one will come forward. In these virtuous days, the greatest crime a man can commit in France is to denounce another, even though the crime should be a plot to assassinate a third

person. Cantillon will go free." He gave one of his unexpected whoops of laughter. "Why, it wouldn't surprise me if
Bonaparte remembered the scoundrel in his will!" Still
chuckling, he offered her his arm once more. "Shall we go
down to the bean feast, m'dear?"

Her gold-spangled muslin skirts dragging softly behind her,
she descended the staircase at the duke's side, parting from
him at the entrance of the crowded banqueting room. Chairs
scraped as the gathering rose as one to respectfully applaud as
the duke made his way to the place of honor beneath the
canopy. His progress to the dais was accompanied by the
strains of a triumphant march.

Caroline stood at the doorway for a moment, and then
slipped unnoticed to stand beneath the Ionic colonnade, close
to the entrance to the butler's pantry. The moment the banquet
began, she would go to the kitchens and see how Gaspard
was.

The assembly sat down once more and there was a great
deal of shuffling and clearing of throats, and in that moment
she became aware that someone in the midst of the gathering
was looking at her. It was not a pleasant sensation, and with a
slight shiver she searched the room. At last she met those
staring eyes, so gray, like her own. Dominic's handsome face
was as chill and full of loathing as it had been when first they
had met. He made no pretense now of liking her; his gaze
was steady and did not waver at all; it was Caroline who
looked away first. To her relief, the line of waiters carrying
the first courses made their entrance, and as the last one
passed into the room, a silver dish borne expertly aloft on his
left hand, she gathered her skirts and hurried along the passageway toward the kitchens.

The atmosphere was strained and it soon became apparent
to her that Gaspard was so upset still that he was, unbelievably,
close to collapse. Mrs. Hollingsworth was anxiously fussing
around him as he sat in a chair by the fireplace, his face
hidden in his hands and his shoulders bowed. There was an
air of wretchedness about him that affected Caroline greatly
as she crouched beside him and put a gentle hand upon his
jaunty-checkered sleeve.

"Monsieur?"

Slowly he raised his head. "It is no use, mademoiselle,"

he whispered, his voice almost lost in the bustle of the kitchens as the efficient *brigade* continued without supervision.

"What is wrong?" she asked anxiously. "Surely it isn't the violets."

"But yes," he replied brokenly. "It is the violets." He looked away, his eyes filled with that hollowness she had seen earlier. "Never before have I so hated one of God's creations. A little flower . . ."

Perplexed, Caroline straightened, looking helplessly into the housekeeper's distraught eyes. "Perhaps he would be better lying down, for to be sure it does him no good to sit here like this."

"I will take him to my rooms, they are closer than his own, and I will be able to go and see how he is more easily."

"Very well, do that. Can everything go on without him?" Caroline glanced around the busy kitchen.

"Yes, that Boisville fellow has taken over."

Caroline said nothing more as Mrs. Hollingsworth coaxed Gaspard to his feet, gently persuading him to accompany her to her rooms. Before he left, he turned once more to Caroline. "Forgive me, mademoiselle, please forgive me."

"Of course I forgive you," she replied, seeing how his haunted eyes flew toward Boisville, who had watched and listened all the while, and whose presence was quite obviously lending an extra edge to Gaspard's fear, for fear it was that had brought the chef to this piteous state.

With a heavy heart, Caroline walked back along the passage, taking up an advantageous position in a shadowy corner of the butler's pantry. From here, by looking in a mirror on a nearby wall, she could see all that was happening in the dining room, which for this one night had become a grand banqueting hall. She could watch the proceedings in complete safety, for no one at the magnificent tables could see her.

For a while she almost forgot Gaspard as she watched the banquet. The many tapers flickered in the rising heat and she could clearly see the flash of the silver star on the duke's breast as he turned to speak to Hal, seated some distance away at the end of the dais. She gazed at Hal, able to do so only because she knew he could not see her. How very handsome he was, and how easily that lazy, almost cynical smile of his twisted in her heart like a knife. Why had everything to be the way it was? Why couldn't fate have decreed that he should look at her with that same love now reflecting so plainly in her own eyes? Suddenly the remoteness and tranquillity of Selford seemed a blessed haven, and it was the first time she had felt like that since leaving all those weeks ago. Weeks? Sometimes it seemed that she had dreamed of Dartmoor, that London was the only life she had ever known—and that Hal Seymour was the only thing ever to have been of deep and lasting consequence to her. Gazing at him now, the utter futility and hopelessness of her love washed painfully over her, and she forced herself to look away.

The waiters filed past her once more, bearing aloft another impressive array of dishes. Course followed course as she stood there, and all the while the orchestra played discreetly in the background, the soft notes almost drowned by the deep drone of male conversation. In spite of the upset with Gaspard, the banquet was going very well indeed, thanks to the efficiency and skill of his wonderful *brigade de cuisine*.

The cheese course was served and she realized with some surprise that the evening had been in progress for nearly two and a half hours now. All that remained to be served were the *entremets*, consisting of the magnificent array of hot and cold desserts over which Boisville had been in charge, and the appearance of poor Gaspard's prized *pièce montée*. Sadly she reflected that in his present state, the chef would not be able personally to light the candles on the *gâteau*, and would therefore forfeit the moment of glory he so richly deserved for all the work he had put into the banquet.

She heard a discreet cough at her elbow, and turned to see Boisville standing there. "Yes?" she inquired, unable to quite conceal the dislike she so instinctively felt for this reptilian Frenchman.

"Forgive the intrusion, mademoiselle, but there is a small problem."

"Problem?"

"It concerns the *pièce montée*. I fear that the filling of cherry ice is proving difficult to keep frozen. I think that it would be best if it was served with the *entremets*. By that I mean that it should immediately follow them to the tables and not be delayed until they have been virtually finished."

"What does Monsieur Duvall say?"

He did not reply, but expressively shrugged his shoulders.

"He is still unwell?" she asked, knowing in her heart that this had to be so.

"Most unwell, mademoiselle, but then he is a very superstitious man."

"So it would seem," she replied, disliking him intensely. "Very well, you may serve the *pièce montée* directly after the *entremets.*"

His smile was almost sleek as he bowed to her and retreated, making as little sound as he had when approaching her. She contained the urge to shudder and returned her attention to the banquet. She watched as toasts were drunk and the gentlemen then relaxed to linger over their cheese. At last the line of efficient waiters spirited away the remnants and the tables were cleared in readiness for the numerous desserts.

"Miss Lexham! Come quickly!" Her attention was drawn sharply away from the banquet by the sound of Mrs. Hollingsworth's low, urgent voice.

"What is it?"

"It's Gaspard, madam, he's in a terrible way now and he's saying things I think you should hear."

Caroline's blood almost froze at the fear contained in those few words. "Things? What things?"

"It's a matter of life and death, Miss Lexham, and you must come right away."

Caroline gazed in growing horror at the trembling, ashen-faced woman, and without another word followed her along the passage in the direction of her rooms.

Unknown to either of them, their brief exchange had been overheard. A stealthy, elegantly clad shadow slipped from the brightness of the banquet into the relative quiet of the butler's pantry. Dominic Lexham's honey-colored hair was unmistakable as he moved silently after the two women. From his place at the table he had witnessed the housekeeper's hurrying, anxious approach along the passage, and his curiosity had been immediately aroused. Now he was intent upon learning what lay behind their intriguing words.

Chapter 32

Gaspard had broken down completely. He rocked to and fro, whispering to himself as if in prayer, and his whole body shook as if he were ice cold. There was no trace now of the buoyant, cheerful little chef whose charm and kindliness had won him so many friends and admirers. Now he was stricken, overwhelmed with some dreadful fear and guilt, and it was too much for him to bear.

Mrs. Hollingsworth went to him, kneeling on the floor before his chair and lovingly taking his hands. "Gaspard, my love?" she said gently. "Gaspard, you must tell Miss Lexham what you told me."

His tormented eyes fled to Caroline's anxious face. "I cannot," he whispered, shaking his head, "I cannot say it—"

"You must, it's too important."

Tears shone in his soft, melting brown eyes and at last he gave a barely perceptible nod. "I cannot go on with the lies, mademoiselle. I have tried to do as they wish, but now I cannot. Until today, I hoped—I *prayed*—that nothing would come of it after all; now when they sent the violets, I knew that I would have to do their bidding."

"The violets? What do the flowers mean?" asked Caroline, although in her heart she was beginning to guess the answer.

"They were a signal, mademoiselle. Bonaparte once said that when the violets were in bloom, he would return to France. Violets have become the emblem of his followers." He sat forward urgently, his face tormented with the fear and guilt that tortured him. "They have my mother and my sisters, mademoiselle, and they said that if I did not do as they wished, my family would be killed. What was I to do? I am a Frenchman, I love my country, but I am no longer a Bonapartist. I have seen how his grand designs have ruined my country and never would I willingly lend my support to his cause. But I love my mother and my sisters. Their lives depend upon me!" Tears shone on his pale cheeks as he gazed imploringly at her. "I do not wish to be the instrument of their death, but nor do I wish to be part of the assassination of the Duke of Wellington. I hoped, dear God how I hoped, that they would not need to call upon me after all, that their plots would be confined to France, but I began to fear the worst when Cantillon was arrested. Today my fears were realized, for the violets meant that the plan would have to be carried out after all. I am upon the rack, Mademoiselle Lexham, and my body, my heart, and my soul are being torn apart by the burden I am forced to bear."

Caroline could only respond sympathetically to the wretchedness in his eyes, and she believed every word he said. "I'm so sorry, monsieur," she said gently. "Believe me I am, but you must realize that I have to ask you what they plan to do, and when they intend doing it."

His lips trembled and he looked faint at the thought of betraying his countrymen, but Mrs. Hollingsworth drew his hands to her lips, kissing both and looking up into his eyes, her great love for him written plainly upon her face, which in that moment was softened to a great beauty. "I love you, Gaspard," she whispered, "and nothing you have said or done will ever change that."

His fingers tightened convulsively around hers and he smiled a little, seeming to find strength in her love. He looked up at Caroline. "It is Boisville, mademoiselle; he is the assassin." He glanced at the clock on the mantelpiece. "You have time enough, for it is to take place when he accompanies *pièce montée* to the duke. Originally he was to have been one of the four men carrying it, but now he will probably take my place and appear to be there only to light the candles upon it. Instead he will draw a pistol and he will shoot the duke. At that range he will be sure to kill him instantly."

Caroline stared at him, a numbness settling coldly over her. "But we have no time at all," she whispered, "for Boisville has changed the plans. The *pièce montée* will already be on its way to the dais!" Gathering her skirt, she fled to the door.

Mrs. Hollingsworth rose swiftly to her feet, her concern only for Gaspard. "But, Miss Lexham, what about Gaspard? We cannot let them know about him."

Caroline paused for the briefest of seconds. "Keep him here, hide him, I'll do what I can." Then she had gone, her heart pounding in her breast. Pray God she would be in time! Pray *God*!

Dominic emerged slowly from the shadows nearby. He had overheard everything and now his mind was racing. Somehow he must turn all this to his own advantage. Somehow there had to be a way of defeating his beautiful but tenacious cousin and of winning back his property. His gray eyes were sharp and shrewd, lightening a little as he made his way back toward the banquet.

She could hear the applause long before she reached the doorway of the butler's pantry. In the brilliantly lit banqueting hall, all eyes were turned toward the dais. In a frozen moment she saw the duke, she saw Hal, she saw the magnificent *pièce montée* resting on its bed of ice, its little illuminations flickering over the lifelike battle scene; and she saw Boisville, his attention solely upon the duke. His hand began to move slowly toward the inside of his coat.

With a scream of warning she hurried into the blinding light, and it was Hal's name that was on her lips. Everyone turned sharply toward her, a stir passing through the assembly. Hal moved like lightning, darting to the startled duke and flinging him bodily from his seat to the floor behind the dais. Boisville's pistol discharged harmlessly into the crimson velvet of the canopy and immediately there was pandemonium. With a lightness that was astounding, Boisville vaulted over the table, scattering the wax tapers in all directions and knocking over a decanter of cognac. Immediately there were flames everywhere, and people began to shout as the assassin vanished behind the drawn curtains. Caroline heard the shattering of the glass in the tall windows as he plunged through into the darkness and anonymity of the gardens. She was vaguely aware of Hal giving pursuit, his figure barely discernible through the smoke which now rose from the blazing table.

The atmosphere swiftly became choking as the smoke filled the room, and men milled everywhere. She heard someone ordering people to form a chain to pass pails of water through from the kitchens. The smoke irritated her eyes and burned in her throat. It seemed that the noise and clamor went on forever as the chain of men formed, and pail after pail of water was tossed over the flames. Anxiously she searched the smoke and vapor for a sign of Hal, but he was nowhere to be seen. The duke was being attended to by several of the army officers present, and although he was a little disheveled, he did not seem any the worse for wear. She was trembling with the shock of everything, and tears stung her smoke-burned eyes as she made her way down through the devastated room toward the curtains, which someone had now drawn back from the flames. She saw the shattered glass in the windows, the fragments shining on the flagstones outside. Cool, refreshing air swept in, passing revivingly over her. How calm and peaceful the gardens looked, the lanterns shining so prettily in the trees, the spring flowers nodding in the night breeze, but Hal was somewhere out there, pursuing a desperate armed man. "Please keep him safe," she whispered. "Don't let him come to harm."

"Miss Lexham?"

She turned to see a scarlet-uniformed gentleman looking inquiringly at her. "Yes?"

"His Grace wishes to thank you for your timely warning. If you would please come this way?" He stood aside, ushering her toward the duke's small party.

Feeling anything but elegant and composed, she followed him. The duke turned to her, a smile on his lips, and he hastily prevented her from sinking into a deep curtsy. "No, no, m'dear, it is I who should be making obeisance to you! Although damn me if I can think how you guessed what that villainous *parlez-vous* was up to!" Still smiling, he drew her hand to his lips. "I thank 'ee from the bottom of me heart, m'dear, for I owe my life to you."

Another voice broke in suddenly. "Your Grace, I believe

you should know that you owe her your life only because at the last moment she lost her nerve and could not go through with it. She is one of the conspirators.''

With a horrified gasp, she whirled about to see Dominic standing there, a cool smile upon his lips. ''That is a lie!'' she cried. ''An infamous lie!''

''Is it, coz?'' he replied, coming closer and bowing reverently to the startled duke. ''Forgive me, Your Grace, I do not mean to insult you in any way by my conduct now, but things have come to my notice which prove that my kinswoman is anything but the loyal patriot you now believe her to be; she is an adherent of the revolutionary cause and a Bonapartist of the first order.''

His words carried clearly through the room and an amazed silence fell over everyone. Caroline's face had drained of color; her shock was so great that she could not speak. She stared in stunned silence at her cousin.

The duke's smile had faded. ''I trust you can prove your accusations, my lord, for if you cannot then I swear I will have your elegant hide for my next pair of boots.''

''I can prove them well enough, Your Grace. Perhaps my cousin would care to tell us if the felon Seymour now pursues was working alone. Well, coz, was he?''

Her lips parted, but she could not speak. ''I—''

''Why do you not reply, cousin?'' he inquired reasonably. ''Could it be that you have someone you wish to protect? Someone who, like yourself, had not the courage to carry out the murder?''

''No!'' she cried. ''It isn't like that at all!''

''So, you admit that there is someone else!''

She looked away, tears wet on her cheeks.

Dominic was triumphant. ''You see, Your Grace? She convicts herself by her silence. In her housekeeper's rooms you will find hidden the chef, Duvall. He, my cousin, and the wretch who has escaped tonight were together in the conspiracy to assassinate you. I thought my cousin's conduct was a little odd tonight and I made it my business to keep an eye upon her. I overheard her speaking with the chef and it was quite obvious that she was party to the whole thing, but that the two of them had lost their nerve and had decided the plot should be abandoned as it was so unlikely to succeed. That was why she arrived in so timely a way to rescue you, Your

Grace; she did it simply and solely to cover her iniquitous tracks—which she would have done, had I not listened to all that was said."

"Is this true, Miss Lexham?" asked the duke.

"No!"

Dominic smiled. "The chef is in the housekeeper's parlor and he can be questioned."

Caroline looked up swiftly. "He is in no condition to answer questions."

"So," answered the duke heavily, "the chef *is* where Lexham says he is?"

"Yes, Your Grace," she replied. "But—"

The duke turned to several nearby officers. "Bring him here."

"Your Grace—" persisted Caroline desperately, but he turned a stern, cold eye upon her.

"Please be silent, Miss Lexham."

She could do nothing but obey, but she did so with dread in her heart, for she knew that what she had said was right. Gaspard was *not* in any state to answer questions, especially questions from the Duke of Wellington!

Silence reigned in the great room, where pools of water lay upon the floor, flames and smoke had ruined the costly furnishings, and panic had overturned chairs and wrenched hangings from the walls. The once proud and glittering assembly of dignitaries waited in silent groups, and everyone looked at Caroline, whose air of agitation made her appear to be very guilty.

At last the officers returned, half carrying and half dragging Gaspard, who was so terrified of the fate which might now await him that he could hardly stand. He did not at first see the duke; he saw only Caroline. Hope leaped into his eyes. "We were in time, mademoiselle?"

That word "we" sealed her fate. A stir passed through the room and she closed her eyes, nodding. "Yes, we were in time, monsieur."

The duke's face was very still as he folded his arms, the silver star glittering on his breast. "So, monsieur, you admit that you knew of this intended crime."

With almost a squeak, Gasped turned his head in the direction of the new voice, and recognition dawned instantly upon his pale, terrified face. *"Monsieur le duc!"*

"Do you admit that you were party to a plot to assassinate me?"

"Not willingly, milord, never willingly!" cried the chef.

"Your complicity is nevertheless proved by your reply, monsieur," replied the duke, nodding briefly at the officers. "Remove them to secure rooms for the time being!"

"I am but a chef!" cried Gaspard desperately, seeing the net closing inexorably around him. "I was forced to do as they wished! But I stepped back from the abyss, milord. I stepped back in time to save you!"

"Remove them both," repeated the duke, his face cold.

Gaspard struggled helplessly as they dragged him away, but Caroline held her ground for a moment more. "Your Grace!" she said. "Please do not—"

"I will hear nothing more from you, madam," he replied. "The Frenchman's acts I can understand, but you are English and your crime is therefore all the more heinous!" He glanced at the waiting officers. "Get her out of my sight until she can be taken to the correct place of detention."

It was as if she were in the grip of a nightmare from which she could not escape. She saw Dominic's grinning, victorious face, she saw the condemnation in the eyes of all those gathered in the room, she saw Gaspard being hauled to the doorway, and she saw Mrs. Hollingsworth, so shocked and horrified by what had happened that she could only cling to one of the columns for support, her face quite ghastly.

In a daze, Caroline allowed the officers to take her away. She stumbled a little as they crossed the inner vestibule, halting in dread as she realized that they intended to immure her in the cellar.

"Please! No!"

"It's the most secure place, and it's fitting for traitors," replied one of them, opening the door and thrusting her into the chill, dank darkness beyond. The door closed swiftly behind her, the sound reverberating through the invisible cellar rooms, and the rattle of the key in the lock seemed to carry on forever, echoing over and over again until it became so faint that she could no longer hear it.

Hesitantly, she edged her way down the steps, clinging to the icy rail. The atmosphere was as cold and clammy as an imagined shroud, and she became aware of the eerie gurgle of the unseen Tyburn, flowing endlessly by somewhere beneath the foundations. Slowly she sank to the floor, burying her face in her hands, and the echoes took up the sound of her sobs, tossing them scornfully back at her as if they were in league with Dominic, whose evil triumph was surely now complete.

Chapter 33

How long she remained there, alone and terrified in the darkness, she did not know. She fell into a light, restless sleep, finding little solace in the dreams that haunted those dreadful hours, but at last she was roused by the sound of the key in the lock again.

She struggled to sit up, her eyes turned hopefully toward the light that poured down into the cellar. A woman's figure appeared, and with a cry of gladness she rose to her feet, for it was Mrs. Hollingsworth.

The housekeeper carried a laden tray, her way illuminated by a candle. She set it down and then turned to embrace Caroline. The two women wept in each other's arms, and at last Caroline drew away, wiping her eyes.

"There-there is news of Sir Henry?"

Mrs. Hollingsworth's expression became distinctly cooler. "No, madam."

"I don't know how long I've been here, but it seems like forever. What is to become of us? Have you seen Gaspard?"

Tears filled the housekeeper's eyes. "No," she whispered. "They've taken him away somewhere, I know not where. Oh, Miss Lexham, I'm so afraid for him, he was forced to do what he did, but he could not bring himself to become party to murder! I know that he will pay with his life!'' The tears wended their slow way down Mrs. Hollingsworth's cheeks, and then she looked swiftly and ashamedly at Caroline. ''Oh, my dear, I did not mean to imply that I was not equally concerned for you—''

''I know.'' Caroline glanced at the tray. On it was a jug of milk, some cheese, and bread. ''Is this my banquet?'' she asked a little wryly.

''I would not leave them alone until they allowed me to see you. I am not permitted to stay long—''

''And you saying that nothing has been heard of Sir Henry?''

''No, but it is still dark outside.''

''I pray nothing has befallen him.''

''That is indeed to be hoped.''

''I must see him when he returns,'' went on Caroline. ''He knows that I had nothing to do with the plot.''

''Madam—''

''Yes?''

''I know that now is not the time to tell you this, but I cannot let you hold out hope that Sir Henry will rescue you, for I know that the opposite is the case.''

Caroline stared at her, her eyes huge and dark in the wavering light of the solitary candle flame. ''What do you mean?''

Mrs. Hollingsworth took a long breath. ''I was in the kitchen when word was sent that refreshments were to be taken to the duke, who has temporarily occupied Lady Carstairs' apartment. I decided to wait upon him myself, thinking that if I could speak to him, I could persuade him that you were entirely innocent and that my poor Gaspard should be treated leniently, for he is not a bad man. When I reached the apartment, however, I found that he was not alone; he was seated with a number of gentlemen and they were so deep in conversation that they hardly noticed my presence as I served them. I overheard the duke relating a tale Sir Henry had told him.''

''What tale?''

''Oh, my dear, I would give anything now not to have to say this to you,'' said Mrs. Hollingsworth, reaching out to take Caroline's hand. ''Sir Henry told the duke of the night you caught him eavesdropping upon Gaspard and Boisville, and of how he convinced you to say nothing. The duke roared with laughter, telling the others that it spoke volumes of Sir Henry's skills as a lover that he could persuade a member of the plot to believe him to be pursuing her.''

In the dim, faintly moving light, Caroline's cheeks flamed with humiliation.

"So you see, my dear," went on the housekeeper. "You must not hope for anything from Sir Henry, for he has believed you to be part of it all along, or at least, he has done for some time."

"I cannot believe it," whispered Caroline hollowly. "I cannot believe he thinks that of me—"

"I know that you love him, my dear, but he is not worthy of your love. Forget him; he has brought you nothing but pain and it would have been better for you had you never met him. You will be saved, of that I am sure, but your salvation will not come at his hands."

Numbly, Caroline turned away.

The key turned in the lock again and a soldier looked in. "Your time is up, missus; you're to leave the prisoner alone again now."

Mrs. Hollingsworth squeezed Caroline's cold fingers comfortingly and then left, and almost absently Caroline noticed the absence of the chinking of her keys. Those keys had been confiscated, for fear that she might contemplate helping her mistress to escape.

The darkness and silence folded over Caroline once more, but she was hardly aware of it. She felt and heard nothing, only the distant pounding of her broken heart.

Dawn was beginning to break, and the great crowd still thronged the courtyard. News of what had happened had spread like wildfire and the whole of London had learned of the events at the Lexham Hotel. The capital buzzed with it, and lights had burned in the windows of Mayfair mansions throughout the night. Everyone now knew that the Earl of Lexham's fair cousin, the lady whose enterprise had taken London by storm, was guilty of being a wicked Bonapartist, that she had almost carried off a dastardly plan to assassinate the hero of Waterloo.

A solitary hackney coach made its way slowly through the crush in Mayfair Street, turning with difficulty into the crowded courtyard, the coachman shouting and cracking his whip in an attempt to clear a way.

Inside, Hal sat wearily, his head resting against the ancient upholstery. His cravat hung loose and his shirt was torn. Mud stained the costly velvet of his coat, and a bloody mark scored his right cheek, a reminder of how very close Boisville's dying shot had come to finding its target. Hal had fired first, picking the Frenchman off the parapet of the appropriately named new Waterloo Bridge, and as he began to fall to his death, Boisville had instinctively returned the shot. How close it had scorched, whining through the cold night air, leaving a scar forever.

He was roused from his thoughts by the sudden halting of the hackney as it at last reached the steps of the hotel, where the flowers were now crushed beyond redemption. He flung the door open and climbed down. Immediately he was recognized and a jubilant shout went up for the man whose swift actions had thrust the great duke to the safety of the floor. He hardly glanced around as he hurried up the steps and into the hotel. The door closed behind him and he came face-to-face with Mrs. Hollingsworth.

He managed a weary smile. "Good morning, Mrs. Hollingsworth."

"Sir." She gave him the briefest of nods, her eyes cold and unsmiling.

"Where is Miss Lexham?" he inquired.

"I would have thought that you could have guessed that well enough for yourself, sir," she replied stiffly.

"Mrs. Hollingsworth, I don't know what is the matter with you, and I am certainly not in the mood for parlor games. Where is Miss Lexham?"

"She is under lock and key, Sir Henry, where the ill-founded suspicions of you and your like have placed her!" cried the distraught housekeeper, her anger and bitterness making her forget her place. "She is innocent, the poor lamb, and you will no doubt be congratulating yourself upon your cleverness. You've destroyed her as much as has the Earl of Lexham, Sir Henry Seymour, and I hope you one day pay the price for what you have done!"

Hal stared at her, but then he recovered. "Where is the duke?"

Mrs. Hollingsworth made to walk away from him, but he

caught her angrily by the wrist, twisting her so sharply to face him that her skirts brushed against the nearby orange trees. "Damn you, woman! Answer my question!"

"The duke occupies Lady Carstairs' apartment until later this morning!" she cried, rubbing the wrist which he abruptly released, and watching him as he pushed his way through the avenue of little trees, thrusting aside a hanging banner and then moving swiftly up the grand staircase.

The duke was taking a very Spartan breakfast and he looked up with a smile as Hal was admitted. Wiping his mouth with a napkin, he rose from his table. "Seymour! By Gad, I'm glad to see you! Did you snare the ruffian?"

"His body will be recovered from the Thames, no doubt."

"Excellent. I must thank you for your quick thinking, Seymour, although if I am to be tumbled to the floor I think I would prefer a pretty wench to do the honors next time, eh?" He gave his strange whoop of laughter again, sitting down to pour himself another cup of thick black coffee and gesturing to Hal to sit down with him.

"With your leave, Your Grace, I would prefer to stand."

The duke looked shrewdly at him. "Come on then, out with it. What's on your mind?"

"I'm told that Miss Lexham is under lock and key."

"That is so, for unfortunately she was part of the plot."

"That cannot be so!"

"It *is* so, Seymour, there's no doubt of it, and we've Lexham to thank for exposing her."

"Lexham?" Hal's eyes narrowed.

The duke stirred his coffee busily. "Yes, the fellow decided to pry a little and overheard an interesting and revealing conversation. She and Duvall were Boisville's accomplices, they admitted it."

Hal stared at this information. "She *admitted* it?"

"What is this, a damned inquisition? Yes, Seymour, she admitted it. Now, if you are going to be disagreeable and sulky, you can take yourself elsewhere to do it. If you have any doubts about Miss Lexham's guilt, then you would be best advised to question her cousin about it. You'll find him somewhere around, conducting himself as if the house has returned to him already." The duke looked up, but Hal had gone. With a shrug, and a slight frown at the continuing noise of the crowds outside, the duke continued with his breakfast.

Dominic lounged elegantly on a sofa in the red saloon, a cigar in one hand and an exceedingly early glass of cognac in the other. He held court, glorying in his triumph and fame and repeating the whole story yet again for the benefit of some new arrivals who were eager for every detail. He set a splendid scene, with a cast of wicked, intriguing assassins and with himself as the intrepid hero, risking life and limb to reach the truth and prevented from warning the duke himself only by the wretched cowardice and funk of his treacherous, despicable cousin, the fair Caroline.

From the doorway, Hal listened in disgust to this highly embroidered tale, and gradually the others in the room became aware of his presence. One by one they turned to look at him, something in his cold glance making them silent, and at last only Dominic's drawling voice could be heard.

"Oh, she was a scheming little adventuress, all right; conniving was second nature to her. She made many an advance to me, you know. I suppose she fancied the notion of being Countess of Lexham, eh?" He laughed, but the sound drew no response. Slowly his smug smile faded and he sat up, his eyes going at last to the reason for the silence. His face paled a little as he saw Hal. His tongue passed nervously over his lips and he gave an uneasy laugh. "Well, the paladin returns—and bearing suitable marks of mortal combat. Your health, Seymour." He raised his glass.

With an oath, Hal came forward, striking the glass from his hand and reaching down to drag him from the sofa.

Dominic gave a startled cry. "Take your hands off me, Seymour!"

Hal flung him contemptuously to the floor where he sprawled ignominiously on the carpet, winded. His face was pale but defiant as he gazed up at his attacker.

"Now, my brave fellow," breathed Hal, his soft, menacing voice very clear in the silent room, "you will tell the truth about what happened."

"I've told the truth—" Dominic ceased abruptly as a muddy boot pressed down roughly upon his chest, and then all color drained from his face as Hal slowly drew his pistol and leveled it at him.

"I'm not a patient man, Lexham," he said softly. "Indeed, at this moment patience is a virtue in which I am singularly lacking." He cocked the pistol and a stir passed through the watching gentlemen.

Dominic stared at the pistol and then at the ice-cold determination in his assailant's eyes. "All right," he cried suddenly his defiance collapsing. "All right, Seymour, I'll tell you."

"I'm waiting."

"Miss Lexham is innocent, she had nothing to do with it." Dominic's tongue passed dryly over his pale lips and he was a picture of craven fear as the pistol barrel moved closer.

"That is not enough, Lexham," said Hal softly.

"I heard everything. Duvall told her about the plot, and she went straightaway to warn the duke. That is the truth, I swear it."

A disgusted murmur greeted this and slowly Hal lowered the pistol. "You are beneath contempt, Lexham, so low that a snake could aspire to the name of gentleman before you. Now then, up you get!" Reaching down, he dragged Dominic to his feet again. "We'll toddle along to the duke and we'll see to it that your innocent cousin is released, her good name and character unharmed by your foul lies. And after that, you would be best advised to get yourself out of the country, for unless you do, I shall be looking for you, dear fellow, and our next meeting will be the last thing you know in this life."

Dominic's gray eyes bulged with dread, his whole body trembled, and he could only nod his head vigorously in agreement. "Anything you say, Seymour, anything at all!"

Unable to look at such abject cowardice, Hal pushed Dominic toward the door, the others parting instinctively to allow them through.

The duke listened in amazement to Dominic's miserable confession and then turned away in disgust. "Great God above," he muttered. "And this creature is an English gentleman! Get him out of my sight before he makes me sick!"

Gladly Dominic escaped toward the door, but Hal's icy voice followed him. "Remember what I said, Lexham, for if you forget, then it will be a fatal mistake."

Dominic fled, stumbling down the grand staircase in such haste that he almost lost his footing upon the petals which still lay scattered there from the previous night. In his scramble to reach the outer door, he knocked over several of the

ong-suffering orange trees, a number of which had met with
disaster during the night's excitement.

The duke looked at Hal. "I think I owe Miss Lexham a
considerable apology, Seymour, and I certainly must admit
that I know I owe her my life." He nodded at a waiting
soldier. "Have her brought to me immediately."

In the intervening minutes, nothing was said in the room.
Hal waited by a window and the duke drummed his fingers
upon the table. At last they heard the sound of footsteps
approaching. The door was opened and Caroline was shown
in. She did not see Hal; she saw only the duke.

Hal watched her, thinking how very lovely she was, even
now. Her hair was disheveled, the honey curls tumbling
down over her shoulders, and her gown was smoke-stained
and a little torn, but still she was quite breathtaking.

She faced the duke, who had immediately risen to his feet.
"You sent for me, Your Grace?"

"I did indeed, my dear Miss Lexham," he said, coming
around the table toward her. "And I have done so in the great
hope that you will forgive me for doubting you."

She stared, hardly daring to believe what she heard.

He took her hands. "You have been gravely wronged,
m'dear, and it was my wretched fault for believing the word
of that rodent of a cousin of yours. He has admitted his lies
and I now know that you are entirely innocent, that you
behaved in a most loyal, brave, and patriotic way last night."

Tears of utter relief filled her eyes and she swayed a little.
The duke steadied her. "There, there, now, it's all over,
m'dear, and you are free to go. But first you must tell me that
you forgive me."

She nodded, half blinded by the tears. "Of course you are
forgiven, Your Grace."

He raised her hands to his lips, kissing them upon the
palms. "Thank you, m'dear, it's more than I deserve."

Her fingers closed over his. "There is one thing—"

"Yes? Name it."

"It's about Monsieur Duvall. Please be lenient with him,
Your Grace, for he was made most wretched, he was forced
to do their bidding because they threatened to kill his mother
and sisters. He is not a wicked man, sir, he is very kind and
gentle, and I regard him with great respect. He could not go
through with it, he told my housekeeper and then me, and he

told us in time to save you. There would have been much more time had not Boisville decided to hasten things by serving the *pièce montée* very much sooner than originally intended. You must think of these things, Your Grace, and I beg you to deal as lightly as you can with him, for it would be tragic if he paid the full price for a crime he could not contemplate without breaking down.''

The duke looked at her for a long moment. "How very compassionate you are, m'dear, and how very eloquent a counsel for the defense. Very well, you have my word upon it that Duvall will be dealt with as leniently as possible.''

"Thank you, Your Grace.'' At that moment she saw Hal by the window, and the little smile that had warmed her lips faded immediately.

The duke perceived the change in her and glanced a little uncertainly at Hal. Then, clearing his throat, he muttered something about having things to attend to, and he left them alone.

"Good morning, Caro.''

"Sir Henry.'' Her eyes were cold.

"Your pleasure at seeing I am safe and well quite overwhelms me.''

Briefly her eyes lingered on the mark on his cheek. "Did you apprehend Boisville?''

"I did.''

"Is he—''

"Dead? Yes. Very.''

"I congratulate you.''

"Do you? Your tone suggests that you wish me in the Thames with him.''

She hid her anguish with the consummate skill of devastated pride. She was more glad than he would ever know that he was safe and well. She knew great pain on seeing the mark of Boisville's shot upon his cheek, for it told her how very close to death he had come. But she could not forget what he had said of her, what he had thought of her. "You are wrong, Sir Henry. I do not wish that at all. I rejoice that you are safe and that you have defeated the assassin, and I trust that for Jennifer's sake you will now leave such dangerous things to others.''

The coldness in her eyes and the aloofness of her manner angered him then, his own pride stiffening him against her.

"Thank you, madam," he said shortly. "Again I am overwhelmed by your warmth and concern."

"I do not know how you can expect anything else of me," she said in a shaking voice. Afraid she was about to cry, she gathered her skirts and fled from the room.

He remained where he was for a long moment and then he brought his fist bitterly down upon the table. "God damn you, Caro, God damn you for that!"

Chapter 34

Another day had passed and Caroline stood with Mrs. Hollingsworth in the ruined dining room. The smoke had dulled the chandeliers and stained the magnificent ceiling. The broken window had been roughly boarded up for the time being and the curtains taken down to be restored. One of the Sheraton sideboards had been badly burned and everywhere there was the acrid, pervading stench of the fire. Most of the military banners and union jacks had been taken down and the room cleared of the tables and chairs, but still the echoes of the banquet sounded eerily, as if it was still taking place but could not be seen.

A moment earlier Mrs. Hollingsworth had been smiling, glad of the news that Gaspard would soon be released, the duke carrying out his word to Caroline, but now her face was shocked. ''Close the hotel? You cannot mean it!''

''My mind is made up.''

''But—''

''To begin with we have no dining room.''

''There are other rooms, and the *brigade* is more than anxious to continue! Please, my dear, don't take this dreadful step.''

"My heart has gone out of it, I just want to turn my back on it all."

"This isn't like you," said the housekeeper gently.

"Yes, it is," whispered Caroline. "It's very like me to turn my back on things when I cannot endure them anymore. I turned my back on Selford, now I will do the same to London."

"That will give victory to the earl after all, and that can *never* be right!"

A new voice broke into the echoing room. "It certainly cannot!"

Caroline turned swiftly, smiling as she saw Jennifer standing in the doorway, looking very splendid in pale pink, silver tassels trembling from her little hat. She came toward them. "From all accounts it is as well that Charles and I returned from France when we did, for now maybe we will be able to stop you from being silly, Caroline Lexham!"

"France? But were you not—"

"Destined for Venice? Yes, we were, but Charles confessed that he does not travel well and so we lingered on the French coast instead. Then we became restless, thinking all the while of coming back and doing up Carstairs Place, and so we decided to return to England. We arrived last night, and found my brother had high-handedly moved himself into our house."

Caroline looked away. "Yes, I know."

Jennifer looked shrewdly at her. "Are you going to tell me, or do I have to wring it from you by force?"

"There is little to tell."

"Little to tell?" echoed Jennifer incredulously. "My dear creature, London is bristling with tales about the events here. I've heard so many conflicting tales that I am positively dizzy, and you stand there and say airily that there is little to tell. Now then, I shall stamp my pretty foot with pique if you do not come across properly and behave as a best friend should. Besides which," she added more meaningfully, "I wish to know what has passed between you and Hal."

"Nothing whatever," said Caroline quickly.

"I know when I am being humbugged, Caroline," replied Jennifer briskly, "and I know what the present situation calls for."

"What?"

Jennifer smiled. "Why, toast in Mrs. H's lair, of course."

The smell of toast was as appetizing as ever, even arousing Caroline's appetite when she had had no interest in eating since the night of the banquet. Aided and abetted by Mrs. Hollingsworth, she related the whole story, and Jennifer listened enthralled.

"Why," she said when all had been said, "it is better than the latest novel. And to think that I had the bad sense to be away when it was all going on." Her teasing smile faded then. "But you have not told me it all, have you? You have not told me why Hal left here so suddenly and why he avoids mentioning your name as much as you avoid his."

"There is nothing to tell."

"Please, Caroline, you must tell me, for how can I help if no one will admit anything? I *know* that something has happened between you and my brother, something of sufficient seriousness to make him quit these premises and to make you now consider closing the place completely and go back to Devon."

Caroline couldn't tell her, she couldn't tell her how much she loved Hal, how much she would always love him.

Mrs. Hollingsworth glanced at her and then put down the toasting fork. "Lady Carstairs, she will not say anything because she is in love with Sir Henry."

"Mrs. Hollingsworth!" cried Caroline in dismay. "You should not have said that!"

"No, but I think that her ladyship should be told."

Jennifer looked sadly at Caroline. "Oh, my dearest Caroline, I had no idea—"

"No, and that was how I wished it to remain." Caroline got agitatedly to her feet. "You are not to say anything to him, do you hear me? I don't want him to know."

"If that is what you wish, but—"

"No buts, Jennifer, he is not to know because he already despises me."

Jennifer's eyes widened. "Surely you are wrong."

"No, he thinks me a very low creature, Jennifer, capable of anything, even involvement in the assassination attempt on the Duke of Wellington."

"Now I know you have taken leave of your senses!" cried Jennifer. "Hal would never think that of you!"

"But he did for a while, Jennifer, long enough to say as

much to the duke, who then related the tale to others. Mrs. Hollingsworth overheard him.''

"Did you?'' inquired Jennifer.

The housekeeper nodded reluctantly. "I am afraid that I did, your ladyship, though it grieves me to have to say so.''

Jennifer was brisk and disbelieving. "It has to be a misunderstanding. I know in my heart of hearts that my brother would not think that of you, Caroline. No, it's no use telling me all over again, I just know that it isn't true.''

"Please don't say anything to him, Jennifer.''

Jennifer remained silent.

"Please, Jennifer,'' cried Caroline desperately, "you must give me your word.''

Jennifer shook her head. "I cannot, Caroline, for if I did, I would be being an unworthy friend to you and an unworthy sister to him.''

"Please, Jennifer.''

"No. Oh, don't look at me so reproachfully, for I take this stand for the most noble of reasons. I cannot undertake not to say anything, since I believe him to be innocent, and if that is so, he deserves the right to speak in his own defense.''

"He will not care what I think of him, he will laugh about it,'' cried Caroline. "But I will care very much that he knows my secret. I could not bear it, Jennifer.''

Slowly Jennifer rose to her feet, the tassels on her little beaver hat trembling just a little as she bent to gather up her reticule and parasol. "I will not set out to tell him that you love him, Caroline, of course I will not, but I think I should tell him what it is you think he has said and thought of you. I know my brother, he has never been such a monster that he would say untrue things about a lady, and I know that before I left he held you in very high esteem. He still held you in sufficiently high esteem to wring the truth from Dominic, did you know that?''

"It makes no difference, Jennifer, for the fact remains that he *had* thought me guilty, and he thought many other untrue things about me, things which I am ashamed to say to you. Tell him what you wish, it will no doubt amuse him.''

Jennifer lowered her eyes at the bitterness in these words. Glancing sadly at the silent Mrs. Hollingsworth, she took her leave.

*   *   *

Hal was in the billiard room with Charles, and he straightened from the green baize table as his sister came in. "How
charming you look, sis, and where have you been that takes
you out before we mere males have even risen?"

"I've been to see Caroline."

His smile faded. "I trust she is well."

Charles glanced from one to the other. "What exactly is
going on? I return from my honeymoon in a state of delirious
happiness to find my brother-in-law as bad-tempered as a
bear with a sore head and my bride obviously preoccupied
with things other than my good self."

Jennifer hurried to him, taking his hand and resting it momentarily against her cheek. "Forgive me, my love, but it
seems my disagreeable brother's life needs a little of my
attention." She turned quickly then, snatching up the cue ball
from the table as Hal resolutely made every sign of continuing with his play. "Oh, no, brother mine, you shall not carry
on as if nothing has happened."

"Don't be tiresome, Jennifer," he replied.

"I am permitted to be as tiresome as I like in my own
house, especially with an uninvited guest." She held his
gaze. "Did you believe Caroline to have been part of the plot
to kill the duke?"

Hal stared at her. "Don't be so damned foolish!" he
snapped.

"Is it foolish?"

"You know that it is. Of *course* I've never thought that."

"She thinks you did, among other sins you seem to have
perpetrated against her good name since my back has been
turned."

She related what Mrs. Hollingsworth had overheard, and
then he gave a short, wry laugh. "So, that was why the
omnipresent Mrs. Hollingsworth spoke to me the way she
did!"

"Is that all you have to say?"

"No, it isn't, for I will tell you that the duke's version is
somewhat incorrect, embroidered upon by the fact that he
related it after Caro had been arrested."

"Caro?" she asked quickly. "That is an unexpectedly
intimate way to refer to her."

He turned away. "A mere slip of the tongue."

"Is it, Hal Seymour? Or could it be that your pride is making you as obstinate now as Caroline's is making her?"

"Don't interfere in something of which you know nothing, Jennifer," he replied shortly.

"I intend to interfere as much as I possibly can," she retorted, "And for once in your life you will stand there and say nothing more until I have finished. Today a great deal has become clear to me and things which puzzled me a little in the past are now presented to me as solved. I remember how you spoke of Caroline when first you traveled to London with her, and I remember how you enjoyed her company at the opera house. You looked at her time and time again, and I thought you did so with more than amused interest, and now I know that it was indeed something more. Your secret duties forced you to remain at the Oxenford, that I also now understand, but you leaped swiftly enough to her defense when Dominic Lexham posed any threat to her. And you never again felt the same about Marcia once you knew what she had done; you had turned from her even more after the wedding and those beastly cockroaches, hadn't you? You showed the world the truth then when you kissed Caroline's hand in front of us all—didn't you?"

He said nothing.

"Didn't you?" she persisted. "Look at me, you wretch, and admit the truth!"

He smiled a little then, gently touching her cheek. "What a terrier you are at times, Lady Carstairs. Very well, I admit it, but after my foolishly public display—which display I thank God only you appeared to understand—I discovered that she had been seen fondly embracing and kissing her cousin Lexham."

"And you were jealous!"

Again he said nothing.

"The truth, Henry Seymour," she pressed, "for I will hear you say it. Admit that you were jealous and you hid the fact by accusing her of improper conduct. Am I right?"

"Yes, dammit, you are right! Now, will you please be satisfied and leave the matter alone?"

"No, I will not leave it alone, for it is too important. Why were you so concerned and jealous that she kissed her cousin?"

Hal glanced momentarily at Charles, who gave him a

sympathetic smile. "You may as well come clean, Hal, for she will not leave you alone until you do."

"What manner of support is that from a brother-in-law?" demanded Hal.

"It is the support of common sense, Hal, for I do believe that Jennifer has discovered you in the wrong."

"I have indeed," declared Jennifer triumphantly, "and you are going to admit it if it is the last thing I do, Hal. I want you to tell me exactly why you were so upset that Caroline should show affection for her kinsman."

"For the life of me I cannot see what difference it makes now. Caro loathes the very sight of me now and I cannot say that I blame her after what I've said and done."

"Don't avoid the issue," she said crossly. "Admit that you love her!"

He gave a heavy sigh and tossed his cue down upon the table. "Very well, I admit it, Jennifer. I was jealous because I loved her."

"Past tense?"

"By *God*, you are persistent! I love her—present tense. Will that suffice?"

Tears shone in her eyes then and she smiled, suddenly flinging her arms around his neck. "Oh *yes*, Hal, that will indeed suffice! You must go to her, you must tell her what you have just admitted here."

"Never." He drew away.

"Because your insufferable pride gets in the way? Oh, Hal, can't you see that that is what is happening to her too? She loves you, she told me that she did, but she thinks you do not care for her. You must go to her, for unless you do you will lose her forever—and I will lose the sweetest of sisters-in-law."

He caught her hand urgently. "She told you she loved me?"

"Yes." She smiled. "She is the only one for you, and you know it. If you do not go to Mayfair Street now, you will regret it for the rest of your stubborn life."

He looked at her for a moment longer and then pulled her close, kissing her warmly on the cheek. "Very well, I will go to her, but first there is something which must be unpacked from my trunk." He reached over to take up the little handbell.

"Something to *unpack*?" she cried incredulously. "What
can possibly be of sufficient importance that—"

He smiled. "You will understand when you see it."

A footman entered. "Sir?"

"Tell my valet to unpack the green trunk immediately and
bring me the small leather box he will find in it."

Caroline was seated on the bench where first she had had
her startling idea to turn Lexham House into a hotel. She
wore her old turquoise gown, for somehow it seemed more
appropriate now that she had decided to return to Devon. Her
hair was dressed loosely, several long curls falling down over
one shoulder, and the ends of the ribbons tied in it fluttered a
little in the soft spring breeze. The daffodils nodded on the
lawns, and the gardeners tended the flower beds, weeding
carefully between the sedate rows of tulips. How beautiful the
house looked, just as it had done on that other occasion.

She saw Hal approaching, his tall figure very elegant and
distinguished beneath the trees. Swiftly she lowered her eyes,
her cheeks flushing. How she wished that Jennifer had not
learned her secret.

"Caro?"

"Please don't call me that, Sir Henry," she replied a little
stiffly.

"Why?"

"And please don't play games with me, sir, for I do not
feel able to parry words."

"I will not waste time then. I will tell you straightaway
that I did not tell the duke I thought you were one of the
conspirators, nor did I tell him that I persuaded you to silence
by making love to you. It is my belief that he placed such
meaning into what I said because when he related the tale,
you had been apprehended. Look at me, Caro, and know that
I am telling you the truth."

Unwillingly she raised her eyes. "Very well, Sir Henry,"
she said at last. "I believe you about that."

"Will you also then believe me when I say that never in
my life have I so much regretted a thing as I have regretted
saying those hurtful words to you, and saying them not only
once but on several occasions."

Agitatedly she looked away. "Why have you come here
like this?" she cried, suspecting him of somehow still mock-

ing her. "Do you do it simply to please Jennifer? Or perhaps you enjoy toying with me?"

"I have come here because I wish to forget that we have become estranged, especially as that situation has come about through my own actions. And if I have seemed to toy with you in the past, it has been because I have wanted you so very much. I wish with all my heart that I had never given in to my jealousy, but I did, and I hurt myself as much as I hurt you. I could not bear to think of Dominic Lexham's arms around you, Caro; it made me want to cause you the pain you caused me." He saw the uncertainty in her gray eyes, and the first stirrings of something more. He took the little leather box from his pocket and gave it to her. "Perhaps this will convince you that you have been in my heart for almost as long as I have known you."

With trembling fingers, she opened the box. Inside, flashing and glittering in the sunlight, was her grandmother's necklace. With a gasp, she looked up into his eyes. "Oh, Hal—"

"I did not want you to lose it forever, Caro. I knew how much it meant to you. I persuaded Jordan to go along with the deception, for I did not think the moment was right to tell you, and besides, it could somehow have looked like a contravention of your uncle's damned will! I did it because I loved you, Caro, and I still love you."

The little box tumbled to the grass and the necklace spilled brightly among the daffodils as she reached out to him. Then she was in his arms, held as close and cherished as she had always dreamed. "I love you too, Hal Seymour," she whispered, before his kiss stopped her words.

About the Author

Sandra Heath was born in 1944. As the daughter of an officer in the Royal Air Force, most of her life was spent traveling round to various European posts. She has lived and worked in both Holland and Germany.

The author now resides in Gloucester, England, together with her husband and young daughter, where all her spare time is spent writing. She is especially fond of exotic felines, and at one time or another, has owned each breed of cat.

JOIN THE REGENCY READERS' PANEL

Help us bring you more of the books you like by filling out this survey and mailing it in today.

1. Book title:_____

 Book #:_____

2. Using the scale below how would you rate this book on the following features.

Poor		Not so Good			O.K.			Good		Excellent	
0	1	2	3	4	5	6	7	8	9	10

                                                              Rating
Overall opinion of book................................._____
Plot/Story..._____
Setting/Location......................................._____
Writing Style.._____
Character Development.................................._____
Conclusion/Ending......................................_____
Scene on Front Cover..................................._____

3. On average about how many romance books do you buy for

 yourself each month?_____

4. How would you classify yourself as a reader of Regency romances?
 I am a ( ) light ( ) medium ( ) heavy reader.

5. What is your education?
 ( ) High School (or less)   ( ) 4 yrs. college
 ( ) 2 yrs. college   ( ) Post Graduate

6. Age_____   7. Sex: ( ) Male ( ) Female

Please Print Name_____

Address_____

City_____State_____Zip_____

Phone # (   )_____

 Thank you. Please send to New American Library, Research Dept, 1633 Broadway, New York, NY 10019.